Brandy

by

Christine Davies

Cover Art by *The Wild Rose Press, Inc.*

The Wild Rose Press, Inc.
PO Box 708
Adams Basin, NY 14410-0708
Visit us at www.thewildrosepress.com

Publishing History
First Edition, 2024
Trade Paperback ISBN 978-1-5092-5357-9
Digital ISBN 978-1-5092-5358-6

Published in the United States of America

Dedication

To Daddy

Prologue

England, Summer 1793

Mick darted through the dark alley, oblivious to its rank odors. Clutching a blanketed bundle to his chest, he maneuvered around piles of discarded garbage and puddles of stagnant water dimly lit by the moon, searching frantically for a solution to his dilemma. His mind raced as he discarded one idea after another. He had been so sure his sister would take the babe, but she'd complained she had enough mouths to feed and didn't need another. What should he do now? The thought of killing the child turned his stomach. His mother may have raised a thief and a liar, but she hadn't raised no murderer. That he'd been paid handsomely to do the deed mattered not at all.

He continued down the alley, and the babe, as if sensing his predicament, moved restlessly in his arms. "Don't ye worry," he cooed. "Mick will take care of ye." He skidded to a stop when the alley ended abruptly in a small courtyard. The smell of hay and horses identified the dark building on one side of the area. He glanced around and, finding the courtyard deserted, snuck into the livery stable. He laid the bundled child on a mound of hay and quickly and quietly harnessed the nearest horse.

Scooping up the babe, he swung into the saddle and

rode down the narrow streets of London, the bundle nestled safely in the crook of his arm. While spiriting away the horse, he'd come to a decision and, armed with his new directive, headed out of the city. For several hours he rode purposefully through the quiet English countryside.

The moon had dipped low in the star-strewn sky when Mick came upon a manor house sprawled at the bottom of a small rise. Guiding his horse through the large trees surrounding the place like trusty sentinels, he dismounted at the back of the dark, silent house and crept toward a gate. He set the babe on the ground, unsheathed his knife, and hunkered down to pick at the lock until it clicked open. His knife again sheathed, he gathered up the bundle and pushed open the gate. When the rusty hinges squeaked in protest, he froze, head cocked to one side, listening. Hearing nothing, he sighed with relief and studied his surroundings.

In one sweeping glance he took in the grounds, noting the trim layout of flowers and shrubbery in the garden—sadly, a garden his mother had always wanted but never got. *This be a good place.* A more agreeable solution than murder had been found. Drawing aside the blanket, he looked down at the little face, pale in the moonlight, into eyes that gazed steadily back at him.

"I hope ye have a good life, wee one," he whispered, reaching into his pocket and withdrawing a thin gold chain. He held it aloft, watching the play of moonlight on the suspended oval locket. *It would fetch a pretty penny, and the good Lord knows I could use the extra coin.* A faint whimper drew his attention back to the babe. Those eyes were watching him, tugging at his heart. He heaved a sigh and, chiding himself for being too good-hearted, slipped the gold chain around the babe's neck.

"This be yers by right," he declared quietly as he bent down and placed the blanketed bundle on the ground among the fragrant roses climbing the wrought iron trellis. "Be well, wee one," Mick whispered, and with a last glance back, he closed the gate, mounted the horse, and disappeared into the night. He prayed those fancy folks who had paid him to do away with the child never discovered what a pigeon his mother had raised.

Chapter 1

England, June 1811

"The Earl of Hathshire is dead." Ross Blanchard made the announcement before handing the missive to the Duke of Marbury.

As the duke scanned the paper, his frown deepened. He looked up in disbelief. "Drummond took his own life? Good Lord, he must have been in dire straits. What do you make of it, Ross?"

"I'm not sure. You're aware the Earl of Norwood's property abuts Drummond's? Mind you, we don't yet have solid proof, but Drummond could have been involved with Norwood and his outfit. Could be why he killed himself. We will have to notify Michael, of course."

"Of course," the duke echoed. He arched a brow, anticipating the inevitable directive. He took a sip from his snifter of brandy, waiting.

"I need you to go to France." Ross raised his hand in response to the other's sardonic grin. "I know, you were told the last job would indeed be the last. But this development has changed everything. Michael must be told. If this bloody war would only end—"

The duke laughed, not at all put out by the request. "I suppose my affairs at Marbury Hall can wait a while longer." He thought quickly, making plans as he voiced them aloud. "I will leave for Alden Ridge in the morning. I want to inform Jeffrey of this latest news. Although I'm sure he's already heard, since he and Drummond were neighbors. I'll leave for France from there. Jeff is having a soiree the following weekend, and I promised to make an appearance. Since I should be back from France by then, I will attend. That would put me back in London in a fortnight. If you need me sooner, you can leave word at Alden Ridge. You will take care of the arrangements?"

Ross nodded. "While you're in France, see if you can uncover any more information on Norwood. There has been an increase in goods slipping in and out of England. We're not interested in the luxuries finding their way into our homes—cognac, wine, silk. Someone is sending guns and ammunition into France, which obviously could prove devastating to our troops in Portugal. Our navy has a stranglehold on their ports, and the French are in dire need of many items, military equipment being high on their list."

"What have you been able to gather so far?"

"Only that shipments are crossing the Channel and arriving somewhere near Calais."

The duke set his glass on a nearby table and rose to his feet. "If any further information comes in regarding those behind it, send me a message. Otherwise, I will contact you when I return to London."

Ross escorted the duke to the front door. He shook his hand firmly. "I'll make this up to you, I promise."

The duke chuckled and, as he turned to leave, shot back over his shoulder, "Yes, you will."

Standing in the doorway, Blanchard watched the duke stride down the front walk. He had complete faith in Chandler Townsend, the duke. He could be a formidable enemy but a true friend, unwavering in his loyalty to his country. He was a valuable asset to England—he had proved himself a hundred times. Ross hated to see him step down from service but fully understood his reasons. He, too, had officially retired, until war broke out again. After France and Spain invaded Portugal, with England sworn to support Portugal, he had been called back to assist the new Foreign Minister.

As he watched Chandler mount his black stallion and turn down the road, his wife came up behind him, slipping her arm through his. "Is your business with the duke concluded?"

"For tonight."

"He's a handsome man, isn't he?"

Ross looked down at his wife, one brow arched. Seeing the merriment in her eyes, he remarked dryly, "I suppose the ladies do find him attractive."

"Attractive? He's downright gorgeous!" She patted her husband's arm. "But not to worry, my dear. I much prefer snow on top and deep brown eyes, not coal-black hair and eyes the color of…" She raised her hand and wiggled the finger bearing her favorite ring, a large blue sapphire solitaire that sparkled even in the candle's glow—a gift from her husband.

Ross placed a kiss on the back of his wife's hand. "Waxing poetic, my dear. Should I be worried?"

"Well, he is quite the talk of my sewing circle, so elusive and one of the most sought-after bachelors in Society. I think he keeps speculation about his life at an all-time high with very little effort, I might add. He cares nothing for the gossip that circles the *ton*."

Ross chuckled to himself, having no cause for

alarm. He knew full well his wife loved him completely. As they turned back into the house, he wondered how Michael would take the news of his father's death. He hoped it wouldn't interfere with the mission. The thought was not cold-hearted, merely practical. He knew all too well there was no room for emotion when dealing with affairs of state. He quit the foyer and followed his wife up the stairs to their bedchamber.

Chandler Townsend headed for home, unaware of the conversation centered on him. He thought briefly of visiting Vivian before he left for France but decided against it. She had become tiresome of late. They all at some point became tiresome, the ladies of Society. With barely concealed amusement, he suffered their fawning attentions, was entertained by their covert machinations to gain his favors, all trying to outdo one another in their bids to lead him to the altar. They were tenacious, he'd give them that, and stubbornly determined despite very little encouragement. Whoever succeeded in capturing him would win the ultimate prize—a title and wealth.

It wasn't that he didn't appreciate women. On the contrary, he enjoyed what they offered, quite freely tendered, but, out of bed, they all had one thing in common—greed. Oh, they tried desperately to hide it, but it glittered in their eyes just the same. His friend Jeffrey was wont to say he need only bend his gaze on a woman and even the most seasoned courtesan trembled with desire. *Hah!*

Frankly, he had become bored. This unexpected trip to France couldn't have come at a better time. His life needed some shaking up, and traveling into enemy territory was a good remedy for his mundane routine.

As long as he made it out alive.

****

The next morning, Chandler, following a small stream to Alden Ridge, stumbled upon a scene he would not soon forget. Anything but dull, in fact it was quite exhilarating, a feeling he hadn't experienced in a very long time—if ever.

He watched her for some time, this woodland angel. The slump of her shoulders and the sound of her weeping tempted him to gather her in his arms and ease her sorrow. He tamped down that unfamiliar feeling and, instead, slid from the back of his stallion and leaned his shoulder against a nearby tree, its low-hanging branches shielding him from view. Arms folded across his chest, he watched with bated breath as the girl unhooked the top of her black dress. Hoping it would collapse about her waist, disappointed when it didn't, he was, nevertheless, afforded a fine view of the voluptuous curve of her breasts.

Chandler was fast becoming intrigued. *Who is this captivating creature?* Sunlight slanting through the trees glinted off her auburn hair, and, when she turned her head to stare across the pond, he glimpsed the delicate features of her profile. He inadvertently moved, rustling the leaves beneath his boots. When she glanced in his direction, his breath caught in his throat. She was without a doubt the most beautiful girl he had ever seen.

He waited for her to acknowledge him, and when she didn't, it was apparent she hadn't seen him. He relaxed and continued his vigil while she dipped a handkerchief in the pond and used it to wipe her exposed throat and chest. Lifting her abundant curls, she ran the handkerchief across the back of her neck. Allowing her hair to cascade down her back, she tossed the cloth aside, lay back, arms crossed beneath her head, and stared up at the sky.

Chapter 2

Brandy studied the canopy of tree branches above her as she lay on the grass. The sky between the leaf-covered limbs resembled a blue-and-green patchwork coverlet, one she wanted to pull over her face and pretend the last several weeks of her life had never happened.

In the hushed stillness of the tree-circled glade, she breathed deeply of the forest-scented air, trying to calm her spinning emotions. A hard task, that. It was all too dreadful!

So many unanswered questions, and she hadn't a clue where to begin to find the answers—except perhaps from the beginning...

****

Her father, Philip Drummond, had never been an overly loving parent. Kind, yes, fulfilling her every need, but never doting. She had strived to win his love, but after years of trying had learned to accept matters as they were. Her mother and brother had more than made up for her father's absent love. He had never been mean-spirited, nor had he been abusive—until that night. That night had been the turning point in their relationship.

What had caused him to lash out? To do what he had done? More importantly, what had happened between him and the stranger who had come to visit him that fateful day? Her mind drifted, reflecting, piecing together events in her attempt to understand.

Her father had entertained the visitor, closeted in his study with him for a good part of the afternoon. After he left, Philip remained in his study, emerging only for supper. Brandy joined him in the dining room but kept to herself—his dour, distracted mood leaving her unwilling to engage him in conversation. His wine glass was repeatedly replenished from the decanter at his elbow, and, after supper, he withdrew with a bottle of his favorite French cognac tucked under his arm.

She sought her bedchamber early but, unable to sleep, and thinking her father had retired, she padded into the library in search of a book. She crossed to the expansive shelves covering one entire wall, scanned the titles, and finally selected a slim book of poetry. As she turned to leave, she spotted her father sprawled in one of the wingback chairs flanking the fireplace. A glass dangled from his fingers as he stared into the orange-and-yellow embers of the dying fire. His thick brown hair was tousled as if he had repeatedly run his fingers through it. She stood in silence, watching him, an unexpected wave of sympathy washing over her at the naked grief etched on his face.

He must have sensed her presence, for he turned toward her, his expression now shuttered. He lifted the glass to his lips, realized it was empty, and with a muttered curse, pushed himself to his feet and staggered to the sideboard. He splashed a liberal amount of cognac into the glass and looked back at her. "No, don't go," he said as she moved toward the door. "I have some news for you."

She tensed at his tone, and, judging from his expression, was fairly certain she would not like what he was about to impart.

"You are betrothed to the Earl of Norwood," he announced baldly.

"I'm—what?" she gasped.

"You are to marry Roger Blackwell."

"Papa, you know I can't tolerate the earl. I couldn't possibly marry him." She waited for him to erupt, but he merely arched a brow at her blatant refusal. Emboldened by his silence, she continued, "Whyever would you agree to that? He's only interested in your piece of land that borders his property. Why, he's been after you for years to sell it to him!"

"It is not for you to question, Brandy—'tis done."

She eyed her father. He had been drinking heavily and, therefore, was unpredictable. She decided to change tactics and in a much softer tone, try reasoning with him.

"Papa—"

"Don't call me that!" He drained his glass and turned back to the sideboard.

"Please, don't drink anymore," she beseeched him. "It only makes—"

"Don't tell me what to do either, missy. I'll bloody well do what I want when I want…understand?" His voice was husky, as if he had run a great distance.

"As you wish," she murmured, deciding it would be wise not to argue with him in his present state of inebriation.

"Don't patronize me, either, damn it!" He hurled the snifter, which sailed across the room and shattered against the hearth.

She cringed in alarm, staring. His face flushed, he gasped for air, and fearing for his life, she ran to his side. "Come sit down, Papa," she said, trying to coax him back into his chair. Despite his callous treatment and blatant disregard for her wishes, he was still her father.

He growled and flung her away, sending her flying across the room to collide with the wall. She crumpled to the floor. Dazed, she looked up, and for a second their gazes locked—hers shocked, his cloudy with confusion. In the stunned silence that followed, her father's erratic breathing echoed through the still room.

When he took a step toward her, she struggled to her feet and backed away from him, but the wall impeded her flight. "Stay away from me," she whimpered brokenly, her palms flat against the wall. "I mean it, Papa!" she stated more firmly when he took another step.

He stopped short and stared at her blankly. Then shaking his head as if coming out of a stupor, he snarled, "Don't call me *Papa*. You are no daughter to me! My daughter would not question my actions! She would obey me!" He pointed an accusing finger at her. "You are merely an ungrateful chit! You have no idea—!" He turned back and reached for the crystal decanter of solace, then looked at his other hand as if wondering why his glass wasn't there.

"What do you mean?" she whispered. "What don't I know?"

He grabbed another glass and emptied the bottle of cognac into it. He drained it in one swallow, abusing the fine, expensive liquor with a flick of his wrist. "Get out!"

She backed toward the door, but didn't leave the room quickly enough, for when he spied her standing wide-eyed in the doorway, he snarled, "I said—get out!"

She turned and raced up the stairs to her bedchamber, but before she could close the door, Maddie came rushing in. With a muffled sob, Brandy turned into her housekeeper's comforting embrace.

"He's certainly in a fine mood tonight." Maddie's voice shook with suppressed anger. "How could he treat you so?"

"He has betrothed me to Lord Norwood."

"I know, child. I heard." She helped Brandy into her nightdress and settled her into bed.

"He'll be gone soon enough." She caught Brandy's look of surprise. "He's leaving in the morning. He instructed Arthur to have his portmanteau packed."

Brandy closed her eyes. She would not be sorry to see him go. His drinking was a constant habit, and he had become completely unpredictable, his moods erratic. And, to top it all off, he had betrothed her to a man she could barely abide.

Brandy did not leave her chamber again that night.

Chapter 3

Next morning, Brandy watched her father's carriage bowl down the drive between parallel rows of ancient oak trees. When it faded from view and the dust had settled, she breathed a sigh of relief.

"Is he gone?" Maddie asked from the doorway.

"Yes." Brandy let her curtains drop into place. Turning to the housekeeper, her eyes widened in surprise at the bundle of gray-and-white fur in her arms. Strands of gray hair had escaped Maddie's usual tidy bun.

"Oh, where did you get the darling thing?" she cried as Maddie disengaged the kitten's sharp claws from the front of her apron and held out the wriggling ball of fur at arm's length.

"Happy birthday, Miss Brandy." Brandy stared at Maddie in amazement. "You've forgotten your own birthday?"

Brandy had indeed forgotten. She was eighteen today. "Thank you," she whispered, cuddling the kitten beneath her chin. "He's adorable." She ruffled the soft fur, then set the kitten on the plush carpet. He immediately scampered off to investigate his new domain.

"How are you, child?" Maddie peered at Brandy, her brown eyes filled with concern.

"I'm fine." Brandy crossed to the mahogany armoire and pulled open the doors. Rifling through the dresses, her hand settled on a plum-colored day dress, which she laid across the bed.

"What will you do about Lord Norwood?"

"Do? Why, I will do nothing. I don't care what Papa says, I will not marry that bounder. Good heavens, Maddie, his own father put his mother in an early grave and then proceeded to squander the family fortune. Or so I've heard. I will not be responsible for replenishing the Blackwell coffers." She reached for the dress, gently disengaging the kitten from its hem.

"Do you remember when Michael and I were children and Roger sometimes played with us— uninvited?" She slipped her arms through the sleeves and settled the garment over her trim figure, tying the sash just below her breasts. "He was always trying to prove himself, that he was the better tree climber, the faster rider. Even as a child, he was a demanding, arrogant little boy." She pulled a brush through her tangle of auburn curls.

"I remember one time, when we were playing in the woods, I found a little bird floundering on the ground, its wing broken. I wanted to take it home and mend it, but before I could gather it up, Roger grabbed it, threw it in the air and laughed as it fell to the ground, its one good wing flapping wildly. Laughed!" She shook her head. "He thought it amusing to watch a helpless little bird fall like a rock. It broke my heart. Michael pushed him to the ground, scooped up the bird, and handed it to me. I nursed it back to health and set it free. I will always carry that memory with me." She tossed her head, auburn curls spilling over her shoulders, and raised her hands in supplication. "Now I ask you, how could I possibly marry a man like that?"

"You'll get no argument from me, child. I never did care for the likes of him." Maddie handed Brandy several hairpins. "Well, at least his lordship is gone. You can come out of your room now," she added with a comforting smile.

"I know I'm acting like the worst kind of coward, hiding up here until Papa left, but honestly, Maddie, he frightened me. I have never seen him so angry." She twisted her hair into a bun and pinned it securely at the nape of her neck. "There was something else troubling him, though. He was upset long before our disagreement about Roger Blackwell." She glanced out the window. "I wish Michael were here," she whispered. "He could talk Papa out of this madness."

Yes, her brother could put a stop to their father's insane plan. Not that it was unusual for a father to betroth his daughter to a man of his choice—it was standard practice. But Roger Blackwell! He had a most disreputable reputation. Even ensconced in the country, away from London, she'd heard the gossip. Why would her father betroth her to such a man? Did he despise her that much?

****

Later in the week, Brandy was in the kitchen with Maddie, her hands wrapped around a cup of spiced tea. The air was fragrant from the yeasty dough of Maddie's weekly bread-baking. Outside, rain pelted windows and wind rustled leaves on trees, but inside the warm and cozy room, she was sheltered from the summer storm.

"Have you any word from Master Michael? He's been gone quite a while."

"No, I haven't." She cupped her chin in her hands. "We used to be so close. He would always confide in me.

But lately, he's been guarded."

"You two were inseparable as children," Maddie agreed with a laugh.

"God's truth, Mother despaired of me ever becoming a lady. I only wanted to climb trees, hunt, and ride. There weren't any other girls to play with—Roger had a sister, I think, but she didn't live at Blackwell Hall."

Michael had been her constant companion. Father was always so proud of him; his son could do no wrong. But instead of resenting her brother, Brandy had emulated him—learned to ride a horse, shoot a gun, and hunt with the best of them—for she had naively thought that would make her father proud of her too. Similarly, to please her mother, she had balanced those skills with the requisite crafts prescribed for every young woman.

Life had been so carefree, each day a new adventure. She remembered the day they discovered the glade. Tucked within the trees, a narrow stream meandered through moss-covered rocks and emptied into a small pond. Leafy boughs arched overhead, creating a haven from the rest of the world. They spent many happy hours in that secluded glade. It became a source of contentment for Brandy.

Because of that closeness with Michael, it was especially difficult to accept the distance now between them. As far as she knew, her brother had never kept anything from her, as she had kept nothing from him.

In childhood, Brandy had been happy, quick to laugh, finding humor in most situations. She was hard pressed to find any such esprit in her life now. Since her mother's death and her father's transformation into a hard, bitter man, life was not as gay as it once had been.

So when Michael walked into the salon later that afternoon, he found his sister pensively staring at the cold fireplace, idly stroking the gray-and-white kitten nestled in her lap. With the rain ended, the sun slanted through the windows, bathing her in soft light, turning her hair into curls of fire. He took a moment to admire her profile—the small firm chin, the delicately shaped nose, and high cheekbones. He shook his head in awe at the lovely picture she created, sitting there quietly… He frowned. Something was wrong. It was unusual to find his sister idle.

"Brandy?"

She turned and looked up in happy surprise. "Michael, you're home!" She jumped to her feet, spilling the kitten to the floor, and hugged her brother as if he'd disappear if she but loosened her hold.

He pulled back. "What's the matter, little one? Are you upset I missed your birthday?" he teased.

She shook her head and gave a radiant smile. "Your being here is gift enough." Her gaze lingered on him. Dark-haired and gray-eyed, with thick black lashes and neatly trimmed sideburns, he was, to Brandy, the most handsome of men.

Not wishing to spoil his homecoming but unable to contain her unhappiness, she sank onto the settee, pulling him down beside her. "He has betrothed me to Roger Blackwell," she announced bluntly.

"I know. He told me of his decision before I left." He watched her valiantly try to stifle her tears. "Brandy, 'tis all right. You don't always need to show a brave front." He leaned back against the settee, crossing one leg over the other. "I do not approve of what he has done, nor do I understand why he did it. Father is not the man he once was."

"He's always been distant with me, but he never intentionally hurt me, not until the other night when he threw me against the wall," she uttered without thinking. She paused, alarmed by the thunderous expression on her brother's face. "He was flinging me away, `tis all, and I accidentally hit the wall."

"Don't defend him, Brandy. You have spent most of your life defending him."

"Well, I certainly can't defend him for betrothing me to Roger Blackwell." She glanced at Michael. "I don't like him. He's a cruel man." At her brother's look of astonishment, she nodded. "Remember the little bird with the broken wing? If Roger could harm a defenseless creature, just imagine what he is capable of!"

"He was a child, Brandy. Granted, I don't care for him either, but I don't believe he would hurt you."

"I don't trust him, either. Since his father died, he's become quite ruthless. I hear stories—"

"Stories? From whom?"

"Well, Arthur…"

"What has the butler been telling you? And how in the world would he hear stories?"

"Arthur's brother used to work for the Blackwells. After the old earl died, Roger let him go. No notice, no stipend, nothing a`tall. Just told to pack his bags and vacate the premises. And Roger spends most of his time in London. Rumor has it he's destitute and searching for a wealthy wife to restore Blackwell Hall to its former glory. Before our purported betrothal, that is," she added with an arched brow.

"There's nothing odd about that. Plenty of men do the same thing, but frankly, I'm not too keen on the idea of you marrying him. I'll speak to Father when he returns. Where is he? London?"

Brandy shrugged. "I have no idea. He doesn't tell me where he goes nor when he'll return. If I do ask, he mutters, 'Business,' and reaches for a snifter."

Michael hid his growing concern. His sister was bringing up some alarming information. Turning the topic, he brought up a subject he knew would be more to her liking. "Why don't we go to the glade? Just the two of us," he encouraged with a smile.

"Oh, yes! That would be heavenly!" She jumped to her feet, and the two ran from the room, hand in hand, just like when they were children.

The following week restored Brandy's spirits. She was able to forget the black cloud hovering over her and simply enjoy her time with her brother.

Her euphoria ended abruptly when a messenger arrived at the manor. After scanning the missive, Michael announced, "I have to leave."

Her eyes clouded with sadness. "Now?"

"I'm sorry, Brandy. I will speak to Father when I return."

"Oh, I can handle Papa. It's just that I miss you so much when you're gone. Will you be back soon?"

He averted his gaze to look out the window. "I'm not sure," he answered vaguely, and turning back with a smile, ordered gently, "Now, erase that frown from your pretty face. I'll be back before you know it." He kissed her on the forehead before his long strides took him swiftly out of sight.

Brandy sank into a chair, tears slipping down her cheeks as her brother left her alone once again.

Chapter 4

Brandy strolled through the garden's neatly tended flower beds, her kitten bounding along beside her, exploring. A bee buzzed from flower to flower, dipping in lazy circles as it searched for nectar.

Plucking a crimson rose from a vine climbing the ornate trellis by the gate, she inhaled the sweet fragrance, the silken petals tickling her nose, before she placed it with other flowers in the basket. At the wrought iron bench by the brick walk, she sat, basket at her feet, and removed her bonnet, raised her face to the sun, and breathed deeply of the fresh, scented air.

Except for the birds warbling, the garden was quiet, and bordered by shrubbery that provided a modicum of privacy, it had become a sanctuary. Michael had been gone a fortnight, her father longer. She didn't mind. There was plenty to keep her busy. One thing she had to do, quickly, was determine a way to dissuade her father from this outrageous betrothal. She would never marry the Earl of Norwood. Never!

A gust of wind blew through the garden, tousling the auburn tresses framing her face. The sun had disappeared behind a bank of ominous, swift-moving clouds.

Tucking the kitten under her arm, Brandy grabbed her bonnet and the basket of flowers and dashed into the kitchen just as the dull gray sky unleashed a torrent of rain and a slash of lightning answered by a loud clap of thunder.

Maddie turned from the oven, holding a tray of freshly baked turnovers, their crusts flaky and golden brown. Glancing at Brandy's basket, she asked with a smile, "Are there any flowers left in the garden?"

"I suppose I did get carried away, but I just couldn't resist. They do so brighten a room, don't you think?" She cringed, trying to ignore the clamor outside, where wind thrashed the trees and rain battered the countryside. She did not like storms.

"Just like your mother, she loved her flowers." Maddie set aside the turnovers and gave a quick stir to the venison stew simmering in a large black kettle over the fire.

Brandy placed the basket on the huge oak table and reached for a vase from the shelves lining the wall. She chose several red and pink roses and a few sprigs of orange and yellow daisies and artfully arranged them in the vase, then stepped back to admire her handiwork, pleased with the riotous bouquet of color she had created. Setting the vase in the center of the table, she announced, "I think I'll take supper in here tonight. Will you and Arthur join me?"

Maddie nodded and glanced up as her husband entered the kitchen. With a wide grin, Arthur withdrew a plain brown package from behind his back and placed it on the table with a flourish. "This just came, Miss Brandy."

"For me? What is it?" She reached for the package.

"I don't know. Why don't you open it?" He smiled at his wife, his brown eyes crinkling at the corners.

Brandy turned it over in her hands but found no clue to its sender. She ripped it open to find inside a small black velvet box. As she lifted the lid, she gasped in delight. A pair of diamond earbobs twinkled like stars against the dark velvet. A note was tucked inside. "They are from Michael."

"Does he say when he will return?" Maddie asked, setting out a loaf of freshly baked bread.

"No. He apologizes for the lateness of the birthday gift. He is well and hopes everything here is sound. He promises that, when he returns, he will take care of the matter with Roger Blackwell."

Brandy tucked the note inside the pocket of her blue-and-white-striped gown. "You know, I haven't heard from Papa."

"I'm sure Master Michael will be home soon enough. As for his lordship, well…" Maddie busied herself setting out three places at the table.

A flash of lightning slashed across the sky, followed by a burst of thunder so loud it rattled the dishes on the shelves. The wind howled through the trees, raking the branches against the window.

"'Tis no secret what happened between Papa and me. He simply isn't the same since Mama died. It was hard on him," Brandy said.

"Humph! If you ask me, he should have turned to you in solace, not in anger—"

"Maddie!"

"Don't *Maddie* me, Arthur. You know as well as I do that what he did was unthinkable." Maddie ladled the steaming stew into large floral-bedecked porcelain bowls before grabbing the loaf of bread and slicing it into thick slabs, nearly butchering it in her displeasure.

Brandy reached for a crock of freshly churned butter and a jar of marmalade. "'Tis all right, truly. I'm not going to make excuses for his actions, but—Papa!" Spotting her father standing in the kitchen doorway, she sputtered to a stop. *How long had he been standing there?* Judging from his expression, she guessed long enough to hear the gist of their conversation.

The Earl of Hathshire was not a tall man, his lack of height exaggerated by his stocky build. His brown hair lay plastered to his head by rain, and his bushy brows lowered over dark eyes now flaring with disapproval.

"Since when do we eat with the servants, Brandy?"

Brandy froze in indignation. "Maddie and Arthur are family. With you and Michael gone so much of the time—"

"Well, I'm home now. Maddie, you may serve us in the dining room." He turned on his heel without another word.

Brandy glanced at Maddie, heartsick at her father's derogatory manner. She patted her arm and whispered, "I'm sorry he was so rude," and followed her father into the dining room.

Her father sat at one end of the long table as she took her place in the middle. She hadn't seen him since that fateful night in his library, and she was shocked by his appearance. His face was ravaged by deep lines, and dark circles underscored his eyes. He looked haggard.

Deciding to pretend the confrontation had never happened, crediting his bad behavior to momentary madness and drink, she asked in a pleasant tone, "How was your trip, Papa?"

"Fine."

"Did you accomplish what you set out to do?"

"Yes."

"Were the roads terribly flooded coming home?"

"They were passable."

Brandy fell silent, his curt answers compelling her to cease attempts to draw him into conversation.

Throughout the meal, Philip glanced occasionally at Brandy but for the most part ignored her. He filled his wine glass several times, paid little attention to his meal, and Brandy became increasingly concerned. She knew all too well liquor blinded his judgment. Thunder boomed outside amid flashes of lightning, stretching Brandy's already taut nerves. Eyeing his sullen expression, she ceased her pretense of eating and rose to her feet, preparing to leave him alone.

"Have you seen Roger Blackwell?"

"No, I have not."

"He has not called on you?"

"Yes, but I did not receive him."

"He is your betrothed."

"By your decision, not mine. I do not intend to marry him."

Philip's brows drew together. "Listen to me, girl. I have given him my word. You will not disgrace me."

"Disgrace you? What about me? If you intend to force me to marry that blackguard, I'll—"

"You'll what? Eh? I've had enough of your impertinence. You are stubborn, willful—" He struck his glass on the table with enough force to shatter the fine crystal stem. Wine stained the delicate white silk table runner like blood. Getting to his feet, glaring, he opened his mouth to continue his tirade but paused when Arthur entered the room. "Not now, man! Wait, bring me a bottle of cognac." He turned back to Brandy while Arthur went to do his bidding. "You will marry him," Philip averred, his eyes shooting sparks of rage.

Brandy held her ground despite his anger and her rising fear. "Why, Papa? Why must I marry him?"

Philip stared at her with a strange almost tortured expression on his face. He was visibly relieved when Arthur returned with the cognac. He grabbed a snifter from the sideboard and poured a deep draught, then stared into the glass, a frown creasing his brow, seeming to have forgotten she was in the room.

After a few moments of strained silence, Brandy turned to leave. She had caught a glimpse of pain in his dark eyes, but it had disappeared so quickly she wondered if it had been her imagination.

Arthur stopped her in the hallway. "There's someone here to see his lordship. I have put him in the study."

"Who is it?"

"Mr. Osbert." Arthur shot a quick glance at the closed study door. "He's an unsavory sort, Miss Brandy. I don't care for the likes of him."

Brandy could well understand his displeasure. The last time Mr. Osbert had paid a call, it had sent her father into a tirade that ultimately caused the ugly scene in the library. *What would happen this time?*

"You go on, Arthur. I'll tell Papa he's here." Brandy turned back into the dining room. Philip was slumped in his chair, his glass in one hand, the bottle of cognac within easy reach.

"Mr. Osbert is here to see you. Arthur has put him in your study." Philip paled at her words. "What is it, Papa?"

He sliced the air with his hand, cognac sloshing over the rim of the snifter and onto the rug. He set the glass on the table and stood up, yanking his waistcoat into place. "'Tis fine, girl. Leave me be." He went out, his steps unsteady. Brandy glanced at the half-empty bottle of cognac, the reason for his precarious pace.

Drained from the events of the day, Brandy climbed the stairs to her bedchamber and curled up on the cushioned window seat. The storm had subsided, leaving behind a warm, misty twilight.

She gazed out over the gently rolling hills of Stonebrooke, the wide-open spaces of lush grassland. She loved her home, especially this old house. The brick had mellowed with age and large oak trees shaded the house from the hot summer sun. Her window faced the long, front drive bordered by ancient oak trees whose branches bowed over the lane, creating a leafy dome. A stray breeze blew in, ruffling the curtains and the wisps of hair around her face.

A movement caught her eye, and she looked down at the front stoop, just visible over the window ledge. Mr. Osbert was descending the steps, making his way to his horse tethered at the front post. He glanced up at the house, and Brandy caught a glimpse of his face. His features were shadowed by his hat, but even from this distance she sensed the evil aura surrounding him. She watched him mount his horse and race down the drive.

When he had disappeared from view, Brandy stood and moved to her dressing table, pulling the pins from her hair. The heavy mass cascaded down her back, a faint scent of lavender drifting from it. She sank onto the bench, took the silver hairbrush that had belonged to her mother, and pulled it through her unruly hair, trying unsuccessfully to tame the auburn curls. She stared at her reflection in the mirror, into emerald-green eyes filled with apprehension.

The sound of the gunshot didn't at first register. Maddie's horrified scream, however, brought Brandy instantly to her feet and bolting from the room.

Grabbing the smooth balustrade for support, she flew down the stairs, her skirt raised high above her ankles. She stopped on the bottom step, suddenly chilled. An eerie silence had descended on the manor. She looked toward her father's study, where Arthur stood in the doorway like a sentry, his expression grim. Maddie was by his side, clutching his arm, her expression one of horror. Brandy moved toward them, engulfed with a premonition of disaster so strong it nearly felled her. Arthur blocked her way into the room.

"Arthur, please, let me by!" She pushed him aside and entered the shadowy room. "Oh, my God," she whispered, rearing back in horror. She clutched both hands to her chest, hardly able to comprehend the grisly scene.

Her father was slumped over his desk, a smoking pistol clutched in his hand. Blood and gore splattered the bookcase behind him and stained the papers that littered the top of his desk. In the ashtray beside his lifeless hand, a pile of ashes still smoldered.

She raced to her father's desk and stopped short, clapping her hand over her mouth. The acrid smell of gunpowder burned her nose and her stomach clenched with nausea at the sight of the blood seeping from the hole in his head. She gagged, turned away, and leaned over the waste can, violently sick.

"Come away, child." Maddie draped her arm around Brandy's shoulders and led her from the room, her eyes averted from the gruesome sight. "Arthur, you had best send for Sir Bodsworth."

Brandy sagged against Maddie, her legs suddenly void of strength, and allowed herself to be guided into the salon. Maddie pressed her into the settee and crossed to the sideboard. She poured a finger of cognac into a crystal snifter and handed it to Brandy. "Drink this, child."

Brandy downed the cognac in one swallow. Her eyes watered and she gasped for air as the fiery liquid burned its way down her throat. After a few moments, the fire died to a dull warmth. She turned a distraught gaze on the housekeeper.

Maddie shook her head at the unspoken question. "I don't know, child. His lordship was a troubled man."

"But to take his own life?" She covered her face with her hands and cried with such force her slim body shook like a frail leaf in a raging storm. And like that leaf, she desperately tried to cling to the strong branch of sanity.

"I need Michael," she said. "I'm not sure I can handle this without him."

"You will, child. You always do."

Chapter 5

Due to the heat, they buried her father two days later. There weren't many in attendance, which bothered Brandy not at all, with fewer questions to be answered. After the service, wanting to be alone with her thoughts, she headed to the stables, not taking time to change from her black crepe mourning dress into her riding habit. She needed to work through her grief, and she knew the perfect spot to do just that. Cobey saw her coming and brought out her favorite mare, Misty.

Brandy waved the stableman away and slipped the bit into the mare's mouth. Forgoing a saddle, she tucked the hem of her mourning dress into the sash around her waist and swung up onto the mare's back, astride, dug her heels into the horse's flanks, and tore out of the yard. Turning toward open grassland, she gave Misty her head.

Brandy did not know how long she rode, nor did she care. The warm wind kissed her cheeks, dried her tears, and plucked the pins from her hair. She crossed the meadow and rode through the cool forest until she reached the secluded glade. Her glade. The sun slanted through the trees, illuminating some, shadowing others.

Dismounting and dropping the reins, she left Misty to munch on the tender grass while she kicked off her black silk slippers, rolled down her stockings, and dropped to the cool grass encircling the pond.

Father dead! And by his own hand!

Just remembering that horrific scene in his study, Brandy became flushed, her skin clammy. In the warm surroundings, the black crepe dress clung to her overheated body. She freed the top hooks, spread open the bodice, and untied her chemise, exposing the gently rounded tops of her breasts. She heard a rustling sound and glanced over her shoulder at the fringe of trees. Seeing nothing unusual, she turned back to the pond and dipped her handkerchief in the cool water. After wiping her throat and chest, she lifted her hair and ran the cloth across the back of her neck, releasing a trembling sigh. The cool, wet cloth felt wonderful against her hot, sticky skin. She tossed the handkerchief aside, lay back on the lush carpet of grass, and crossed her arms beneath her head—completely unaware she was being watched.

As Brandy's memories floated by, reliving the past several weeks, she still didn't have any better understanding of her father's downfall.

I might never know the reason for his actions.

Chapter 6

It was time to return home. Brandy rolled to her feet, straightened her chemise and dress, pulled up her stockings, and slid her feet into her black slippers. She strode to her horse, tucking the hem of her dress into the sash. She pulled Misty over to a large rock and, using it as a mounting block, threw one leg over the horse's back. Sitting astride, she pulled on the reins and horse and rider melted into the trees.

Chandler Townsend, enchanted by the beautiful woodland nymph, had not stirred from his hidden position in the trees. He had been tempted to make his presence known, but she had looked so lost in thought, so thoroughly engrossed in her own world, he hadn't dared to intrude. But when she climbed onto her horse and disappeared into the forest, he mounted his stallion and followed her at a discreet distance.

When Brandy reached open grassland, she dug in her heels and sent Misty charging forward. Racing with the wind, she delighted in the feel of the horse beneath her, her muscles bunching with power as her hooves churned up the ground.

The first inkling she had she was not alone was a band of steel encircling her waist and lifting her clear off her horse. She screamed in surprise as she landed with a jolt on top of another horse, the vise still clamped around her midriff. When the horse slowed to a stop, she turned around to confront the one who had unseated her, her tangled auburn hair whipping across her face. Her emerald-green gaze collided with one of deep blue, like brilliant gems sparkling against bronzed velvet. The force of that optical collision nearly tossed her to the ground.

"Are you well?" Chandler gazed down at the young woman sitting before him, his expression filled with concern. Feeling quite pleased with himself for rescuing the damsel in danger, he slowly became aware of her thunderous expression, making it glaringly apparent he had been mistaken. She did not need saving, far from it. Her first words confirmed his growing suspicion.

"What were you thinking, to yank me off my horse like that? I could have been killed! Let me down this instant!" She struggled from his grasp and, in her haste, nearly tumbled to the ground.

Chandler slid off his stallion's back, pulling her down with him, his arm still wrapped securely around her waist. She was not tall—the top of her head just reached his shoulders. Her slight stature, however, did not dissuade her from venting her anger.

"You may release me now!" Still breathing hard, her breasts rose and fell with each labored breath.

Chandler let his arm drop. He bowed low. "My most humble apologies, milady. I feared for your safety, 'tis all. From a distance I thought you were atop a runaway horse. Obviously, I was mistaken," he added with a lopsided grin.

"Yes, you were," she retorted, brushing impatiently at her hair, now a riot of windswept curls. She caught a glimpse of amusement in his eyes—brilliant blue eyes— and bit back the laughter welling up inside her. Though she was still disgruntled, his good humor, not to mention his endearing grin, was infectious. She found her irritation evaporating under his admiring regard.

"Excuse my outburst, sir. I should not have berated you for being a gentleman and coming to my aid, regardless of the fact you were wrong." She was unable to suppress her grin. Oddly, finding herself alone in the middle of a pasture with a stranger, she wasn't afraid, merely astonished.

"You are quite a horsewoman," he conceded. He cocked a brow and tilted his dark head to one side, watching her intently.

Except for her brother, he was the most handsome man she had ever laid eyes on. He had strong sculptured features—cheekbones well-defined, jawline square yet gentled by softly rounded edges, and sporting sideburns. His hair was coal-black, worn slightly longer than the style, curling at the top of his shoulders. He exuded an aura of self-assurance, a man completely in control and used to command. He was elegantly dressed in fawn-colored breeches that disappeared into dark brown riding boots. A snowy-white shirt beneath a chocolate-brown frock coat completed his outfit. His admiring regard pleased her—she didn't know why, but it made her strangely warm. Being sheltered out in the country as she was, she'd not had the opportunity to meet many men, certainly none as handsome as this one. She blushed at her shameless thoughts and lowered her eyes in embarrassment, watching him from beneath her lashes.

Chandler's demeanor changed immediately. Well versed in the telltale signs of flirtation, his lips softened into a smile and his eyes began to smolder. With one finger, he lifted her chin, leaned down, and kissed her on the mouth. A jolt of electricity shot through them.

He lifted his head, tilted it to one side, as if trying to understand what had just happened. With a shrug, he covered her mouth with his, pulling her tighter into his embrace. Knots entangled in her stomach as all sensibility flew out of her head. When he deepened the kiss, she was filled with an unfamiliar yet not unpleasant sensation. His tongue pushed against her lips, seeking entry—and jerking her to awareness. She panicked, coming quickly to her senses. Sliding her hands between their bodies, she pushed against his chest, freeing herself from his embrace. He stepped back but not fast enough. Her open palm cracked against his face.

"How dare you?" she shouted, hiding her mortification behind righteous anger. She changed her earlier opinion of him—he was no gentleman!

He shrugged and leaned nonchalantly against his horse.

"Well?" she demanded.

"Well, what? I won't say I'm sorry I kissed you. I enjoyed it," he commented, adding, "And I think you did, too."

"Oh, you…you…!" She stuttered to a stop, amazed at his audacity. "You are insufferable! First you pull me off my horse like a sack of grain. Then you take liberties. I don't know who you are, but if I ever find you on my land again, I will call the authorities. Better yet, I will shoot you myself!"

With that, she spun on her heel and stomped toward her horse. Grabbing the reins, she looked around for a rock large enough to boost her up. She heard a low chuckle a split second before she was unceremoniously tossed onto Misty's back. She opened her mouth to deliver a stinging retort then, deciding not to waste her breath, she stuck her nose in the air, and rode off at a gallop.

Chandler watched her charge away, sitting tall, her back straight. *What a spitfire!*

Up close, she was even more lovely. When he had watched her by the pond, from that distance, he had not been privileged to observe her unique coloring—hair the color of cognac, eyes the color of emeralds. Even clad in black, from head to toe, she was breathtakingly beautiful. He recalled her weeping by the pond and wondered if she mourned a husband. He frowned, not fully understanding why it would matter.

Fascinated by the play of emotions that had crossed her face, to his jaded mind, she had been flirting with him, and he was quite familiar with flirtation. He rubbed his cheek. Quite a convincing display of outrage, complete with a stinging slap.

He supposed he shouldn't have kissed her, but since he had discovered her beside the pond, desire had overruled common sense. Hell, even now, despite her violent reaction to his kiss, he was tempted to go after her and kiss her again.

Watching her disappear in the distance, he wondered again who she was. If he wasn't mistaken, they were on Blackwell land. Had Roger another sister?

He turned and mounted his stallion, his questions unanswered—for now.

Brandy, fighting through her humiliation, was thinking of him with just as much interest. Her thoughts banged into one another. *Who is he? What was he doing on my land? And why in Heaven's name did I allow him to kiss me?* She had taken leave of her senses! He was a total stranger. She could just as easily been murdered than kissed! Oh, but what a kiss! She had no others to compare it to, of course, but her lips still burned deliciously.

As she neared the manor, she decided to put it down to temporary madness. She would never see him again—they did not move in the same circles. It was evident by his dress that he was gently born, possibly of nobility. She dismissed the encounter, having more important things to think about than her lapse in not only judgment but decorum.

****

Jessie MacCartin and her daughter, Anne, arrived at Stonebrooke Manor a sennight later. Brandy had not seen her aunt and cousin since her mother's funeral two years past, but since they had corresponded often, she hadn't hesitated in sending for them at this turbulent time. Though her father had been laid to rest, a memorial service at the family chapel was scheduled for the next day.

Brandy now stood on the front stoop, her hands folded in front of her, and watched the coach carrying her aunt and cousin careen up the oak-lined drive. As it rounded the circular drive and pulled to a stop, she rushed to meet it as its door flung wide. A small, gray-haired woman tumbled out.

"Aunt Jessie!" Brandy cried, immediately enfolded in her aunt's comforting embrace.

Jessie grasped Brandy's chin in her tiny hand and studied her face with concerned gray eyes. "My poor girl. What an ordeal you have been through! Well, Aunt Jessie is here now." She stepped aside as her daughter alighted. Anne was small and pretty and endowed with an abundance of dark red curls, and eyes like her mother's, gray. A few years older than Brandy, she too was unmarried.

The two girls hugged, tears coursing down their cheeks. "I'm so glad you've come," Brandy whispered.

Jessie herded the two girls up the steps and into the house. Maddie waited just inside the door. "Lady Whyte, Miss MacCartin, welcome to Stonebrooke." She smiled at Anne. "And just look at you! You've grown into such a beautiful young lady!"

"Thank you, Maddie. 'Tis wonderful to be here again." She looped arms with Brandy and the two girls proceeded into the salon, while Jessie stayed behind to talk with Maddie.

"Lady Whyte, I'm sure happy to see you. Miss Brandy has been beside herself with grief. Oh, she's put up a brave front, that's her way, you know, but she's hurting inside. She was calm answering the magistrate's questions, but I know my girl. She was not calm on the inside. And, too, she's missing Master Michael something dreadful."

"Is he on his way?"

"Miss Brandy sent him a note, but we have not yet received word."

"Still no word? Hmmm…I wonder where he could be. Well, let's see what we can do to lift her spirits. I'm sure, with Anne here, she will soon snap out of her melancholy. And we'll do our best to ease her grief." Jessie turned into the salon after asking Maddie to bring tea. She took in Brandy's feigned smile and eyes bright with unshed tears. "'Tis all right, my dear, there's no need to pretend with us."

"It has been awful," Brandy admitted, her smile

dissolving.

"Why don't you tell us exactly what happened? It was hard to understand from your note, dear." Jessie settled herself on the floral settee in front of the large picture window while Brandy and Anne took the two dark green high-backed chairs across from her.

Maddie brought in the silver tea service, placed it on the low table in front of Jessie, and left, closing the double doors behind her. While Jessie poured tea, Brandy began her story starting from the time following her mother's funeral. She told them of the gap that had widened between she and her father, of his quick temper and rather large consumption of spirits, all of which caused him to lash out at her. "So, you see, I don't quite understand everything myself. I don't know where he went on his trips nor why he took his own life."

"'Tis a mystery, to be sure. Was the magistrate at all helpful?" Jessie gazed worriedly at her niece, whose beautiful face was gaunt from grief and exhaustion.

"Not really. He, too, was at a loss."

"Have you gone through your father's papers? Perhaps you'll find a clue to his activities."

Brandy shook her head. "I haven't the strength."

"I'll help you, Brandy," Anne offered, clasping her cousin's hand.

Brandy smiled with gratitude. "Thank you, Anne. Maybe after the memorial service. Perhaps we will find something to shed light on this mystery."

****

"Good heavens, I'm tired." Brandy threaded her fingers through her unbound hair. "I'm glad everyone is gone. I know they mean well, but I didn't think they would ever leave. Not that there were many in attendance." She closed her eyes, letting her head fall back against the settee, and thought for the hundredth time—*Where is Michael?*

Brandy straightened as Maddie entered the salon with the tea service. "Oh, Maddie, you've done quite enough for one day."

"Tsk! I'm not so old that I can't take care of my girls." She placed the tray on the low table and looked worriedly at her charge. "How are you, child?"

"Now that Papa has been buried—" Her words trailed off. Years of trying to win her father's love battled with her recent aversion. She was sorry he was dead, of course, but she just couldn't summon up any other emotion than relief. He had changed so much in the past two years she had actually begun to dislike him. When he had betrothed her to Roger Blackwell, without any regard to her feelings, well— She blinked away tears. *What was done was done. 'Tis in the past and I will leave it there.*

"I'm glad her ladyship isn't here to see this day. She loved the old earl, she did. Now, I have her young one to look after," Maddie said with a teary smile, passing cups of hot tea to the two young women.

Despite her somber mood, Brandy chuckled. "Really, Maddie, I'm hardly in the schoolroom."

"Well, never you mind," she admonished with a wave of her hand. "Where is Lady Whyte?"

"She's upstairs resting. She'll be down for supper."

"Oh, dear, I nearly forgot. Mr. Arbuckle sent word that he would be here tomorrow to go over his lordship's estate. He's aware that Master Michael is not here, but he said he had some things to go over with you."

Brandy nodded. "Why don't you and Arthur relax

41

before supper? `Tis been a long day for all of us." The front door chimes sounded and Brandy looked up expectantly when Arthur appeared in the doorway.

"Lord Norwood to see you, Miss Brandy." His displeasure was evident in his tone. "Would you like me to send him on his way?"

"That won't be necessary," she answered, smothering her smile at his anticipative question. "Send him in, Arthur."

Maddie shook her head and, muttering under her breath, followed her husband from the room. Anne made as if to rise, but Brandy held out her hand. "Please stay. I could use your support."

"What do you suppose he wants?" Anne whispered. "He wouldn't be so uncouth as to bring up the betrothal agreement after just burying your father."

"I would not put it past him," Brandy replied, mentally preparing herself for a confrontation. She gathered her scattered wits and rose to greet her unwanted visitor.

Roger Blackwell sauntered into the room. He was tall, slim, and walked with an easy gait that exaggerated his arrogance. His weak chin and fair complexion gave him a decidedly effeminate appearance, thereby ruining the masculine effect he sought with his swagger. His wavy blond hair was tousled from the ride and his brown eyes shone with sympathy. He clasped Brandy's hand and brought it to his lips, looking at her from beneath his lashes. When he held fast, she gently disengaged her hand.

"Lady Brandy, I am heartbroken at the news of your father's demise. What a tragedy, my dear. And, too, I am distraught that I was unable to attend the service. I only just returned from London. Is there anything I can do for you? Anything you need?"

Ignoring his inquiries, she waved her hand toward Anne. "May I introduce my cousin, Miss Anne MacCartin? She and her mother, Baroness Whyte, are visiting for an indeterminate period of time."

"A pleasure," he murmured, barely glancing at Anne. He waited for them to resume their seats and then, without being invited, took a seat across from Brandy. "As I said, I came as soon as I heard. I quite admired your father, you know."

"I'm afraid we're not quite over the shock."

Roger cleared his throat. "There is something I wish to discuss with you." He looked pointedly at Anne. "If we could have a moment alone?"

"You may speak freely in front of my cousin."

Roger hesitated a moment, then leaned forward with an air of extreme confidence. "With your father gone, I think we should marry as soon as possible—after an appropriate mourning period, of course."

"Roger, I don't believe this is an appropriate time to discuss that subject. But since you felt the need to bring it up, let me tell you this—I do not want to marry you. It was my father's wish, not mine."

At her words, his eyes narrowed in vexation that, to Brandy, disappeared as fast as it had surfaced. His face resumed an expression of acquiescence. "Well, perhaps we should speak of this at another time," he agreed, completely ignoring her refusal. He rose to his feet. "I really must be going. There are many things to attend to at Blackwell Hall." He bent over Brandy's hand. "I hope I have not offended you. We will continue this discussion at a more appropriate time. Good day, ladies." He nodded to Anne and bowed out of the room, his smile fixed, his back stiff.

Brandy leaned back on the settee. "Good heavens, Anne. I thought for sure he was going to put up a fierce argument. Did you see his expression harden when I turned him down? His whole demeanor changed."

"It seems to me that he's not likely to give up. He completely ignored your refusal to marry him."

"I think he covets the land more than me. He has been after Papa for years to sell it to him. Papa was against it, of course, but then suddenly he agreed to give him not only the land but my hand in marriage. Thank heavens a contract was never written." Knowing instinctively this confrontation with Blackwell would be the first of many, she prayed Michael would return soon. He would undoubtedly become more persistent, and she could deter him for only so long. She needed her brother here to ward off any future meetings.

"I thought he was going to insist that I leave the room."

"I'm glad you stayed. I'm too tired to have dealt with him alone. I'm quite sure the visit wouldn't have ended as civilly if you were not here to keep him on his best behavior."

Anne rose to her feet. "I'm going to lie down for a while. Will you come upstairs and rest before supper?"

"No, I'll stay here and relax, but you go ahead." Brandy smiled as Anne left the room, eternally grateful she and her mother were here. She hoped they would stay for a long time. Her thoughts turned to the upcoming meeting with her father's solicitor, Mr. Arbuckle. The idea of meeting with the solicitor to settle her father's estate was hard to comprehend. *Michael needs to be here. He is the new Earl of Hathshire and has inherited Stonebooke Manor and all it entails.*

She laid her head back against the settee and closed her eyes. Unbidden, the image of a man with vivid blue eyes appeared, the one who had dared kiss her in the meadow. She had wondered about him, blushing each time she remembered their kiss, but with all that had transpired since then, she had more times than not, pushed him from her thoughts.

But now, the solitude of the quiet afternoon brought forth the myriad of feelings she had experienced in his presence—his touch, from his arm encircling her, his voice, deep and resonant, to his lips covering hers that created a delicious sensation in the pit of her stomach. She shivered, goose bumps dimpling her arms. With firm resolve, she once again pushed him away. *Let it go!*

Overcome with exhaustion, sleep wrapped her in its arms, melting away her worries, fears, and fanciful dreams until such a time they would again haunt her waking moments.

Chapter 7

Arthur answered the summons at the front door and promptly led the gentleman into the drawing room. He made his way to the dining room where the ladies were breakfasting to announce the visitor. "Mr. Arbuckle is awaiting you in the drawing room, Miss Brandy."

"Thank you, Arthur. We'll be there directly." Brandy laid her napkin beside her plate. "Shall we?" she asked, glancing at her aunt and cousin. They rose as one and went to greet the late earl's solicitor.

Mr. Arbuckle was seated in a mahogany armchair, a brown case at his feet. He was a short man with a girth that age had widened. His round face was framed by brown hair liberally peppered with gray, and sideburns that reached nearly to his lower jaw. Wire spectacles perched precariously on his nose. He stood as they entered the room. "Lady Brandy, allow me to express my deepest condolences to you at this tragic turn of events. It is regrettable, too, that business kept me from attending the memorial service."

"Thank you, Mr. Arbuckle. I know how hard this must be on you. You and Father spent many years together." Brandy extended her hand to him, then introduced Jessie and Anne.

"It's a pleasure to meet you, Miss MacCartin. Jessie, how are you?"

"Why, Thaddeus, you're still as handsome as ever."

Jessie smiled warmly at the solicitor, who was now beaming at her compliment.

"You two know each other?" Brandy glanced from her aunt to the solicitor. It was obvious they did, and indeed were quite fond of one another.

"Oh, yes, we've known each other for a number of years. We met at your parents' wedding."

"Has it been that long?"

"Indeed, it has."

Mr. Arbuckle resumed his seat after the girls had seated themselves on the red-and-gold settee, and Jessie had settled herself in the matching chair beside him. He straightened his spectacles, glanced briefly at Jessie, then clearing his throat, he faced Brandy.

Alarmed at his odd behavior, she leaned forward and surreptitiously wiped her damp palms on the skirt of her black crepe dress. "Is there something amiss?"

"Well, not exactly amiss. You must understand that your parents loved you very much. They had every intention of telling you themselves, of course, but when Lady Hathshire passed away, well, your father decided against it. Now, with Lord Hathshire passed on, I suppose it's left to me." He paused and straightened his already impeccably tied cravat. Jessie smiled encouragingly and his agitation lessened.

Brandy witnessed this exchange. "Aunt Jessie? Do you know this news?"

"Yes, but it was not mine to tell. I begged Philip to tell you after Doreen died, but he flatly refused. It was odd. I know he was in full agreement with Doreen at one time, but after she died, he apparently changed his mind."

"What is this news?" Brandy asked Mr. Arbuckle,

her hands clasped tightly in her lap. She had a dreadful feeling she wasn't going to like what he was about to say. She swallowed past the lump in her throat.

"Just tell her, Thaddeus," Jessie urged when the solicitor seemed to be searching for a delicate way of imparting the news.

"You were adopted," he blurted out, pulling on his cravat, and unintentionally unraveling the expertly tied knot at his throat.

Brandy blinked, then stared wide-eyed at the man. Surely, she hadn't heard him correctly. "Adopted?" she whispered, her heart thumping loudly in her chest. As if from a distance, she heard Anne gasp.

The solicitor cast Jessie a look of sheer helplessness. Legal matters concerning gentlemen he was quite familiar with, but dealing with genteel ladies? This was an entirely different matter, a most complicated matter.

Jessie tried to soften the blow. "'Tis true, Brandy. I was here when Doreen found you by the back gate. She was out in the gardens—you know how she loved her flowers—when she found you among the roses. Let's see...I believe Michael was four at the time. After his birth—it was quite difficult, you see—Doreen was informed that it was unlikely she could have more children. And how she wanted a little girl! Don't you see? You were a Godsend, my dear, her special miracle."

"Why didn't Papa tell me?"

"You said yourself he changed a great deal after Doreen's death. Perhaps he believed it was no longer important."

"No longer important?" Brandy stared blankly at Jessie as her world crashed down around her. She felt like a pebble caught in an eddy, tossed hither and yon.

Her mind spinning, she tried desperately to latch on to just one coherent thought.

Jessie grasped Brandy's cold hands in hers. "They both loved you as if you were their own. Don't ever doubt that. Regardless of Philip's recent behavior, he loved you."

Mr. Arbuckle laid his case across his knees, opened it, and withdrew a slim blue velvet box. "You were wearing this around your neck when Lady Hathshire found you in the garden. She intended to give it to you when she told you the story. She was waiting until your eighteenth birthday."

Now that the secret was out, the solicitor had quickly regained his composure and had adopted his usual businesslike tone. "There is a miniature portrait inside the locket we believe could be your natural father. We tried to identify him at the time but were unsuccessful." He handed the box to Brandy. "We have kept it in the safe in my office all these years."

As Brandy reached for the box, a shiver went down her spine. Holding the box in her hands, she felt the softness of the velvet. Her hands trembled as she lifted the lid. Nestled inside, on a blanket of the same blue velvet, was an oval gold locket suspended on a thin gold chain. She removed the delicate locket from the box and studied it. One side was unadorned but turning it over, she noted the intricate engraving of two entwined hearts. She laid the locket in the palm of her hand and, with the tip of her finger, traced the detailing, observing the initials etched in the center of each heart—*T* and *M*. She lifted the latch and spread the locket open. Inside was a faded color portrait of a young man with hair the color of mahogany. It was hard to ascertain the color of his eyes, for over time the paint had faded, but the artist had deftly captured the love shining in them.

"I know this is quite a shock to you, but believe me, Jessie is correct. They loved you dearly." Mr. Arbuckle straightened his spectacles. "Of course, Master Michael inherits the title and estate, but his lordship did provide handsomely for you, regardless of the circumstances of your birth." He cleared his throat. "There is a matter that has recently surfaced that I will need to discuss with Master Michael. Perhaps I should return another day—when he has returned?"

"No, please, won't you stay? If it affects Stonebrooke Manor, it affects me. I should like to hear everything now. Besides, we aren't entirely certain when Michael will return home." Brandy pushed the startling news of her birth to the back of her mind, placed the locket back in the box, and laid it on the settee, her hand resting on the soft velvet as she focused on the solicitor.

"If that is your wish, Lady Brandy." Mr. Arbuckle straightened his spectacles on the bridge of his nose. "As I said, Lord Hathshire did provide amply for you and Michael, but after the debts are paid, I'm afraid there will not be much left."

"What do you mean, not much left? What debts are you talking about?" Brandy gaped at him in disbelief.

"Quite frankly, your father—his lordship—owed a lot of people a vast amount of money. He was becoming deeper and deeper in debt. He came to me for advice just last month. I'm afraid I wasn't much help. You see, he had kept a great deal of his activities hidden from me, so I was working as a blind man. Since his death, however, the notes have been coming in fast. I'm sorry, Lady Brandy. I will, of course, take care of everything for you—if you wish."

"What of the house?"

"I have done a preliminary report of what is owed compared with what you possess. For the time being, you may keep Stonebrook Manor. However, it is imperative that Master Michael return to fatten the coffers. Have you heard from him?"

"No, I have no idea where he is nor when he'll return. He told me he was traveling on business for Mr. Oakley, who owns a shipping company in London. I penned him a note in care of Mr. Oakley, but I have not received a reply."

"With your permission, I will also send word."

Brandy nodded, suddenly feeling lightheaded. The walls were closing in, and the sympathetic looks directed her way would be her undoing if she remained in the room much longer. She rose to her feet.

"Will you excuse me? I need to clear my head." She fled from the room, rushed up the stairs and into her bedchamber. She collapsed onto the dressing table's bench and stared into the mirror. She looked the same, but she wasn't. Her world as she knew it no longer existed. Her entire life had been a lie.

Questions pummeled her mercilessly: *Who are my real parents? Why would they abandon me?* She gasped in dismay as an unpleasant thought swirled into the mix. *Am I a bastard?* She cringed over that ghastly possibility and quickly pushed the thought away.

She looked around her bedchamber. She loved this room, the soothing colors a balm to frayed nerves. She remembered how her mother had allowed her to choose the décor, pairing two of her favorite colors together. Yellow-and-green floral damask covered the walls; a plush forest-green carpet lay under foot; and lemon-yellow silk curtains framed the window. A matching yellow-and-green flowered ceramic pitcher and bowl resided on the commode. A multi-colored cushioned window seat brought it all together.

But Doreen hadn't been her mother, had she? She just happened to find her in the gardens one day. Brandy let out a cry and, covering her face with her hands, she wept.

Just this morning she was the only daughter of Lord Philip and Lady Doreen Drummond. And now—now she didn't know who she was! Her beloved mother had not been her mother? Her father, well, she now better understood his aloofness as well as those hateful words he had flung at her head. Indeed, she was no daughter of his!

She rubbed her throbbing temples as her aunt's words echoed in her head. *Perhaps he believed it was no longer important.* Well, it may have become unimportant to Philip, but it certainly mattered to her! *How could they have kept this from me?*

She tilted her head to one side. *Did Michael know?* Is that why he had always been especially caring toward her? Did he feel sorry for her? She couldn't bear it if he only cared for her out of a sense of duty, or worse—pity.

Chapter 8

Brandy sat at the large kitchen table across from Arthur and Maddie, twisting her already crumpled handkerchief. Heartbroken at what she had to do, yet seeing no reason to skirt the issue, she came right to the point. "Maddie, you and Arthur have served Stonebrooke Manor for a long time, 'tis your home. You're more like family than not, which makes this even more difficult." She leaned forward, placing her folded hands on the table. "My fath—that is, Philip—amassed many outstanding debts. Mr. Arbuckle has made a list of what we owe and finds it necessary to sell most of our possessions to pay off these debts. After that, well, I'm hopeful Michael will be home to fill the coffers. I'm sorry, but there just isn't enough coin to pay your wages." Her eyes filled with tears at their forlorn expressions.

"What are you going to do?" Maddie asked, dabbing at the corners of her eyes with the hem of her apron.

Brandy grasped the housekeeper's hands in hers. "I don't know. After we pay the creditors, there will be a little money left over, but not much."

"But who will take care of you? You can't stay here alone, Miss Brandy. It's just not done."

"I can't worry about propriety now, Arthur. Besides, Aunt Jessie and Anne plan to stay here indefinitely."

Maddie looked over at her husband, who silently

nodded his assent, then turned back to Brandy. "We will stay. Now, don't argue, Miss Brandy. As far as we're concerned, we are family. And you needn't worry about our wages, either. We won't take a shilling until all is right again." She took Arthur's hand. "We have a little set aside and what we have is yours, if you need it. Everything we could possibly want or need is right here at Stonebrooke—with you."

"That's right, Miss Brandy. Our lives are here with you." Arthur wrapped his arm around his wife's shoulders.

Brandy sighed with relief. "God's truth, I didn't want you to leave. But until Michael returns home, it might be difficult. Cobey has agreed to stay, too. He declared he's just too old to look for other employment. I think he doesn't trust anyone else to tend the horses," she added with a chuckle, lightening the somber mood.

Brandy found her cousin in the sitting room, seated in front of a large canvas perched on an easel. The morning sun spilled in through the picture window. In one hand, she held a palette of varied colors of paint, in the other, a slim brush.

"Maddie and Arthur have agreed to stay," Brandy announced. "Cobey, too. Lord, I'm thankful. I wouldn't have known what to do without them. Doreen despaired of me ever running a home even while pounding household duties into me." She couldn't contain her grin, remembering how Doreen had insisted she forgo her boyish pursuits and take an interest in womanly pastimes and the many tasks of running a household. Brandy had consented without argument as long as it hadn't interfered with time spent with Michael. Unfortunately, she had not excelled in those pursuits as well as Doreen had hoped.

"I suppose between the two of us, and Mama, we can manage it," Anne said with a laugh. "Unfortunately, needlepoint and dancing do not come in handy at a time like this." She laid her brush aside and placed her hands in her lap. "Brandy, aren't you the least bit curious about your real parents?"

"No." She turned to stare out the window. "They deserted me. They thought so little of me they left me in someone's garden. I'm not interested in them at all," she averred, knowing even as she said the words, they were a lie. But she refused to let anyone, even her beloved cousin, know of the anguish that filled her at the very idea of being abandoned.

Brandy had tucked the gold locket away in her bureau. Aunt Jessie had tried to convince her to wear it, that there had to be a perfectly good explanation as to why she'd been left with the Drummonds, but Brandy would not—not yet.

"Liar." Anne's softly spoken censure pulled Brandy from her cloud of misery. "I think you are, indeed, very interested in them."

Brandy straightened her shoulders. "Never mind about that, Anne. There is a more dire need to be addressed. Just what we will do for money? Any ideas?"

They had both agreed not to bother Jessie with this problem. She was in the midst of a nasty battle of her own with her late husband's family, fighting among themselves over his estate. Never mind that Jessie and her Scottish Baron had been deeply in love, and that Jessie had spent a good part of her life in Scotland—his family had turned their collective backs on them.

"I could try to sell my paintings. I have often

wondered if others think I'm as good as my family believes I am."

"You are indeed talented, but the village of Hathshire is not a wealthy one. No, we'll have to think of something else." Brandy paced the length of the room and stopped to gaze again out the window, as if searching for an answer to their dilemma.

"What about a loan?"

"I received a letter from Mr. Arbuckle this morning. On my behalf, he contacted the Bank of London for a loan. It was declined. They will only generate a loan to Michael, as the new Earl of Hathshire. Even so, with this blasted war raging on, there isn't much money to be found." Brandy leaned her forehead against the windowpane, fighting the wave of helplessness threatening to drown her.

"We'll think of something," Anne assured her. Her tone, however, revealed she, too, hadn't the faintest idea of what to do next.

****

Chandler waited impatiently for the signal, drawing his cloak tightly around his tall frame, pulling the collar up around his neck. As the sun descended, so did the temperature—becoming cooler with each passing minute. It seemed summer had yet to reach the coast of France.

At last, he spotted a flash of light in an upstairs window. He made his way to the back of the house, keeping well to the shadows. As he neared the door, it swung open on silent hinges, allowing him entry. Removing his hat, he stepped into the dimly lit foyer.

"*Bonsoir, bon ami*. It is good to see you again."

"How are you, Pierre?" With a firm grip, he clasped

Brandy

the other man's outstretched hand.

"*Excellente*. Come, *bon ami*, they are gathered upstairs."

Chandler followed Pierre up a dark, narrow flight of stairs. The boards creaked beneath their boots; the smell of damp wood permeated the air. At the landing, they proceeded down a similarly darkened hallway and stopped before a door at the end of the corridor. After striking a quick knock, Pierre pushed it open and stepping aside allowed Chandler to enter. Without a sound, he pulled the door closed behind him and retraced his footsteps downstairs, to stand sentry at the outer door.

With a sweeping glance, Chandler surveyed the small, sparsely furnished room. Three men were seated at a round table, a pair of squat candles, lit, a bottle of red wine, and several short glasses upon its scarred surface. Chandler acknowledged them with a nod as he shrugged out of his cloak.

"You were not followed?" asked the older of the three men. His bushy gray beard covered most of his face, and tufts of gray hair peeked from beneath the brim of his green-and-black beret. Chandler knew him well— Claude was a trusted friend. Chandler shook his head in answer and turned to the man seated next to Claude. "Good to see you, Andrew."

The man was endowed with thick, black hair and eyes of brown that were now alight with pleasure. "'Tis good to see you, too. We've been on tenterhooks since we received your note. What brings you to France?"

"Yes, what is the urgency?" echoed the third man. He, too, was dark-haired, but his eyes were gray, and he sported sideburns. "You have us all quite curious."

Chandler took the only other available ladder-

57

backed chair and accepted the glass of wine Claude slid across the table. He faced the third man. "I'm afraid I have some bad news, Michael."

Michael leaned forward, resting his arms on the table. "What is this news?"

"Your father is dead."

"Good Lord." Michael slumped back in his chair. "How?"

"He shot himself."

"He...what?"

"'Tis true." Chandler drew in a deep breath, hating to be the one to break the news. "Rumor has it, and Blanchard has since confirmed, he was involved in smuggling. We're not sure just how deeply he was involved, whether it was merely goods—or spies—he was helping transport into England." He cocked his head to one side. "You are acquainted with Roger Blackwell?"

"I know him, yes. What has he to do with my father?"

"Blackwell is heavily involved in not only smuggling but espionage as well. We have been unable to place the two of them together, or what, if anything, it has to do with your father's suicide, but it's possible Philip was involved with Blackwell. Blackwell's place borders yours, does it not?" At Michael's nod, he continued, "We have suspected Blackwell for some time, but he is shrewd. We've been unable to get him on anything concrete. Word is he frequents a town in northern France. The people there claim allegiance to England, but we think they help their own with their fight in Portugal." Chandler reached into his pocket and withdrew a slim, silver case, flipped it open and held it out to Michael. "I suppose whichever hand holds the most coin at the time, eh?"

Michael accepted a thin brown cheroot and leaned toward the proffered flame, his mind spinning. His father, the respected Earl of Hathshire, involved in smuggling? It was too fantastic to be believed! But there was no reason for the duke to fabricate the story. His stomach sank with the awful realization that it was more than likely true.

Michael had been away from home for a good portion of the past two years. When he was home, he never stayed long, certainly not long enough to delve into his father's affairs. But why would Philip get involved in smuggling? Or worse yet—treason? His eyes widened in alarm, and he focused on Chandler's face. "My sister— how is she?"

"I don't know," Chandler replied, having forgotten the existence of a sister. "Is she at Stonebrooke Manor?"

"Yes, I must go to her. She will be devastated."

"You can't leave France."

Michael started to argue, then recalled the duke's earlier concerns. "She is betrothed to Blackwell." He raised his hand as all three men leaned forward with matching frowns. "Father arranged it against her wishes. Believe me, she was not happy about it. In fact, she outright refused to honor the betrothal." He looked back at Chandler. "Would you look in on her? Make sure she has everything she needs? Maybe keep an eye on her, if possible? She'll be all alone now. And I don't trust Blackwell. If he did involve my father, she could very well be in danger. She's a curious sort, and if she suspects anything, she won't rest until she has her answers.'

"I will stop at Stonebrooke Manor on my return to

London."

"As time goes by with no word from me, she will become frantic with worry. And who knows what Blackwell will do next? She could be in danger." Michael took a long drink of the red wine, his brow creased in worry.

"Could she have been involved in your father's activities?" Claude asked. "Or Blackwell's?"

"Good Lord, no!" Michael stood, his fists clenched at his sides.

"Settle down, *bon ami*. I meant no disrespect."

"How involved is Blackwell?" Andrew asked, motioning for Michael to sit down.

"Since his father died and left the family destitute, he will do anything for money. Marrying a young, wealthy woman would be right up his alley, as would smuggling and spying for the French. Any way to make quick coin," Chandler added with a shrug of his shoulders.

Michael laughed bitterly. "My sister may be a wealthy woman, but as long as I'm alive, I have control. Frankly, money has never interested her. But with my father gone, Blackwell will no doubt press his suit." He grinned. "How I'd love to be there to watch her set him back on his heels."

"You may be next on Roger's list," Chandler warned.

"How so?"

"Roger needs money. He sees his problems solved by marrying your sister. You said yourself that you control the money—as long as you're alive."

"Oh, hell! I hadn't thought of that."

"But he can't reach us here," Andrew interjected.

"If he has people working for him in France, he could, very easily."

"Will you take a note to her?"

"I can't. She mustn't know where you are or what you're doing. She also can't know we are acquainted. But I promise I will look in on her."

Michael nodded, despondent, and reached for the bottle of wine.

"I have to go now," Chandler said, rising to his feet. He reached for his cloak. "Good luck to you both. Claude will fill you in on the details. Andrew, I'd like a word with you outside."

Andrew followed Chandler out of the room. Standing in the darkened hallway, Chandler turned to his brother. "How are things going?"

"I think we are close to finding out the information."

"Look after Michael, Andrew. I know he must be devastated."

"I will. Lately, his father had become a difficult man to like. But I know the news of his traitorous actions has hit him hard. He will worry about his sister."

"Will it affect the mission?"

"No. Michael lets nothing interfere with what must be done. Reminds me of someone else I know," he added with a grin.

Chandler chose to ignore the good-natured jibe. "One more thing. If Roger is as involved as we think, you both could be in a great deal of danger. Watch your backs," he warned. Andrew assured him they would. "Well, then, I will see you in London." They clasped hands, and Andrew waited until his brother descended the stairs before turning back into the room.

Pierre was waiting for Chandler in the shadows near

the back door.

"If you need me, I will be staying at Mona's. You can contact me there." Chandler donned his cloak. "I will head for England tomorrow night. Please make sure the boat is ready and waiting."

Pierre nodded. "God speed, *bon ami*."

Chandler stepped into the night, staying close to the buildings until he had reached the main street. He hailed a passing hackney and in flawless French gave the driver his destination. He leaned back and mentally went over the dangers Andrew and Michael faced as they moved deeper into France. He couldn't shake this feeling of uneasiness. He was tempted to join them on this mission, but he was needed in England.

How I hate war. He was weary of the intrigue, tired of the demands on his time. He longed to settle on his country estate. The solitude of Marbury Hall was what he needed. Maybe he would even bend to his grandmother's constant urging and wed. Then she'd stop needling him about marriage. He grinned. It would also take him off the eligible bachelor list and he'd be free of the ladies' collusions. It still amazed him how a title and wealth could turn even the most pious of women into whores.

Yes, he would find a quiet, unassuming woman. Certainly, not one of the ladies of the *ton* who hunted him with hungry eyes. He wanted a woman he could leave in the country while he continued his pleasurable pursuits in London, if so desired. Just as soon as this mission was over, he would concentrate on finding a suitable wife. But he would keep his grandmother in the dark. No need to up her game in finding him a wife.

But first things first. He had promised Michael to

check on his sister. He was sure he would find her overwrought with grief, and he had no idea how to handle a woman in crisis. He would pay a brief visit to Stonebrooke Manor, introduce himself to Michael's sister, and be on his way.

Oh, bloody hell, he had neglected to get the chit's name.

Chapter 9

The moon was not cooperating. In fact, it was being downright mischievous. Cavorting behind the clouds, occasionally peeking out to dance upon the land. Brandy was ready to scream in frustration—not only from the uncooperative moon but finding herself in this predicament due to her present circumstances.

Michael had not yet returned. Aunt Jessie, bless her, had contributed what she could, but the battle with her late husband's family still raged. Mr. Arbuckle had sold many of the Drummond possessions to pay off the creditors, but with no funds coming in, it was all they could do to keep the roof over their heads. The merchants in the village would no longer grant her credit, and with the price of food sky high, she had little coin to pay for it. The continuing war with France was causing hardships for everyone. The one saving grace was that their well-tended vegetable garden was thriving and producing enough food to stave off complete starvation.

Desperate, Brandy had become a thief.

She had come up with the scheme, disguised in Michael's old clothes, to pilfer food from the wealthier neighboring estates. Anne had argued against it, of course, but despite her cousin's tears, Brandy began to venture out at night. It wasn't as if they couldn't afford to lose a little, she argued, trying to justify her thievery. Those that had, had a plentiful lot.

She had been fortunate thus far. She had not been caught, nor had her identity been found out. She only hoped her luck held. She could well imagine what her Aunt Jessie would do if she became aware of what her niece was doing in the middle of the night. Or, heaven forbid, the authorities!

Brandy gritted her teeth in frustration, then vented her anger aloud when the clouds opened and released a torrent of rain. She raised a clenched fist skyward. Nature was not making it easy for her this night. The obstinate moon and now the blasted rain were hindering her dash to safety. The rain quickly soaked through her cloak and woolen cap, and she shivered from the chill.

Crouching low, she pressed against the side of the stable, waiting impatiently for the rain to stop. The wind picked up in intensity and blew the clouds across the sky, taking the rain with it, and leaving behind a cool, damp mist. Breathing a sigh of relief, she cautiously stepped from behind the concealing shrub. She peered at the stand of trees a short distance away. If she could just make it there…

Glancing up, she watched the silhouette of a large cloud approach the moon. She looked over her shoulder at the brightly lit manor house, the sound of music drifting faintly to her on the rain-scented breeze. Her muscles tensed in anticipation. The dark silhouette was getting closer, closer—

The cloud covered the moon. Taking advantage of the darkness, she sprinted toward the trees, the dark stand looming just out of reach. She was very nearly there when, suddenly, her feet were swept out from under her by an iron band clamped around her stomach. She doubled over, her breath momentarily knocked out of her.

For one split second, she froze in fear, then snapping quickly out of her shock, she struggled to free herself, twisting and turning and blindly kicking out. She connected solidly with a shin and was rewarded with a grunt and the grip loosening from around her waist. She twisted sideways, fell to the ground, and jumped to her feet. As she started to dash off, she was brought up short by a firm grip on her arm. Jerked backward, she gasped in pain, certain her arm had been wrenched from her shoulder.

The moon shook off the cloud, its light fully illuminating the face of her captor. Good Lord! She recognized those strong, sculptured features. Her breath caught in her throat. It was him—the one who had so unceremoniously pulled her from her horse. Her gaze dropped to his mouth, the full lips now stretched into a thin, tight line. Despite her fear, she remembered their kiss—vividly. The warmth from that recollection nearly set her damp cloak steaming.

Her captor looked down and smiled without mirth. "What have we here?"

She blinked in surprise. She had been prepared for anger, but contempt? "Let me go!" she demanded, remembering to lower her tone to match her lad's attire. She increased her struggles, but to no avail. She was caught in a steel trap. Kicking out, she again struck his shin.

"Ouch, damn it!" He shook her, hard. "What are you doing, sneaking around out here? Answer me, or God's truth, I'll beat it out of you."

Brandy stilled and lifted her chin a notch. She clenched her lips together, her brows drawing down in a scowl.

"Have it your way." He started to pull her toward the manor house. "We'll see what our host has to say about a thief on his property."

"Unhand me, you—you beast! I ain't no thief."

"That is his chicken, is it not?" He looked pointedly at the bird dangling from Brandy's hand.

She had completely forgotten about her booty.

"Are you telling me 'tis yours? Out for a midnight stroll with your pet? A dead pet?" He laughed at his own joke. He peered into her shadowed face and, scowling, jerked her arm. "Come along, thief."

When he again started to drag her toward the manor house, and the inevitable irate owner of the chicken, Brandy dug in her heels.

"Chandler? Chandler, darling, are you out here?"

Brandy heard his muttered curse and glanced toward the house. The silhouette of a woman was drifting toward them through the mist. Quickly taking advantage of the distraction, she leaned over and bit his wrist.

He grunted in pain and when his grip slackened, Brandy wrested her arm free and spun on her heel. She was gone in a flash. The moon, deciding to cooperate, hid behind a passing cloud to conceal her flight into the trees.

Chandler rubbed his wrist, staring at the point where the lad had melted into the darkness, his eyes narrowed. The urchin seemed familiar, but his usually sharp mind was clouded by whiskey, so he was unable to ascertain in what way.

The woman drew his arm through her silk-clad one. "There you are, darling, I've been looking everywhere for you." The invitation in her voice was unmistakable, a promise of passion in her tone.

"Now that you have found me, Vivian, shall we go inside?" he drawled, drawing her toward the house. He glanced over his shoulder at the stand of trees, resolving to ponder this turn of events when in a clearer frame of mind.

****

"Brandy?" The voice whispered anxiously from an unlit corner of the room.

"Ssh, 'tis me." A small, booted foot appeared in the window, followed by a trim form dropping to the floor with a soft thud. Brandy straightened and peered at the spot of white slicing the darkness. "Anne, why are you still awake? Is something amiss?" Brandy lit the candle on the bedside table.

"I had a bad dream and awoke frightened. I had to assure myself of your safety. I don't like this one bit." Her voice quivered with fear.

"We have to eat, don't we?" Brandy snapped, her nerves stretched taut from her near disaster.

"Yes, of course."

"We must fend for ourselves. There's no one else to help," Brandy continued, softening her tone at her cousin's obvious distress. She drew off the soggy woolen cap, allowing the auburn braid to fall free. "Good heavens, the entire country is in a miserable state of affairs. Except for the rich," she muttered beneath her breath.

"Michael will be home soon," Anne said with encouragement.

Brandy took a deep breath, twisting the cap in her hands. "There is something I haven't told you. It's about Michael. I received word from Mr. Arbuckle that he could not locate Mr. Oakley's shipping company in London."

"I don't understand."

"Neither do I."

"But then where is Michael?"

"I don't know."

Anne stared at Brandy in confusion. It was then she noticed her cousin's disheveled state. "Brandy, what happened? You look like you've been in a scuffle. Why, your cloak is torn!"

Brandy doffed the damp cloak and, after brushing away the drops of rain, laid it over the back of a chair. Not wanting Anne to become more alarmed, she thought it prudent not to tell her of the close call she'd experienced.

"'Tis nothing, truly. My sleeve got caught on a low-hanging tree branch." She leaned out the open window, turned toward her cousin and exclaimed, "Look what I have!" Raising her hand, she proudly displayed the night's booty.

"Oh, my! Here, let me take it to the kitchen. I'll be back to help you to bed." Holding the dead chicken at arm's length, its head dangling at an odd angle, Anne left the room.

Brandy was bone-tired, her body aching from head to toe. She reached up to loosen her hair, and immediately grimaced in pain. Silently cursing the stranger's rough treatment, she unraveled the braid, allowing her hair to tumble around her shoulders. She tugged off her scuffed black boots, then shed her britches and shirt and stuffed them into the bottom of the armoire. Wrapping the boots and cap in the cloak, she hid them with the other clothes. She unwound the bindings from around her breasts, sighing with pleasure as the restriction was lifted, and was donning a pink cotton nightdress when her cousin returned.

Anne picked up a cloth and dipped it in a bowl of water on the commode. She washed the dirt from Brandy's face, studying it as she did. Brandy studiously kept her gaze averted from Anne's inquisitive one.

"Was there a problem this evening? You arrived later than usual." Anne placed the cloth on the commode and picked up the silver hairbrush from the dressing table. She turned her cousin around, and slowly pulled the brush through the mass of auburn hair, the motion soothing Brandy's frayed nerves.

"No, it just took longer to catch the bird. It led me a merry chase. Do stop worrying, Anne. I'm home now. I appreciate you waiting up for me, but I'm fine, truly I am." She reached for the brush. "Now go to bed. I will see you in the morning."

"Well, if you're sure. Until the morning, then." Anne closed the door softly behind her.

Brandy sank to the bench in front of the dressing table and stared at her reflection in the mirror. A close call, it was, too close. She shuddered as she recalled dark eyes boring into hers, the steel grip of his hand wrapped around her arm. Thank the Lord that woman had arrived when she had, giving Brandy the opportunity to twist out of his grasp and flee. It was just lucky she hadn't dropped the bloody bird in her flight to safety.

Chandler. She now had a name. She had thought of him often since their first encounter, but her adoption, Philip's death, and the consequences from Michael's continued absence had weighed heavily on her mind. There hadn't been room for much else, least of all fanciful dreams of a handsome stranger with startling blue eyes. Except at night, when her dreams were active.

She had thought it a perfect night to raid the Aldens' barn, what with him hosting a house party. She hadn't counted on one of the guests skulking around the grounds in the rain. She had thought herself quite safe, for what idiot would shun the warmth and gaiety of a party for the cool dampness of an English country night? *An extremely handsome idiot.* Even overwhelmed by fear and frustration, she had not failed to be affected by his presence. She also couldn't forget the feel of his lips on hers. That one kiss had kept her up many a night. To think of it now fairly took her breath away.

The moon had highlighted his features to perfection—features that were already etched in her memory. His chin was strong, his nose perfectly sculpted. His mouth—well, maybe she'd stay away from that body part.

Her kitten jumped into her lap, and absently stroking the soft fur, she continued her musings of the mysterious man. After her first run-in with him, she had searched her memory but had been certain she had not seen him before that day. The Drummonds had been on friendly terms with the Aldens, when they were in residence, but they did not travel in the same circles.

She inhaled sharply, suddenly panicked, and jumped to her feet, spilling the kitten to the floor. If she could see his features, then couldn't he see hers? But—wait! When the moon had escaped its cloud cover it was behind her, illuminating his features, not hers. She sighed in relief. She was perfectly safe, for now. She'd need to be more careful in the future, she decided, climbing onto her bed and sliding beneath the soft linen sheets. She pulled the coverlet under her chin and fell asleep instantly, her fears eased for a time.

She would have been alarmed to learn that the object of her musings was just as occupied with thoughts of her.

****

After the guests had found their beds, Chandler relaxed in his chamber in front of the huge hearth where a fire crackled cheerfully. He leaned back in the chair and dragged on a cheroot. Vivian had retired to her room an unhappy woman after her not so blatant invitations were received with barely concealed frustration. Why couldn't she grasp the fact he was finished with her? Perhaps time and continued refusals would do the trick, though he didn't truly believe it would be that easy. He'd been tempted to leave for London but had promised Michael to check on his sister. He would honor that promise before he left Alden Ridge.

Blue eyes narrowed as he thought through the events of the evening. He had gone outside to escape the attentions of the women buzzing around him like bees—and he'd been nearly trampled by an urchin. He conjured a vision of the lad glaring up at him with a mixture of anger and fear. Peering into the urchin's dirty face, he had difficulty making out features, yet there was an air of familiarity. He'd also experienced the oddest sensation as if he were—drawn to a lad? Absurd! No, there was something else here—all wasn't what it seemed. Too bad the hellion had escaped. If Vivian hadn't come looking for him, he might have his answer to this riddle.

He smoked his cheroot in silence, dismissing the incident, and thought about his recent trip into France. It had gone well enough, although he hadn't been able to obtain any hard evidence against Blackwell. It was frustrating, to be sure. He threaded his fingers through his hair, exhausted from the journey. He suddenly felt much older than his twenty-eight years. Deciding he needed a few days to relax before returning to London, he made the choice to stay on at Alden Ridge with Jeffrey and the other guests. It would do no harm to wait a few more days before checking in on Michael's sister.

She would still be there.

Chapter 10

The morning sun streaming through the window touched Brandy awake. She opened one eye, squinting at the sunlight. She had neglected to close the drapes when she retired. Rolling over, she screamed in pain. Just when had she been slammed repeatedly against a wall? Tentatively, she stretched one slim arm toward the edge of the bed, wincing at the throbbing ache in her shoulder. Gritting her teeth against the pain, she flung off the coverlet and swung her legs over the side of the bed. She wiggled her toes. Good heavens, even that small movement was torture. Oh, of course, she had landed a well-placed kick. Two, in fact.

Memories of last night's escapade washed over her like a mountain stream. Her heart pounding, she lay back against the pillows, desperately trying to calm her fear, worried again he might have seen through her disguise to discover the dirty lad was in truth a lady—the same lady he had kissed in the lea.

No, she reassured herself, not possible. The moon had illuminated his features, not hers. He wouldn't have been able to make out her features. Besides, he didn't know who she was. If he reported the theft, who would suspect Lady Brandy Drummond of sneaking about the countryside in the dead of night to pilfer food? She prayed he hadn't reported the theft. She wanted to continue taking from Alden Ridge—it being the best stocked larder around.

She closed her eyes and wondered for the hundredth time, *Who was he? More importantly, why did just the idea of him have such an unsettling effect?*

No doubt he would return to wherever he hailed from—most likely London. She had read about peers of the realm descending upon their country estates, elaborately dressed with guests in tow, for endless rounds of parties. Although, he had not been garbed as she would have expected, on the contrary, his attire was of simple elegance. He obviously shunned the bright colors that rivaled a peacock's brilliance, rather opting to be clad in black, with only his white ruffled shirt and impeccably tied cravat visible in the moonlit grounds.

She pulled the coverlet up under her chin and fingered the gold locket nestled between her breasts. At first, she had refused to wear it, but Aunt Jessie had convinced her otherwise, stating that whatever the reasons for her abandonment, she was certain it was not for lack of love. Brandy wasn't sure about her logic but decided to wear it just the same. She hadn't the courage to delve too deeply into her feelings yet, but the locket was the only link she had to her natural parents. It gave her an odd sense of belonging, without even knowing to whom she belonged.

Anne had studied the portrait of the man in the locket and announced that she saw some resemblance to Brandy. Brandy didn't see it, but it did make her wonder about her mother. Did she have the same auburn hair? The same emerald-green eyes? Was she tall or short? Was she even alive?

Brandy had changed since the day she had learned of her adoption. To some extent, she was relieved to learn that Philip Drummond was not her true father. It explained his actions, his aloofness. She had felt guilty about her declining affection for him. Now she felt only anger—anger he had never told her the truth about her birth, anger he had taken his own life and left hers in such a mess, but mainly anger that he was the cause of a little girl's heartache and misery.

She shook off the depressing thoughts. She would think on it after she found a way to put food on the table. She hoped in a more ladylike and lawful manner.

A solution to Brandy's dilemma had been presented, but the very idea of marrying Roger Blackwell made her flesh crawl. It wasn't that he was hard to look upon— some even considered him handsome with his wavy blond hair and brown eyes, but she was certain his handsome looks hid a cruel streak as wide as England. She would starve before she married that bounder. If the rumors were true, he hadn't a farthing to his name, so he would be no help to her immediate problems anyway.

She rolled her head to look out the window. Her gaze followed the puffy white clouds drifting lazily across the azure expanse. The sunny day and sweet songs of the birds helped revive her wilted spirits. Deciding it was time to leave the relative safety of her bed, she suddenly laughed aloud imagining the authorities knocking down her door and dragging her off to prison. How ridiculous!

She threw back the coverlet, preparing to rise, when a knock sounded at her door. She froze and stared at the closed portal, eyes wide with fright. The authorities! She called out, fully expecting to see the magistrate stride into the room, chains in hand. When it was Maddie who bustled in, she berated herself for her fancies and smiled as the housekeeper placed a cup of chocolate on the bedside table.

"Good morning."

"Good morning, Miss Brandy. I trust you slept well?"

Brandy nodded, watching Maddie cross to the armoire. "'Tis not necessary for you to wait on me."

"Tsk, I enjoy doing it." Maddie dismissed the subject with a wave of one plump hand. "Miss Anne is already up and out in the garden painting. Her ladyship is in the salon with her needlepoint. She's waiting to breakfast with you."

"Oh, Maddie, what would I do without you? I only wish I could pay your wages."

"I will hear none of that." Maddie held up her hand. "We wouldn't dream of leaving you, especially now when you have fallen on hard times. I'm certainly not one to run at the first sign of trouble. And I believe circumstances will improve. Why, just this morning I found a chicken in the cooler!" She turned back to the armoire, ignoring Brandy's wide-eyed expression. "What will my child wear today? It promises to be another warm one."

"You pick out something," she answered, feeling a spark of gratitude and love for the older woman. Whatever Maddie suspected she would keep to herself. She swung her slim legs over the side of the bed and rushed over to the housekeeper. Wrapping her arms around her ample waist, she hugged her tight. "Maddie, you're wonderful!"

"Now, none of that. Let's get you dressed and downstairs to greet the day."

Brandy bounced back with her usual high spirits.

She splashed cool water on her face and allowed Maddie to brush her hair and bind it with a colorful ribbon. She donned a cotton shift, threadbare but still serviceable, then reached for the cornflower-blue muslin dress Maddie had laid out on the bed. It had short, capped sleeves with a square neck, and the waist belted with a white ribbon, accenting her trim figure.

"I'm glad you gave up wearing those dreary black dresses, Miss Brandy. They didn't suit you, and we're close enough to the end of the mourning period."

Brandy silently agreed and, toilette complete, descended the wide staircase, her hand sliding down the smooth banister. She found Jessie in the salon seated near the window, her gray head bent over her tapestry, her nimble fingers expertly plying the needle. Jessie was older than her sister, Doreen, yet her step was lively and, though at times a bit vague, when warranted she had the constitution of an ox.

Jessie looked up from her embroidery and smiled. "Good morning, Brandy."

"Good morning, Aunt. How is your tapestry coming along?" She edged around the chair and glanced over her aunt's shoulder. Ablaze with color, the silken threads were intricately intertwined, the delicate stitches depicting a scene from another era—an armored knight and his lady fair. "'Tis beautiful," she breathed, clearly impressed with her aunt's show of talent.

"Thank you, my dear."

Brandy looked out the window to where Anne was engrossed with her painting, a large canvas placed within reach, a palette of varied colors in hand. "Will Anne be joining us?"

"No, she broke fast earlier. She was eager to take

advantage of this glorious morning." Jessie set aside her sewing and rose to her feet. "Shall we?" She slipped her arm through Brandy's and the two strolled into the dining room.

On the sideboard was a covered dish and a large basket of rolls, a selection of preserves beside it. Arthur came in and placed the tea service next to the basket.

"What have we this morning, Arthur?" Brandy peered over the butler's shoulder. He lifted the lid, allowing the steam to escape in gray ribbons to the ceiling.

"Porridge, again? Oh, what I wouldn't give for one decent meal. Just think, Aunt Jessie…" Her mouth watered as she envisioned the feast. "A lovely pink ham, mounds of fluffy eggs, lightly toasted brioche with jam, and fresh fruit with coddled cream." With a resigned sigh for what was not to be, she spooned porridge into a bowl, and selected a roll and a small jar of marmalade while Jessie poured them each a cup of tea.

Brandy tasted the porridge and silently blessed Maddie for trying to enhance the bland flavor by adding generous portions of cream and honey. She fingered the rim of the bowl, off-white porcelain peppered with little pink and yellow flowers. She treasured Doreen's chinaware and had refused to part with it. Not only was it beautiful and in perfect condition, it had been a wedding present to Doreen from her mother. She was determined to hold onto it, no matter how destitute they became.

"Good morning," Anne called out as she entered the dining room.

"Good morning, Anne. How's the painting?"

"Coming along nicely." She poured herself a cup of

tea and joined them at the table.

"What are you girls going to do today?"

"I thought I might take Misty for a ride. Thank heaven we haven't needed to sell her. I'm sure I'd go mad without my horse."

"Yes, we do have some things to be thankful for, even with your less than desirable circumstances."

As they chatted among themselves, Brandy surveyed the dining room. It was a bright, sunny room. Two floor-to-ceiling windows framed by blue velvet drapes let in plenty of sunshine. The large mahogany table was centered on a thick rug of bright blues and greens. It could easily seat at least twenty guests, however only six cushioned chairs remained grouped around it. The white decorative silk cloth runner had to be discarded due to the red wine stain caused by Philip's anger. They managed to hold onto the matching sideboard, but the beautiful cabinet that had housed her mother's chinaware had to be sold. Her glance took in the many bright spots of wallpaper where here and there gilt-framed paintings depicting the English countryside had once graced the walls.

They were enjoying a second cup of tea when the doorbell chimed. Brandy listened to the muted voices drifting down the foyer, trying to recognize the caller.

"I wonder who could be calling this early in the day?" Jessie looked over at Brandy. "My dear, you look positively peaked. Are you ill?"

Brandy forced a smile. "I'm fine, Aunt. I fear I ate too fast, 'tis all."

Brandy waited with bated breath for Arthur to appear in the doorway. "Miss Brandy, Sir Bodsworth is here to see you. I put him in the drawing room. I informed him you were breakfasting, and it is too early to be calling, but he insisted on seeing you," he added with a frown.

Brandy's uneasiness blossomed into panic. Her cup slipped from her fingers, clattering noisily against the saucer, and sending tea sloshing over the sides. "Thank you, Arthur. Please tell him I will be there directly."

"I wonder what the good magistrate wants." Jessie looked at Brandy with a puzzled expression. "We've already answered his questions about Philip's death."

In a show of nonchalance, Brandy shrugged her shoulders and, studiously avoiding Anne's anxious expression, placed the napkin beside her bowl, stood, and smoothed her skirts. "Well, I will find out soon enough. No, stay and finish your tea," she said as they made to rise. "I will call you if it is of any importance." Brandy swept from the room, her spine straight, her shoulders back, ready to face her fate.

"Lady Brandy." Sir Bodsworth rose to his feet as she moved into the drawing room. He was a tall, lanky man with a thin face and a long mane of white hair. Since leaving the mean streets of London, his expression had become one of perpetual contentment, the sleepy town of Hathshire obviously agreeing with him. His now drawn countenance and troubled eyes only served to increase Brandy's trepidation.

"Good morning, Sir Bodsworth. What brings you to Stonebrooke Manor?" She winced as she heard the slight tremor in her voice. Praying he hadn't noticed it, she perched on the edge of a chair as he resumed his seat on the settee.

"My apologies for disturbing you at such an early hour, milady. I hope I have not inconvenienced you. But

I have just learned something quite disturbing, and I didn't want to wait a moment longer to inform you."

"Sir Bodsworth, what is it?" She took a deep breath, a vision of being carted off to jail darting through her head. She clasped her hands in her lap, her knuckles white.

"Lady Brandy, I've known you for many years, and since your family and I have always been on friendly terms, I wanted to tell you myself before you heard it from another. There is a bit of news circling London—"

"Is it Michael? Have you news of my brother?"

"No. Why?" He cocked his head to one side. "Is your brother in some kind of trouble?" His expression remained nonplussed as he waited for her to explain.

Brandy shook her head. "I'm sorry, please forgive me for interrupting. You were saying?"

He hesitated, then leaned toward her. "'Tis news of Lord Hathshire."

"News of Papa, er, Philip?" A feeling of relief knifed through her that it was neither about Michael nor her midnight activities. She tried to maintain her composure beneath his unrelenting stare.

"It seems—that is, rumor has it—his lordship was involved in smuggling. I have spoken to several of the merchants in town, but they are all very close-mouthed." He held up his hand when she started to protest. "Wait, there is more. It is also being bandied about that he was a spy—for the French. I wanted to spare you the anguish of hearing this from someone who would not be as considerate of your feelings." He leaned back on the settee. "I apologize for blurting this out, but I couldn't find an easier way to spare your feelings but to just say it."

Brandy took a moment to digest this news. Fully expecting him to tell her he had learned about her covert activities; she was unprepared for this startling revelation. "Philip, a spy? Why, that is ridiculous!" But as she thought back to his frequent business trips, the change in his behavior coupled with his excessive drinking, she began to wonder if mayhap it was true.

"That's my opinion as well, Lady Brandy. Absurd. I just thought you should know, `tis all."

"I appreciate it, of course, but I can't believe the rumors are true."

"Yes, 'tis hard to credit. Please don't worry yourself. I will dig further on my own and certainly tell you of anything I uncover." He rose to his feet and reached for his hat. "I will leave you in peace."

"Thank you, Sir Bodsworth."

He stopped in the doorway and turned back. "How are things here?"

"Why, everything is fine." She looked him straight in the eye, her heart beating erratically.

"And Lord Michael? He fares well?"

"He is travelling now, but he is well." She hoped he wouldn't question her further after her earlier blunder.

He stepped forward and took her hands in his. "I would do anything for you, Lady Brandy. If you need anything, anything a'tall, please let me know." He chose his words with care, causing her to wonder if he knew more than he was disclosing.

"Thank you, Sir Bodsworth. You have been more than kind." She escorted him down the hallway and waited for Arthur to open the door. When the door closed behind him, she went into the salon and stood in front of the window, rubbing her hands up and down her bare arms. She glanced over her shoulder and found Anne standing in the doorway.

"You heard?"

Anne nodded. "I feared it was about you, so I listened outside the door."

"'Tis all right. What think you of this news?"

Anne shrugged her shoulders. "I don't know. As hard as it might be to accept, it is something to consider."

"But a spy! For the French? It's just too incredible." She shook her head. "Well, I can't worry about that, too. He's dead, so it no longer matters."

"You don't suppose Michael—"

"No! Don't even think it!"

"I'm sorry. I didn't mean to imply—" Anne rushed forward and grasped her cousin's hands.

"I know, Anne. So much has happened in such a short time."

"What else has happened?"

Startled, Brandy searched for an answer.

"Last night?" Anne prompted.

"I told you nothing happened."

Anne eyed her closely. "If you thought it would worry me, you wouldn't tell me, would you?"

Brandy was saved from answering by Jessie asking from the doorway, "Is the magistrate gone? What did he want?"

"He wanted to see how we are faring and to again extend his condolences. And to be sure to call on him if we need anything." Brandy exchanged glances with Anne. She had not exactly lied, but she had left out a good portion of the real reason for his visit. Her aunt, however, accepted the explanation without question and picked up her tapestry.

As Jessie plied her needle, humming quietly beneath her breath, Brandy read aloud from the *Hathshire Times*, regaling her aunt and cousin with articles she found amusing.

Arthur appeared in the doorway, wearing his second frown of the day. "Miss Brandy, Lord Norwood is coming up the drive."

"Please tell him that I am unavailable."

Arthur nodded and with grim satisfaction walked down the foyer as the door chimes sounded. The three women turned toward the door at the sound of a commotion just as Roger Blackwell strode into the room, Arthur close on his heels. "I'm sorry, Miss Brandy." Arthur was tugging on his waistcoat, his face flushed. "He went right past me."

"Milord, I believe you were informed that I was unavailable." Brandy arched an auburn brow.

"My apologies, Lady Brandy." He bowed at the waist. "But I wished to continue the discussion we started after your father's funeral."

"And I informed you then that the subject was closed. Now, if you don't mind, we were in the middle of a family discussion."

He gaped at her, a flush darkening his fair complexion. He glanced briefly at Anne and Jessie, and turned back to Brandy, a strange glint in his eyes. "Again, my apologies," he said stiffly and strode from the room.

"He's going to cause trouble," Anne warned.

"Maybe we should inform Sir Bodsworth," Jessie suggested, her tone worried.

"He hasn't done anything against the law."

"Maybe we should let the magistrate know just to be

on the safe side," Anne pleaded.

"Nonsense." Brandy waved her hand in the air. "I can take care of Roger Blackwell."

"Well, if you're quite sure, dear." Jessie rose to her feet. "If you girls will excuse me, I think I'll visit with Maddie for a spell. She's been pleading with me to divulge my recipe for shortbread."

Anne waited until her mother had left the room before turning to Brandy. "He threatened you. Not in so many words, mind you, but his demeanor was quite intimidating. What are you going to do?"

"Nothing. Like I said, he hasn't done anything the magistrate could hold him on."

"Remember, Michael is not here to lend his protection."

Brandy bent down to pick up her kitten, who had been rubbing persistently against her skirts. "You may be right," she agreed, adding pensively, "He was furious when he left." She stroked the kitten's soft fur. "I wish there was something I could do, someone I could talk with to find out where Michael is. I'm worried, Anne. He lied to me about his employment. And I haven't heard from him in weeks." A glint of determination flashed in her eyes. "I think it's time to go through Philip's papers. Perhaps I will find something that will lead to Michael's whereabouts or at the very least an explanation as to why I was betrothed to that bounder."

"You know, `tis all right to think of him as your father. After all, he was the only father you knew."

Brandy sighed. "I know, Anne, but…" She rubbed her temples. Life was becoming increasingly more challenging, and it was becoming more difficult by the day to keep up her spirits.

She deposited her kitten on the carpet. "If you need me, I will be in Philip's study."

Chapter 11

Brandy walked into Philip's study, her usually sure step broken by uneasiness. She found his desk littered with papers, splotched with brownish-red stains. Arthur had cleaned away the blood and gore as best he could but otherwise had left the room much as it had been the day Philip took his life. She shut the door quietly as if afraid of disturbing his spirit.

With halting steps, she approached the desk. The image of Philip slumped over it, the still-smoking gun clutched in his hand, the raw gaping hole in his head, caused bile to rise in her throat. She took a few deep breaths and stiffened her spine. *I'm on a mission. This is no time to be squeamish.* She sat in the large leather chair behind the desk and proceeded to read each piece of paper, search every nook and cranny of the desk. She had no idea what she was looking for, nor what she would find. However, if there were any clues to Philip's downfall or the reason behind her betrothal to Roger Blackwell, or what, if anything, her brother was involved in, she was determined to find them.

Twilight crept in, shadows grew into long ribbons of black against the dun-colored carpet, yet still she pressed on. When she could no longer see clearly, she lit a candle. Most of the papers she'd sifted through were of little importance, and she set them aside. Peering into each drawer, she studied the contents carefully, looking for any information. She reached to the back of one drawer and withdrew a crumpled piece of paper. She smoothed it out. It was an official-looking document, an unfamiliar seal stamped in the center of the page. She couldn't make sense of most of the words, as if written in code. But she readily made out one word, and her heart thudded in her chest. *Michael.* And whenever her brother's name was mentioned, coupled with it was another's—*Andrew Townsend.*

Brandy leaned back and chewed the tip of her finger. She vaguely remembered Michael mentioning a school chum by the name of Townsend. Could it be the same one? What were they involved in? And why did Philip have this document with their names on it stuffed in the back of a drawer? Crumpled into a ball, no less!

She folded the wrinkled piece of paper and placed it back in the drawer. Leaning down, she pulled open the bottom drawer and was met with resistance. It was locked. She searched through the other drawers for a key. Finding none, she slammed the last drawer shut in annoyance and heard a faint clinking sound. She yanked it back open and found a key on the bottom of the drawer, obviously knocked loose from its hiding place. She fit the key into the lock and the bottom drawer opened to reveal a brown leather journal. She picked it up, running her hand over the smooth cover, filled with a sense of foreboding. What secrets, if any, did it hold? Was she prepared for what she was about to learn? She hesitated but a moment before turning it over—and found it, too, was locked. After a careful search of the drawer, she found a small key hidden under a piece of wood in the bottom of the drawer.

She opened the journal and flipped through the

pages, stopping occasionally to scan selected pages. She read of her adoption, but no mention was made of her natural parents. She continued until she arrived at the entries beginning several months before Philip took his life.

Michael and his cohorts are in trouble. I have heard their names mentioned among my superiors. I must warn them. But how? Lest I get caught myself.

Brandy drew in her breath, a strong premonition of disaster beginning to dawn. She read on.

Blackwell is quite persistent. He will not rest until he has the promise of Brandy's hand. I hate to do that to her, but all will be lost if I don't comply with his demand. Blackwell knows too much. Damn it, he holds my future in his hands.

Brandy's brow knitted in confusion. Philip had felt remorse betrothing her to Lord Norwood? Had he, indeed, been coerced into it? And what had he meant about Michael? What trouble did he speak of?

She closed and locked the journal, having no answers to her questions. She slipped the key into her dress pocket and left the study, the journal tucked under her arm.

Pleading a headache, she spent the rest of the evening in her bedchamber curled up on the window seat with the journal. She read each word until, well past midnight, she finished reading the last entry, placed the journal in the bedside table drawer, extinguished the candle, and slid into bed.

Unable to sleep, she tossed and turned while time crawled by at a snail's pace. By dawn, she had come to a decision. She would go to London. She had to find this Andrew Townsend. She was certain he was the key to finding Michael. She was worried—her brother had lied to her, a rarity in itself, and she sensed he was in trouble. She could no longer afford to wait for word from him—she had to act now.

After pinning her hair into a loose bun at the nape of her neck, she splashed water on her face and dressed in a pink-and-white flowered dress. Searching for Anne, she found her in the kitchen with Maddie, enjoying a cup of tea.

"Good morning," she greeted them, entering the warm, inviting room.

"Good morning, Brandy." Anne assessed her cousin's mood. "Did you sleep well?"

Maddie looked up from a tray of plump loaves of golden bread she had just taken from the oven. "Good morning, Miss Brandy. Sit down, child, and I'll fix you something to eat. You missed supper last night," she admonished with a frown.

"I wasn't hungry. But that bread does smell delicious."

Maddie grasped a crusty loaf with a towel and proceeded to cut it into thick slices. She placed a platter of bread, a crock of creamy butter, and a pot of honey on the table within easy reach.

Brandy slathered a slice of warm bread with butter and honey, and grabbing a napkin, she signaled to her cousin. "I need to talk to you," she whispered, making her way to the sitting room.

"What is it?"

"I found Philip's journal yesterday and spent most of last night reading it. He wasn't explicit, but from what I could gather he was in a great deal of trouble. I think 'tis true what Sir Bodsworth told me. Philip was involved in smuggling. He makes several mentions of shipments arriving from France and of depositing them in secret places throughout the village. Wait, it gets worse." She placed the plate of untouched bread on a small, spindly table. "It seems that he was roped into becoming a spy— for the French. The rumors circulating London are true," she ended in a ragged whisper.

"Oh no!" Anne's hand flew to her mouth, her eyes widening in disbelief.

"I didn't want to believe it at first, but after reading the entire journal, I am almost certain 'tis true. Michael is in trouble too. But he's not a traitor. Apparently, he and Philip were working on opposite sides of the war."

"That would explain why he lied to you about working for a shipping company."

"True, but it also means he could be in danger." She started to pace, her hands clasped tightly in front of her. "It seems that Roger was behind everything. He demanded marriage to me and forced Philip to do his dirty work."

"Poor Uncle Philip. What are you going to do now?"

"I am going to London. I believe Michael is involved with a man named Andrew Townsend. Perhaps he can lead me to Michael or at the very least assure me he's safe. Philip also mentioned a man named Blanchard. Roger's cohorts apparently fear him. He must be quite powerful to instill that emotion in those miscreants."

"Whatever will you tell Mama? I don't think she'll allow you to go alone."

"We will not mention a word of this to Aunt Jessie. I am only confiding in you because I need your help."

"What can I do?" Anne sank into a flowered damask chair, her hands clenched in her lap.

"If Aunt Jessie wonders where I am, I'll need you to cover for me."

"You can't think to travel alone? I have heard such horrible stories of young ladies—"

"I will not be traveling as a lady." Brandy stared out the window facing the back garden. It was early autumn and most of the summer flowers were gone. The trees, however, were turned out in a profusion of warm colors, the leaves splotched against the cerulean sky like a painter gone mad.

"You can't think to travel in disguise! I won't allow it!"

"I have no other choice. I can do nothing about Philip. He is dead. But Michael is not, and I will find him. Roger is becoming far too persistent. Michael needs to be here to help me squash this ridiculous betrothal agreement once and for all. And, lest we forget, we're practically destitute." She waved her hand through the room. "Look around you, Anne. I have sold virtually everything we own and there are still creditors hounding me. I have no other choice."

"You've made up your mind, then?"

"Yes."

"Then I will do whatever needs to be done. And don't worry about Mama—I will think of something to explain your absence."

"I knew I could count on you. Now, I will leave tonight—at midnight. I will take Misty and a satchel with a few clothes and some food. I suppose I should take a couple of dresses in case I have need to be a lady."

"Where will you go first? Do you know where Blanchard or Townsend reside?"

"No, I don't. I've decided to try to locate Andrew

Townsend first. If he is of no help, I will search out Blanchard. The problem is, I don't know if that's his first or last name. I will start in the West End of London. I believe that's where the nobility lives."

"How do you know he is nobility?"

"I don't, but it's as good a place as any to start."

Anne tilted her head to one side. "Did you say Townsend? That name sounds familiar." After a moment, she snapped her fingers. "I've got it! Mama had a friend named Townsend. Although, I don't believe they've corresponded in years."

"Townsend is not an uncommon name. It might not be the same, and we certainly cannot ask Aunt Jessie. She will want to know why we want to know. And then my plans will be for naught."

"True, but—"

"I will find out soon enough when I get to London. Now stop worrying, cousin."

****

Brandy waited impatiently for the clock to strike midnight. When the chimes drifted up from the foyer, she jumped off the bed and by the soft glow of a candle, began to disguise herself in the lad's clothing. She groaned as she wrapped the linen around her breasts, binding them flat. She was not, by any means, a small-breasted woman, and the bindings were not only uncomfortable but painful.

Anne slipped into the room with a large cloth bag of food and stood to one side, shaking her head at her wayward cousin. "Mama and I could accompany you to London."

"I would rather the two of you stay here. What if Michael comes home? He would wonder where

everyone is. Besides, I will be able to travel faster alone."
She shrugged into a wrinkled shirt and caught Anne's
worried expression. "I'm tired of just sitting here waiting
for something to happen. I must do something! Now,
come help me with my hair." Anne quickly plaited
Brandy's mass of curls, twisted the braid around her
head, and stuffed it under the wool cap.

Brandy peered into the looking glass, pleased with
the transformation. Lady Brandy Drummond had
disappeared, replaced by an urchin. Now for the final
touch. She reached into the fireplace and grabbed a
handful of soot. With a grimace, she rubbed it on her
face, concealing the creamy glow and feminine lines of
her complexion. "There, what think you, cousin?" She
faced Anne, arms akimbo, one knee bent, her head
cocked saucily to one side.

"As long as you don't smile or look directly at them,
no one will mistake you for a lady," Anne announced
with a nod. She grasped Brandy's hands in hers. "Are
you sure you want to do this? I'm frightened for you."

"Well, don't be. I can take care of myself. Will you
and Aunt Jessie be all right by yourselves?"

Anne nodded and moved to hug her cousin. "God
speed, Brandy," she whispered. Then, a little louder and
a little more fearful, "I don't know what I'm going to tell
Mama."

"You'll think of something." Brandy held onto her
bravado as tightly as she held onto Anne. "Be sure not to
tell her until tomorrow evening. I should be in London
by then. I will send a message as soon as I can."

Anne picked up the cloth bag of food and stuffed it
into the satchel while Brandy pulled on her boots and
shrugged into the black cloak. They left the room and

walked downstairs to the back door. Anne gave her cousin one last hug and waited until Brandy had faded into the night before shutting the door and making her way to her bedchamber, her whispered prayers drifting behind her.

Brandy made haste in saddling her mare, then walked Misty out into the cool night air. She cast one last glance at the big house, silent in the dark of night. She mounted astride, keeping her horse to a walk until she reached the long drive where, setting her heels to the horse's flanks, she cantered down the drive.

The moon was a sliver of silver, emitting little light, and stars were strewn haphazardly against the black velvet sky. She turned onto the main road to London, skirting the deep ruts left by wagons that travelled daily from the country to the city transporting produce and livestock. Hugging the side of the road, she kept a wary eye out for bandits and ruffians.

The horizon swallowed the moon as dawn emerged in pink and yellow grandeur. Brandy, nodding wearily in the saddle, had jerked awake more than once in time to catch herself from toppling to the ground. Thinking she had made good time thus far, she decided to catch a few hours of much-needed sleep. Guiding her mare deep into the forest, she came upon a small clearing where she dismounted, tied Misty to a tree, and handed her a handful of oats from a bag hanging from the saddle. She retrieved her satchel and rummaged through it until she found the bundle of food Anne had stowed. Selecting a fat, red apple, she leaned against a tree and devoured her treat. She tossed the apple core to Misty and stared off into the distance, her thoughts focused on the task ahead. The early morning sun filtered through the trees, caressing her face with warmth, making her eyelids heavy. She pulled the cloak around her and settled down to take a quick nap.

****

Several days after Chandler had returned from France, he ventured to Stonebrooke Manor to honor his promise to Michael. Having decided on the reason for his visit—to offer his condolences on her father's death—he would assure himself that Michael's sister was faring well, then head for home. The few days of relaxation at Alden Ridge had lifted his spirits, and he was now eager to return to London and report to Blanchard.

He topped a small rise and reined in his horse. At the bottom of the incline, nestled among large oak trees, sprawled Stonebooke Manor. It was not a large home, compared to most country estates, but it had a warm, inviting look about it. It was two stories high, the brick mellowed with age where ivy scaled the walls, clinging to the eaves of the roof. He urged his stallion down the hill and dismounted before the front stoop. He ascended the steps and knocked loudly upon the door. After several moments, it was opened by a young woman with dark red curls. Her gray eyes were wide with curiosity, her expression guarded.

"May I help you?" She tilted her head to one side.

"I am Chandler Townsend, Duke of Marbury—"

"Townsend?"

"Yes, Chandler Townsend. Are you Lady Drummond?"

"Brandy?"

Ah, the chit's name. He nodded. "Yes, Lady Brandy Drummond?"

"No, I'm her cousin."

"Is Lady Brandy at home?"

"No. Is she in some kind of—I mean to say—is there a problem?"

Chandler eyed her curiously, having seen the shadow of fear darken her eyes. "Not that I'm aware of. I simply wanted to offer my respects. I am acquainted with her brother, Michael."

"Michael! Have you word of him?" She reached out and clutched his arm.

Chandler frowned. "No, I am merely acquainted with him. I was visiting a friend of mine who lives nearby and thought to offer my condolences on the loss of her father."

"Oh, I see," Anne said, releasing his arm, her face tinted pink. She glanced over her shoulder and stepped out, pulling the door closed behind her.

Taking note of the odd conversation they were engaged in, and mindful of her reaction to his name as well as Michael's, he turned the subject. "Do you know when she will return?"

She opened her mouth to answer, apparently thought better of it, and merely uttered, "No."

Chandler's brows drew together. What in the hell was going on here? And why was she acting so mysterious about Lady Brandy's whereabouts? Deciding he would get nothing further out of the woman, he bowed and took a step back.

"Thank you for your time."

"Of course. I will inform Brandy of your visit."

He nodded and descended the steps, mounted his stallion and cantered off down the drive.

Anne remained on the front stoop until he disappeared, wondering if he was any relation to the one

Brandy sought in London. She glanced up, frowning at the darkening sky. It had turned an eerie shade of gray, and the wind was now blowing wildly, kicking up leaves and playing havoc with the tree branches.

She prayed her cousin had found shelter from the coming storm. Shivering from the chill in the air, she moved back into the house, mentally preparing herself for the confrontation with her mother. She had yet to inform her of Brandy's departure. She would be upset—to say the least.

Chapter 12

Brandy awoke from her nap completely disoriented. She was chilled to the bone and her bed was cold and unyielding beneath her back. Coming fully awake, she jumped to her feet, crying out in dismay at the long shadows slicing the clearing. She had slept the day away!

Quickly mounting Misty, she urged her out of the forest and, resuming her trek, stayed close to the side of the turnpike. It was deserted, and eerie shadows danced in the stand of trees bordering one side. The thunder of approaching horses broke the silence. With a quick glance over her shoulder, she pulled off the road just as a large black barouche went bowling by, the team of horses lathered from the fast pace the driver had set. She watched it disappear around a bend in the road as she choked on the dust churned up by the horses' pounding hooves.

She glanced up, saw the sun hugging the horizon, the sky streaked yellow and orange. She berated herself again. *How could I have been so witless to sleep so long?* Frowning, she watched a bank of dark clouds rolling in, heavy with unspent moisture. She didn't relish the idea of spending a night on the road, especially in what promised to be inclement weather.

The sun descended behind the horizon and the wind picked up in intensity. Turning a bend in the road, she spotted a faint light up ahead, a welcome sign of habitation, and mentally counted the coins in her pocket. When the first cold raindrops landed on her head, it didn't take long to come to a decision. She would just have to conserve her money when she arrived in London. Tonight, she would seek shelter.

A flash of lightning split the sky as she rode into the yard of the inn. A sign swung crazily in the wind, proclaiming the establishment as *The Rusty Rooster*. She left Misty in the care of the stable boy and ran around to the front of the inn just as a gust of wind blew across the yard, nearly knocking her to the ground.

She wrestled with the door, finally succeeding in pushing it open, but gasped in alarm as it slipped from her hands and, with a resounding bang, collided with the wall. The sound echoed loudly in the room where several people had gathered. A few curious souls cast glances in her direction.

The innkeeper came bustling over and easily shut the door behind her. He was a heavy-set man with a ruddy complexion and bushy black brows perched over equally dark eyes. His muscles bulged beneath his dingy shirt, stretched taut over his upper arms. He eyed her suspiciously. "What do ye want, lad?"

Brandy started at the appellation, then remembering her guise, lowered her voice to a hoarse gruff. "A room for the night."

"Have ye coin?"

"Aye."

"Well, come along then, but I'll be wantin' the coin first, mind ye." He held out a large grubby hand and quickly pocketed the coin she'd fished out of her pocket.

Brandy followed the innkeeper up the stairs, coming up beside him when he stopped at the first door. Pushing it open, he stepped over to the bureau and lit a squat candle. The room was small, the only furniture inhabiting the room was a narrow bed, a small bureau, and a washstand with a small bowl and pitcher. Faded paper peeled away from the walls near the ceiling, and the air smelled musty. A wealth of cobwebs hung like silver lace from the rafters.

"Ye can come downstairs and eat, if ye a mind to. It comes with the room."

"Thank you—ye." Brandy shut the door behind him and turned the key in the lock. She rubbed her bruised posterior and aching back. Her entire body felt as if it had been beaten against a rock, compliments of the many hours she'd spent in the saddle as well as sleeping on the hard ground. The thought of hot food and a warm bed perked up her spirits, and with a renewed spurt of energy, she doffed her damp cloak, checked her appearance in the small, cracked mirror above the washstand, and ventured downstairs. The smell of roasting beef made her mouth water as she made her way to the back of the room near the roaring fire ablaze in a stone hearth. She kept her cap on, her head down, and took one of the tables near the hearth.

A barmaid sauntered over. "What'll ye have?" She studied Brandy with appraising eyes as she took her order. "Will ye be wantin' anything else?" She bent over the table, exposing her bountiful bosom. Brandy nearly choked as the barmaid's meaning became clear. She shook her head in response to the barmaid's veiled suggestion. That one just shrugged and ambled away, hips swaying.

With her head lowered, Brandy glanced around the room but, with her limited vision, was only able to see chair legs and the bottom half of the people who occupied them.

The barmaid returned shortly with a trencher of roasted beef and potatoes along with a tankard of ale. Without a word she placed them in front of Brandy and sauntered off toward a group of men drinking and talking among themselves.

Brandy turned her attention to the food. The meat was slightly tough, and the potatoes overcooked, but it was hot and filling. She made quick work of the meal, and her plate was soon scraped clean. Sated and feeling relatively safe from discovery, she sipped the warm ale, wrinkling her nose at the unfamiliar flavor.

She could hear the wind howling outside and the slash of rain against the windows. She would not have liked to be outside in what had turned out to be a healthy squall. She was thankful she had found the inn to ride it out, despite the coin it cost. The ale began to soothe her frayed nerves and her thoughts turned to London.

The first thing she needed to do was find Andrew Townsend. Failing that, she needed to locate this Blanchard. Assuming she found one or the other, she still had to get information out of them. If the stories about her father were true, they might not believe she was innocent of any wrongdoing. Well, she would just have to handle that, too. She was deeply afraid something had happened to her brother. It mattered not at all that he wasn't her true brother—she loved him and wanted him safe.

Maddie had confided in her that she and Arthur had known about her adoption but had been sworn to secrecy. She thought to tell her after the earl died, but her aunt and cousin had arrived, and she left it to Jessie. After careful consideration, Brandy couldn't blame them for keeping it to themselves—it was not their secret to tell. Brandy had been relieved to learn that Michael didn't know, afraid he had tolerated her presence out of a sense of duty.

Brandy edged closer to the fire, allowing the warmth to steal through her still chilled body. Without warning, the fine hairs on the back of her neck began to bristle. She looked up in alarm and her eyes locked with curious ones of blue. She blinked. What was he doing here? Her gaze slid to his right and her eyes widened. Roger Blackwell! Oh Lord, to be beset by both men! She lowered her gaze lest she be recognized.

Chandler Townsend had noticed the arrival of the lad, loudly announced by his struggle with the inn's door. Something had sparked his memory as he watched the boy follow the innkeeper up the stairs. When they were out of sight, he had turned his attention back to his uninvited dinner companion, dismissing the lad until he'd reappeared minutes later and took a table on the other side of the large hearth. Chandler had watched him clean his plate but was still unable to place the nagging memory his presence stirred. Blackwell drew his attention back to their conversation.

"I'm sorry, Blackwell. You were saying?" His black brows drew down in a frown. It had been a mixed blessing, his running into Blackwell. He couldn't abide the man, and if what Blanchard had told him proved true, he had even more reason for his aversion.

"I said that barmaid looks quite willing. She's been eyeing you most of the evening. Obviously caught sight of your heavy purse." Roger chuckled, resentment oozing from the veiled barb.

Chandler shrugged nonchalantly, not the least bit perturbed by Blackwell's sarcasm. "Not interested. Too many others have passed there before me." He lifted his glass to his lips and sipped the sweet wine, taking the opportunity to study the other man while he was busy flagging down said barmaid. It was a well-known fact that Blackwell's father, the old earl, had lost most of the family fortune gambling. Rumor had it his womanizing and scandalous behavior had put his wife in an early grave. Apparently, Blackwell had inherited his father's bad habits, mixing smuggling and spying into the pot. Chandler grimaced in disgust. If it was the last thing he did, he would stop Blackwell from his treachery.

From under the brim of her cap, Brandy watched both men. She wished she could hear their conversation but didn't dare move any closer. She did not want to bring any undue attention to herself. The dark-haired man had already noticed her, and she thought she had spotted a flicker of recognition in his eyes. She studied his visage, caressed by the fire's glow, and felt giddy. She had to admit he was indeed handsome. In fact, she could still feel his lips on hers from that stolen kiss in the meadow.

Her gaze swung over to Roger. He was handsome, she'd admit, but looked insignificant beside the other man. His blond hair and fair complexion paled beside the bold coloring of the other. Roger was not as tall nor as well built, his shoulders weren't as broad nor was his frame as finely clothed. Remembering his last visit to Stonebrooke Manor, she frowned. He was proving to be a most persistent suitor, and she feared he could become an adversary of the worst kind with her continued refusals to marry him. And what connection did he have to Philip's death? If he was responsible, she would see that he paid for it—dearly. She may not have loved Philip Drummond, but he had provided for her over the years.

She noticed a scowl darkening the handsome man's face. Curious, she leaned closer, hoping to hear their conversation but not be noticed. She set her tankard on the table and scooted her chair around. The leg caught on a splinter of wood and tilted, spilling her unceremoniously to the floor. She landed sprawled on the floor. Luck rode with her, for her cap stayed on, securing her identity as a lad. Scrambling to her feet, she dared a covert glance their way and was mortified to find one corner of the stranger's mouth pulled up in a sardonic smile, black brows arched high above eyes filled with amusement. Roger Blackwell was too busy eyeing the barmaid to notice her tumble to the floor.

Brandy spun on her heel and raced for the stairs but was bought up short by a steel band closing about her upper arm and spinning her around. She looked up into his face and watched, horrified, as recognition dawned in their sapphire depths.

"Let me go, you clod," Brandy cried, her voice a low-pitched squeal.

"You're the little thief I caught stealing a chicken." His accusation was laced with amused disbelief.

"I know nothin' of thievin'. Let me go!"

Chandler stroked his chin with his free hand. "I suppose I could be mistaken." He tightened his grip on her arm. "Nevertheless, I dislike eavesdroppers as much as I do thieves. Would you care to explain yourself?"

"I ain't been eavesdroppin' and I don't have to explain nothin' to the likes of ye." She twisted from his grasp, tearing the still-damp shirtsleeve. "Now see what ye did? Ye tore me bloody shirt!"

"My apologies. But honestly, one more rip in your raggedy clothing is hardly cause for tears."

To Brandy's mortification, a single tear born of fear and frustration had slipped down her cheek, leaving a flesh-colored path in its wake. With a trembling finger she brushed away the tear. "I ain't cryin'. It's water from me cap, 'tis all." She drew herself up. "Now, if ye have no more clothes to be tearin' or accusations to be makin'—" She took a step back from him, poised for flight.

Chandler felt the same odd stirring he had that night at Alden Ridge. He waved his hand toward the stairs. "By all means, don't let me keep you." He turned, dismissing her, and headed back to his table.

Brandy spun around and ran up the stairs, her quick movement causing her cap to slip from her head. She gasped, made a grab for it, and quickly stuffed the thick braid back under it. She sped up the stairs, praying he hadn't turned around to witness what would have been a dead give-away.

When she reached the safety of her room, she slammed the door shut, turned the key in the lock, and leaned back against the door, panting from the close call.

But Chandler had turned around. At the sight of the thick braid of hair snaking down the lad's back, his eyes widened, and his jaw fell slack. Well, of all the bloody— A spark of interest flared. Reluctantly, he rejoined Blackwell, who had missed the exchange while flirting with the barmaid, and hoped he would soon leave so he could contemplate this latest development.

Blackwell patted the buxom barmaid on the buttocks

and stood up. "I'll be retiring now, Townsend. Would you care to join me in my barouche in the morning?"

"No, I have my horse."

Blackwell nodded and disappeared up the stairs to his room.

Chandler signaled for another wine and leaned back, watching the flames dance in the hearth. He stretched his long legs out in front of him and rested his arms across his chest. So, the thieving lad was a girl! That would explain his unnatural attraction. Why was she masquerading as a lad? He was certain she was the same little thief he had caught at Jeffrey's country home. He mentally rubbed his hands together, sensing a mystery. And he loved a good mystery. It was just the sort of thing he needed to get his blood going again, not to mention keeping his mind off his brother's dangerous mission in France.

He envisioned the urchin's face. Now that he knew she was a woman, he wondered how he could have been so blind as not to have seen it. Of course, to his credit, it had been dark that night, what with the moon dodging the clouds, yet underneath all that dirt, her face had a fine, delicate bone structure. The nose was short yet straight, her cheekbones high. Large green eyes were framed by thick dark lashes and accented by dark auburn brows. His blood warmed—he could lose himself in those eyes. He straightened. Of course! That was the ringer—those eyes! He had seen those startling green eyes before—how could he forget? She was the same girl he had *rescued* from her horse the day he had spent watching her in the secluded glade. The same girl he had stolen a kiss from and been slapped for in the meadow. He would bet his life on it!

He relaxed back into his chair and lifted the glass of wine to his lips. He had been so preoccupied with his trip to France he had forgotten to mention the incident to Jeffrey. He had half a mind to beat down her door and demand the truth. He grinned. No, he would bide his time. He would follow her, instead. He would trail her and discover her intentions. He found it passing strange a young girl would be traveling alone—as a lad, no less. Probably stealing from every house she came across, he muttered to himself.

As the storm raged outside the inn, his thoughts turned to his own life. He had spent a relaxing week at Alden Ridge, and after his forthcoming meeting with Blanchard in London, and a short visit with his grandmother, he would travel on to his own Marbury Hall. He hoped Blanchard had no more jobs for him, for he would be forced to decline. He needed to look after his own affairs. Besides, Michael and Andrew were well qualified for the mission they had undertaken, and he had complete confidence in Pierre and Claude to guide them through it. He would also keep watch on Blackwell. If he knew about Michael and Andrew, he would most assuredly make a move against them. That was something to prevent, at all costs.

The first thing he needed to do was survive his time in London, unscathed. His grandmother was residing in his townhouse, and with her ardent wish he wed, she had been parading beautiful young women in front of him despite his declaration that marriage was not an institution he was eager to embrace. Yet she had declared this was the year she would triumph in her quest.

His parents' marriage had been arranged. His father had loved his mother and she had been passing fond of him. He had provided her with a title and wealth, everything she could ever want, but she had to have more, including the attentions and pleasures of other men. She had taken more men to her bed than probably even she could count. After he was born, his father had, on occasion, discreetly sampled what was available but only after being turned away repeatedly by his wife.

Chandler pulled a cheroot from a silver case and lit the end. Inhaling the fragrant smoke, his eyes narrowed in thought as painful, unwanted memories marched through his head. There was a time when he had adored his mother. Camille had been beautiful and gay—her laughter filled the house. Then came the day his opinion of her changed—forever. A lad of twelve, he had finished his schooling early and gone in search of her. He had hesitated outside her bedchamber door, where he'd heard muted voices and soft laughter. Then, pushing it ajar, he had peeked around the edge.

The sight that had greeted him was burned in his memory. His mother had glanced around, the look of horror on her face mirrored on that of the naked man beneath her. Chandler had despised her ever since.

As he grew older, he'd watched his father become a broken man, haunted by his wife's infidelities. When Chandler witnessed what his father's love for his wife was doing, he had vowed that he would never love a woman. Love made one vulnerable—wasn't his own father proof of that? He believed Camille's actions had killed his father, and until his mother's death several years later, Chandler had barely tolerated her in his life. He was not grief-stricken when she'd died.

As he aged, Chandler's belief that women were not to be trusted cemented. He enjoyed what they had to offer, true, but for his own pleasure. He didn't give a damn about their feelings; as far as he was concerned, they possessed none. They hung onto his every word, their eyes glowing with greed they tried to hide. His grandmother scoffed at his opinion of the fairer sex, insisting that not all were like his mother. He just had not met the right one yet.

The only woman Chandler respected was his grandmother. She, too, had despised Camille for what she had done. He knew, to a lesser extent, his grandmother understood how he felt, but she was nevertheless determined to show him not all women were cut from the same cloth. And she intended to prove it.

No, he had no desire to wed, but knew he must, vowing the woman he took to wife would not be one he had met in London. She would be a quiet, unassuming woman he could keep safely ensconced at his country estate, preferably with his heir.

He tossed the cheroot into the fireplace and made his way to his room. At the top of the stairs, he paused outside the room the girl had disappeared into and whispered, "'Til tomorrow, my little thief."

Chapter 13

During the night, the storm peaked and ebbed, leaving behind a slow, steady drizzle. Brandy snuggled beneath the thin blanket, searching for warmth. Finally, the chilly air forcing her from bed, she threw back the blanket and swung her legs over the side, her toes curling at the contact with the cold floor. She dressed quickly, relieved to find the boy's clothing had dried enough to be passably comfortable. She pulled aside the limp linen curtain and glanced out at the gray day, resigning herself to a wet, cold day in the saddle. No matter. She'll be in London soon and, hopefully, by this time tomorrow, have some answers.

She braided her hair and stuffed it under the cap. She pulled it low, grimacing as the damp wool scratched her forehead. There was no fireplace in the room, so she'd have to chance being seen before she could pinch some soot from the hearth downstairs. She stuffed her nightdress into the satchel, gave a quick glance around the room, and opened the door.

Peering out, she looked up and down the hallway and, finding it deserted, made her way to the common room. Few people were about at this early hour, and she breathed a sigh of relief when she didn't see the handsome stranger nor Roger Blackwell. She scooped up a handful of soot and quickly smeared it over her face before settling herself at the hearthside table she had occupied the previous evening. Seeking its warmth, she sat as close to the fire as possible without falling in. The barmaid sauntered over with sleepy eyes and a wide yawn.

Mentally counting her remaining coins, Brandy decided a cup of hot tea and a slice of toasted bread were all she dared purchase to break her fast. She had an uncertain future ahead of her and it would be wise to hoard what little coin remained. What she'd already spent by staying at the inn was an expense she hadn't counted on.

She sipped the hot tea, sighing as it began to warm her chilled body. At the sound of heavy footsteps on the stairs, she quickly ducked her head and peered out from beneath the brim of the cap. Her heart sank. Striding into the room, as if he owned it, was her nemesis. *What rotten luck.* Making herself as small as possible, she kept her head down, but to her utter dismay, a pair of polished black boots came into view. Her gaze traveled up his form, vaguely registering what a fine form it was—strong thighs encased in buckskin trousers, a white lawn shirt tucked into the waistband, with a dark brown frock coat completing the outfit. Her gaze paused on his full lips, one side curled in a grin, and slowly rose to meet his eyes. His black brows were arched in amusement.

"Do you hope to grow up and become a man like me?" He didn't wait for a reply but chuckled at the murderous expression that fell across her face. "You're up and about early," he noted the obvious, his voice like warm honey sliding over her body.

"Aye," she retorted, thankful for the soot that covered her blush. "What of it?"

"Mind if I join you?" Chandler was fast becoming

aroused, not the least bit daunted by her surly tone. Her slow perusal of him had ignited his blood. If this dirty urchin was, in fact, the same girl he had *rescued,* he was hard pressed not to snatch her out of her chair and kiss her senseless.

Brandy pointedly looked about the nearly deserted room. "There be plenty of other tables." She kept the brim of the cap pulled low over her forehead, her eyes averted lest he see the fear of discovery. "Seat yerself elsewhere. Leave me be."

"My apologies, I thought you might like the company." Chandler willed himself not to succumb to the laughter building inside him and moved to sit at a nearby table. The barmaid hurried over, bending low to reveal her ample bosom as she took his order.

Brandy sneered, watching him take in her charms. She pulled her gaze from him and, feeling him watching her, managed to finish her meager breakfast. Hefting her satchel, she headed for the door, pointedly ignoring him. She left the common room, the door slamming shut behind her, and stepped out into the chilly, wet morning. She waded through the mud to the stables, and finding no one about, saddled Misty. As she cinched the saddle, she heard a soft nicker coming from a stall at one end of the stables. Curious, she peeked in to find a large black stallion contently munching his oats. She marveled at the graceful lines of the animal. No doubt it belonged to *him*. There was no way Roger Blackwell could afford such a beast. As much as she wanted to, she could find no fault with the stallion. *A handsome steed to match a handsome man.*

She dragged a stool over to Misty's side and mounted astride. Urging her horse out of the stables, neither of them anxious to be out in the cold drizzle, she placed her heels against Misty's flanks, and huddled into her cloak. With her cap pulled low on her forehead, she did not see the man in the doorway of the inn, watching her ride away.

For several miles, Chandler followed Brandy at a discreet distance. He cursed aloud as the rain found an open space between his neck and cloak and drew the collar tighter around his throat. It was then his stallion started to limp. He dismounted and lifted its hoof, to find a small stone wedged in the underside. He carefully removed it, and resumed his trek, keeping the stallion to a walk. With no sign of further limping, he urged him to a canter. He turned a bend in the road and found the road deserted. Bloody hell! The chit had disappeared. The rain was falling in earnest now and visibility was sharply curbed. He kicked his heels into his steed's flanks and made haste for London. He would find her if it was the last thing he did, he vowed, not stopping to think how he'd accomplish that feat.

****

Brandy reined in on the outskirts of London. The rain had ended and the afternoon sun illuminated the skyline of the city. As she trotted across the bridge, she stared in awe at the magnificent dome and gold cross of a cathedral in the distance, the silhouette of the imposing Tower climbing high in the sky. She trotted down Fleet Street, threading her way through the hustle and bustle. Throngs of people, animals, and carts vied for room on the narrow street, making her progress slow. Excitement gripped her, the chaos heightening her sense of adventure.

She stopped before a street crier and waved at the

vendor to gain his attention, trying in vain to ignore the enticing aroma of meat pies wafting from his cart. She knew she could ill afford one of the pies and willed her grumbling stomach to silence.

"Do you know where I might find the Townsend residence?" she asked, hoping she was correct in her assumption that he might be nobility and therefore well known.

The vendor eyed her from beneath bushy red brows that nearly obscured his deep-set eyes. He wiped his hands on his dingy, white apron. "Ain't heard of it," he grumbled and turned back to hawk his wares.

"Can you tell me where the West End is?"

He looked at her as if she were daft. "Why, it be on the west end of town."

"I realize that. Where is—" She crinkled her brow trying to recall the articles she had read. "Where is Grosvenor Square?"

He jerked his thumb over his shoulder. "Go down a few blocks and turn down Park Lane. About three blocks down ye be there. So, unless ye be wantin' some pies here, be on yer way."

She cast a last, longing look at his cart, nodded her thanks, and wended her way through the throng of humanity. After a time, the streets became straighter and wider, yet she kept Misty to a walk, marveling at the sights and sounds. She passed magnificently tended squares and elegant houses set behind wrought iron fences. It was still afternoon, but the lamp-lighters were out, for the fog enshrouding the city made it darker than the hour. She called out to one of the men, "Can you tell me where the Townsend residence is?"

"Aye, Grosvenor Square." At her inquiring

expression, he continued, "Turn down Ashford Lane. Third house on the left."

She pulled her cloak around her body, the temperature having lowered with the sun, and trotted down Ashford Lane, counting the houses as she went. When she drew up before the third house, she gasped in awe. Never had she seen such a beautiful home—an imposing brick townhouse set back from the street, behind a tall wrought iron fence. Four stories high and covered with ivy, it had a warm, regal look about it. A gate opened onto a brick walkway leading to the front steps. A wide front door resided at the top, handsomely framed by indigo-blue sashed windows.

Brandy dismounted and looped the reins over the front post. She grabbed her satchel and pushed open the gate, making her way down the walkway through neatly manicured shrubs. After climbing the steps, she tugged on a rope hanging beside the door and heard the faint ringing of bells. She swallowed her trepidation when the door opened.

An austere-looking man dressed entirely in black appeared. With one look at her, his eyes widened in distaste. Peering down his nose at her, he stated in dignified hauteur, "The delivery entrance is in back." He started to close the door.

"Wait, please!" she cried out and the door stopped. "Does Andrew Townsend reside here?"

"He does."

Brandy breathed a sigh of relief. "Is he at home? May I have a word with him?"

"No." His gaze traveled over her raggedy clothing, and he sniffed in disdain. The door started to close again, but she stayed it with one small, booted foot.

"No, he's not at home? Or no, I can't have a word with him?"

"He isn't presently at home."

"Can you tell me when you might expect him?" Brandy persisted, not about to be rebuffed by the butler.

"I'm sure I don't know."

"Can you tell me anything without being so bloody rude?" Brandy glowered at the man.

Startled, he took a small step back. "I'm sure I don't know what you mean."

She glared at him in frustration and turned away, her shoulders slumped in defeat.

"Deaton, what is all the commotion?" A feminine voice drifted over the man's shoulders.

The butler presented his back to Brandy. "There is an urchin here, Your Grace."

"An urchin, you say? Well, what does he want?"

"He is requesting to see Lord Andrew."

"I see. Well, step aside."

Deaton frowned but did as bidden, allowing the owner of the voice to move into view. She was an older woman, attractive, her steel-gray hair pulled back into a bun at the nape of her neck. Her complexion was peach-tinted, with very few lines, and her eyes were blue. Her dress was apricot-colored, and around her neck was a strand of lustrous pearls. She was the epitome of stately grace.

"Hello, my dear. You want to see my grandson?"

"Yes, but I understand he is not at home. Please, milady, if I may have a minute of your time. It's very important."

The woman stared intently at Brandy. Then, as if coming to a decision, she stepped aside and nodded to

Deaton. Brandy picked up her satchel and stepped into the foyer. It was large and airy, the white marble floor gleaming in the light from the overhead chandelier. What looked to be the dining room was on her right and a wide, indigo-blue carpeted staircase at the end of the foyer disappeared upstairs.

"I am Abigail Townsend, Dowager Duchess of Marbury. What do you want with my grandson?" She smiled kindly at Brandy. "And why are you dressed as a lad?"

Brandy tilted her head. "You guessed?"

The Dowager Duchess nodded. "You'd have to be blind not to see through the rough garb and dirt."

"There have been a few," Brandy rejoined, thinking of those she had fooled, including the handsome stranger. Belatedly remembering her manners, she dropped into a quick curtsy. "Thank you for receiving me, Your Grace." She took off her woolen cap and her thick braid slid down her back. The butler had turned back from closing the door and at the sight of the auburn braid, his mouth dropped open and quickly slammed shut. Brandy swallowed her laughter, pleased she had set the haughty man back on his heels.

"My name is Brandy Drummond, Your Grace. I have come to see Lord Andrew on a most urgent matter."

The Dowager Duchess held out her hand, beckoning Brandy to follow. "Why don't we go into the morning room, and you can tell me all about it. Would you care for tea, my dear? Deaton, please ask Mrs. Farnham to bring us a tray."

"Very well, Your Grace." Deaton hesitated, apparently loathe to leave his mistress alone with this oddity, but at an impatient wave of the Dowager

Duchess's hand he left to do her bidding. Brandy couldn't blame him for his reluctance. After all, he was only protecting his mistress, much like Arthur's possessive attitude toward her.

The morning room was large, the walls covered in light blue silk. Two overstuffed chairs upholstered in blue-and-green-striped damask hugged the hearth. A pair of royal blue settees on either side of a low rectangular table were placed before a tall window that opened onto a courtyard. A small writing table sat in one corner of the room next to a round table decorated with a vase of orange and yellow flowers.

Mindful of her dirty clothes, Brandy perched on the edge of the settee across from the Dowager Duchess. She looked up as a short, plump woman clad in a voluminous black skirt and white starched blouse entered the room, pushing a cart bearing an elegant peach-and-white-striped porcelain tea service. A round platter piled high with small square-cut sandwiches accompanied the tea. Brandy watched with hungry eyes while the woman set the tea service on the low table between them.

"Thank you, Mrs. Farnham. Please close the door behind you." Abigail noticed the direction in which her young guest's gaze had travelled and scooted the platter of sandwiches toward her. She waited until Brandy had chosen one, then poured two cups of tea. "Now, my dear, do tell. Why are you dressed as a lad?" She handed a cup of tea to Brandy.

"I thought it best, since I am travelling alone."

"I see." Abigail nodded, although her expression remained nonplussed.

"I am here to find my brother, or at least some news of his whereabouts. I have reason to believe that Lord

Andrew may know something. You see, my father died recently, and I found your grandson's name in his papers." Brandy paused, realizing she was rambling, and took a bite of the little sandwich.

"Hmmm—you say your brother is missing? And what would his name be?"

"Michael Drummond, Earl of Hathshire." Brandy gasped in dismay. "Good heavens! He is not even aware he is earl—he does not know of our father's death." Brandy took another bite of the sandwich. "It is imperative that he come home to run the estate. I cannot do it alone. There is so much that needs his attention."

"Do you mean to tell me that you are living alone?" Abigail's eyes widened in disbelief.

"No, my aunt and cousin are living with me. They arrived for my father's funeral and are staying until Michael returns home."

"Why didn't they accompany you to London?"

Brandy tried to evade the question, but not wanting to appear rude, answered simply, "There wasn't enough coin for all of us to travel here." She started to reach for another sandwich but, not wanting to appear greedy, placed her hands in her lap instead. "I should send my aunt a note to let her know I have arrived safely."

"If you like, I will have Rochester post a letter for you," Abigail offered, sliding the plate a little closer to Brandy.

"You are very kind, Your Grace." Brandy chose a second sandwich, finished it, and, though wanting to eat the entire platter, did not make a move for a third. She blinked, suddenly exhausted, and stifled a yawn.

"Where are you staying?" Abigail leaned forward to pour tea into Brandy's empty cup. Noticing her young guest's sudden blank expression, "You have nowhere to stay? No other relatives or friends in London?"

Brandy had no idea if she had relatives in London, but she wasn't prepared to confide that to the Dowager Duchess, as kind as she might be. The look of genuine concern on the Dowager Duchess's face, however, crumbled Brandy's rigid self-control. All the pain, sadness, and insecurity she had endured the last few months suddenly overwhelmed her, and to her utter mortification, she burst into tears.

"There, there, my dear." Abigail handed Brandy a delicate white handkerchief. "How far is your home from London?"

"It took me two days to get here, but I think it's much closer. I slept the day away yesterday and then the storm descended upon me…" Her words trailed off. Drying her tears with the pretty square of lace, she straightened her shoulders. "I will find lodgings. Yes, and there I will wait for your grandson to arrive home. When will that be?"

Abigail smiled at the young girl who sat so courageously before her. "I don't know when Andrew will return," she admitted, then stopped, her eyes widening. She raised a brow in surprise. "Drummond, you say? Your mother wasn't Doreen Drummond, was she? Doreen Harrison Drummond?"

Well not exactly. But aloud said, "Yes, did you know her?"

"Indeed, I did. Although her older sister, Jessie, and I were better friends."

"You know my Aunt Jessie?" Brandy recalled Anne thinking the Townsend name sounded familiar.

"I most certainly do! Although, we have not seen

each other in many years. Not since she married that red-haired rogue and moved to the wilds of Scotland. We used to cut quite a path through Society in our day. How is she?"

"She's a widow now, has been for several years."

"Oh, yes, I remember hearing her husband had died. Archibald, wasn't it?"

"Yes, Archibald MacCartin, Baron Whyte."

Abigail nodded, clearly mulling over this news. She leaned forward and patted Brandy's hand. "You have quite a bit on your plate right now, but don't you worry, my dear. I insist you stay here with us. When my eldest grandson returns, we'll ask him for his advice. He will know what to do. He knows loads of people in very high places. I'm sure he will help solve this little mystery of yours."

Brandy sniffed and brushed away the remaining tears from her cheeks. Glancing down at the handkerchief, she gasped in dismay. Black ribbons of soot streaked the delicate white lace. She flushed in embarrassment.

"It can be laundered, my dear."

"Thank you, Your Grace. You've been most kind."

"Nonsense. It's the least I can do for the niece of an old friend. What I can't understand is why Jessie would let you travel to London alone, and dressed as a boy, no less!"

Brandy bowed her head, frantically searching for an answer.

"Aha! What's this? She doesn't know?" Abigail eyed her young visitor, one brow arched.

"No, madam. I confided in Anne, my cousin, but I knew if Aunt Jessie were told ahead of time, she would put a stop it."

"She most certainly would have! Well, enough of that, what's done is done, and you are here now. I will have Mrs. Farnham show you to your room. I'm sure you would enjoy a bath, my dear. Have you any other clothes?"

"Yes." Brandy pointed to the beaten satchel Deaton had placed by the door.

"Very well." Abigail stood up and pulled on a velvet rope hidden in the folds of the curtains. Mrs. Farnham appeared in the doorway.

"Please show our guest to the green bedchamber. Liza can tend to her needs. Have water sent up for a bath, as well."

"Yes, Your Grace."

"Why don't you rest after your bath? I will see you at dinner."

"Thank you, Your Grace. Oh, my mare is tied out front."

"I will have Deaton take care of your horse."

Brandy curtsied and followed Mrs. Farnham up the wide staircase. As they walked down the hallway, she glanced at the portraits lining the walls. Brandy, assuming they depicted past Townsends, paused before a portrait of a man with dark eyes and black hair with just a touch of silver at his temples. Brandy tilted her head to one side. There was an air of familiarity about him.

"That was the old Duke, Edgar Townsend, Her Grace's husband. He was the fourth Duke of Marbury. He died many years ago." Mrs. Farnham had retraced her steps and the two stood looking at the portrait. "Handsome, wasn't he?"

"Yes," Brandy agreed. They continued down the hallway, Mrs. Farnham pointing out the people in the other portraits, all of them descendants of the first Duke of Marbury.

Mrs. Farnham opened a door and stood aside to allow Brandy to enter the bedchamber. Brandy took a moment to take in the room, decorated in varied shades of green—a large window accented by forest-green velvet drapes pulled back with gold tassels, a plush carpet woven in moss-green and gold. The four-poster bed, covered in a grass-green coverlet, dominated the room. A large mahogany armoire, polished to a rich sheen, stood against one wall, a matching dressing table beside it, an oval looking glass on the wall above. A hand-painted screen depicting flora and fauna stood in one corner of the room near a fireplace centered on the wall. Two high-backed chairs covered with gold damask were placed before the large hearth. As Brandy surveyed her surroundings, Mrs. Farnham lit the kindling already laid in the fireplace and soon had a fire blazing, banishing the chill.

"'Tis beautiful," Brandy breathed in awe, feeling dipped in luxury.

"This was Lady Norma's room."

A maid entered with Brandy's satchel and several towels under one arm. She was young and fresh-faced and sported a friendly smile. She wore a black dress with a white apron tied around her waist. Her hair was hidden beneath a white mop cap.

"This is Liza. She will see to your every need. You have only to tell her what you require."

Liza bobbed a quick curtsy. "Good afternoon, milady."

Mrs. Farnham stopped at the door. "Dinner is served at eight o'clock. The Dowager Duchess partakes of a glass of sherry in the salon at half past seven."

A discreet knock at the door produced two footmen with buckets of steaming water, which they poured into a large brass tub hidden behind the screen. After they left, Liza helped Brandy off with her dirty clothes and settled her in the tub. While Brandy luxuriated in her bath, she watched Liza withdraw her belongings from the satchel. She grimaced at her worn chemises and faded dresses, looking out of place in the elegant surroundings.

Liza turned to Brandy, the lad's clothing held aloft. "What would you like me to do with these, milady?"

Burn them. "If you could have them laundered, I would appreciate it. I might have need of them again."

Liza nodded and left Brandy to her bath, two dresses and the lad's garments slung over her arm.

Brandy selected a lavender-scented bath oil from among several bottles on a shelf beside the tub and poured a liberal amount into the water. She slid deeper into the tub and sighed as the warm scented water caressed her skin. She squeezed the sponge over her breasts, laughing out loud at the wonderful feeling of being clean once again. She lifted one slim leg and sponged it, watching idly as the water ran in rivulets down her thigh. She washed her hair, rinsing it with clean water from a bucket beside the tub. When the water began to cool, she stood and dried herself with one of the thick, fluffy towels left on the stool. She donned a dove-gray velvet robe Liza had thoughtfully provided, and sat before the fire to dry her hair. The lustrous tresses slowly dried into an unruly, auburn mass that curled down her back, brushing her hips.

Some of her earlier tension had eased. She had located Andrew Townsend. The fact that he was not at home was unfortunate, but she had at least accomplished the first of what she had set out to do. She would wait to see what developed before trying to locate Blanchard.

She climbed onto the bed and pulled the heavy coverlet over her travel-weary but clean body. Snuggling deep within its folds, she was asleep instantly, unaware that she was the topic of conversation downstairs.

Chapter 14

The Dowager Duchess stared into the fire, her thoughts centered on the young girl upstairs. It wasn't her usual time, but she had poured herself a sherry just the same. Hearing footsteps, she turned and watched with pride as her eldest grandson strode into the salon. He crossed the room in long strides and, upon reaching her side, bent down and placed a kiss upon her smooth cheek.

"Good evening, Grandmother. I trust you are well?"

She sniffed, hiding her pleasure at his presence. "As you can see, Chandler, I am alive and well. You were supposed to be here yesterday. You missed my soiree last night."

"You are merely put out because I avoided another one of your matchmaking efforts. Tsk, tsk, Grandmother. I'll have you know, I was caught in that bloody storm and stranded in some lowly inn outside of town. You should take pity on me for the miserable night I spent instead of being miffed because I missed meeting another one of your title-hungry barracudas."

She ignored his barbs and sipped her sherry, gazing at him with love. *He is so handsome, as handsome as my Edgar. But too cynical by far. Blasted Camille.* "Is Andrew with you?"

Chandler moved to the sideboard and poured himself a whiskey. "No, he's still at Marbury Hall."

"Why did you send him there?"

"He needs to do something with his life, so I thought a bit of work was in order." He pulled at a loose thread on his jacket. Despite her piercing stare, he managed to keep his expression shuttered. His grandmother was sharp and the only person he knew who could read his thoughts, despite his adroit ability to hide them.

Abigail threw back her head and laughed. "Good gracious, do my old ears deceive me? I seem to recall saying those exact words to you, my boy."

He bowed to the elder woman. "Then I merely passed on your infinite wisdom. After he sees to my affairs at Marbury Hall, he will be traveling to Scotland to check on a piece of property I just purchased. In fact, he's most likely on his way there now. So, I don't expect him home for quite a while." The lies left a bad taste, but they needed to be said.

"Oh, dear," Abigail exclaimed in dismay. "Can we get a message to him?"

"I doubt it. Why? Is there something amiss, Grandmother?"

"No, well, maybe. We have a guest. She's in the green bedchamber, resting. You will be here for dinner? I would like for you to meet her."

He stared at his grandmother, eyes narrowed in suspicion. "Who is she?"

She laughed and waved her hand. "Not part of a matchmaking scheme, I assure you. However, now that I think on it…" She held up her hand at his scowl. "No, 'tis Lady Brandy Drummond from Hathshire. She's the niece of an old friend of mine. She came here looking for Andrew. I told her we would seek your advice. Which reminds me, I need to write Jessie and let her know the child is safe. Chandler, what is it? You look positively ghastly."

"'Tis nothing." *What the devil was Michael's sister doing here? And what did she want with Andrew?* Recalling Abigail's earlier statement, he asked, "Safe? From what?"

"She arrived here in disguise. She was garbed in the most horrendous outfit. Imagine, dressed as a lad! Deaton almost slammed the door in her face, poor dear. But of course, how was he to know the lad was a lady?"

Chandler's brows drew together. Could it be the chit he'd encountered at the inn? The one he believed he may have caught stealing a chicken from Alden Ridge? This girl was turning up in the oddest places, her actions most peculiar. *What was she up to?*

"A lad, you say? How intriguing," he drawled, sinking into one of the overstuffed chairs. He stretched his long legs out in front of him and gave his grandmother a look of expectation, as if waiting for her to continue.

Abigail hid her smile. "Why the interest, Chandler?"

"'Tis nothing. As I said, the story sounds intriguing. Pray continue."

As he listened to the story unfold, Chandler smiled to himself. *It had to be her!* Now he understood why she was dressed as such—it wasn't safe for women to travel alone. Unexpected anger shot through him at the thought of the danger she had put herself in. The naïve chit!

Abigail watched her grandson's face. His expression was closed, but his usual façade of bored indifference, especially when discussing women, was nowhere to be seen. Staying seated, and listening to her at length, showed he had more interest in this young girl than any she had paraded before him. And he hadn't even met her yet! Or had he? He was not one for idle gossip, and yet he had exhibited an unusual amount of curiosity in her story. She would find out soon enough—she always did.

"Will you talk with her? Perhaps you can help find her brother, Michael Drummond. According to Brandy, he's not even aware he's the new Earl of Hathshire, unaware his father has died."

"Hmmm, I will see what I can do," Chandler said, thinking rapidly and hiding his alarm behind a wall of nonchalance. First, he needed to determine if she was in fact Michael's sister. If she was, what, if anything, did she know about Andrew and her brother's activities? And how did she even know about Andrew? Bloody hell, this was fast becoming complicated. He set aside his glass and rose to his feet. "I have a few things to attend to, Grandmother. I will see you at dinner."

"Please ask Rochester to come in. I need to post a letter." She watched her grandson leave the room, a devilish grin creasing her mouth. She moved to the writing table and quickly penned a note to her dear friend Jessie.

****

Brandy tried to scream past the terror clutching her throat. Caught in a cruel grip, strong hands shaking her shoulders, long fingers viciously pinching her soft flesh—

"Milady, 'tis time to dress for supper. Milady?" Liza stepped back in alarm as a scream pierced the air.

Brandy sat up with a start, eyes wide with fright, her heart beating a wild tattoo. With difficulty, she focused on the young maid standing by the bed. "Oh, Liza, 'tis you."

"You must have been having a bad dream, milady." Liza smiled kindly and turned to lay out the dress Brandy would wear.

Brandy shook her head to clear it of the lingering nightmare. "What time is it?" she asked, brushing aside her hair. She threw back the coverlet and swung her legs over the side of the bed.

"It's nearly seven o'clock, milady. The Dowager Duchess's grandson has arrived. He will be joining you for dinner."

"Lord Andrew is here?" Brandy leapt from the bed, tumbling to the floor in her excitement. She rolled and jumped to her feet in one fluid movement.

"No, His Grace, the Duke of Marbury." Liza cocked her head to one side, hiding her smile.

"Oh, well, then we must hurry."

Liza had selected the best of Brandy's two dresses— a lavender muslin with plum-colored flowers scattered across the bodice and skirt. Short, capped sleeves perched on her shoulders, and a ruffle of lace adorned the neckline. A violet-hued ribbon cinched just above her waist. The dress had seen better days and was terribly outdated, but it had been neatly pressed, and scented. *It would just have to do.*

Liza brushed Brandy's hair until it shone like fire in the soft glow of the candles. Then, she tied the mass of curls with a lavender ribbon, allowing the auburn tresses to flow freely down her back. She pulled a few tendrils loose to curl about Brandy's face.

Brandy left the maid to tidy the chamber and proceeded down the hallway, stopping again in front of the portrait that had intrigued her. She could not dispel the air of familiarity the man in the portrait possessed.

She descended the wide staircase, pausing on the bottom step as the sound of voices drifted to her from the salon. She heard a man's deep laughter.

She proceeded to the salon and stopped in the doorway, surveying the room. Abigail was on the settee, sipping sherry from a small crystal glass. A man stood in front of the fireplace, facing Abigail, one arm resting casually on the mantel. Brandy was presented with his profile. He was garbed in dark brown breeches and matching jacket, a snowy white shirt, and a tan-hued waistcoat. His black hair, worn slightly longer than was considered fashionable, curled at his nape.

Abigail spotted Brandy in the doorway and with a welcoming smile bade her enter. "Good evening, my dear. Why don't you look lovely? Quite a change from this afternoon, eh? May I present my eldest grandson, Chandler Townsend, Duke of Marbury. Chandler, Lady Brandy Drummond."

The duke turned and bowed low in introduction, his blue eyes sparkling. He had been correct—she was indeed the same girl.

Brandy groaned but kept her smile intact. *Of all the rotten luck.* When their eyes met, she knew without a doubt he recognized her from the day in the meadow when he *rescued* her from her horse. Her initial reaction was to flee, but she repressed the impulse, and replied in a voice that didn't even hint at her uneasiness. "Your Grace." She dropped into a curtsy.

"A pleasure, Lady Brandy. Would you care for a sherry before dinner?"

Brandy nodded and blindly took a seat beside Abigail. While his back was turned, she took a moment to collect her scattered wits.

She accepted the glass of sherry, refusing to meet his eyes. He would have none of that, however, for when she took the glass, his finger wrapped around her hand. She jerked her hand away, nearly spilling the wine on the carpet.

Abigail, who had been closely watching their exchange, was surprised by Brandy's reaction. If she weren't mistaken, Brandy looked as if she wished she were anywhere but here. Odd, that. Women usually fawned over her grandson. Moreover, she seemed disturbed and, frankly, embarrassed. She glanced up at Chandler, who had taken up his stance by the hearth's mantel. Yet for all his casual posture, Abigail sensed his close attention.

Chandler took a sip of his whiskey. "I understand you travelled to London as a lad."

Brandy nodded wordlessly, praying he wouldn't put the pieces together and recognize her from the inn or, God forbid, as the thief he had caught at Alden Ridge.

"I hope you don't mind, but I confided in Chandler your reasons for being in London. Unfortunately, Andrew is away for some time. But Chandler might be able to help you. I also took the liberty of informing your aunt of your whereabouts."

"Thank you, Your Grace. I had planned to write to her in the morning. 'Tis better she receives your missive earlier, to alleviate any worry." She chanced a quick glance up at Chandler. The urge to slap that infuriating grin off his face was strong. She gripped the delicate stem of the glass and sipped the sherry, nearly choking on the wine.

When he spoke again, his smile had disappeared.

"So, tell me, Lady Brandy, why are you concerned about your brother's absence? Has he never left home before?"

"Yes, of course, just not for this long." His condescending tone made her sound like she was overreacting. "It is not unusual for Michael to leave home. However, our father recently passed and still he is absent. It has caused me a great deal of concern. There are other factors, too, that are of a more personal nature. I don't wish to discuss them, at this time."

"And my brother, Andrew, what has he do with it?"

"As I explained to Her Grace, his name was linked with Michael's in some of my father's papers. I thought maybe Michael knew your brother from school."

"Fascinating," he uttered, taking a step toward her as if to question her further.

Deaton entered to announce that dinner was served, interrupting the duke's interrogation. Miffed at his cavalier attitude, Brandy ignored the hand he extended and rose from the settee to follow the butler downstairs to the dining room, leaving Chandler to escort his grandmother.

Chandler was mystified by her appearance in his home. If she were in fact Michael's sister, he had to allay her concerns and deflect any suspicions that might arise. And if she weren't? Then who was she and what was she up to?

Brandy looked around the elegant dining room with awe. The large table, laid with fine porcelain and sparkling crystal stemware, dominated the room. It could easily seat twenty people. For tonight, however, three places were grouped together at one end. The walls were painted gold matching the gold damask table runner, and the chair cushions were covered in a burnished copper floral design. Crystal wall sconces were placed evenly about the room, and a fire blazed in the marble fireplace. The entire room was cast in gilded elegance.

While Chandler held out a chair for Abigail, Brandy slid into the one opposite. She caught his grin and had the distinct feeling he was laughing at her. She refused to look him in the eye, concentrating instead on the act of placing the linen napkin in her lap. They were silent as the footmen served the first course.

Abigail discussed the latest gossip, with Chandler chiming in with a question or comment. Brandy listened idly to their conversation as she swirled the spoon around her bowl, creating ridges in the cream soup. Unfortunately, her appetite had disappeared with her introduction to the duke. She had the sneaking suspicion he was about to make her life miserable, so it was unfortunate, indeed, if he was to help her, she had to be gracious. A hard task, if their brief history was any indication.

After the soup bowls had been removed, the footmen brought in the main meal. As they dined, Brandy peeked at Chandler from beneath her lashes. He didn't seem at all affected by this unexpected turn of events. He ate with relish, nodding to his grandmother every so often as she talked of the latest happenings in town. Brandy pushed the food around on her plate, taking an occasional bite of the roasted goose and currant pudding. Watching him enjoy his meal while she could not fully appreciate the rich tempting fare only increased her resentment. She hadn't seen, much less tasted, food this marvelous in months.

She sipped her glass of Madeira and tried to ignore the man sitting beside her. But he filled her senses. She could smell his cologne, feel his body heat, and his deep voice sent shivers down her spine. When she sensed his regard, she glanced up, yet he averted his gaze and took a deep drink of his wine, his expression inscrutable.

Abigail placed her fork on her plate and eyed them both. "Would one of you like to tell me what is going on? Chandler, you look as smug as the cat who got the cream, and Brandy, you the one that didn't get a drop." She raised her brows, her inquisitive gaze sweeping over them.

Brandy lowered her eyes and placed her hands in her lap, heat rising to her cheeks.

Chandler leaned back in his chair. "Grandmother, it seems we owe you an apology. You see, I have indeed met the fair Lady Brandy before this evening, although we were not properly introduced at the time."

Abigail looked over at Brandy. "Do you have anything to add?"

"Yes, Your Grace. I had no idea who he was at the time. Otherwise, I certainly would have told you I had already met him. You see, he was on my property one day and, ah, saved me from my runaway horse." She couldn't suppress her grin.

Chandler actually blushed at her subtle sarcasm. "And after that?" He tilted his head to one side, one black brow arched.

Brandy stared mutely at him. Of course, he had caught her stealing the chicken from the Alden Estate, but he couldn't know it was her—could he? Was he aware it was her at the inn last night? At his wide-eyed innocent expression, she knew without a doubt: he knew. She gritted her teeth. "And at the inn last night," she whispered, sounding more like a question than a statement.

Brandy turned to Abigail, who had heard Brandy's whispered confession, but chose not to comment. "As I said, I did not know his name. Therefore, I was as surprised as he most assuredly was when we met this evening."

Abigail looked at Chandler. He was holding his wine glass aloft watching the candlelight illuminate the amber liquid, an amused smile playing about his mouth. She guessed there was more to the story but decided to leave it alone for now. She looked down at her plate to hide her delight. The strained tension between them was palpable. "'Tis no matter how you came to know each other. What we do need to do is find out about her brother." She looked at her grandson. "When will Andrew return?"

He gazed thoughtfully at Brandy, who was studiously avoiding his gaze. "I don't know, Grandmother. But I will do what I can for Lady Brandy. Perhaps tomorrow we can discuss it further."

Brandy looked up at him in surprise. He had sounded, well, almost agreeable. "Thank you, Your Grace."

He nodded and their gazes met briefly before she lowered her lashes and took a sip of her wine. Still exhausted from her long day, she found herself drowsy from just the small quantity of spirits she'd consumed. She wanted nothing more than to crawl back into bed and forget she had ever met the Duke of Marbury. She found his presence unnerving, making her feel curiously warm with knots in her stomach. Eyes lowered so as not to give away her thoughts, she missed the contemplative look that entered his eyes as he regarded her bent head.

Abigail, however, missed nothing. She knew little of what Chandler was involved in, for he kept his affairs close to his chest, but she had noticed his reaction, which he quickly concealed, when she had mentioned Michael Drummond. She would wait to question him, though. She did not want to voice her concerns in front of the girl. She was satisfied her grandson would do what he could to help. She was also eager to see how long it would take for the two of them to come together. If the tension in the room was any indication, she would wager on sooner rather than later. She had taken an instant liking to Brandy and vowed to do what she could to encourage the match. Abigail picked up her fork and resumed her meal, content to let the matter rest for now.

Brandy pushed back her chair and rose to her feet. "Please forgive me, Your Grace, but I should like your permission to retire."

"Of course, my dear, you have had a long day. I will see you in the morning."

Brandy nodded to Chandler, who returned the gesture with a faint smile as she moved from the room to seek the relative safety of her chamber. Pushing open the door, she found Liza waiting. Smiling absently at the young maid, Brandy began to disrobe, but Liza brushed her hands aside to assist. When she was stripped to her chemise, she said over her shoulder, "Thank you, Liza, I can handle the rest. Good night."

"Pleasant dreams, milady."

Brandy changed into her nightdress and climbed into bed to stare thoughtfully at the canopy. What should she do? Should she stay and suffer Chandler's arrogance and condescension? And what about those unfamiliar feelings he aroused? But most importantly was the fear of exposure. For if the duke did learn of her midnight pinching and reveal her secret, she would pay—dearly. They threw men in prison for less. Would a woman suffer the same fate?

****

Abigail kept Chandler company in the salon while he enjoyed a snifter of cognac. A log shifted in the fireplace, spitting sparks from the hearth. Startled from her thoughts, she turned to her grandson, who had also been contemplating the dancing flames. "Where have you met Brandy before?"

"We told you, on her estate. Although we neglected to get each other's names at the time. And once again at the inn last night."

"I'm aware of what you told me. I'm more interested in what you didn't tell me. There is more, isn't there?"

Chandler smiled fondly at his grandmother. "Not much slips by you, does it?" He refilled his glass from the decanter Deaton had left on the side table.

"As she said, we stayed at the same inn last night, seeking a haven from the storm. She was dressed as a lad, a dirty urchin, to be exact. But you saw for yourself this morning." He chuckled. "I saw through her disguise, although she was unaware of that fact until just now."

"It seems to me you should have offered your protection. Why, any manner of danger could have befallen her."

"How was I to give her my protection when she obviously wanted her gender kept secret? Besides, it wasn't until she had retired to her room that I discovered the ruse. And I did attempt to follow her to London this morning, but the rain was coming down so blasted hard and my stallion took a stone in its hoof—I lost sight of her outside the city."

Abigail became quiet as she pondered this information. Then, "How did you know she was the same girl you had met on her property?"

"I didn't at first, although after I discovered the lad was a woman, I suspected it. Her eyes are quite unforgettable, aren't they? The most beautiful shade of green."

Abigail, fascinated by his wistful expression, was speechless. Watching her grandson quietly, she waited for him to continue their conversation.

"It was only after seeing her in the salon this evening that I was certain."

"She seemed quite upset. Had you seen her before last night?"

He knew she would pester him until he told her the entire story. The woman really would have done well in foreign affairs. He leaned back in his chair with a resigned sigh. "I caught her stealing a chicken on Jeffrey's estate. When I recognized her at the inn, I thought her nothing but a little thief."

"Stealing chickens? Hmm, I wonder why. 'Tis passing strange and doesn't sound a`tall good. You're not sure she *is* Michael's sister, are you?"

Chandler hesitated before answering—it was the same question he's been asking himself. Not wishing to divulge what he knew, he answered evasively, "I don't know. I only know that my experience with her has been anything but forthright. However, if she is not who she claims to be, we will find out soon enough when you receive a reply from her aunt. You sent the note?"

"Yes, one of the footmen left today for Hathshire. I believe her, Chandler. What earthly reason would she have for lying about who she is and making up a story about a missing brother?"

"I agree, Grandmother, but, nevertheless, I would like confirmation."

Abigail hid a yawn behind a slim, blue-veined hand. "It's time you retire. I will see you in the morning."

Abigail accepted his assistance and, patting his cheek, wished him pleasant dreams and left him alone with his thoughts.

Chandler sat down and stared into the fire, his thoughts sliding back to dinner. He had listened absently to his grandmother's discourse of the comings and goings of the *ton*, hiding his preoccupation with the beautiful girl sitting beside him. He could smell the soft essence of lavender wafting from her hair, the scent intensified by the warmth from the fire, and he had become physically affected by her nearness.

If she is Michael's sister, why in the hell was she stealing chickens in the middle of the night? The Drummonds were not poverty-stricken—the Earl of Hathshire had a vast estate. Not on the level of Jeffrey Alden or a few of his neighbors, but they certainly weren't destitute. Or, God forbid, was she in league with Blackwell out scouting the area? And when it was learned she had met the Duke of Marbury, Blackwell had charged her with infiltrating his home and gleaning information? They were, after all, purportedly betrothed. He took a sip of cognac. None of this made sense. He needed time to put the pieces together. It was a fact he didn't trust the lovely young lady who had graced his table and was now sleeping under his roof. She was a thief, perhaps a liar, and most definitely a woman. And everyone knows women are not to be trusted.

He swirled the cognac in the snifter, watching the firelight catch and dance in the drink. She was quite lovely, with her reddish-brown hair and green eyes. He could lose himself in those eyes. And her mouth! Perfect for kissing. How he ached to kiss her again. He envisioned her bent over his arm, his mouth capturing hers in a soul-stirring kiss. She would reciprocate, of course, and kiss him back just as passionately, molding her body to his…

His body reacted to his imaginings, and he shifted uncomfortably in his chair. Disgusted with himself for behaving like a green lad who had not yet tasted his first woman, he drained his glass, quit the room, and sought his bedchamber. *She was just an attractive chit, 'twas all.*

He dismissed his valet, who was patiently waiting for him to retire, and after removing his clothing, slipped on his robe. With only a moment's hesitation, he entered the adjoining chamber through the connecting door. He crept over to the side of the canopied bed, careful not to wake her, and gazed down at her sleeping form. Her hair fanned out on the pillow, and one slim hand was tucked under her cheek. Her mouth was slightly open, her slow even breathing a whispery sound in the quiet room. Her lashes lay like delicate fans against her ivory cheeks. She looked so soft and vulnerable Chandler had the overwhelming urge to crawl into the bed and draw her up against his side, wrap his arms around her, and keep her safe. The sensation was reminiscent of the one he had experienced in the forest the first time he had seen her.

Who are you? He tended to agree with his grandmother that she was who she said she was, but the mystery remained—why was she roaming the countryside at night?

He returned to his chamber, unsettled by the unfamiliar emotion she had unwittingly stirred in him. It wasn't like him to give a woman, any woman, a second thought. Sleep was elusive that night.

Chapter 15

The next morning, Brandy entered the dining room and found Chandler seated at one end of the long table, alone. She hesitated in the doorway. She had hoped the Dowager Duchess would be present to offset her grandson's irritating habit of frustrating her. She took a step back, wanting to escape before he noticed her presence.

"I trust you slept well?" he asked, peering at her over an elaborate arrangement of autumnal flowers.

Inclining her head, she moved into the room and took a seat at the table. She accepted a cup of tea from the footman and, studiously ignoring Chandler, selected a warm roll from a pretty porcelain platter and slathered it with marmalade.

Chandler waited until she had taken a bite. "I didn't recognize you at first," he commented, waiting with quiet amusement as she, with some difficulty, swallowed her mouthful. She looked up at him with her brows drawn down in confusion. "When you walked into the salon last night," he clarified. "Now, if you had been clutching a chicken and the moon had shadowed your smudged features, I'm sure I would have instantly, *Lady* Brandy."

"So, you do know," she whispered, her worst fear coming to pass. He nodded slowly and popped a slice of sugared pear into his mouth. Fighting through her mortification, she sipped her tea, studiously examining the floral design on the delicate porcelain cup, and waited for his next move.

"Why were you stealing chickens?" His demanding tone of voice immediately put her on the defensive.

She tossed her head back in a gesture of pure hauteur. "I don't believe I owe you any explanations, Your Grace. Your grandmother was kind enough to offer me accommodation until your brother returns from your country estate. He will hear my story." She looked the duke squarely in the eye, challenging him.

"This is my house, not Abigail's. I suggest if you don't want your cute little derriere thrown out into the streets, you will deign to answer my questions. Besides, I believe you asked for my help?"

"I did not. Your grandmother did."

He stared at her in astonishment, obviously floored by her audacity to defy him. He half rose from his chair and with a scowl, dropped back down, slashing his hand through the air. The footman, who had been standing quietly to one side, turned and left the room.

Brandy watched him leave and turned back to Chandler, her jaw set. "You do not frighten me."

"I am not trying to. I merely thought to save you further embarrassment in front of the servants." He took a sip of his tea, ignoring her rebellious expression. "It would not matter one whit to me to send you on your way, but I promised Abigail I would try to help you. But while you are here, I expect a certain amount of respect."

"Does that go both ways?"

His eyes narrowed, and grudgingly he inclined his head. "If I am to help you, I will need some answers."

She had a brief, private struggle with her pride. On

one hand, she would dearly love to shove his generosity down his throat, thereby wiping that superior smirk off his face. But on the other, she did need his help in locating her brother. That was surely more important than her pride! Stubbornly, she nodded her head in acceptance of his demand.

"Why were you stealing chickens from the Alden Estate?"

"We needed food."

"Why?"

"Because we were hungry."

"Naturally. Why did you have to *steal* food?" As her chin raised a notch, he warned, "Brandy…"

"Oh, all right. Because we had none and no means to acquire any other than what we grew in our garden."

"Your father left no wealth? He was not a poor man, I think."

"No, he was not," she snapped, taking exception to his sarcastic tone. "There were debts to be paid. When news of my father's death became known, anyone he owed a shilling came around with their hand out. My father's solicitor informed me our funds were fast dwindling. We have sold most of our belongings to survive this far."

Chandler digested this information. "How did you find my grandmother?"

Brandy related the story she had told the Dowager Duchess the previous day. When she had finished, Chandler nodded, his expression shuttered. "Are you acquainted with Roger Blackwell?"

"Yes, I'm acquainted with him. In fact—" She clamped her mouth shut and refused to elaborate.

"In fact—?"

"'Tis nothing. Michael and I have known him since we were children."

"I would think he would have offered his assistance." He sipped his tea, watching her closely. Would she admit she's betrothed to him? "Are you two close? Do you spend much time with him?"

"First of all, I didn't ask him for his assistance. And secondly, no we are not close. He…" She tilted her head to one side. "Why are you asking me so many questions about Lord Norwood? I have told my story." Her eyes widened. "You think I am in league with him! You think I'm a spy like—" She immediately slapped her hand over her mouth, horrified at what she had nearly revealed.

"A spy like whom?" Chandler leaned forward in his chair. His expression had hardened, indeed his entire body had turned to stone. "I repeat, *a spy like whom*?" His question boomed like thunder in the suddenly still room.

She valiantly tried to hold onto her composure. Hearing voices in the hallway, she whispered, "Can we change the subject, please?"

"For now," he conceded. "But this discussion is far from over," he warned, disturbed by her revelations. *What wasn't she telling him?* Did she know about her father's purported traitorous actions? And Blackwell— what did she know of his?

"Good morning." Abigail swept into the dining room with a smile, taking the chair Chandler pulled out for her.

"Good morning, Grandmother."

"Good morning, Your Grace," Brandy murmured, picking at her roll and listening idly to their talk of an upcoming social event.

"Would you like to attend the Barringtons' ball, my dear?"

"Well, I'm not sure, Your Grace," Brandy answered, uncertain about attending an elaborate event.

"Oh, you must! It'll be diverting. Chandler, you will escort us, won't you?"

"It would be my pleasure. Someone needs to keep an eye on the Barrington silver." One brow arched in amusement.

It took a moment for the barb to strike home. When it did, Brandy gasped in anger and clenched her hands into fists. Before she could retort, however, he smoothly interrupted with, "Does the, er, lady have the appropriate attire?"

Brandy pushed back her chair and stood. "I've had just about enough of your rudeness, Your Grace." She turned to the Dowager Duchess. "I believe I will find lodgings elsewhere. I'm sorry, but I just cannot abide your grandson's deplorable manners one minute more. If you will excuse me?" She spun on her heel and headed for the door.

"Just a minute!" Chandler roared, jumping to his feet. "You duped me, my dear, so I have ample reason to doubt your motives. You will agree that your tale of woe is just a tad hard to swallow? You show up on my doorstep with some sad story of a missing brother and we're supposed to take you in with open arms? You forget, *Lady* Brandy, I know you as a thief and a liar, and God knows what else!"

"I don't give a bloody fig what you think! I did not ask for your assistance, nor do I want it! You are the most infuriating, arrogant..." She stuttered to a stop, too angry to continue her diatribe.

They stood glaring at each other, sparks of electricity blazing between them, and nearly igniting the room on fire. So engrossed were they in their battle for control, when Abigail spoke, they both flinched, having forgotten she was in the room.

"The two of you stop this instant! I will not tolerate this kind of nonsense! Brandy, you are our guest, and I will not hear of your leaving. Chandler, do sit down and stop badgering the girl, and kindly keep your opinions to yourself. Now come and finish your breakfast, both of you." Abigail waited until they had taken their seats. "Do you have a ball gown with you, my dear?" she asked calmly, trying to restore order to her dining room.

Brandy had just taken a sip of her tea and, at the Dowager Duchess's question, choked as it went down the wrong way. Chandler leaned over and graciously came to her rescue, slapping her so hard on the back she lurched over the table, knocking her plate askew, and sending the half-eaten roll sailing across the room. He was rewarded for his assistance with a scowl.

"No, madam, I'm afraid I didn't bring one. I didn't expect to attend any such affairs on this trip." *Not only do I not have a ball gown with me, I haven't one to my name.*

"The ball is in two days, so we won't have time to have one fashioned. But I do believe we can find something for you to wear. If I'm not mistaken, there's a trunk of Norma's dresses in the attic. Norma was my daughter. She died several years ago." Her expression softened for a moment before she continued, "I will send a footman to bring it down. I'm sure we'll find something suitable. It may need to be altered, but we can take care of that." She looked up as Chandler pushed back his chair.

"If you will excuse me, ladies? I have work to do."
With that and a curt nod, he strode from the room, hiding
his chagrin behind a mask of aloofness. He was at a loss
to explain his outburst. Never had he treated a woman so
abominably, and she his grandmother's guest. But then
again, no woman had ever dared stand up to him,
matching him word for word. They were too busy
fawning ingratiatingly over him. But this one—*this
one*—could get under his skin.

"Don't mind Chandler, my dear. He isn't such a
difficult man once you get to know him. He can actually
be quite charming."

"Hah!" Brandy scoffed and immediately blushed.
"I'm sorry, Your Grace. I suppose you rather like him."

Abigail laughed out loud, thoroughly enjoying
Brandy's frankness. How alike she and her grandson
were!

****

Brandy and Liza rifled through the trunk of dusty
clothes the footman had brought down from the attic.
"This be a nice one, milady. The color would look good
on you, I think." Liza held up an emerald-green velvet
gown shot through with golden threads.

With a discerning eye, Brandy studied the bodice
and long sleeves and decided that with a few alterations
it could pass as fashionable. She picked up the latest
copy of a lady's magazine she had been reading and
flipped through the pages until she came to the picture of
a gown she had admired earlier. She showed it to Liza.

"Are you handy with a needle? Could you fashion it
to this style?" At the maid's nod, she replied, "Good.
Now, let's see…" Brandy rose and stood before the full-

length mirror, holding the gown in front of her. "Be sure to ask Her Grace if we can alter it, before you do." She handed the gown to Liza, who bobbed her head and hurried from the room, the gown draped over her arm.

Brandy picked up a book of love sonnets as she left her chamber and wandered down to the garden. She strolled along the brick walk that split the garden in two, admiring the landscape—both sides symmetrical. Trees, some green, some decked out in their autumn colors, dormant flowering shrubs, and neatly manicured evergreen bushes filled every inch of space.

She spent a good part of the afternoon seated on a bench beneath a wide-spread tree, its pendent branches shielding her from prying eyes, especially disconcerting blue ones. Losing interest in the book of sonnets, she placed it on the bench beside her. Still keyed up from the scene at the breakfast table, she was unable to concentrate on the beautiful words.

A deep, masculine voice echoed through the garden. She stilled, hoping *he* wouldn't discover her sanctuary. No such luck. Chandler stopped in front of her and peered through the tree limbs. "Good afternoon, Brandy," he said, his sweeping glance taking in everything—from her periwinkle-blue dress to the tips of her shoes, to the high color now staining her cheeks. He reached down and snatched the book from the bench. With arched brow, he asked, "Love sonnets? You? I wouldn't have thought you a romantic."

Brandy shrugged her shoulders and glanced away from the amusement in his eyes.

"I have a library full of books in my study you might find of interest. Now that I know you can read, feel free to peruse them at your leisure."

"Thank you, Your Grace." She plucked a leaf from a nearby branch and twirled the stem between her fingers. His presence was disquieting, and she nearly jumped clear off the bench when he moved to sit beside her. Quelling her uneasiness, she scooted over to make room.

"Why so nervous, sweet? Where's the brave girl I encountered this morning at breakfast?" He lit a cheroot and leaned back with a sigh, the fragrant smoke circling his head and tickling her nose.

"I'm not nervous," she retorted. "I just don't appreciate your sense of humor, 'tis all. And I'm not answering any more of your questions—so save them!" She leapt to her feet and smoothed her skirt, preparing to leave. His hand shot out, wrapped around her wrist, and tugged her gently back down on the bench beside him.

"Very well." He drew on his cheroot.

Surprised by his answer and not wishing to cause another scene, she settled herself on the bench but pointedly ignored him. His soft chuckle brought her head around. "Whatever do you find so amusing?"

"You."

She looked away from his startling blue eyes to gaze out over the garden. "You are no gentleman," she quipped, stifling her smile.

"And you, my dear, are no lady," he countered.

She opened her mouth to dress him down, but instead laughed, the truth of his words too real to be denied. "Yes, I suppose you would think that. My mother would be very disappointed. She tried so hard to instill the finer points of femininity in me." She sobered, murmuring to herself, "How I hate to wear those pitiful clothes."

"Then why do you?" he asked, wondering if there was more to her story than pinching food.

Startled, unaware she had spoken aloud her thought, she shook her head. "I'd rather not—"

Chandler held up his hand. "I concede—again. I'm sure the subject is not one to your liking."

She felt his warm hand cover hers and glanced up. His smile was kind, without a hint of mockery, and her heart bumped against her chest.

He reached out one finger and gently traced the outline of her mouth. His featherlight touch tickled her lips, creating a tingling sensation. His hand slipped behind her head, drawing her near, as his mouth descended upon hers. Their lips touched—the earth moved. His other hand cupped her cheek, keeping her still for his kiss. He needn't have bothered—she couldn't have moved if she wanted to. His mouth slanted over hers, deepening the kiss, before he pulled away to caress her lips, running his tongue lightly over the silky, pink petals before moving his mouth across her cheek to her ear and nibbling the soft lobe. He dipped his head and trailed warm kisses down her long, slender neck, inhaling her lavender-scented skin.

Brandy sighed deep in her throat, a curious seed of sensation beginning to blossom in her belly. Never had she experienced such a feeling of utter pleasure. Her stomach muscles contracted as her insides were pummeled with a hundred tiny fists. His strong arm encircled her back as his mouth once again fastened on hers—wet, hot, demanding.

Chandler tried to curb his desire, tried to restrain the lust urging him on to fulfillment. Elated when she offered no resistance to his kisses—indeed, she was kissing him back!—her passionate response was nearly his undoing. Without breaking contact, he pulled her onto his lap and slid his hand over her bodice, feeling the soft mounds beneath the fabric. He slipped his hand inside the folds of material to touch her soft skin, cup one breast, feeling the hardened bud pressing against his palm. Her faint whimper and warm flesh—

"Chandler? Are you out here?" Abigail's voice blasted through their euphoria. With a gasp, Brandy pushed hard against Chandler's chest.

"Let me go! Oh!" She glanced down to find the bodice of her gown misshapen, her chemise untied. *Now when had he done that?* She jerked her head up and glared at him, eyes dark with outrage.

He held up his hand. "Before you say a word, sweet, observe where you are seated. I did not force you onto my lap." His sigh was heavy and loud. "Damn it, Brandy, admit you enjoy my kisses."

"I will not!"

Chandler scowled, thoroughly displeased with her retort, even more so with his grandmother for choosing this inopportune time to seek him out. But when Brandy's hand started descending toward his cheek, he nearly lost all control. He grabbed her wrist, twisting it slightly in his frustration.

"Ow! You—you—beast!" She yanked her wrist away and jumped off his lap. Flushing hotly, she quickly straightened her dress, turned on her heel, and hurried down the brick walk. She passed Abigail, who was coming from the house, and nodded her head in greeting as she flew by her. When she reached her bedchamber, she threw herself face down on the bed, tears of mortification streaming down her face. Why did she let him take such liberties? Had she no shame? And she'd been practically lying on top of him, for heaven's sake! She couldn't understand the attraction. He was the most vexing man she had ever met. He was arrogant, derisive, condescending, and...oh, all right, handsome, but that didn't give him the right to grab her every time she was within reach, did it? Brandy let out a loud sob. *Admit it, you coward, you enjoy his kisses.*

"Oh, be quiet!" she shouted and pummeled the pillows with her fists. When Liza came in an hour later, she found Brandy sprawled across the bed, sound asleep, a pillow hugged tightly to her chest.

****

Brandy stopped in the doorway of Chandler's study and glanced around the masculine room with admiration. The walls were paneled in mahogany. One wall held shelves filled with leather-bound books, another housed a huge stone fireplace half-circled by three dark brown leather chairs. The late afternoon sun streamed through two arched windows framed by royal blue velvet drapes held aside with gold tassels. The view was of the back gardens. Across from the windows was a black walnut desk and—Chandler.

She caught her breath in surprise, having not been aware he was in the room. She hovered in the doorway, watching him work quietly at his desk. His forehead rested on his palm, his fingers tangled in his black hair. He had removed his waistcoat and rolled up the sleeves of his white lawn shirt, revealing tanned, muscular arms. He was studying a sheet of paper; a tall stack of papers at his elbow awaited his attention. She had to stop herself from leaping over the desk, wrapping her arms around his neck, and curling her fingers in his hair. That thought so unsettled her she turned to leave. The sound of his voice stopped her in mid-flight.

"Is there something you wanted?"

She turned back and waved a hand toward the bookshelves. "You said I could avail myself of your library. But you're busy, so I'll come back another time."

"No, 'tis acceptable. Come in and choose what you like." His tone was one of dismissal, his actions even more so, for before he had even finished speaking, he had turned his attention back to his papers.

Brandy hurried to the shelves and scanned the titles. She selected a slim leather-encased book and turned to leave, surprised to find Chandler watching her, his eyes narrowed in thought. She smiled shyly and rushed from the room the book clutched to her breast.

Chandler ran his hand through his hair. What in the hell was he going to do with her? He found himself considerably charmed by her laughter and, when not vexed with him, her easy-going manner. To say nothing of his physical reaction to her shapely form. He didn't like the feeling, not a'tall. He recalled her lament about the lad's garments and prayed it was only for stealing food that she donned the clothing, and not for something more nefarious. He had not questioned her further since breakfast, so he still had no answers to the questions that plagued him.

When his grandmother had found him in the garden earlier, she had been none too pleased. She hadn't missed Brandy's flushed face and rumpled gown as she sped past her to the house. Abigail had admonished him not to take advantage of the sweet girl and to please stop baiting her. Rather, he should spend the time trying to find her brother, as he'd promised.

Chandler shook his head and went back to his papers, trying in vain to concentrate on his work, but all he could think of was Brandy's sweet, pliant mouth and intoxicating scent.

Chapter 16

Brandy stared blindly into the fire as the ticking of the clock echoed the passing minutes, heralding impending disaster. She dreaded the upcoming evening. She was to attend her first ball, and, as such, had to navigate Society, comport herself accordingly, in front of not only the duke but the *ton*.

She had been in London for three days and was still no closer to learning Michael's whereabouts. She had questioned Chandler about the one named Blanchard, but his answer had been evasive, telling her nothing. She could do naught but wait until his brother returned home. For the most part, Chandler had absented himself from the townhouse, thereby avoiding her questions and saving her from his arrogance—and kisses. She had spent most of the time reading or walking in the gardens. She had to admit, though, after the last several months of emotional upheaval, it felt good to just do nothing. Soon her aunt and cousin would be here, the Dowager Duchess having received a short note from Jessie stating that she and Anne would be arriving within the sennight. Brandy was eager for their arrival.

Her thoughts returned to the matter at hand. She had never been to a ball and prayed she wouldn't embarrass herself or the Dowager Duchess. Chandler was probably rubbing his hands with glee at this opportunity to further humiliate her. Well, it wouldn't take him long to succeed. She would undoubtedly make the veriest fool of herself. She chewed the tip of her finger as an idea began to form. As the plan took shape, she broke into a grin.

She would merely pretend she had been to dozens of balls! Not once would she give the duke even the slightest inclination that a ball was as foreign to her as the exotic sights on the Continent. If she could masquerade as an urchin, she could certainly pretend she was a sophisticated, worldly woman. She would show him she was more than a simple country girl. With the plan set firmly in her mind, she became excited at the prospect of setting the insufferable duke back on his heels.

She dearly hoped those endless hours of dance lessons she had endured at Doreen's insistence would come back to her when she heard the music. It was unfortunate she hadn't had a Season. If she had, she'd have at least a little knowledge of what to expect, and what was expected of her. But when she had come of age, she had shunned such nonsense. And after Doreen died, it had seemed even less important. Philip had never mentioned it, and she hadn't broached the subject with him.

After a light luncheon, she took a short nap in preparation for the late evening. The borrowed gown now hung in the armoire—altered, scented, and pressed.

At the appointed time, Liza woke Brandy for her bath and, after seeing her ensconced in the tub, left her alone. Brandy soaked in the warm, lavender-scented water until it began to cool. Rising from the tub, she reached for a thick white towel and froze in mid-action, having the distinct feeling she was being watched. She heard the faint click of a door closing and spun to look behind her. Now why hadn't she noticed that door in the wall before? Staring suspiciously at the portal, she stepped from the tub, dried herself, and donned the velvet robe Liza had laid out on the bed. She tiptoed across the room and placed her ear against the door. She could hear the murmur of voices but not what was being said, nor who was saying them.

"Milady?" Liza stood in the doorway holding a tray with a crystal decanter of Madeira and a single glass upon it.

Brandy, caught eavesdropping, flushed to the roots of her hair. "Whose chamber is beyond this door?"

"Why, 'tis His Grace's, milady." Liza poured the Madeira into the glass.

"I see," Brandy murmured, mortified. She sank down on the bench in front of the dressing table. How long had he stood there watching her bathe? Even though she was filled with indignation at the duke's blatant disregard for her privacy, she sighed in disgust as her treacherous body tingled with warmth. *What is wrong with me?* She picked up the glass of wine and nearly drained it of its sweet contents.

Liza pulled and twisted Brandy's auburn tresses, artfully arranging them atop her head in the latest fashion. She left a few tendrils to curl about her face, unintentionally creating a more alluring effect. Brandy had never seen her hair more beautifully done and said as much to Liza. The maid beamed with pleasure and went to fetch the emerald-green ball gown from the armoire.

The gown was a bit snug across the bosom but otherwise fit her trim form perfectly. Liza had slit the long sleeves to add a filler of golden lace and a matching sash was tied just above her waist. The neckline was cut low, daringly so, and the cotton stays pushed her breasts up and out, revealing quite a bit of creamy flesh. Brandy glanced down and the blood drained from her face. Never had she shown this much bosom. She looked up at Liza in alarm, but that one merely shrugged her shoulders.

"'Tis the fashion, milady."

A wicked grin curved Brandy's mouth. She couldn't wait to see Chandler's expression when he saw her in this gown. She laughed aloud as she spun around, the golden threads sewn into the green velvet fabric shimmering in the candlelight. The folds of the skirt swirled around her ankles like the ocean lapping at rocks. She stepped into the matching green silk slippers that now fit snugly after a bit of padding had been placed in the toes.

"Oh, Liza, I don't think I've worn anything half as lovely." She put on the pink topaz earbobs, on loan from the Dowager Duchess, then bent her head so Liza could fasten the gold locket around her neck.

"'Tis lovely you are, milady." Liza handed her a matching green beaded reticule.

Brandy descended the stairs, following the voices to the salon. She paused in the doorway, unnoticed. Abigail was seated on the settee, sipping a glass of sherry, dressed in a white-and-teal gown, diamonds sparkling at her throat and on her wrists. Chandler was leaning casually against the fireplace mantel, a tumbler of whiskey in his hand. Her breath caught in her throat. He was a vision of expensive simplicity, resplendent in evening attire. The snowy white ruffled shirt and expertly tied cravat contrasted sharply with his midnight black jacket and breeches. He had donned an emerald-green waistcoat and a large emerald winked in the folds of his white cravat. His clothes fit him like a second skin—the jacket strained across broad shoulders; the breeches molded to powerful thighs.

She lifted her eyes to his face and was startled to find him watching her, his eyes glowing with an inner fire. She melted like a snowflake in summer. "Good evening," she murmured.

Chandler was stunned. Never had he seen a more breathtaking vision than the one now gracing his salon. Still battling his lust, since watching her bathe in the tub, he found himself quite at a loss. He didn't trust her, yet he wanted her—badly.

Quelling his desire, he bowed at the waist and, finding his tongue at last, greeted her, "Good evening, Brandy. You look lovely." His gaze traveled over her breasts straining at the gown's neckline. They looked ready to escape their confinement, such as it was, with just the smallest movement. He nearly fainted from the sight.

Brandy smiled and entered the room, extremely pleased. She had not missed the appreciative light in his eyes. *So far the plan was sound!*

Abigail nodded. "I agree, my dear. That gown is quite becoming on you. Come and have a glass of sherry before we depart for the ball. Chandler was just telling me the most delightful story about the Barringtons. They are our hosts for the evening, you know."

Brandy sat on the edge of the chair, careful not to crease her gown, and accepted a thin-stemmed glass from Chandler. She sipped the sherry and, after a few minutes, felt herself begin to relax.

Deaton appeared in the doorway to announce Jacob had brought the carriage around. Draped over his arm were three cloaks.

"Thank you, Deaton. Please tell Nash I will be home quite late and not to wait up for me. Don't frown so, Grandmother. I have business to attend to later this evening." Chandler laughed as Abigail's brows rose even higher, nearly disappearing into her perfectly coiffed hair. "Not that sort of business," he assured her with a chuckle and a shake of his dark head. Brandy listened to their exchange, not understanding the undertone.

Abigail set aside her glass of sherry and rose to her feet. Chandler laid a white, fur-lined cloak around her shoulders and, retrieving a dark green velvet one from Deaton, he placed it around Brandy's shoulders. She glanced up at him in surprise.

"Norma's," he replied to her unspoken question. Taking his black cloak from Deaton, he escorted the ladies outside and handed them into the carriage. He stretched out on the seat opposite and rapped on the ceiling. The carriage lurched forward and they were on their way. On the short ride to the ball, Abigail talked quietly with Chandler while Brandy surreptitiously studied Chandler from beneath her lashes. As she stroked the soft velvet of her cloak, she wondered why he was being so nice to her. What surprises did he have hidden up his sleeve, ready to spring on her when she least expected it? Well, she would just have to keep her guard up and be ready for anything he threw at her—while she was playing the seasoned debutante, of course. She had a busy evening ahead of her.

The Barringtons' townhouse was large, three stories

high, every window ablaze with light. Carriages lined the street, waiting to discharge their occupants. After a few moments, they ascended the steps to the foyer beyond the front door. It was a large area, as wide as it was long and tiled in black and white squares. A chandelier hung overhead, illuminating the space and casting prisms of light around the room. Chandler introduced Brandy to their hosts for the evening. Lord Alfred Barrington was a jovial fellow with a ruddy complexion and a receding hairline. Lady Beatrice Barrington looked nearly identical to her husband save for her full head of white hair.

After exchanging a few pleasantries, they were ushered up another flight of stairs, to pause at the entrance of the ballroom. Perched on the landing was a man, resplendent in black and gold livery, introducing the guests as they filed past him into the room. "His Grace, Duke of Marbury. Her Grace, Dowager Duchess of Marbury. Lady Brandy Drummond of Hathshire." At his announcement, several guests turned to stare at the new arrivals. A group of ladies near the entrance put their heads together, whispering behind their fans, their eyes caressing the duke, their eyes narrowing as they assessed the lady on his arm.

Brandy took a moment to take in the scene. She had never seen anything as grand as this room. On closer inspection, she noted it was actually several rooms, the folding doors having been opened to create one large space. The floor was pine, the walls covered with silk wall-hangings, and elegant gold chairs with tapestried cushions lined two of the walls, providing comfortable repose for those tired from dancing or merely wishing to chat. A larger version of the chandelier in the foyer hung overhead, its candlelight reflecting in the cut-glass pendants and sending fragmented rainbows around the room. Crystal scones dotted the walls, candles flickering, and adding to the ambiance.

The women's gowns created a rainbow of color, vying with each other for attention. Their jewels sparkled like colored fire at their ears and throats. For the most part, the men were garbed in evening black, although Brandy spied a colorful outfit or two among the dandies.

As they moved into the ballroom, Brandy felt a hundred pairs of eyes on her. The women were eying her with a mixture of envy and curiosity, while some of the men openly gawked. Under such watchful gazes, the threesome made their way through the crowd.

Roger Blackwell was among those who had turned to stare after hearing their names, turning his back on a young woman in pale pink, who'd had his attention. His eyes narrowed as he watched Brandy enter the ballroom flanked by the duke and the Dowager Duchess. He pushed through the crowd to gain her side, only to be thwarted by the throng of people surrounding them.

Chandler stopped briefly to speak to friends and acquaintances. He kept Brandy by his side, his hand resting on the small of her back, and allowing only a moment or two of conversation with each guest.

Abigail laid her hand on Chandler's arm. "I see Lady Dolores and Lady Annabelle across the room. You'll see that Brandy is introduced around? Bring her to me later." She patted Brandy's cheek and made her way to two splendidly dressed matrons who occupied chairs along one wall. Brandy watched her disappear, her stomach knotting in anxious anticipation of being left alone with Chandler.

"Quite a crush, isn't it? I gather from your expression you have not attended many of these affairs."

So, he was back to being sardonic. "I'll admit it has been quite a while, but I can assure you I have attended dozens of balls." She turned away from his mocking smile.

Chandler watched her gaze around the room, obviously fascinated by the lavish affair. He was quite certain she had never been to a ball, regardless of her claims to have done so. There was an innocent wonder in her eyes and pure pleasure on her face. Her excitement was tangible.

"Would you like to dance?" He offered her his arm.

Brandy shook her head. She had seen the guests dancing and hadn't an inkling to what they were doing—step, slide, step, turning and embracing. She had never seen the likes of it before.

"Don't tell me you don't dance?" he asked in mock horror.

She blushed and refused to meet his gaze. "Of course, I dance! It's just—" She thought quickly not wanting to appear naive. "'Tis too crowded right now."

He gazed down at her flushed face and arched a brow. "Admit it, Brandy. What woman who dresses like a lad, steals chickens, and Lord knows what else, would have the time or inclination for the finer art of dancing?"

She turned away from his ridicule, her eyes filling with unshed tears. He opened his mouth to apologize but slammed it shut; he would not be swayed by her tears. He ignored the stab of guilt that pierced from clearly ruining her evening, reminding himself that until he was sure of her motives, he couldn't afford to let his guard down. He took her arm and dragged her over to Abigail.

"Grandmother, I bring you Lady Brandy. I have business to discuss with Jeffrey." He released Brandy's arm, bowed to the other women, and melted into the crowd. He felt his grandmother's disapproval burning into his back as he crossed the room.

Jeffrey Alden was a handsome man with dark brown hair and hazel eyes that shone with a love of life. He was nearly as tall as Chandler, and the two of them together set the ladies' pulses racing. However, where Chandler shunned marriage, Jeffrey had embraced it. The two had known each other all their lives and were fast friends. He beckoned to Chandler, who was striding across the room toward him, scowling.

"Good to see you, Chandler. Did you just arrive?"

"I did." He stopped a passing footman and grabbed a glass of champagne from the silver tray. He lounged against the wall and surveyed the room, sipping the sparkling wine. He sought out Brandy, but she was obscured from his view. Just as well. He didn't think he could bear her unhappy face. He was exceedingly ashamed of himself. He had treated her poorly and she hadn't deserve it. Where his sudden vexation came from, he didn't know. And it didn't sit well.

Jeffrey laughed. "Don't look so glum, old chap. I saw Vivian earlier. She's looking fine and quite eager, I might add."

"I told you Vivian and I are no longer together."

"I daresay she has not taken it for the truth."

"I am not remotely interested in what she thinks. 'Tis a fact."

"Why so cross tonight? I know these affairs are not to your liking, but you are usually able to charm some lovely lady into helping you make the night more pleasurable." Jeffrey eyed his friend, puzzled. "If not Vivian, I daresay you'll stumble across another willing lady."

"Abigail is becoming more persistent. She is determined to see me married, and soon."

With that dour admission, Jeffrey threw back his head and roared with laughter. "Abigail is the only woman, or for that matter the only person, I know who can give it as adeptly as you."

Chandler ignored his barb and turned the subject. "Did Blanchard request to see you this evening?"

"Yes. What do you suppose he wants?"

"I'm not sure. I informed him I am through, that this last assignment will be my last. I feel a need to retire to the country for some peace and quiet. I fear I have neglected my duties for far too long."

Jeffrey nudged him with his elbow. "Don't look now, old chap, but someone's bearing down on you with a very determined look on her face. If you will excuse me?" He disappeared before Chandler could stop him.

Chandler watched his former mistress approach, mentally preparing himself for the confrontation. Lady Vivian Beaumont was a beautiful woman. Her dark hair and dark eyes contrasted with her ivory skin, creating an exotic, alluring effect. Her beauty, however, hid a malicious nature she kept well hidden, unless challenged.

"Chandler, darling, I've been looking everywhere for you," she purred, extending her hand for his kiss. He bowed low and accommodated her, placing a light kiss upon her scented skin. His eyes traveled over her bosom, the sight of the exposed bounty stirring memories of times past. She had been quite an eager bed partner, but her actions were mechanical, nearly ruining the encounter.

"Good evening, Vivian. You're looking well."

"Who is the little girl you escorted tonight? A relative, perhaps?"

"She's a friend of the family, 'tis all."

She smiled and slipped her arm through his. "I've missed you, darling. Will you visit me tonight?" She lowered her voice, mindful of the watchful eyes and ears surrounding them.

"I cannot," he replied, feeling hunted by the hungry look in her eyes, not to mention nauseous from her perfume. Why had he never noticed the overpowering scent? "If there is nothing else you need—"

Her eyes narrowed. "What I need, darling, is you—back in my bed."

"I thought I had made myself clear, Vivian. It's over."

"Chandler, forget what I said about marriage. I—I was wrong to mention it. We can keep our relationship just as it's been."

His expression hardened, his eyes becoming chips of ice. He could feel her panic, it was palpable. He could almost pity her, except for the scene in her salon when he ended their relationship. She had threatened, cajoled, then acted the whore. He had left disgusted.

He pulled his arm free and bowed low. "If you will excuse me?" he said, and headed toward the library, eager to get away from her clutches.

Chandler joined Jeffrey and a group of men near the entrance to the library. He grasped Jeffrey's arm, nodded to the other men, and dragged him into the room.

"And how is our dear Vivian? Demanding, as

always?"

"I swear she has vises for hands and cotton for brains." Chandler shook his head in exasperation and accepted a cognac from Jeffrey. He took a seat in a maroon leather chair and ran his hand through his hair in a gesture of pure frustration. "Did Lydia accompany you tonight?"

"No. Her parents are visiting. She took pity on me and gave me leave to attend alone." Jeffrey took the other chair.

"How accommodating of her," Chandler drawled, pulling a cheroot from his silver case and lighting it. He blew a stream of smoke toward the ceiling.

"She knows I love her madly and would not even think of looking at another woman. Hell, she'd make a eunuch of me in no time!" He laughed and Chandler joined him, both envisioning Jeffrey's petite wife brandishing a knife. They looked up as Alfred Barrington strode into the room.

"Hello, my friends! I see you have made yourselves at home. Good, good. I see you are also enjoying some of my fine cognac. The French are good for something, eh?" Chandler and Jeffrey exchanged amused glances as their host rambled. He laughed at his own joke as he poured himself a healthy draught of cognac.

Barrington was well liked by the *ton*. He was, however, the brunt of many jokes, behind his back, of course, for no one would dare hurt his feelings. They all knew his wife had him on a short leash, but they overlooked that fact and agreed with him when he stated he controlled her with an iron fist.

"So, Townsend, who's that ravishing young lady who accompanied you tonight? Lady Brandy, wasn't it?"

"What's this?" Jeffrey set down his glass and leaned forward in his chair.

"Lady Brandy Drummond. She's visiting with my grandmother." He tapped the ash from his cheroot on the edge of a silver tray.

"Drummond? Her bro—" Jeffrey stopped at the warning look Chandler shot him. "Her father wouldn't be Philip Drummond, Earl of Hathshire?" he amended. "I understand he passed away recently."

"Have you met her before?"

"'Tis true Alden Ridge is near their home, and I know my parents were acquainted with hers, but I don't believe I ever met their lovely daughter. I assume she is lovely, to have caused such a stir?"

"She's not bad to look at."

Barrington slapped his knee and chortled. "She's downright gorgeous, she is." He took a deep swallow and set down his glass. "If you will excuse me, I must see to my other guests. You are welcome to stay here as long as you want. I trust I will see you both later."

Chandler leaned back in his chair, fully aware of Jeffrey's curiosity. He held the snifter of cognac up to the fire blazing in the large stone hearth. An image of Brandy appeared, her auburn hair fanning out about her as she slept. Her lips, like soft petals, aching to be kissed. His features softened as the recollection brought on remembered desire.

Jeffrey watched the play of emotions cross his friend's face. He had never seen Chandler so preoccupied nor his countenance so...dreamy? He leaned over and tapped him on the knee. "Chandler?"

Chandler focused on his friend. "What?"

"Just wondering if you're still with me. You look

positively diverted." He quit his needling as the duke's brows lowered ominously. Sensing there was something truly bothering his friend, he asked, "What is it? Is she aware you know Michael?"

Chandler drained his glass and rose to refill it. "No, she is unaware of my relationship with her brother. But there is a hitch. She's here to find him. She found Andrew's name linked with Michael's among her father's papers. It seems that Abigail is acquainted with her aunt, so she has allowed Brandy to stay and wait for Andrew to return from Scotland."

"But he's not in Scotland."

"I know. I told them he was checking on a piece of property I recently purchased. For obvious reasons, I can only use that excuse for so long. Now, with Brandy here, we will have to move quickly. I will fill Blanchard in on this development when we see him later this evening."

Jeffrey nodded. "That would be wise." Then, "She must be quite young."

"If I'm not mistaken, ten and eight years. I had forgotten about her until Michael asked me to look in on her."

"Did you?"

"Yes, but she wasn't at home."

"Are you sure she is his sister?"

"No, I'm not. Why do you ask?"

"A stranger shows up at your door claiming to be the sister of a man who is," he paused and glanced toward the door, lowering his voice, "carrying out his duty for our country."

"We received a note from her aunt, who will be arriving in London within a sennight. My doubts, at least on that score, will be laid to rest once she arrives."

"Well, then, I'd like to meet this Brandy Drummond," Jeffrey enthused with a grin.

They made their way to the ballroom, pausing in the doorway so Chandler could scan the room for the one he sought. He found his grandmother still sitting against the wall with her two cronies, but there was no sign of Brandy. He turned his head and caught a glimpse of her disappearing through the set of doors leading out to the gardens.

"There she is, heading outside."

"Gentlemen! Would you kindly settle a bet for us?" Before the two could escape, they were surrounded by several men, all in high spirits.

Roger Blackwell, seething with fury, had been watching Brandy all evening. He'd had no idea she was in London, much less acquainted with the duke. He had been shocked when her name had been announced upon her arrival. Since then, she had been by the old lady's side, and he hadn't been able to get close. When he saw her slip through the doors to the gardens, he quickly headed in that direction, eager to get her alone.

Chapter 17

Brandy paused at the top of the steps leading into the gardens, breathing deeply of the crisp night air. It was refreshing after the crush of the ballroom which, as time went by, had become stuffy and overcrowded. She was also tired of being stared at and whispered about behind raised fans. She literally could feel the animosity coming from some of the ladies.

She glanced up and marveled at the twinkling stars dotting the coal-black sky. She could almost imagine she was at home in the country, but for the sounds of merriment drifting through the open doors. She lifted her skirt and made her way down the steps to amble aimlessly down the stone walk. The autumn moon was high overhead, casting its soft light upon the grounds. Here and there lamps were placed, a glow to light the paths for those who chose to venture outside.

Spying a bench set back from the walk, she headed toward it and sat down, arranging her skirt around her legs. The evening was certainly not going to plan. Chandler had disappeared, leaving her alone with Abigail and her friends. A few of the men in attendance were relentless in their quest to meet her. She declined their many invitations to dance, no doubt breaking an unwritten, de rigueur rule of Society.

She had so wanted to dazzle Chandler with her sophistication and wit but had allowed his cruel remarks to upset her instead. Where was her resolve to set him back on his heels, to show him she was not just a simple country girl? She had lost her chance to regain her composure when he had deposited her with the Dowager Duchess and closeted himself with his cronies. She had not seen him since.

She turned at a sound and saw the figure of a man striding down the walk. "Who's there?" she called out, peering from the shadows. Her heart raced at the thought it might be Chandler.

"'Tis me, Roger."

"Roger! What are you doing here?"

"I could ask you the same thing. I wasn't aware you knew Townsend. Why are you in London?"

"The Dowager Duchess is an old friend of my aunt's. I'm visiting for a while." Her tone was unusually sharp. She was tired of being questioned, and she certainly did not owe Roger Blackwell any explanations.

"Then it's lucky we ran into each other." Without waiting for an invitation, he sat down on the bench.

"Why is that lucky, Roger?" she asked, hiding her sudden trepidation at finding herself alone with him in the dark.

"I've been wanting to speak with you privately. It was most inappropriate to discuss the subject at our last visit, and I apologize for my insensitivity. I do, however, intend to make you my bride. Your father and I had a contract and he fully intended for us to marry."

"That may have been his wish, not mine. I do not intend to marry you."

He turned and grabbed her shoulders with both hands, all pretense of regret and civility disappearing. "You will marry me, Brandy. I had your father's word on it."

She jerked back, trying to dislodge his hands. "My father is dead. His word means nothing now."

His grip tightened, bruising her soft skin. "We are betrothed," he said through gritted teeth. His expression turned dangerously dark. "'Tis a moot point that your father is dead. He promised you to me."

Brandy disengaged herself from his grip and jumped up in fury. "Now you listen to me, Roger. My father may have betrothed me to you, but it was done against my wishes. I have no intention of fulfilling his promise. I don't know what you threatened him with to get him to make that promise, but I can assure you of this—I will never marry you!" By the time she had finished her tirade, her voice had risen to a shout. She took several deep breaths trying to calm the anger raging through her.

Blackwell flushed darkly, his eyes narrowed, his nostrils flared. He rose to his feet and raised a fist as if to strike her. After one suspended moment, he let it drop to his side.

"Rest assured, you will marry me. Your father and I had an agreement."

"What agreement, Roger? I have seen no contract." Brandy waved her hand around the gardens.

He ground his teeth together. "You won't get away with this, not after everything I have—" He grabbed her by the arms. "It was a verbal agreement, and I will hold you to it. You have not heard the last of this. You will marry me!" He shook her so hard she thought her head would snap from her neck.

"Get your hands off me," she said through gritted teeth. She opened her mouth to scream but he quickly covered it with his own—wet, sloppy and breath foul with stale smoke and whiskey. She brought her hands up between their bodies and shoved as hard as she could against his chest. Unprepared for her actions, he stumbled back but didn't loosen his grip on her shoulders.

"How dare you!"

"I'll dare anything—" he threatened, looming over her.

"Brandy?" The sound of her name echoed through the shadows. "Brandy?"

Chandler strode into view, another man close on his heels. "Get your hands off her, Blackwell. What in the hell do you think you're doing, man?"

"This is none of your concern, Townsend. Brandy is my betrothed." Roger sneered at his nemesis.

Chandler heard Brandy's gasp of outrage and stopped short, looking over at her. *Was her indignation for Blackwell's benefit or mine?*

"Are you daft?" she shouted in the ensuing silence. "I've had quite enough of this ridiculous conversation." She started to step around Roger, intent on returning to the ballroom, but he blocked her way.

"I wouldn't if I were you," Chandler warned, his voice low and frightfully calm.

Roger dropped his hands and hissed, "This subject is not closed." He turned on his heel, shoved Jeffrey out of his way, and strode back toward the house.

Chandler grabbed Brandy's arm. "What were you doing out here with him?"

She pulled out of his grasp. "Take your hands off me. I have endured all the ill-treatment I am going to take for one evening." She took a deep breath. "And besides, I do not have to explain myself to you."

"Are you two betrothed?" Before she could answer him, he continued sharply, "I forbid you to see him."

"Forbid me? *You* forbid me? You have no say over me!" Brandy settled her hands on her hips, her eyes flashing green fire.

"Brandy, you don't know him—"

"Your Grace," she cut in curtly, "you are not my guardian. I will do what I want when I want and with whom I want. Do I make myself clear?" She spun on her heel, leaving the two gentlemen staring after her, their mouths agape.

Jeffrey whistled through his teeth. "I can see why you're so taken with her."

"I am not taken with her! She is the most stubborn, exasperating—"

Jeffrey held up his hand. "Whatever you say," he agreed good-naturedly. "You certainly know how to endear yourself to her," he added with a chuckle.

"Shut up, Jeffrey."

"I still want to be formally introduced to her. Exasperating or not, she is gorgeous."

Chandler ignored him and followed Brandy back into the ballroom, utterly perplexed. She had been furious when Blackwell had announced she was his betrothed. Was she angry because Roger lied? Or because he was unknowingly informing Chandler she was involved in his treasonous schemes? Chandler didn't know, and that was the catch.

Brandy was miserable. She sat once again with Abigail and her friends, listening idly to their chatter. She kept one eye on the door, waiting for Chandler to appear. She had no doubt he would be mad as Hades. When she spied him striding through the door, she turned toward Abigail and pretended to be avidly engrossed in their conversation.

"Brandy?"

She turned and looked up into his eyes. Expecting fury in their blue depths, she was totally unprepared for amusement. Her gaze shifted to the man standing beside him, bowing before Abigail. He had been in the gardens.

"How are you this evening, Abigail?"

"Just fine, Jeffrey. 'Tis good to see you again. How is your lovely wife?"

"She's doing well, thank you for asking. Her parents are visiting, so she chose not to attend tonight."

"Please give her my regards."

"I will." Jeffrey nodded to the other two women, then gave his full attention to Brandy.

"Brandy, I would like to introduce you to a very good friend of mine." Chandler stepped aside, his mouth twitching with suppressed laughter. "Jeffrey, may I present Lady Brandy Drummond? Brandy, Jeffrey Alden, Marquess of Montaldene."

Brandy smiled at Jeffrey and rose to her feet, extending her hand. Chandler was watching her closely so knew the exact moment Jeffrey's name registered. Her body stilled, her green eyes narrowed, and she blushed from her head to her toes. She glared at Chandler, who was trying in vain to smother his laughter, an innocent expression fashioned on his face. He quirked one brow in a silent gauntlet.

Jeffrey looked from Brandy to Chandler and back to Brandy. "I say, am I missing something?"

"No—" Chandler choked out. "'Tis nothing, Jeff. Brandy, say hello to Lord Montaldene."

Mortified, she turned her full attention to the tall,

dark-haired gentleman. "Please ignore the duke. How do you do, milord?" She planted a brilliant smile on her face, and prayed Chandler would not divulge her secret.

"'Tis a pleasure to meet you, Lady Brandy. I understand we're neighbors. 'Tis a wonder we have not met before this evening."

"Yes, a wonder..." Chandler echoed.

"'Tis a pity we have not," she agreed. "My parents spoke very highly of yours."

"My country home is Alden Ridge. Do you know it?" He glanced at Chandler, confused by the muffled sounds he was making.

Brandy managed to maintain her composure. "Yes, I believe I am acquainted with Alden Ridge. It's very beautiful."

"I was sorry to hear of your father's untimely death."

"Yes, it was quite sudden."

Jeffrey turned to Chandler. "It's getting late. We had better leave for our appointment. I'll have my carriage brought around." He turned back to Brandy and bowed. "It was indeed a pleasure, Lady Brandy. Will you please excuse me?"

"Of course, milord." Brandy watched as Jeffrey bowed to the elder women and turned to leave. She waited until he was out of earshot before turning on Chandler. Shaking with fury, she said between clenched teeth, "How dare you?"

"Dare I what?" His blue eyes were filled with merriment.

"You were just dying to tell him, weren't you?"

"Tell him what?" He cocked his head toward Abigail and her friends, who were avidly listening to their exchange.

"Oh, you…" Brandy turned away, her chin in the air.

"Chandler, stop torturing the girl. I don't know what is going on between you two, but I demand you cease badgering her at once." Abigail struck her fan against his arm, eyes flashing with indignation.

Chandler nodded, and bowed before Brandy, looking up at her from beneath his lashes. "My apologies, Lady Brandy."

She ignored him and sat back down on her chair.

Chandler turned back to his grandmother. "Jeffrey and I have an appointment. Our host has assured me he will escort you both home. I will see you ladies in the morning." He kissed Abigail on the cheek, nodded to her two friends, glanced at Brandy and, taking note of her stony profile, turned on his heel and disappeared into the crowd.

With his departure went her evening. Despite the infuriating trick he had played on her, she wanted him to stay. She didn't know why, and wasn't about to examine the reason, but she didn't like to see him leave.

Fortunately, she didn't see Roger again that evening. She was still shaken from their meeting in the gardens— he was becoming more persistent and quite frightening in his goal to make her his wife. One more reason Michael needs to be home.

It wasn't until she and the Dowager Duchess were headed for home, she realized that, because Chandler had cut his evening short, she'd not had the chance to set the infuriating duke back on his heels.

Now that was disappointing.

****

Ross Blanchard pulled open the door at the first knock. He was of medium height with perfect posture and a friendly disposition. His years in government service had fine-tuned his ability to put anyone at ease, even the most seasoned cynics. He stepped aside to allow his guests entry. "Good evening, Chandler, Jeffrey. Thank you both for coming at this late hour."

"Not a problem, Ross. How is your wife feeling?"

"Improved. She'll be up and about in no time." He led the way to his oak-paneled study and shut the door. While Chandler and Jeffrey settled themselves in two of the tan leather-covered chairs circling the fireplace, Blanchard poured them each a cognac and settled himself in the other chair. He came straight to the point. "Michael and Andrew are missing."

"Damn it!" Chandler threaded his fingers through his hair. "I was afraid of that."

"I received word earlier today. They failed to show up at the appointed time and place." Ross gazed at Chandler with compassion. "I'm sorry, Chandler. I know how devastating news of this sort can be."

"Do you have any idea where they could be? Or what might have happened?"

"My men are on it, Jeffrey. I have complete faith in them. But it's tricky. There are just too many turncoats out there. I may need your help, Chandler. We'll wait a few days, but if my men can't come up with any news, I'll need you to go in and find them. I know it's dangerous, so we'll wait until the last possible moment to send you in." He took a long drink of his cognac. "Jeffrey, I'll need you to go to Alden Ridge and keep an eye on Blackwell. We have reason to believe a shipment of supplies will be going out within the next few weeks."

He took the proffered cheroot from Chandler and lit the end before leaning back in his chair. "One more thing. Because of the disturbing news about Drummond, it wouldn't do to ignore the others at Stonebrooke Manor. There are the servants and, of course, Michael's sister. We also received word two women are residing there as well."

"That would be Philip's sister-in-law and her daughter. They are due to arrive in London within the next few days to visit with Abigail." At Blanchard's blank look, he quickly outlined the events of the past few days. "So, you see, Brandy is waiting for Andrew's return so she can question him about Michael."

"Can we create a letter from Michael? That might appease her curiosity."

"She would most certainly know Michael's hand."

"Then she will have to continue to wait for Andrew's return."

"I don't know how long I can continue to stall her with the vague answers I've been handing her. She also asked about you, Ross."

"Me?"

"Yes, she found your name in Drummond's papers."

"What did you tell her?"

"That Andrew had a friend from school by the name of Blanchard."

"Well, let's hope we don't meet. I am quite a bit older than your brother."

"I will deal with that problem if and when it arises."

Ross was silent a moment before speaking aloud his suspicion. "I will expect you to keep an eye on Lady Brandy. She could very well be involved."

"I am one step ahead of you, Ross. Since she's been

in London, she has not left the house, until this evening. Even now, while at the Barringtons' ball, she is being watched." He leaned back with a frown and contemplated his statement while Blanchard refilled their glasses. True, there were still many unanswered questions about Lady Brandy Drummond, and he would get to the bottom of this matter when he returned from France—if indeed he went. In the meantime, he would spend as much time as possible with her. He suddenly grinned. That wouldn't be too difficult a task. She was quite enchanting—even when furious.

Jeffrey had been pacing the length of the room. He snapped his fingers and turned to the other two men. "I've got it! I will hold a rout at Alden Ridge. I will be certain to invite Blackwell, which I'm sure will surprise the hell out of him, but that way we can keep a close eye on him."

Blanchard nodded. "Good idea, but we must move cautiously. Chandler, I will keep you posted about Michael and Andrew. Jeffrey, plan the party for three weeks' time. If we find it necessary to send Chandler to France, that will give him enough time to ferret out the information we need and return to England."

Jeffrey nodded, then having paused in front of the fireplace, asked "Who is this woman?" He was gazing at a portrait hanging above the mantel.

Blanchard followed his gaze and his eyes filled with sorrow. "My daughter, Marian."

"Yes, of course. She was a beautiful young woman, Ross. You never found any clues to her disappearance, did you?"

"No. She vanished without a trace."

After a few minutes more discussing their plans,

Chandler and Jeffrey departed. Blanchard glanced up at the portrait of Marian, his eyes burning with unshed tears. *So long ago—where could you have gone?* The pain of her disappearance still bit with sharp teeth. He shook his head to rid himself of the painful memories and turned, finding his wife standing in the doorway.

"Are your guests gone?"

"Yes, I was just coming to bed."

Madelyn saw the unshed tears. "'Tis no good, you know."

"I know." He reached for her hand, and they quit the room, tucking away their shared sorrow.

Chapter 18

The following days were a whirlwind of activity. Out of deference to the Dowager Duchess, Brandy and Chandler put aside their differences and came to a truce. More often than not, Chandler was on his best behavior as he squired her about town. She found that when he wasn't mocking her or hurling insults, he could be quite amiable. They took walks in the park, attended an outdoor concert at Vauxhall Gardens and an opera at the King's Theatre in the Haymarket. They attended a soiree with Abigail, and Brandy was pleased to discover that her dance lessons had not been for naught. Since the dance steps had been familiar ones, she had not been self-conscious when taking the floor with Chandler. She had proved that she could indeed dance.

The more time they spent together, the more comfortable she became in his presence. He had ceased grabbing and kissing her at every opportunity, which—she told herself—was a relief. Still, she became flustered if she inadvertently brushed up against him or when he clasped her hand in his large one. Yes, he could be quite charming but then he would make some sly reference to her chicken pinching, and she'd remind herself that she needn't worry about her growing attraction to the duke— he drove her mad.

Chandler, too, was feeling the effects of spending time with the beautiful and captivating Brandy. She was full of incredible enthusiasm, quick to laugh, her green eyes glowing with excitement at all her new adventures. She was childlike in her eagerness to experience all the sights and sounds of London. It was obvious it was all new to her, despite her claims to the contrary. He knew instinctively that her world, up until now, had been limited to the county of Hathshire. He found himself enjoying her company and decided looking after her was no hardship at all. Still, he had to continually remind himself that, despite her childlike wonder and delight, she could be involved in activities against the Crown, and that possibility lurked behind his every move.

The only time Brandy's gaiety dimmed was when she spoke of Michael. Still unsure if he was her brother, when her aunt came to London and he was assured she was, at least that one lingering doubt would be put to rest. Though he could still not confide in her and would have to continue stalling her many questions with vague answers, momentarily satisfying her curiosity.

Abigail had insisted Brandy be fitted for a new wardrobe. Brandy had argued vehemently, knowing she could never repay the Dowager Duchess. But Abigail was resolute. Thus, Brandy found herself fitted for a new wardrobe, including three evening gowns, one of pale purple silk, one of sea-green silk, and one of sapphire-blue crepe, and several day dresses of muslin and lawn. She was also fitted for chemises of the softest cotton. Abigail took her to the milliners in Leicester Square for caps and bonnets and to the cobblers for shoes in colors that matched her new gowns as well as a pair of half boots.

Chandler was kept busy—doing what Brandy didn't know. He absented himself from the townhouse for two days, and when he returned on the second evening, he surprised her with tickets to the opera. Brandy had read about the ladies and gentlemen with the incredible voices who inspired such awe in their audiences, and she was excited by the prospect of hearing them first-hand. For the occasion, she wore her new gown of pale purple silk. The gown was high-waisted, the bodice cut low and exposing not only her shoulders but a great deal of her breasts. Elbow-length gloves of a matching hue completed the outfit, and matching shoes peeped out from beneath the frilled hem of the skirt.

Chandler was resplendent in tight-fitting black breeches, a matching black frock coat, snowy-white cravat, and a gold embroidered waistcoat. The sight of him so splendidly outfitted set her pulse racing.

On the carriage ride to the King's Theatre, Brandy could hardly contain her excitement. She looked over at Chandler and caught him watching her. "Excited, sweet?"

"Oh, yes. I must admit I have never been to the opera."

"Really? Well, then this will be a new experience for you."

When they entered the theatre, they were the recipients of many admiring glances and Brandy was proud to be on his arm. Chandler nodded to a few acquaintances as they made their way to the Townsend box.

Brandy sat as quiet as a mouse, drinking in the sights and sounds of her first opera. As the music built to a crescendo, the notes flowed over her, bringing an inner peace she had not felt in a very long time. Chandler watched Brandy, her eyes misty with unshed tears, completely enthralled with the performance. His heart softened a small degree.

When the curtain came down on the first act, they followed the crowd to the hall for the intermission. Chandler left her momentarily, to obtain two glasses of champagne, and while he was gone, Brandy was content to watch the other ladies and gentlemen. As Chandler crossed the room toward her, her heart skipped a beat. He really was the most handsome man in attendance. She smiled at him, accepting the glass of champagne.

"Enjoying yourself, sweet?"

"Oh, yes! Chandler, this is the most wonderful night of my life. I love the opera!"

He laughed, thoroughly enjoying her obvious pleasure. He glanced over her head and frowned. Bearing down on them was Roger Blackwell, Lady Vivian Beaumont on his arm.

Brandy felt Chandler stiffen and looked up at him in concern. Following his gaze, she murmured, "Oh, dear."

"Lady Brandy, it is indeed a pleasure to see you again. Townsend…" Roger nodded at the duke as he pulled his companion forward. "I believe you're acquainted with Lady Vivian?" His smile was evil laced with sweetness.

"Vivian," Chandler bowed over her hand.

"Chandler, darling. 'Tis so good to see you again."

"May I introduce Lady Brandy Drummond?"

"A pleasure, I'm sure," Vivian purred, her eyes fixed on Chandler, barely glancing at Brandy.

"How do you do?" Brandy uttered, doubting the woman even heard her, she was that focused on the duke.

With an effort, Vivian dragged her eyes away from Chandler and looked down at Brandy with a delicately raised brow. "Are you enjoying the opera, my dear? I must say I am surprised to find you here. I believe Chandler told me you're visiting from the country..." Her words trailed off as if finding herself bewildered by the thought.

Chandler draped his arm across Brandy's shoulders. "Brandy has exceptional taste, even for a country girl."

"Have you been in London long, my dear?"

"Long enough," Chandler answered with a lazy grin.

At the thinly veiled intimation, Vivian's eyes narrowed, and if looks could wound, Brandy would be flat on the floor, bleeding. "I see," Vivian bit out between clenched teeth. With a toss of her head, she grabbed Roger's arm and pulled him away without extending a word of farewell.

"Good evening, Brandy, Your Grace," Blackwell flung over his shoulder, his eyes filled with resentment.

"Who was that woman?" Brandy watched them walk away, anger simmering just below the surface at the woman's snide remarks and rude manners. "Didn't I see her at the Barringtons' ball?"

"Nobody important, sweet. And, yes, I do believe she was there."

"She seemed as though she has prior claim on you. Does she?"

"Not anymore, sweet."

"I wonder what she's doing with Roger."

Chandler watched her closely. He hadn't missed Brandy's stiff expression and wondered if the sight of Roger with another woman had upset her or if Vivian's rude demeanor was what rankled.

"Come along, the second act is about to begin," he stated more brusquely than he had intended, unable to dispel the onslaught of uncertainty now besetting him. And, if truth be told, a twinge of feeling he couldn't quite put a name to.

Brandy dismissed the unpleasant encounter and thoroughly enjoyed the rest of the opera. Later, when they were ensconced in the carriage heading home, she thanked Chandler once again for the evening.

"Do you really want to show your appreciation?" His smile was seductive, and before she knew what he was about, he dragged her onto his lap.

"Chandler! Let me go!" She struggled, but it was like trying to escape a steel trap.

Ignoring her efforts, he settled her on his lap before his mouth descended on hers with a fierceness hard to contain. She tried twisting her head to one side, but his hand kept it firmly in place, denying her freedom from his kiss. His mouth devoured hers, searing her lips with white-hot heat. His kiss deepened and his hands slid down her back until suddenly it was no longer necessary to hold her still. Brandy surrendered to the passion his kisses aroused. Without conscious thought, she wrapped her arms around his neck, settling herself more intimately on his lap, and returned his kisses with enthusiasm.

Growling low in his throat, he parted her lips with his tongue before slipping it inside to tangle with hers. She quivered with delight, her stomach knotting in the most wonderful sensation. She melted into him, clinging to him as she was sucked deeper into an eddy of hot desire.

The carriage hit an especially large hole, jostling them apart. Brandy's eyes flew open and, jolted back to reality, she pulled from his embrace. Blushing, more than unsettled by her uninhibited reaction to his kisses, she scooted off his lap and straightened her skirt, all the while avoiding eye contact with him.

"You really must refrain from kissing me whenever we're alone, Chandler. 'Tis just not done." Her voice sounded husky and not quite as reproachful as she would have liked.

"Would you prefer Blackwell's kisses?"

"What?"

"I said—"

"I heard what you said. What I meant was—are you daft?"

Chandler didn't answer, his mouth drawn in a tight line, his body rigid. He dismissed her with an abrupt shake of his head and stared out the carriage window.

Brandy eyed his expression, now shuttered, unable to tell what he was thinking. He certainly didn't look happy. Soft light from the carriage lantern threw his features into sharp relief. His jaw was set and a muscle worked in his cheek. No, he was definitely not happy.

The duke's quicksilver change of mood was bewildering. One moment he was attentive, if not downright courteous. Then he'd become stone-faced and irritable. She straightened her shoulders and resolved to avoid his company henceforth, at least when there was no one else around. It would just not do to continue with these stolen kisses. They could only lead to disaster.

****

The afternoon before Aunt Jessie and Anne were due to arrive, Brandy headed to the gardens to spend a quiet afternoon reading. As she passed Chandler's study, she heard lowered voices from within. The door was ajar, so she stopped for a moment, curious as to who was visiting the duke. She heard only a few words before Deaton came around the corner and caught her listening. She quickly moved away from the door and made her way outside.

Finding her favorite tree, she sat on the bench beneath it, setting the book aside. She had clearly overheard three words, and those three words were echoing in her mind: *Michael, Andrew, France*. What did it mean? Should she confront Chandler with what she had overheard? No, he would just accuse her of eavesdropping and make up some convoluted story. She bit her lip, uncertain. Picking up the book, she tried to concentrate on the written words, having decided to wait and talk with Anne before she did anything about this mystery.

Chapter 19

"Milady? 'Tis time for you to rise." Liza whispered, mindful of the last time she awoke her mistress and her ensuing scream.

Brandy opened one eye, squinting against the shaft of sunlight slanting across the bed. "What time is it?"

"'Tis ten o'clock, milady. Your aunt and cousin have arrived. Her Grace bade me fetch you." Liza pulled a honey-colored muslin gown from the wardrobe and laid it across the chair while Brandy threw back the coverlet and rose from the bed. She hurried to the commode to wash the sleep from her eyes, then sat at the dressing table to allow Liza to comb the tangles from her hair. She dressed quickly, eager to see her aunt and cousin, and was out of the room in less than an hour.

The sound of feminine laughter drifted up as she ran down the stairs and raced into the salon. "Aunt Jessie— Anne! I'm so glad you've come!" She hugged each of them and curtsied to the Dowager Duchess. "Good morning, Your Grace."

Jessie resumed her seat on the settee and contemplated her niece, frowning. "Well, young lady, you have some explaining to do. Anne has already felt my displeasure."

Brandy blushed, joined Jessie on the settee, and reached for her hand. "I know, Aunt, and I am sorry for worrying you. Please don't be upset with Anne. I made her keep my secret. I knew you wouldn't let me go alone, and I just had to come to London!"

"I know, child. And though I understand your reasons, it was foolish of you to travel here by yourself, regardless that you were in disguise. It was dangerous. Why, any manner of evil could have befallen you." Her frown disappeared and she hugged Brandy. "We'll find Michael, we will." She glanced over at Abigail. "In any event, it's good to see my dear friend again."

Brandy rose to her feet and beckoned Anne. "Let's leave them to get reacquainted. Come walk with me in the gardens."

"Brandy, we have been so worried about you. Mama scolded me something fierce when I told her you had gone to London. She was packing our bags to come find you when the Dowager Duchess's missive arrived. We were so relieved." Anne linked her arm through Brandy's as they strolled down the walk.

"I'm sorry, Anne. I realize now I hadn't thought it all through. But everything is fine now." She smiled brightly at her cousin.

"How was your trip here? I worried about you traveling alone."

"As you can see, no harm befell me. I didn't have any problems a'tall."

"What aren't you telling me?" Anne peered closely at Brandy.

"Nothing of any consequence. I slept the day away, unfortunately, and had to seek shelter from the storm that night. But as you can see for yourself, I arrived safe and sound." She waved her hand around the gardens.

"A gentleman came to Stonebrooke Manor looking for you, right after you left for London. Chandler

Townsend, the Duke of Marbury. Any relation?" Anne cocked her head to one side, smiling.

"He came to the manor? Hmmm, I wonder why," Brandy mused aloud. "He never told me." She turned back to Anne. "He is Abigail's grandson."

"He's quite handsome, your duke."

"He is not *my* duke. Good heavens! The man is the most arrogant, self-serving, vexing man I have ever met. Frankly, Anne, he tries my patience."

"Something you have plenty of." Her tone was dry.

"Well, I would show more if he didn't needle me so. You'll see for yourself when you meet him. Although, I must admit he has been on his best behavior recently. *Until the night of the opera.*

"What I can't understand is why Chandler's brother, Andrew, has not returned home. Whenever I bring up the subject, Chandler skirts the issue. I have half a mind to go to Scotland just to prove him wrong."

"Scotland?"

"Yes. The duke told me he's in Scotland, supposedly inspecting a piece of property Chandler purchased."

"And you don't believe him?"

"I do not."

"Why?"

"I overheard Chandler talking with one of his friends. I only heard a few words before the butler caught me eavesdropping." She lowered her voice. "I think Michael may be in France. Why, I don't know, but it wouldn't be hard to figure out what he's doing. I found out something else, too. Blanchard, the Marquess of Merrick, was the Foreign Minister. He's retired now but was called back in to assist the new Foreign Minister when England was needed in Portugal to battle the French army."

"What has this to do with Michael?"

"Don't you remember Philip's journal? He linked Michael and Andrew's names together. The name Blanchard was also mentioned."

"Oh, yes, of course," Anne replied with a nod.

"When I asked Chandler, he made it sound as if Blanchard was his first name and a friend from Andrew's school days."

"So?"

"I think he was lying."

"Why would he lie?"

"I don't know. But think about it, Anne. Chandler knows Ross Blanchard, the Foreign Minister, Andrew is away, Michael is away. I receive vague answers to my questions. It all seems rather odd, don't you think?"

"It could be a coincidence."

"I think not, Anne. But I'm not ready to do anything just yet. I want to find out as much as I can before—"

"Before what—? Just what are you planning to do, Brandy?"

She became overly interested in the bare branches of a willow tree. She didn't want to alarm Anne with the plan she was contemplating, nor was she ready to further discuss the infuriating duke. And she most certainly didn't want Anne to know she had met the duke before coming to London, not only at the inn but during one of her midnight raids. No, that wouldn't do a'tall.

Anne noted the stubborn tilt to her cousin's chin and knew she'd get no more information until Brandy was ready to share.

"Well, there is nothing to be done until he returns.

In the meantime, we can explore London together."
Anne sat on the bench, pulling Brandy down beside her.
"Now, tell me everything you have done since you
arrived here."

"I attended my first ball! It was a most extravagant
affair. I drank champagne..." Brandy related all her
experiences in London, successfully turning Anne's
attention away from her suspicions.

At dinner that evening, Anne was introduced to the
formidable, haughty, and vexing Duke of Marbury. He
was charming. He entertained the ladies with amusing
stories of the *ton* and juicy bits of gossip. He soon had
them all laughing with delight, except Brandy. She
glowered at his outrageous behavior, smiling stiffly
throughout the meal, thoroughly displeased. She had
only been afforded a mere glimpse of his charms, and
that was only after a good dose of his insults. What was
he up to? And why wasn't he like this with her—relaxed,
easygoing and, well, affable?

Chapter 20

Chandler still had his doubts about Brandy's involvement with Roger Blackwell. Each passing day, he reminded himself that he had met women before who'd made a living at deception. So, was she innocent of any wrongdoing? Or was she deserving of a career on the stage? He could not let his growing attraction to her blind him to reality, a hard task.

One fine autumn day, while Jessie and Anne were in town shopping for evening gowns, Chandler took Brandy away for an adventure. The air was mild, the sun warm as they strolled through the park. Chandler led her down to a lake at the bottom of a small hill where drops of sunlight rained down on the water, a thousand prisms on the liquid surface. Ducks basked in the sun or swam lazily around the perimeter of the lake.

Brandy unceremoniously flopped to the ground, arranged her burgundy-and-white striped lawn skirt modestly around her legs, and pulled Chandler down beside her. She fell back and gazed up at the cerulean-blue sky. She glanced over at Chandler, who lounged beside her, leaning back on his elbows, his legs outstretched. He looked quite handsome in his smoke-gray, square-cut tailcoat, his white cravat tied in a small knot below his chin. His dark gray pantaloons disappeared into black Hessian boots, polished to a rich shine.

Chandler turned his gaze on her. "I will be leaving in the morning. I'll be away for a few days."

She glanced at him in surprise, the sun dimming a little. "Why?"

"Business."

Brandy sat up with a frown. Philip had often used the exact reason for his many trips, and he had turned out to be a spy! "Where do you go?"

He averted his gaze. "To the north country."

"What business do you have in the north country? Another piece of property just purchased?"

Chandler sat up, and looked at her with furrowed brow, wondering at her sarcasm.

"Are you going to France? Is Michael in France?" she blurted out, unable to contain her burning curiosity and need for information.

Startled by her questions, he cocked his head to one side, gazing at her intently. "Why do you ask?"

She shrugged her shoulders, hesitated, then decided to forge ahead. "I heard you talking with someone in your study the other day, and I thought maybe— Oh, don't look so disgruntled. I wasn't eavesdropping. I happened to be passing by the door, 'tis all. I wish you would tell me. I just know you're keeping something from me." She looked out over the glistening lake. "I suppose you've heard the rumors about my father." It was more a statement than a question.

Chandler nodded slowly but didn't utter a word.

"I can't believe they're true, but who knows? He was often away, and I didn't have the vaguest idea where he went." She plucked at the folds of her skirt. Should she confide in Chandler? Tell him Philip Drummond was not her natural father? No, she wasn't ready to reveal that fact. She still carried the shame of being deserted at birth.

"Do you know why he took his own life?"

Brandy looked over at him and thought carefully before answering his question. "I wasn't aware you knew that fact. I suppose there isn't much you don't know," she conceded, looking back over the lake. "In answer to your question, no, I don't know the reason."

Her crestfallen expression tugged at his heart. He decided to let the matter rest for now. In an effort to lighten her mood, and regain her earlier joy, he lifted her chin with his finger and smiled down into her face. "I won't be gone long, sweet. Will you miss me?"

"Certainly not!" She jerked her chin away and gave him a good frown.

"And why not?"

"Because you are insufferable. It will be heaven, indeed, not to have to abide your dreadful presence."

He made a gasping sound as if mortally injured and clutched his chest. "How your words do wound!"

She glanced askance at him, one corner of her mouth twitching before becoming a grin. Helpless beneath his teasing banter, she pushed against his chest. Falling back on one elbow, he captured her hand and held it pressed against his heart. She stilled, all playfulness gone. She read the desire in his eyes, desire for her. She panicked and tried to pull her hand from his, but he held it fast. He lifted it to his mouth, turned it over, and placed a soft, warm kiss on her palm. Time was suspended as their gazes locked and held.

An outraged duck, squawking and flapping its wings, shattered the sudden spell they were under. They broke eye contact and turned to watch one annoyed duck chasing another.

Chandler released her hand and lay on the ground, stacking his hands behind his head. He looked up at the sky, watching the white puffy clouds glide by. "Are you looking forward to the Blanchards' soiree tonight?"

"Blanchard—Andrew's school chum?" He didn't answer. "The Foreign Minister?"

"Former." His expression remained closed, yet he raised a brow in question.

Brandy plucked a blade of grass and twirled it between her fingers. "I read his name in the newspaper. Andrew doesn't have a school chum named Blanchard, does he?"

"For all I know, he could." He changed the subject. "Which of your new gowns will you wear tonight? I'm particularly fond of the blue one."

"Oh, yes, that's one of my favorites, too. I will wear it tonight." She felt her body relax now that the strained moment had passed. "Chandler, your grandmother has been wonderful. I fear I can never repay her for her generosity."

"She doesn't expect you to. She lost her own daughter not long ago and misses having a girl around to spoil. Indulge her, Brandy." He rolled to his feet and bent down to assist her up from the ground.

"If you insist," she said, accepting his hand. She extended her arms and spun around in the warm autumn sun, laughing with pure abandon.

Chandler watched her whirl and couldn't contain his smile. Her enthusiasm was contagious. He grabbed her beneath her arms and lifted her high in the air. Squealing with delight, she placed her hands on his shoulders to steady herself.

Mindful of the stares and whispers of the other park

goers over the undignified display between the two, Chandler brought Brandy back to earth, and they headed for home, each lost in their own thoughts. Brandy, excited for the upcoming soiree, envisioned her ensemble, while Chandler was focused on Brandy.

How could she be involved against the Crown? The idea was inconceivable. She was naught but a child. There was a moment he'd thought she was going to reveal some inner secret—a confession, perhaps? He scoffed. If she were involved, she certainly wasn't going to blurt it out in the middle of a park. He shook his head. He couldn't wait to get to the bottom of this whole sordid affair.

****

The Blanchards' townhouse was located in Bedford Square. It was large, the brick whitewashed, and sat back from the street, protected by a tall iron fence. Light from every window spilled out into the front yard, welcoming the guests. The Townsend carriage inched its way around the front drive, stopping briefly to discharge its passengers, and continued around back to where the coachmen would gather to pass the evening.

Chandler escorted Brandy and Anne up the steps and into the foyer. Abigail and Jessie had chosen to stay home and catch up on the years they had been separated. Anne was beside herself with excitement, this being her first taste of London Society. Brandy was eager to finally meet the heretofore unknown Blanchard. If the opportunity arose, she would be sure to inquire about her brother.

The Marquess and Marchioness of Merrick, Ross and Madelyn Blanchard, stood just inside the entrance of the foyer. They had forgone the formality of a majordomo, preferring instead to greet their guests as they entered their home and escort them to a large drawing room where the others were gathered.

Ross Blanchard wasn't a tall man, but he exuded such a commanding aura that one tended to overlook his medium build. He had a full head of white hair and caramel-colored eyes that crinkled at the corners when he smiled. Madelyn Blanchard was petite, with hazel eyes framed by long dark lashes. Her chestnut brown hair, streaked with just a hint of silver, was piled high atop her head. When she smiled, she revealed a small space between her two front teeth that only added to her attractiveness.

"Lady Brandy, 'tis a pleasure to meet you." Blanchard clasped Brandy's hand, flashing her a friendly smile. He turned to his wife, who was staring wide-eyed at Brandy, and made the introductions.

Madelyn Blanchard recovered herself and extended her hand. "A pleasure to meet you, Lady Brandy."

"You have a lovely home, Lady Merrick. I am honored to have been invited."

"Thank you, my dear."

"May I introduce my cousin, Miss Anne MacCartin?"

"Miss MacCartin, welcome to our home. I understand you have just arrived in London. I do hope you enjoy yourself this evening."

As Brandy and Anne exchanged pleasantries with the Marchioness, Ross drew Chandler aside. "She looks innocent enough. But looks can hide the most evil heart, eh?" Blanchard looked askance at Brandy. "Even beauty."

"She is a beauty," Chandler agreed, gazing at

Brandy's profile. Her chin was tilted as she smiled, and her small nose was in perfect symmetry with her oval face. When she laughed, the sound ignited his lust. He rubbed his forehead, willing his desire to abate. "We had an interesting conversation this afternoon. We spoke of her father. She seemed surprised that I was aware he had taken his own life. She also made reference to the rumors that he was a spy. Then she asked me if I was traveling to France. And was Michael in France."

"What? How would she—"

"She overheard Jeffrey and me one afternoon discussing my upcoming trip. It's apparent she didn't hear much, but enough to ask. I avoided answering the questions, of course, but she's not a stupid woman. She is slowly putting two and two together and becoming suspicious with the ambiguous answers I've been handing her about Andrew. And she knows that you were the Foreign Minister."

"Chandler, go to France. I will see to Lady Brandy," Ross assured the duke. "When you return, come and see me."

Brandy turned and caught Chandler watching her with quiet intensity. It was fraught with meaning, the essence of which she was unable to interpret. Her gaze dropped to his mouth, and she immediately regretted it, as a rush of warmth stole over her body. She blinked once and turned back to Lady Merrick, who was gazing at her with head tilted, as if awaiting an answer. Brandy blushed and asked her to please repeat her question.

"I asked how long you plan to be in London."

"I'm not sure, milady. I'm here—"

Chandler stepped up, interrupting whatever Brandy was about to say. He nodded to Madelyn and presented an arm to both Brandy and Anne. "Ladies?" he offered and escorted them through the door and into the drawing room. It was a large room with a high-beam ceiling and two sets of doors leading outside. The walls were a muted yellow, the wood floors a smooth warm brown. The perimeter of the room was lined with colorful settees and potted plants. Several doors led to other rooms where some of the guests had clustered into groups. One large crystal chandelier rained light upon the gathering.

Brandy recognized quite a few people she had seen at the various functions she'd attended with Chandler. As usual, the women were turned out quite fashionably, their gowns creating an undulating sea of color. Here and there, the men's black evening attire dotted the sea like rocks amid the kaleidoscope of colors.

Brandy was dressed in another of her new gowns, a sapphire-blue crepe, that just happened to match Chandler's eyes. It was décolleté like her other gowns, showing quite a bit of her ivory skin. She wore the diamond earbobs from Michael, that Anne had brought from home, and a sapphire-and-diamond necklace, borrowed from Abigail, graced her slender neck. Anne wore her new gown, a mauve silk with short, capped sleeves. A silk square of the same hue had been tucked into her bodice, creating a more modest neckline. Chandler was splendid in evening black, a white embroidered satin waistcoat, and, in a nod to Brandy's gown, a large sapphire pin nestled among the white folds of his cravat.

Chandler was quickly surrounded by friends. He nodded in greeting but declined to be engaged in lengthy conversations as they continued to the other side of the room, where Jeffrey stood alone, sipping a whiskey.

"Hello, Jeff. You remember my houseguest?"

Jeffrey reached for Brandy's hand. "Lady Brandy, how are you, my dear? Ravishing as always," he added with a wink.

"Lord Montaldene," Brandy murmured, her face tinting pink as she remembered their last encounter.

"And who is this lovely creature?" He bent his gaze on Anne.

"My cousin, Miss Anne MacCartin. Anne, Jeffrey Alden, Marquess of Montaldene." She heard Anne's gasp and grabbed her hand, squeezing her to silence. She ignored Chandler's quiet chuckle.

"It is a pleasure to make your acquaintance, milord."

"I hope I will have the pleasure of a dance later?"

"Of course, milord."

"Is Lydia with you?" Chandler asked, having recovered from his fit of humor.

"No, she decided not to come to London this time. Can I steal you away from such lovely company for a moment?"

Chandler nodded and turned to Brandy. "I will be back momentarily, sweet." He bowed and strode toward the cardroom with Jeffrey.

Anne stifled a giggle. "Little does he know that of late he has been feeding the occupants of Stonebrooke Manor," she whispered behind her fan.

"I thought for sure he would read the guilt written all over your face. You nearly gave us away," Brandy admonished gently.

"It was such a shock to come face to face with him. You should have warned me he might be here tonight."

"I almost swooned when I met him at the Barringtons' ball." She clenched her lips together at the underhanded way Chandler had made the introductions. It was lucky for him he was not within reach, she thought with a scowl, for the recollection made her itch to slap him.

"Isn't it wonderful? I can't believe I'm at a London soiree." Anne gazed around the room in awe. Musical notes drifted across the crowded room from musicians seated behind a wall of plants. "Do you suppose it would be rude of me if I didn't dance with Lord Montaldene? I'm afraid those years of dance lessons are long forgotten. I would hate to embarrass him or myself," she lamented. She glanced over at the dancers gliding about the floor. "And I don't think I'm acquainted with this dance," she added, appearing shocked by the closeness of the couples as they turned around the room. "It looks indecent."

"I thought so, too, but it's quite diverting. The country dances we learned will come back to you. At least they did for me."

A handsome young man bowed before Anne and requested a dance. Brandy smiled encouragingly and, with shy acceptance, Anne took his arm and allowed him to lead her onto the floor, into a dance she was familiar with.

A maroon-and-silver-liveried footman paused to offer refreshment. Brandy accepted a glass of champagne and, sipping it, glanced around the room. She flicked open her fan, moving it rapidly in front of her to circulate the air. The room was becoming quite warm, despite the cool night air slipping in through the tall doors standing ajar.

As her gaze swept the room, it slid over a group of three clustered near one set of doors. It immediately swung back to rest on one of the men. He was tall and slim with thick, mahogany-brown hair that brushed the top of his shoulders. Standing next to him was a nondescript woman with thinning strawberry-blonde hair. She wore a plain straw-colored gown unadorned with jewelry. The other man was short and stocky with full mutton-chop whiskers framing his ruddy face.

Ross Blanchard appeared before her, drawing her attention away from the dark stranger. "Are you enjoying yourself, Lady Brandy?"

"Yes, I am. It's a wonderful soiree."

"I understand you are from Hathshire. What brings you to London?"

"I am visiting the Dowager Duchess of Marbury. She is a friend of my aunt's. I am also waiting for Chandler's brother to return from Scotland."

"Are you acquainted with Andrew?"

"No, but I'm hoping to garner his help in a personal matter."

"I see. Do you have family back in Hathshire?"

"Yes, a brother. My parents are deceased."

"I'm sorry to hear that. If you'll pardon my boldness, I must say you have the most beautiful eyes I have ever seen. A brilliant shade of green."

"Thank you, milord. I understand you were the Foreign Minister."

"Ah, yes, but that was many years ago. Would you care—"

"With England at war again with France, have they not called you back into service? I understand the current Foreign Minister is rather new to his position."

"Not officially, no, although I do lend my services when needed. Who would have thought one so lovely would be interested in world affairs?"

"My mind is not hindered by my looks, milord." She hesitated but a moment. "There is another reason I am in London. I wanted to meet you."

"Really? And why is that, my dear? Is there something you wish me to know?"

"No, of course not."

"Something you wish to tell me? Ask me?"

Brandy, flustered by his probing questions, wondered if it had anything to do with Philip and his less than patriotic activities. "Nothing like that, I can assure you. I was wondering if you were acquainted with my brother."

"Your brother?"

"Yes, the Earl of Hathshire."

Chandler strode up just then, catching the last of their conversation. "Your lovely wife is looking for you, Ross."

Blanchard nodded and over Brandy's head lifted his brows in consternation. To Brandy, he said, "I'm afraid duty calls, my dear. Perhaps we can finish our conversation another time? I would also like to claim a dance, if you'll permit."

"Of course, milord."

When he left, Brandy turned to Chandler. "Is he always so assertive? And evasive?"

"It's what made him so successful in his position. Don't let it upset you." Turning the topic, he glanced around the room. "Where is Anne?"

"She's dancing." Brandy chuckled. "She was afraid to. She hasn't danced in years."

"You did—splendidly."

"Yes, I suppose I did." She pointed to the man she

had noticed earlier. "Do you know that man? The one with the brown hair."

"Yes, Thomas Alexander—a friend of mine. We're also partners in a shipping business. The woman with him is his wife, Lacey. She was raised by the Blanchards after her parents died. She was quite young." He glanced down at Brandy. "Why do you ask?"

Brandy shrugged her shoulders. "'Tis nothing, really."

"Would you like to meet him?"

"Yes," she replied, not fully understanding her interest in the man.

Chandler laid his hand on the small of her back and escorted her across the room. As they approached, Thomas glanced up and met Brandy's gaze. He closed his eyes briefly, missing a question from his wife, who glanced up, turned to see what had him so engrossed and stiffened.

"Thomas, Lacey, 'tis good to see you again." Chandler pulled Brandy up beside him. "May I introduce Lady Brandy Drummond. Brandy, the Marquess and Marchioness of Ashton. Brandy is visiting my grandmother, along with her aunt and cousin. Her aunt is a dear friend of Abigail's."

Thomas extended his hand to Brandy, grasping it warmly. "'Tis a pleasure, my dear. I was briefly acquainted with your father, some years ago. My condolences on his untimely death."

"Thank you, Lord Ashton." Upon a closer look, Brandy thought Thomas Alexander quite handsome. He sported sideburns that reached to his jaw line, and his mahogany-brown hair had a definite curl to it. His eyes, a warm mixture of green and brown, reflected his pleasure at meeting her. He was well-mannered and soft-spoken.

Lacey Alexander held out her hand, her pale brown gaze holding no warmth. "I, too, am sorry to hear of your misfortune." She hesitated a moment. "I believe you are acquainted with my brother—the Earl of Norwood?"

Brandy's smile faltered. "Roger Blackwell? You are his sister?" She paused then continued, "Yes, I do recall he had a sister."

"Yes, 'tis a shame we haven't met before. If you will excuse us? Lord Worthmont is waving to us, dear." With that, she slipped her arm through her husband's and led him unceremoniously away.

Brandy turned to Chandler. "Lady Ashton took an instant dislike to me and I don't even know her!"

Chandler shrugged his shoulders. "I don't know her that well." He leaned down to whisper conspiratorially, "Grandmother says she isn't very pleasant. One never knows what she's thinking behind those cold brown eyes of hers." He straightened. "But I tolerate her for Thomas's sake."

Brandy had to agree with him. She didn't care for Lacey Alexander a'tall. Her expression was dour, her smile not quite reaching her eyes. On the other hand, she had immediately taken to Lord Ashton. His smile had been warm and genuine. She touched Chandler's arm. "I'd like to freshen up. Where is the lounge located?"

"Through those doors and up the stairs." He escorted her to the bottom of the stairs, and after waiting until she reached the landing, he disappeared inside the cardroom.

Brandy found the lounge a comfortable room with royal-blue silk wallpaper and a grass-green carpet. Two striped chaise lounges of the same hues reposed against one wall and a long table with several tapestry-cushioned stools lined another. Mirrors were placed on the table at evenly spaced intervals for the ladies' convenience and gilt wall sconces cast a soft glow over the entire room.

Brandy sat down on one of the cushioned stools, took her handkerchief from her reticule, and dabbed at the moisture on her brow. She glanced into the mirror and patted a few stray wisps of hair back into place.

An overpowering cloud of perfume assailed her senses, and she turned to the woman who had taken the stool next to hers. She stiffened, instantly recognizing her.

The woman looked at Brandy with one brow delicately arched. "I am Vivian Beaumont. I believe we met at the opera. You're Chandler's little houseguest." It was more a statement than a question.

"I am the guest of the Dowager Duchess, yes." Brandy turned back to the mirror.

"I hope you don't have designs on the duke. We have a very special relationship, an understanding if you will. He has informed you of this, I hope?"

Brandy gritted her teeth. "How nice for you," she bit out. "And, no, I do not have designs on His Grace." She picked up her reticule and rose to her feet. Dismissing the nasty woman, she headed toward the door, her head held high, back stiff.

"See that you don't." Vivian looked at Brandy in the reflection of the mirror. "He is a man with a strong sensual appetite. I doubt you have it in you to sate his desires."

Brandy stopped in her tracks and spun around, her mouth open. She had half a mind to rush back and pull the witch's dark hair out by the roots. Resisting the urge, she clenched her fists by her sides. "I don't take orders from anyone, especially not a—"

"I saw the way you were looking at him. I don't like it. Stay away from him. He's mine."

"As I said before, I don't take orders. If you have a complaint, I suggest you take it up with His Grace. It seems to me you just might be reading more into your relationship with him than is there. I have yet to see him escort you to any of the functions I've attended. Why is that, I wonder?" She knew she sounded like a bitch, but the woman's words had a sobering effect. Just how special was their relationship? He hadn't seemed overjoyed to see her at the opera, but perhaps he was trying to make her jealous because she'd been with Roger. And, come to think of it, at the Barringtons' ball, he had left rather abruptly, and she had not seen Lady Vivian again that evening.

Brandy turned on her heel and swept from the room in a cloud of sapphire-blue crepe. As she descended the stairs, she suddenly wished she were back home in Hathshire. She was tired of London—the false smiles, the whispering behind raised fans, the envious glares from the women. She yearned for quiet country days at Stonebrooke Manor.

She glanced around the guest-filled drawing room, tears blinding her vision. She needed to calm herself before she faced Chandler. She just might strike out at him after her confrontation with his mistress. She spotted Anne and cornered her near the buffet table.

"Will you join me for supper, Anne?"

"Yes, I'm starving. Why, Brandy, what is it? You've been crying!"

"No, I haven't. I had something in my eye, 'tis all."

Anne looked skeptical but didn't question her further. She waved her hand toward the heavily laden table. "Let's enjoy it while we can."

Her laughter brightened Brandy's mood, and the two girls circled the table, piling their plates high with a variety of delicacies—slices of cold roasted goose and chicken; salmon and scalloped oysters; slices of rich, crumbly cheese surrounded by autumnal fruits; and a mouthwatering assortment of breads and sweetmeats—all artfully displayed on pretty porcelain platters and bowls. They found a quiet place in an alcove to dine undisturbed. They were just finishing their meal when Roger appeared, as if he had been waiting for them to finish.

"Good evening, ladies. Are you enjoying yourselves?"

"Yes," Brandy replied, setting her plate on the chair next to her.

"Quite an affair, isn't it?"

"Yes, it is."

"Would you care to dance?"

"I—yes, thank you."

Anne glanced at her, confused by her acceptance. She followed Brandy's gaze and saw Chandler heading in their direction only to be waylaid by a beautiful dark-haired woman who had slipped her arm through his, effectively detaining him. She better understood her cousin's agreement to dance with her adversary, especially if her tears had been caused by the duke.

Roger took Brandy in his arms and swept her around the dance floor. She wasn't well-versed in this new dance and tried to follow Roger in time to the music. He held her close, a little too close. As she tried to wiggle space between them, she stole a glance over his shoulder and saw Chandler and Vivian still together. She was holding tight to his arm, pressed against his side, and her more than ample bosom was in full view—if he chose to glance down. A tight knot clenched in her stomach. She tried to ignore them and concentrate on the intricate steps of the dance, but her traitorous gaze kept returning to them, wondering what they were discussing.

She would have enjoyed their conversation.

"Chandler, darling," Vivian purred, her voice lowered seductively.

"Vivian, lovely as always."

"I've missed you, darling."

"I've been busy," he answered absently, watching Brandy glide by in Blackwell's arms.

"Too busy for me?" She tugged on his arm to gain his attention.

He looked down into Vivian's upturned face, his gaze dipping to her exposed breasts. What once had been enticing now didn't stir him at all. He ignored her question and with a slight edge of irritation said, "If you will excuse me, Vivian?" He extracted his arm from her clutches.

"Is that little whore keeping you busy these days?"

He arched a brow. "That is none of your affair, my dear. What we once had is over. I have told you that more times than I can count. It is your misfortune if you cannot grasp the truth." He spun on his heel and threaded his way through the dancers to Brandy's side just as the music came to an end. As he claimed her for the next dance, Roger had no choice but to cede her hand.

Brandy was in Chandler's strong arms, moving around the dance floor, sliding and turning in step to the music. She spied Lady Vivian standing on the edge of the floor, fury twisting her beautiful face. Roger had reached her side and the two of them had murder in their eyes.

"I'm sorry to have neglected you so you were left to dance with Blackwell."

"It wasn't a hardship, Your Grace. He's quite a respectable dancer. Ow, Chandler, loosen your grip. I can hardly breathe."

"My apologies, sweet." He relaxed his hold but still held her close.

"Whatever is wrong with you? An unpleasant scene with Lady Vivian?"

He lifted a black brow. "Jealous?"

"Hardly," she scoffed, missing a beat and stepping on his foot. "But she is shooting daggers at me. Do I need to fear for my life?" She averted her gaze from his intense blue one.

He ignored her question and drew her even closer. He smelled heavenly—a pleasant mixture of whiskey, smoke, and his own manly scent. His hand enfolded hers as they glided around the floor, the music caressing them with its soft melodious tones. She became aware of a subtle difference in him, a shift in his antagonistic demeanor, and found herself drawn to him, her resentment dissipating. She suddenly felt quite special— to be in the arms of the most handsome and dynamic man in the room.

On his part, Chandler couldn't quite pinpoint what was wrong with him. What was it? What was making him edgy? It was all he could do to hold onto his composure when he had seen Brandy in Blackwell's arms. When he had interceded to claim her for the next dance, he had to physically stop himself from knocking Blackwell's head off.

When the dance came to an end, Chandler escorted her back to the alcove where Anne waited, quietly watching the other guests. "I need to talk with Jeffrey. Will you be all right until I return?"

"Certainly. Unless I'm set upon by jealous women," she quipped. Laughing at his dark scowl, she assured him, "Really, Chandler, I was only jesting. We'll be fine."

He turned on his heel and headed back toward the cardroom. Jeffrey was lounging against the door, watching him approach.

"You two dance well together," he teased. "But by your expression, I would guess it was not so enjoyable for you."

"Shut up, Jeff," he snapped in irritation.

"What, ho! You have become quite surly, old chap. Either these affairs really do bore you, or a certain auburn-haired chit with incredible green eyes has you tied in knots."

"The first reason will suffice. Listen, I found Blanchard questioning Brandy earlier this evening."

"That was our intent, wasn't it? To find out if she is involved."

"Yes, of course."

"Are you having second thoughts?"

"No, I just didn't like the way he went about it." He ignored Jeffrey's nonplussed expression and turned when Ross joined them. "Did you find out what you wanted to know?" he inquired sarcastically.

"Now don't go biting off my head, Chandler. It's imperative we discern her motives. From what I could tell, she doesn't seem to be hiding anything. She seems to be acutely interested in finding her brother. She is quite sharp," he added with admiration. "There was a moment there I thought I was the one being interrogated." His smile wavered. "Still, I think we should continue to watch her until we know for certain whether she has picked up where Philip left off. What of Blackwell?"

"I just saw him slip away. Shall we adjourn to your study?"

Blanchard nodded. "Jeffrey, would you track down Thomas and meet us there?"

"Of course. Oh, hello again, Lady Brandy."

"Lord Merrick, I really must speak to you about my brother, Michael Drummond." Having seen Blanchard from across the room, and having been put off earlier, Brandy was determined to get answers.

"Dance with me," Chandler said, wrapping his arm around her waist.

"But Chandler—"

"Don't bother his lordship, sweet. He has other guests to entertain." Before she could utter another word, Chandler had whisked her away.

"She is persistent, isn't she?" Jeffrey chuckled.

"Very, and by the look on Chandler's face I would say she is also one unhappy lady. I wonder what she is filling his ears with to give him such a pained expression."

"He certainly has his hands full with that one."

"I don't envy him,'" Ross rejoined, laughing, "not one bit."

"Still, it's the most animated I've seen him in years."

Ross nodded his agreement. "They're a striking pair.

Let's hope she's as innocent as she looks. I'd hate to see Chandler fall for her and learn too late of her treachery."

The music ended and they watched Chandler escort Brandy off the dance floor and deposit her with Anne. She smiled up at him when he turned to leave, appearing to be slightly more mollified than before the dance had begun. Ross and Jeffrey shared another laugh as Chandler strode toward them.

Roger Blackwell had slipped into Ross's study, made sure the room was empty, and quietly closed the door. He strode over to the large mahogany desk set against one wall and quickly rifled through the papers on top, a lone candle his only light. Finding nothing of interest, he turned his attention to the drawers. He found one drawer locked, and while he struggled to pick it open, he heard footsteps stop outside the door. He slipped behind the burgundy velvet drapes just as the door swung open.

Ross and Chandler strode into the room, Jeffrey and Thomas close behind them. They gathered in front of the fireplace and spoke quietly for a few minutes. A few words were spoken loudly enough to be heard and, after a few more minutes, the four men departed, closing the door behind them.

Roger waited for the footsteps to fade down the hallway. While he waited, he looked about the study, envying the fine wood paneling and deep-set bookshelves that screamed elegance. His gaze strayed to a portrait above the fireplace. A young woman with chestnut-brown hair and green eyes smiled back at him. He walked to the fireplace and stood for a moment studying the portrait. After a moment, he threw back his head and laughed.

He slipped from the study, anxious to dissect the news he had just overheard…and seen.

Chapter 21

Brandy tossed and turned on the soft mattress, but sleep was elusive. She could not dispel the feeling that something was about to happen—something she had absolutely no control over.

With a tired sigh, she swung her legs over the side of the bed and shrugged into her robe. She crossed over to the open window and breathed the night air. It smelled like autumn—crisp and clear. The peaceful night and moonlit sky invited her to step outdoors. Taking a branch of candles to light her way, she crept through the silent house, making her way outside and taking a seat on the top step leading into the gardens. She drew up her legs and, wrapping her arms around them, gazed up at the indigo sky, at the yellow harvest moon surrounded by white twinkling stars. They were so close she could reach out and capture one.

The cool air caressed her flushed skin, the fragrant scent of autumn grass, the stillness of the night, all provided solace to her unsettled mind. Sensing a presence behind her, she looked over her shoulder and found Chandler leaning against the door frame, his body outlined by the candles she had left lit by the door. He was watching her intently, his black evening jacket slung carelessly over his shoulder, his gaze caressing her body like a lover's hand. Her breath caught in her throat.

"What are you doing awake?" He stepped forward

and, pulling his gaze away, looked out over the gardens. From overhead, the moon cast its light across the cobble-stoned terrace, bathing him in a soft glow.

"I couldn't sleep."

"Beautiful night, isn't it?" He drew a cheroot from a silver case hidden in his jacket pocket and lit the end, the flame glowing brightly in the darkness.

"Yes, it is. It seemed to call to me." She waited for his usual sarcastic retort and, hearing none, immediately wondered what he was up to.

He caught her suspicious expression and gazed at her thoughtfully. "You don't like me, do you, Brandy?"

"I, well, I never really thought about it."

"Liar."

"Well, I don't dislike you. But you can be insufferable, arrogant, beyond the pale—"

"I get your drift."

He tossed the cheroot into the gardens, the glowing end slicing the blackness in two, and placed his jacket across a chair. Before she knew what was happening, he leaned down, grasped her shoulders and drew her to her feet. Enfolding her in his arms, he dipped his head and kissed her—long slow and deep—drawing her into him.

His lips were gentle at first, as if seeking her permission, and when she offered no resistance, he increased the pressure, drawing her body closer still to mold intimately against his.

Drugged by the moonlight, mesmerized by his warm mouth, intoxicated by his scent—her senses were aroused. Her arms had a mind of their own, wrapping around his neck, her fingers twisting in the silky strands of hair curling about his nape. She knew she was playing with danger, knew she shouldn't allow him these liberties, but he was water lapping against a rock, slowly wearing away any resistance. When he drew her closer, she felt the hardness of his body, the heat of his arousal, and a small dose of sanity pushed through her desire-fogged mind. She snatched her arms from around his neck and staggered back, her hands clutching the folds of her robe.

"Do you have to grab me every time we are alone?" It was the first thing she could think of saying. She couldn't, wouldn't admit she enjoyed his kisses. She raised her hand, but this time he was ready and caught her slim wrist in midair.

"Brandy, I don't enjoy being slapped every time I kiss you."

"Then stop kissing me."

"You have yet to deny you enjoy my kisses." He smiled lazily, watching her eyes darken, and mentally braced himself.

"I most certainly will deny it!" she shouted, wishing she could stare him down, but unable to with his advantage of height.

"Ssh, sweet, you'll wake the entire household."

She tossed her hair over her shoulder, lifted her robe's skirt aside and started to walk past him into the house. He stayed her, a hand on her arm. "Brandy, wait."

She avoided his gaze, certain she'd be lost if she looked into his smoldering eyes but complied with his request. He gently cupped her chin and turned her to face him. "You are a beautiful woman," he said quietly. "I won't apologize for my actions." He hesitated a moment and released his hold on her. "Maybe it would be best if you retired now." He stepped back and watched her slip into the house. It was just as well he was leaving in the morning. He didn't know whether to trust her or not, but to be near her was torture. Since the day he met her, his life, as well as his views, had begun to change. He still distrusted women—one could not change one's views overnight—but he was starting to rethink his cynical beliefs, at least about this woman.

When he had come upon her, bathed in the moonlight, he'd stood silently watching her. She appeared so small and innocent; it was hard to believe she might be involved with Blackwell. She had looked delicious, though, dressed only in her robe, the moonlight reflecting off her hair, covering her shoulders like a mantle of fire. He was overwhelmed with desire for her, had been since finding her in the glade that summer day. He usually had such tight control over his lust, but this small slip of a girl took his breath and common sense away.

He quit the gardens and turned into the house, the enchantment of the night having disappeared with Brandy. He entered his chamber to find a fire blazing in the hearth, a crystal decanter of brandy on the low table beside a black leather wingback chair, compliments of his valet. He undressed, tossed his clothes carelessly on the bed, and donned his blue velvet robe. He poured himself a healthy draught of brandy and sat before the fire, staring into the flames. He raised the glass to his lips and as he did so the light from the flames danced in the drink, bringing forth an image of riotous auburn curls.

With a muttered curse, he set the snifter on the table, and rose to his feet. He opened their adjoining door and peered in; her room was cast in shadows. The smoldering embers in the fireplace shed little illumination, but the moon shining through the slit in the drapes spread a wide beam of light. He glanced at the canopied bed. The curtains were pulled back to allow in the night air, and he could make out the white bed linen glowing faintly.

Brandy held her breath. Having heard him enter her chamber, she now watched him walk toward her on silent feet. When he reached her side, she stared up at him through the shadows. "What do you want?"

Chandler sat down on the edge of the bed and brushed the hair from her face. "I don't know." He sighed. "I'm sorry about my earlier behavior. I seem to lose my head whenever I'm near you." He took her hand, turned it over and placed a warm kiss on her palm. "Forgive me?"

A shiver went down her spine, but she didn't pull away. She was nervous, but also highly curious. There was a burning ache inside her, a yearning she did not recognize.

"I forgive you," she said, and when he made no move to leave, she asked him again, "What do you want?"

He chuckled lightly. "Would you believe another kiss?" He leaned over and brushed his mouth lightly across hers. When Brandy didn't object, he kissed each corner of her luscious mouth before covering it with his own, drinking in its sweetness.

Brandy could do naught but yield, kissing him back with all the young, innocent passion she possessed, the burning ache now a raging inferno radiating to every part of her body. Trapped in a fog of desire, she knew instinctively Chandler would be the only one to guide her out.

Chandler, certain he would be rebuffed, was surprised by her reaction—pleasantly so. He hesitated but a moment before lying down beside her and gathering her in his arms. Molding her pliant body to his hard frame, he brushed aside her hair and nibbled on her ear, taking pleasure in hearing her soft whimpers. His mouth moved across her cheek to cover hers as he deftly lowered her nightdress. Slipping his hand inside, he cupped one breast, the warm flesh filling his hand, and rubbed his thumb over the soft bud that hardened under his attention. His warm lips moved down her throat to the deep valley between her breasts and kissed her smooth warm skin.

Brandy, helpless under the sensual barrage on her body—his scent, his touch, his being—could no longer deny him. He was magnet, she was steel. She relinquished the last fragile thread of common sense and succumbed to the moment.

He rolled on top of her, and, pressed back into the pliant mattress, she delighted in his weight. She slipped her hands beneath his robe, the soft velvet caressing her skin, and trailed her fingers down his nape, over his shoulders to his back, splaying her hands across the wide muscled expanse of warm skin.

Chandler was in heaven. He held a flower in his arms, a bud he was urging to full blossom with his kisses, his caresses. Her silky skin, her subtle scent of lavender, her purrs of delight, all moved him ardently. He couldn't ever remember feeling this all-consuming need for anything or anyone. It was as if he was lost in a storm, and she the torch to guide him home—a most sensual beacon of light.

Her nightdress discarded, Chandler's fingers danced over her naked body. He caressed the flat plane of her belly, brushed his fingers along the inside of her thighs, only to move up again and cup her breasts, kneading the soft supple skin.

He rid himself of his robe and rose above her, leaning on his elbows to gaze into her eyes. Within their depths, he found desire battling fear. He leaned down and kissed her gently on the mouth. "I'll stop if you want me to, but you must tell me now. If we wait much longer, I'm afraid it will be too late." He held his breath—not an easy feat—and awaited her response.

"Please…don't stop," she whispered, needing him, and wanting to reach where he was slowly, fervently taking her. Though his caresses and the sensations he was arousing were new to her, she was not afraid. She trusted him to take care of her, trusted him to not let her fall.

He spread her legs and poised over her, their gazes locked. Thrusting his hips forward, he pressed into her warmth. She instinctively stiffened, her eyes widening.

"Relax, sweet. It will hurt a moment, but I promise you the pain won't last." Chandler took a deep breath, trying to calm his raging desire lest, in his fevered haste, he tear into her. He pushed again, stopping at the wall of her maidenhead. Taking another ragged breath, he thrust deeply, breaking through the barrier, and completely sheathing himself.

She cried out, pushing frantically against his chest. "No, stop, please, it hurts." Tears rolled down her cheeks.

Chandler immediately stilled and laid his cheek against hers, feeling the wet proof of her pain. He ceased his movements but did not withdraw. "Does it hurt now?" he whispered against her cheek. He felt her shake her head. He moved inside her. "Now?" Again, she shook her head. He slowly moved in and out until she began undulating with him.

The repeated movements sent a delicious blaze racing through her veins. The pain had subsided as he had promised it would. She wrapped her legs around his waist while he withdrew only to fill her again. She did not understand what was happening, but a seed of pleasure sprouted and a rush of warmth flowed over her. Reveling in the feeling, she was euphoric, wanting, wanting— Oh, she didn't know what she wanted!

Chandler was close to the edge, her passionate response nearly his undoing. Their lips locked, the kiss expressing so much more than words, as they found their ecstasy. Collapsing on top of her, he gathered her close and rolled on his side, still deep inside her. He held her tight, the moisture from their bodies mingling, and, unbeknownst to them, their hearts fusing.

Chandler drew her head to his shoulder, feeling a sense of peace and utter satisfaction he hadn't ever experienced before—with any woman. But when he felt her warm tears against his skin, he stilled, uncertain of what to say or do. Had he hurt her? Were they tears of pain? Regret? His heart sank; he was used to seasoned women, women who enjoyed sex and used it as a means to an end. Confronted with tears, he was at a loss. He didn't know how to handle this one. She was different— so different. Suddenly feeling like an inexperienced lad, unsure of himself, he waited for her to speak first.

Brandy was drained emotionally and physically. With their lovemaking at an end, realization of what she'd done covered her like a blanket of shame. She waited, sniffling back tears. *Why doesn't he say something? Was he disappointed? Had the catch not been worth the pursuit?* Without warning, Vivian Beaumont's taunting words came back to haunt her. *He is a man with a strong sensual appetite.* Was she right? Had she failed next to the beautiful and sensuous Lady Vivian?

Oh, how pleased he must be, laughing at his easy conquest. What a fool I am! Humiliated, she pushed him away, felt him slide from her body, and scooted to the other side of the bed, as far from him as she could go without tumbling to the floor.

"Brandy?" Chandler leaned up on one elbow, puzzled by her actions. "What is it? Did I hurt you?"

"Go away! I hate you! I never want to see you again!"

Chandler was stunned. He had just experienced the most gratifying lovemaking he'd ever had, feeling more intimate with her than any other woman, wanting to hold her close until morning's light. And she was spewing hatred. He reached out, but she shrank back from his touch. Wounded, he spoke out, cruelly, "You didn't hate me a minute ago. Why, you purred quite nicely. I suppose we can add courtesan to your list of talents." With that, he rose from the bed, grabbed his robe, and strode naked from her chamber, slamming the door behind him.

Brandy, steeped in misery, stared at the closed portal, tears slipping down her cheeks. She had just succeeded in alienating the one person she wanted, needed. She ached to call out for him to come back, to tell him she hadn't meant her hateful words. She grabbed a pillow, clutching it tightly to her breasts, and began to cry. *Why did I let that vile Vivian's words affect me?*

Her emotions swung like a pendulum. One minute

she reveled in their lovemaking—he hadn't forced himself; he been kind, gentle, thoughtful. The next minute, she was mortified at her lack of propriety. How could she have so easily dismissed decorum? Giving herself to a man who had taken her maidenhead without uttering a word of love or marriage. What must he think? There was no doubt he had lost respect for her, if he'd ever had any. His parting epithet was proof of that.

She curled into a ball, drew her knees up under her chin, and with a teary sigh, knew it was no use. Yes, he was impossible—condescending, arrogant and—but her fate was sealed, the ties too strong to be severed or denied. She could refuse to admit it all she wanted, but her heart would not be silenced. She was, in fact, in love with the duke. She pummeled the pillow. *He could have at least told me he liked me!*

She searched for a bright spot, but unable to find one speck of light, she came to a decision. It was time to leave London. She did not want to be here when the duke returned from his trip. She couldn't possibly face him, not after tonight, not after flinging those dreadful words at his head. And especially, now, after her true feelings for the duke had been realized.

She rolled over, closed her eyes, and waited in vain for sleep to release her from her anguish.

Chapter 22

Late the next morning, Brandy made her way to the morning room, exhausted. She hadn't slept at all, instead reliving last night in excruciating detail. She had tarried in her room most of the morning, worried she might see Chandler, wondering what she would say if she did. Or worse, what would he say?

She was reconciled to the fact she was no longer a virgin. She was not concerned it would be a problem in her marriage bed, for she had no intention of marrying. Later, much later, after the self-pity had faded, she admitted to herself that she had enjoyed his lovemaking—immensely. What she'd done with Chandler last night, she had done because she'd wanted to. She could place no blame on him.

When she entered the morning room, she found Abigail enjoying tea. A quick glance around confirmed the Dowager Duchess was alone.

"Good morning, Your Grace." Brandy took a seat opposite the Dowager Duchess and accepted a pink-and-orange floral porcelain cup.

"Good morning, my dear." Abigail tilted her head to one side. "I've been thinking, it would please me if you'd call me Abigail."

"Thank you—Abigail. I would be honored." Smiling, she reached for the small porcelain pitcher, poured a dollop of milk into the cup, and added tea from a matching teapot. She leaned back in the chair with a sigh, sipping the tea.

"You look tired, child. Did you get in very late?"

"No, it was relatively early compared to other affairs we've attended." She stared into the fire, her thoughts banging into one another. She'd had no idea, had not been prepared for, what occurred between a man and a woman. Doreen had never mentioned it, and she, herself, hadn't given it much thought while growing up. Why hadn't she been more sophisticated? Why had she let that hateful Vivian's words needle her? Oh, how she wished she could take back those awful words she'd thrown at his head.

Abigail, who had been watching the play of emotions cross the young woman's face, wondered if her grandson had anything to do with her somber mood. The electricity that flared whenever they were in the same room was tangible. Had Brandy been burnt by it?

"Did you enjoy yourself last night?"

Brandy started at the question, blushing furiously. "Oh, the soiree—yes, I did. I confess my feet ache from all the dancing." She opened her mouth, then firmly closed it. She would not ask about Chandler.

"Chandler has already left." Abigail ventured, assuming his absence was another reason for Brandy's melancholy. "He asked me to bid you goodbye and to assure you he would return soon." She didn't miss the tightening of Brandy's mouth.

"What of Lord Andrew? Have you any word?"

"No, I'm afraid not."

Brandy glanced around the room. "Where are Aunt Jessie and Anne?"

"Jessie had an appointment with her solicitor.

Something to do with her late husband's estate. Anne accompanied her. They should return in time for luncheon."

"Would it be all right if I took a stroll through your gardens?"

"Of course, my dear. Please do consider this your home. But take a shawl. It's become frightfully chilly."

Brandy pulled the woolen shawl snug around her shoulders. It was indeed chilly. The seasons had changed overnight. The sun, hidden behind large gray clouds, made the day as bleak as her mood. She sat on a bench beside a now-barren lilac bush and looked around. The last of the autumn flowers were fading with winter's approach. They had been beautiful, and no doubt the spring blooms would be just as lovely. She would never know, having already made the decision to leave London. She could wait at Stonebrooke Manor for Lord Andrew's return as easily as she could wait here. Easier, if truth be known. Blanchard had been no help. In fact, he had been so pointed in his questioning, she had the feeling that he, too, did not trust her. And all because of Philip's nefarious activities.

No, she did not want to be here when Chandler returned. How he must hate her! And she, wrestling with her newly found love. If that elusive brother of his had shown up, she would have left long ago and none of this would have happened.

Aunt Jessie and Anne could stay in London, if they chose. Then, when Andrew returned, perhaps he would come to Hathshire with any news he might have of Michael. With the plan set firmly in her mind, her mood lightened, and she sought the warmth of the house to wait for Jessie and Anne to return from their errand.

****

Chandler contemplated the men before him. He was once again in France, meeting with his men. He ran his hand through his already disheveled hair.

Pierre broke the tense silence. "We think they have either been captured—or killed."

Chandler listened quietly, refusing to let emotion enter the picture. He would treat this situation as he would any other, as if his and Brandy's brothers were not the missing men.

"We have had no word of any executions—"

Hubert glared at Pierre and slammed his palm on the table. "*Mon Dieu!* They are not dead! They must be incarcerated somewhere."

Pierre and Claude exchanged worried glances before Claude turned to the duke. "Do not worry, *bon ami*. We will find them."

Chandler drained his glass of wine, the tepid liquid sliding around the lump in his throat. He stood up, the chair scraping against the wooden floor. "I will contact you in two days. Then I must return to England."

"*Oui, monsieur.*"

"Thank you, my friends, for your diligence and thoroughness in the task ahead." Chandler bid them goodbye and departed the house, staying close to the shadows. He was filled with a sense of helplessness. He could not risk going deeper into France. He was too well known. If he was captured, he would be killed. And he'd be damned if he'd be captured again. As it was, he was risking his neck by just coming to Calais. All he could do was pray that Hubert and his men would find Andrew and Michael—preferably alive. If he didn't receive word in two days, he would return to London. Blanchard would need to know this latest news. He would have to think of something to appease his grandmother. He was having a difficult time satisfying her curiosity about Andrew's continued absence. And he had the added pressure of Brandy relentless in seeking answers about her brother's whereabouts. What a bloody mess!

Two nights later, Chandler was staring out over the dark water of the Channel, the boat gently riding the swells beneath his feet. He had never been so worried. Truth was, he was scared. The cool breeze ruffled his black hair as he tried to combat the fear threatening to consume him. It had been confirmed—Andrew and Michael were incarcerated somewhere in the north of France. But no one could discover exactly where they were imprisoned. Hubert had assured him they were still alive. But for how long?

The situation was indeed bleak. They had been betrayed, ambushed, and locked up. He did not have confirmation yet on who was responsible for the betrayal, but he had a pretty good idea. Blackwell, he cursed silently, and vowed to one day wring the bastard's neck.

Hubert would have his network of men fan out and search the area—no stone unturned, no ear unbent. He had asked only that Chandler's people send in reinforcements. Chandler had assured him he would as soon as he arrived back in London. Damn it, he wished there was more he could do, but knew there was not. That was the rub. It wouldn't do to have two Townsends incarcerated.

A gust of wind blew across Chandler's face, and he turned to observe the dark mass of England looming on the horizon. He was almost home. Unbidden, the image of a young woman with auburn hair and green eyes drifted into his mind. He was full of remorse for leaving her the way he had, regretted the words he had flung at her in wounded pride. Having gone over in detail the entire night, he now better understood her reaction. She had been nervous and possibly embarrassed. Good Lord, she had been a virgin!

He was used to jaded women—who only wanted one thing and would use any means to get it—not virginal girls. And when she had lashed out, what had he done? Instead of holding her close, whispering tender words of comfort, he had thrown insults at her head. Oh, he had been quite the gentleman!

He grimaced recalling her sad eyes, tears streaking down her beautiful face. He needed to make amends, needed to see her smile again. He couldn't wait to get home.

The breeze caressed his face, the spray from the boat kissed his mouth. He licked the moisture from his lips, remembering the feel of her pliant mouth under his, her sweet taste that always made him wild for her. He had never known a woman like Brandy. She had brought sunshine into the shadows of his life with her verve, her kindness, her spirit of adventure. She neither cared for nor desired a title or wealth. She was a fresh flower among withered blooms.

Unbeknownst to him, she had wiggled into his heart the day he had stumbled across her in the glade. His heart softened at his musings, a subtle shift in his opinion. Dare he name it? Dare he admit it out loud? Could it be— love? Chandler sighed. Indeed, for the first time in his life, he was in love. There was no denying it, no getting around it—he was in love with the stubborn, infuriating, beautiful minx.

Chandler laughed out loud, a lightness of spirit replacing the dark, and watched the shadowed mass of home loom larger. He could hardly contain his eagerness to see his beloved again.

Chapter 23

The next morning, Brandy announced she wanted to return to Hathshire. As expected, all three women put up a fuss. In the face of their collective to-do, she relented and agreed to stay a while longer. With each passing day, however, she became more nervous about seeing Chandler. At night, when her thoughts were the loudest, she would lie in bed and stare at the dark canopy. She did not want to face him—she couldn't. What must he think of her? With her admitted love for him, she couldn't take it if he looked at her with cold indifference. She just had to leave London—now.

With resolve set, she went in search of her aunt. She found her in the sitting room enjoying a game of cards with Abigail.

"Aunt Jessie? May I have a word with you?"

Jessie glanced up from her hand. "Of course, dear."

"Because all of you wanted me to stay, I agreed to stay. But I want to go home. Chandler has not returned, nor has he sent word when he will. And we have heard nothing from Lord Andrew. Furthermore, I think we have imposed on Abigail's hospitality long enough."

Abigail sniffed. "Nonsense. I enjoy having you here. This place can be awfully lonely at times."

"That's very kind of you, Abigail, but quite frankly, I miss my home. When either one of your grandsons arrive home, perhaps I will return to London." She nodded her head firmly when Jessie looked as if she wanted to argue. "Aunt Jessie, if you want to stay, I am perfectly capable of going home by myself. It's not as if I'd be alone, what with Maddie and Arthur there," she interjected. "Yes, I think that would be best. You and Anne stay, and I will return home."

"Well—" Jessie started, but Abigail quickly jumped in with her objections.

"You will not be traveling as a lad, young lady. If you are bent on leaving, then you will have an escort. Jessie, will she be all right at Stonebrooke Manor alone?"

"Yes, but she has a point, Abigail. We don't want to further impose on you."

"Bah! You are a joy to have here. However, if Brandy is determined to go, we can't very well tie her down, now, can we?"

"Then it's settled," Brandy said with relief. "I will leave in the morning. You will send word to me when either of your grandsons return?"

"Of course, my dear," Abigail reassured her with a kind smile.

Brandy found Anne reading quietly in her room, a fire crackling in the hearth. She looked up when Brandy knocked and pushed open the door.

"I'm going home in the morning. You and Aunt Jessie will be staying on here," Brandy announced without preamble.

"Why are you leaving? The absence of a certain duke?" Anne teased, laying down the book.

"I'm bored, 'tis all. We have had no word of when Chandler or Andrew will return. Who knows when they will? I can wait at Stonebrooke Manor just as easily as I can here."

"Then I'm coming with you. Mama can stay if she wants, but I'd like to return to Hathshire, too. London does not hold much appeal for me."

"What about Sir Tweedall? He seemed quite smitten with you," Brandy teased her cousin.

Anne laughed. "Yes, but he is quite dull. I believe my paintbrush has more personality."

"Then it's settled, you will come home with me. Actually, I'd enjoy the company."

****

The morning dawned clear and cool, the air touched with the promise of rain and the skies a dusky gray. The older women gathered on the front stoop to see the two young ones on their way.

"We'll be fine, Aunt Jessie. Please stop worrying. Good heavens, we're only going to Hathshire."

Brandy turned to Abigail, whose eyes were suspiciously bright. "Not you too?"

"I know, my dear. It's just that I'll miss you terribly. You've been such a pleasure to have here."

"Thank you, Abigail. I have enjoyed my stay as well. I can never repay you for all you've done for me." Brandy's own eyes filled with tears. She hugged the older woman tight.

"God speed," Abigail whispered, pressing a soft leather pouch into Brandy's hand.

Brandy could feel the coins inside and protested, "Abigail, please, you've been more than generous."

"Bah, what is all my money for if not to spoil those I love."

"Well, if you are sure…"

"If nothing else, use it to stock the larder or whatever else you need until your brother returns."

"Thank you, Abigail," she whispered brokenly, touched by the Dowager Duchess's kindness.

After Anne and Jessie said their goodbyes, the two girls piled into the duke's coach. It was black, with the ducal coat of arms blazoned on the side. As it pulled away from the townhouse, they settled in for the trip home. Brandy laughed, snuggling beneath the blanket and leaning back into the supple leather seat. "By their behavior, you'd think they were never going to see us again."

"Mama and I are seldom apart." Anne looked askance at her cousin. "I believe the Dowager Duchess has grown quite fond of you."

"As I have for her." Noticing Anne's sly smile, she reprimanded her cousin. "I know what you're about, and you can just toss the notion right out of your head. She's a hopeless romantic, 'tis all. I can assure you that neither Chandler nor I are remotely interested in her matchmaking." Even to Brandy the words sounded hollow, so to end the conversation, she turned to stare out the window as the duke's well-sprung coach made its way through the crowded city streets. Once outside the city, they bowled down the turnpike, leaving London behind.

Brandy was eager to return home. She missed the rambling manor house and the soft undulating hills. She fingered the purse Abigail had pressed into her hands. How would she ever repay the Dowager Duchess? She had opened her home and her heart. She recalled Abigail's words when she tried to refuse the coins. *Use it to stock the larder.* Brandy wondered if the woman knew of her escapades. She wouldn't put it past Chandler to have told her out of amusement, the scamp.

Where was Chandler? And when would Andrew return? She was anxious about Michael and was confident Andrew was the link between the two. During her stay in London, she had heard several people mention Andrew Townsend, and even a few were acquainted with her brother. What was the connection between the three men? And where did Ross Blanchard fit into this puzzle?

She decided to go over Philip's papers again. Perhaps she had missed something—anything that would shed light on this mystery. She just knew Michael was in some kind of trouble—she could feel it. And she would wager Chandler knew something about it. Whenever she asked about Michael, Chandler put her off with vague answers, never really addressing her questions. But though her worries were real, the knowledge that Chandler might indeed know something, and was not alarmed, made her feel less anxious.

The ride to Hathshire was uneventful. They made good time, for the weather had remained clear despite the bank of threatening clouds on the horizon. They stopped once to stretch their legs and rest the horses, enjoying a glass of wine and the biscuits Jessie had packed.

As soon as they reached Hathshire, the skies opened with a cold, drenching rain. When the coach pulled up before Stonebrooke Manor, they threw open the door, dashed up the stairs, and ran into the house.

"Maddie! Arthur! We're home!' The house was quiet, and long shadows stretched across the polished wood floor. Maddie came bustling from the back of the house, a silver candlestick in hand.

"Miss Brandy—and Miss Anne!" Maddie hugged each of the girls. "But where is Lady Whyte?"

"She decided to stay in London with the Dowager

Duchess."

"Does she know you have returned?" Maddie eyed them both suspiciously.

Brandy laughed and hugged her again. "Yes, we have her blessing. Where's Arthur?"

"He's visiting his brother. He's taken ill again. He should be home soon, though. Are you hungry? I have a nice mutton stew simmering on the fire."

"Yes," they answered in unison, shedding their damp cloaks and hats.

"Will you send Cobey to the front? Misty is tied to the back of the coach, and our portmanteaus need to be brought in."

"Of course, Miss Brandy. Now you two get yourselves warm before you catch…" Her words became unintelligible as she disappeared down the hallway.

Brandy and Anne moved into the salon, where a fire burned low in the grate. Anne threw a handful of dry twigs and a fat log on the embers and stoked it to a roaring flame.

Brandy moved in front of the hearth, stretching out her hands toward the warmth. "'Tis good to be home. The soirees and balls were exciting, of course, but even they became tiresome. I prefer the quiet country life."

Anne poured two glasses of sherry from a decanter on the sideboard and offered one to Brandy. "Mayhap with a certain gentleman in residence it might not have become so dull."

Brandy sipped her sherry, watching the flames dance in the grate. She was not ready to bring her feelings for Chandler out in the open, and she certainly was not about to tell her cousin what had happened between them. She turned the subject. "I hope this rain abates by morning. If it does, will you join me for a ride?"

"No, I think I will paint. I'm eager to pick up the brush again." Anne looked up as Maddie entered the room with a tray, steam rising from the bowls of stew.

After persuading Maddie to join them for supper, they spent the remainder of the evening regaling her with tales of their time spent in London.

****

The rain did not abate during the night. In fact, by morning, it had become a torrential downpour. The day did bring a surprise, if unwelcome, visitor to Stonebrooke Manor. Arthur, who had arrived home in the middle of the night, appeared in the doorway of the dining room to announce Lord Norwood, disapproval evident in his tone. "He's in the drawing room."

"Good heavens! I saw Roger in London not a sennight ago. How did he even know I had returned to Hathshire?" Brandy's brows lowered and her eyes narrowed. "I hope he's not here to cause trouble."

"Remember the scene in the garden at the Barringtons' ball? You were lucky the duke appeared when he did. I shudder to think what might have happened."

"Yes, but he did behave himself at the Blanchards' soiree."

"Do you want me to come with you."

"No, I can handle him." Brandy strode from the room to face her nemesis.

"Good morning, milord. To what do I owe the honor of this unannounced early morning visit?" Roger Blackwell had made himself comfortable, stretched out in a chair before the fire, his legs crossed at the ankle. He rose to his feet when she entered the room and bent over her hand to bestow a light kiss.

"Brandy, 'tis good to see you again. You're looking lovely, as always." He held up his hand. "Before you say a word, please let me apologize again for my unspeakable behavior. It was not well done, and I do hope you will forgive my lapse in judgment."

Brandy eyed him skeptically, then, nodding, took a seat on the settee. "No, it wasn't, but I will accept your apology. Now can we drop this whole inane subject of our betrothal?"

He nodded slowly. "As you wish. I will not bother you again with our contract. Regardless of the fact it was a binding agreement, I don't relish an unwilling bride. However, I would like permission to call on you. Perhaps I can convince you I am indeed worthy of your attentions?" His face was wreathed in a smile.

"Let me think on it," she agreed reluctantly, not believing a word of his little speech. "But I have just returned from London and there are several matters that need my attention this morning. Will you excuse me?" She rose to her feet.

"Of course, my dear. I will visit at a more convenient time." He bowed. "'Til we meet again."

Brandy watched him stride from the room. What was he up to now? It was not like him to concede anything, especially something he desired as strongly as her hand in marriage.

Anne appeared in the doorway, having heard the front door close. "I heard no raised voices."

"He asked my forgiveness for his abominable behavior and has promised to cease harassing me about the betrothal agreement."

"Do you believe him?"

"I do not. He also asked my permission to call."

"He asked to court you?"

"Yes, I only agreed to think on it because otherwise he wouldn't go away. I don't want the situation to escalate further."

"He's up to something, Brandy. You need to watch him closely."

"Posh! I do not fear him. He is nothing but a weasel."

"Maybe, but all the more reason to—"

"I refuse to cower in my own home. He cannot harm me." She spied the concern on her cousin's face and relented. "All right, Anne. I promise I will be more attentive."

****

Brandy chafed at the inactivity. The rain drenched the countryside, forcing her to remain inside the house. She paced in front of the fireplace while Anne painted, occasionally glancing up when Brandy strode past.

"What think you of this?" Anne beckoned her.

Brandy peered over her shoulder at the easel and drew in her breath. "Why, 'tis me!" she cried, admiring the nearly finished portrait of herself. The resemblance was startling. "'Tis beautiful! Too beautiful!"

"It's a perfect likeness, "Anne announced. "It amazes me how modest you are, Brandy. You are truly a lovely woman. I'm pleased that I was able to capture it on canvas." She sat back with a smile, admiring her work.

Brandy blushed with embarrassment. "I don't know about all that, Anne, but it is good."

"It was a little difficult to do, what with you moving

about. I was going to ask you to sit still, but I wanted to surprise you."

Maddie entered with the porcelain tea service, one of Brandy's treasured belongings they hadn't been forced to sell. She set it on the table in front of the hearth. "I'm going to market now, Miss Brandy."

"Wouldn't you rather wait until the rain stops?"

"I would like to get a few goods before it gets dark. Besides, it looks like it's nearing the end. Arthur is here if you need anything while I'm gone."

"Very well, thank you, Maddie."

****

Three nights later, Brandy—as the lad—ventured out for food. Against Anne's tearful objections, she left at midnight to scour the countryside. Brandy had given Arthur most of the money from Abigail, for his brother, who needed immediate medical attention. Their larder was nearly empty, and with precious little coin to stock it, she was forced to pillage.

As the night aged, Brandy, unsuccessful in her search for food, rode farther afield than usual. Finding herself near the coast, nearly at the point where Drummond land ended and Blackwell property began, she paused, hearing muted voices on the night wind. After quietly dismounting, she made her way through the stand of trees lining the sandstone cliffs. It was a nearly moonless night, only a sliver of silver casting faint light upon the land. She proceeded with difficulty, crawling on her hands and knees until she reached the edge of the cliffs. She lay down on her stomach, surveying the scene below. Two lanterns placed on the beach, illuminated the immediate area. A boat, pulled from the water, rested on its side. It looked like a spider, its oars sticking out like long spindly legs. A circle of men stood talking together near the boat. Though she strained to make out their words, only the sound of their voices was audible. She guessed they were arguing, for though she couldn't decipher their conversation, their voices were raised, and they were making sharp gestures with their hands.

Her gaze swept the beach. Among the rocks dotting the shoreline, large wooden crates were piled on the sand. Brows lowered in confusion, her attention returned to the group of men. Four detached themselves from the others and slid the boat back into the water. They piled into the craft and rowed out into the Channel. Where were they headed in the middle of the night? Good heavens, she gasped, could they be smugglers? Or worse—spies?

She shuddered with a cold premonition of dread and quickly made her way back to Misty, unaware of a lone figure hidden in the shadows of the trees, watching her leave.

Chapter 24

Chandler came home from France to find that Brandy had returned to Hathshire. He joined Abigail and Jessie in the salon, stretching out in a chair, his long legs extended toward the fire blazing in the hearth. He heaved a sigh born of weariness. All he wanted was a hot bath and some much-needed sleep. That, however, would have to wait a spell while he visited with the two women.

He arched a brow toward his grandmother. "When did Brandy leave? I thought she would stay, as eager as she was for Andrew's return."

"She is anxious, of course, but she was becoming restless with you away and no word from Andrew. We told her we would send word when one of you returned."

"Should I send her a note?" Jessie inquired of the duke.

"No, I will pay her a visit at Stonebrooke Manor. Jeffrey is hosting a house party this weekend. I will call on her then." After a few more minutes of conversation, he excused himself to the privacy of his chamber with a promise to join them for dinner.

Chandler leaned back in the tub, the hot water soothing his tired muscles. He had been disappointed not to find Brandy here, of course, but he could not blame her for fleeing. He had left rather abruptly, after rendering his callous remarks, and was sure she had nothing kind to say to him. He let out a soft chuckle. He hoped she wasn't still angry with him for he couldn't wait to be in her presence again. He wanted to see her smile, kiss her pliant lips, taste her sweetness. He could still feel her legs wrapped around his waist, feel himself sheathed inside her. He shifted uncomfortably in the tub.

Squashing his salacious thoughts, he focused on the upcoming weekend. In his brief meeting with Blanchard, Ross had confirmed that Philip Drummond had indeed been mixed up with a ring of spies. How deeply involved, he didn't know. Blanchard had also informed him he and Madelyn would be attending Jeffrey's rout. He wanted to watch Brandy closely, in a smaller, intimate affair. With Blackwell's promise to attend, it should prove to be an interesting and informative night.

On Chandler's part, he continued to hope Brandy wasn't involved in actions against the Crown. Despite his tender feelings, he needed to remain on guard—he could ill afford to let love blind him if she was indeed tangled up with Blackwell. He vowed to find out the truth, no matter what it took, no matter what it might turn out to be.

****

Brandy gave Misty her head as they raced across the countryside. The wind whipped the pins from her hair and the tresses streamed out behind her like auburn ribbons. She laughed out loud, gloriously happy in the warm sunshine and crisp cool air. This was the first day in nearly a sennight it hadn't rained, and Brandy had quickly taken advantage of the weather to give Misty a good run.

Lost in the glory of the day, she did not hear the approaching horse and rider until they were nearly upon her. She glanced over her shoulder and her breath caught in her throat as she came face to face with the man who had been haunting her dreams—day and night. She reined her mare to a stop and hid her apprehension behind a tentative smile. She had been dreading this moment, and now that it was upon her, she was as nervous as a cornered cat.

Chandler tipped his hat. "Well, if it isn't the fair Lady Brandy."

Her smile faltered and she stiffened in the saddle, dashed by his flippant remark. "What do you want, Chandler? What brings you to the country?"

"Why, your lovely charms, of course," he quipped, discouraged by her tone. So, she was still angry.

She blushed and gazed out over the land. He had seen the change from wariness to sadness in her eyes and suddenly felt like a cad. *I'm certainly not handling this meeting with grace. Perhaps humor isn't the best avenue.*

"Brandy—"

"Go away, Chandler." She pulled on the reins, but he was quick, grabbing them from her hands before she could ride off. Misty shied, but Chandler had a firm grip on the leather straps.

"Actually, I was on my way to pay you a visit when I spied you tearing across the land—again. I wanted to invite you to Jeffrey's rout tonight. I believe you are acquainted with his country estate?" His grin was lopsided.

She reddened in embarrassment. "Yes, I know it. But I must decline your kind invitation."

"Oh? Do you perhaps have another engagement?"

She looked him full in the face and smiled brightly. "As a matter of fact, I do."

"Roger Blackwell?" Jealousy bit with sharp teeth, unsettling him further.

She hadn't thought of him, but he would do. "Yes."

"Then you will be attending, for he has accepted the invitation as well."

She knew by his expression she had lost. "Oh, all right. I do not have plans with Roger Blackwell," she admitted with a glower. The man really was a rogue. A gentleman would not have forced the issue. She thought of telling him just that but knew she would be wasting her breath. She would only be rewarded with a smirk.

He handed her the reins. "I will call for you at nine o'clock." He started to turn away but stopped and looked back at her. "You do, of course, have appropriate attire?" He chuckled and rode off without another word.

Brandy stared after him, her mouth open. Of all the smug, arrogant… Despite her thunderous thoughts, her traitorous body sang a different tune. Just the sight of his handsome face and brilliant blue eyes, had caused a warm glow to spread and tie her belly in knots of expectation.

She was infuriated—he'd acted as if he'd never thrown those hateful words at her, as if their night of lovemaking was an everyday occurrence. *Well, for him it might be, but for me it was a delicious journey into a world heretofore unknown.* And she was responding to his presence like a ninny.

Well, two could play the game. She could pretend that night hadn't come to pass as well. She turned Misty and raced toward home, contemplating which of her new gowns she would wear.

Chapter 25

Chandler ascended the front steps of Alden Ridge, Brandy on one arm, Anne on the other. Brandy had coaxed Anne into joining her for the evening. She was being a coward, she knew, but now was not the time for false courage. She needed support for her first outing with Chandler since their night together.

Brandy, dressed in a sea-green silk dress that complemented the color of her eyes, had not missed the appreciative gleam in Chandler's when he had called for her at Stonebrooke Manor. He had seemed a bit surprised when Anne joined them, but had merely lifted a brow, grinning at her hurried explanation that she thought Anne might enjoy the evening.

Chandler, dressed simply in black with a white ruffled shirt and cravat, guided them through the foyer at Alden Ridge. It was spacious, decorated in varied shades of green, yellow, and brown. As parties went, this one was quite informal—they simply made their way to the large drawing room where the group had gathered for the evening.

Jeffrey had been watching for their arrival, and when he spotted them, he bent down and whispered a word to a woman at his side. The woman slid her arm through his and they made their way toward them.

"Lady Brandy, 'tis good to see you again. And Miss Anne, I'm delighted you have joined us this evening.

May I present my wife, the Marchioness of Montaldene. Lydia, Lady Brandy Drummond."

Lydia Alden was the most beautiful woman Brandy had ever seen. She was small in stature and graceful, her dark red hair cut short just brushing her shoulders. Her maroon silk gown complemented her coloring and the matching earbobs and necklace completed her outfit. Her brown eyes were warm and friendly as she extended her hand. "'Tis so nice to finally meet you, Lady Brandy. Jeffrey has told me so much about you."

"Thank you, milady. 'Tis a pleasure to be here." Brandy was quickly drawn to her gracious manner. "May I present my cousin, Miss Anne MacCartin."

"Welcome to our home, Miss MacCartin."

Lydia turned back to Brandy. "I was quite distraught to hear of your father's passing. You are getting on well?"

"Yes, thank you."

"I was acquainted with your parents. In fact, your mother and I spent a delightful afternoon together at a mutual friend's home for tea, many years ago."

Brandy suddenly felt horribly guilty for stealing food from these kind people. She heard a muffled noise and glanced up at Chandler and blanched. As if reading her thoughts, his mouth curved into a mocking grin. Just then Lord and Lady Merrick joined the group. Blanchard took her hand, smiling and staring intently into her eyes. "'Tis an honor to see you again, Lady Brandy. I trust you are well."

"Yes, milord," she responded and turned to Madelyn, resplendent in a silver-and-turquoise gown with a matching shawl. As she spoke a few words of greeting to her, Chandler took Blanchard aside just far enough away not to be overheard.

"Have you seen Blackwell?"

"He arrived a short time ago. He's been deep in conversation with a few others I don't recognize. We'll need to watch them closely. I have a bad feeling."

"Do you think he fell for the ruse we staged in your study?"

"I'm sure of it," Blanchard confirmed confidently. "If he believes the coast will soon be guarded by the Crown, he will make his move soon—most likely tonight. 'Tis a perfect night." He added, "You'll keep close tabs on Brandy?"

"Yes," Chandler snapped, unhappy with the reminder of her possible involvement. He sighed, and ran his hand through his hair. "I'm sorry, Ross. This doesn't sit well with me."

Ross clapped him on the shoulder. "I know, I feel the same way. She looks the innocent, and Michael's sister to boot, but we can't be too careful." He stared hard at Chandler. "Are you falling for her, my boy?"

Chandler snorted in response and left it at that.

When they turned back to the group, Brandy and Madelyn were talking quietly together. Jeffrey, Lydia, and Anne had moved away. Chandler took Brandy's arm. "Shall we head into the ballroom?" Brandy glanced over her shoulder, looking for Anne. "I won't bite, sweet," he whispered in her ear and chuckled when she immediately stiffened. Glaring up at him, she snapped, "I was merely making sure Anne wasn't left alone."

"It appears that Jeffrey and Lydia are introducing her to a group of young people. She'll be fine."

"Yes, of course," she murmured as Chandler led her away.

Chandler stopped a passing footman and lifted two glasses of champagne from the silver tray. He handed one to Brandy and lifted his in a silent toast. As she sipped the sparkling wine, Brandy looked around the room. The walls were covered in midnight-blue damask, the floors oak. A multi-tiered chandelier, heavily swagged with dozens of pendant drops, illuminated the spacious room where most of the guests had assembled. Potted plants graced every available space and settees large enough for two were placed evenly apart against the walls, encircling the room. She let her gaze travel over the guests. Like the other affairs she had attended, the women were gowned in a myriad of colors and styles, the gentlemen in black.

She spotted Roger Blackwell standing in one corner of the room, conversing with two other men. He turned, his gaze briefly capturing hers. His eyes narrowed when he spied Chandler at her side, yet he merely nodded cordially and turned back to his group.

Chandler looked down at Brandy, having witnessed the silent exchange. He set his glass on a nearby table. "Would you like to dance, sweet?"

She hesitated briefly, his remark still stinging, but she would show him she was not afraid. Nodding, she placed her glass with his on the table. He drew her onto the dance floor, guiding her expertly around the room, step—slide—step—turn. Brandy allowed the music to wash over her as she danced in Chandler's arms. The image of their night together flitted across her mind, as his arms encircled her, but she pushed it aside. He had yet to mention it, and she certainly was not going to broach the subject first. If he could pretend it hadn't happened, well, then, so could she. Let him think it had mattered not, as it so obviously held such little importance to him.

When the music came to an end, Chandler guided Brandy to a room off the drawing room where a buffet table had been set. It was laden with a variety of foods— filets of venison, slices of cold chicken poached in wine, wafer-thin slices of juicy roast beef, a selection of cheeses, rolls, plum puddings, and candied fruit and nuts. Chandler handed her a large blue-and-white-striped porcelain plate which she began filling with an assortment of tantalizing morsels.

"Feeding an army, my dear?" Chandler glanced down at her laden plate, one brow arched.

She shrugged daintily and continued to survey the feast on the off chance she had missed something delicious.

"Try the chicken, sweet. It's quite tasty and," he lowered his voice, "you won't go to prison." He chuckled at his own joke.

She stiffened, glaring at him. "Will you be quiet? And please stop bringing that up—it's becoming tiresome. If you must, then tell Lord Montaldene. By all means, tell the entire gathering. It would be preferable to your constant innuendos." She turned to walk away.

Chandler's hand shot out and circled her arm. "I'm sorry, Brandy. I just can't get the image of you and that bloody chicken out of my mind."

"Try."

He laughed out loud. "You have to admit it's quite humorous."

She yanked her arm from his grasp, nearly upsetting her full plate. "Oh—go to the devil!" She stomped off, ignoring the curious stares from a few of the guests as well as Chandler's hearty laughter that followed. She found a quiet place in an alcove and settled herself on a settee. She accepted a glass of Madeira from a passing footman and set the glass on the table next to the settee. Floor to ceiling doors framed the niche, and a large potted plant kept her well hidden from a pair of mocking blue eyes. She stabbed at her food, dismayed that she was so angry she couldn't enjoy the rich fare. She looked around, made certain no one was watching, and carefully rolled most of the food into the linen napkin. She opened her reticule and crammed the bundle inside. Maddie and Arthur would feast this night.

"Pinching again?" Chandler drawled, appearing as if from thin air.

Brandy lifted her chin. "I'm saving it for later, if you must know. I find I'm not as hungry as I thought." She closed her reticule and laid the nearly empty plate on the table. She picked up the glass of Madeira and drained it. Setting it on the table, she rose and prepared to move away.

"Brandy, I will give you money to buy food. You do not have to steal it."

"I don't want your bloody money. I don't want anything from you—except maybe some peace. Just leave me alone, will you?" Highly embarrassed and already on edge, she snapped at him, mistaking his kind offer as another form of humiliation.

Chandler nodded curtly, the compassion disappearing from his eyes. "As you wish, milady."

Heartbroken, she watched him stride across the room and disappear into the library. He could make her so bloody furious, and she was quick to rise to the bait every time, screeching at him like a shrew. Where was her sense of humor? Had it disappeared along with her virginity? All she wanted was for the rest of the world to disappear and to be wrapped in his strong arms. She allowed herself one moment of self-pity. *I was just another easy conquest. He probably doesn't even remember that night.*

On that, she was wrong. Chandler thought of nothing but her, however, he was at a loss at what to do. While in France, Mona's bountiful charms had been readily available, yet he had turned her away, consumed with a vision of auburn hair and green eyes. He had sworn he would love no woman, that no woman would capture his heart, yet this slip of a girl had such a hold on him he could not think of, much less bed, another.

He admired her unfailing determination to find her brother, her loyalty to her family, and her wonderful sense of humor. True, of late the latter had been lacking, but he couldn't help feeling responsible. He supposed he did ride her too hard at times. She was just so easy to torment. She was just so easy to tease. She was just so easy to love.

Scowling, he strode into Jeffrey's library and crossed the room to the sideboard. He splashed a liberal amount of whiskey into a crystal glass and swallowed a healthy portion of it.

Jeffrey was right behind him. "I'll have one, too," he said watching Chandler closely. "What's wrong? Is it Andrew?"

Chandler started. Truth be told, he had not thought of his brother all evening. Damn, that vixen was fast becoming an obsession. She could very well make him forget his duty.

"Or is the fair Lady Brandy causing you to snarl

so?" Jeffrey laughed. "You made quite a spectacle in the drawing room. What was so diverting that made you laugh, and Brandy look ready to murder you?"

"Nothing a'tall, just a private joke."

"One I don't think she found amusing, eh?"

Chandler shrugged and refilled his nearly empty glass. Jeffrey eyed him with curiosity. He had never seen Chandler so affected by a woman, not that they hadn't tried to wring an emotion out of him, any emotion. He honestly just had not ever cared, and it showed, by his cool composure, his bored indifference. But this—this was different. As much as he tried to hide it, Chandler cared for the girl. And that pleased Jeffrey no end. He had a fondness for her and didn't buy into their belief that she could be involved, like her father. He opened his mouth to ask another pointed question, but one look at his friend's murderous expression and he wisely turned the subject. "Do you think Blackwell will make his move tonight?"

"I'm counting on it. And when he does, I'll be ready."

"What does Blanchard think about Brandy?" Jeffrey leaned his hip against a chair, sipping his whiskey.

"He still has his suspicions and plans to watch her closely."

"We'll see if she interacts with Blackwell. Although I don't mind saying I don't think she will. I don't believe she's involved."

"Maybe, maybe not," Chandler said tightly. He had not revealed Brandy's nocturnal activities. He saw no reason to—yet. If she did anything questionable, he would confide in both Jeffrey and Ross. But for the time being, he would keep silent. If she weren't involved, he did not want to cause her undue embarrassment.

Anne found Brandy on the settee in the alcove. One of the doors was ajar, an errant breeze ruffling the fronds of the potted plant. It was hot in the room and, although winter was upon them, the night was mild. Brandy was busy watching a flock of women flutter around Chandler. These women were beautiful, artfully arrayed, dressed to perfection. Yet he seemed not to notice—or care. That pleased her—exceedingly.

"Here comes trouble," Anne whispered behind her fan as Roger Blackwell approached.

"My dear Lady Brandy and Miss Anne. You put the other ladies to shame with your beauty."

"How kind of you to say, milord." Brandy forced a smile. Out of the corner of her eye she saw Chandler watching them and her smile became brighter. "You look quite handsome yourself." She felt Anne's surprise.

Roger started, then grinned at the unexpected compliment. "Would you care to dance?"

"Yes, thank you." She allowed him to lead her onto the dance floor, joining the others turning in time to the music.

With a puzzled frown, Anne wondered what her cousin was up to now. She jumped when a deep voice spoke from above.

"Miss Anne, are you enjoying yourself?"

She looked up to find Chandler looming and shyly lowered her lashes. "Oh, yes. Thank you so much for escorting me."

"Do I make you nervous?" He smiled down at her, thinking her a timid creature.

"Yes," she admitted, suddenly becoming interested in the tips of her slippers.

"You don't need to be frightened, you know. I see Brandy is dancing with Lord Norwood. Tell me, are they betrothed?"

"Good gracious, no! What I mean to say is that, well, Brandy has not given him an answer yet." Anne bit her lip in confusion, not knowing what Brandy would want her to say.

Chandler watched her carefully, controlling his expression. "I see," he responded and glanced at the dancers. Watching Brandy in Roger's arms made his chest tighten. He did not like it—did not like them together.

"May I join you?"

"Of course." Anne scooted over to make room for him on the settee.

"When did her mother pass away?"

"Ah, nearly three years ago."

Chandler wondered at her hesitation. "And her father just passed," he added thoughtfully.

"Yes. 'Tis sad, really. Brandy has had to cope with too much sorrow for one so young."

"True, but she seems to hold onto her high spirits despite the hardships. *Most of the time.*

"Oh, yes, Brandy is very resilient. She prefers seeing the lighter side of life than the darker," she stated proudly. "Though sometimes her circumstances can become too much for her. She tries to hide it, of course, but her eyes give her away." She watched her cousin whirl by in Roger's arms, her dress swirling around her ankles.

"Indeed."

Anne did not miss the tightening of his mouth. "Tell me, Your Grace, why did you inquire after Brandy at

Stonebrooke Manor? I wasn't aware the two of you knew each other."

His expression shuttered, he offered vaguely, "I wanted to offer my condolences on her father's death."

"So you said at the time."

He gazed down at her. She had more mettle than he'd realized. "And you don't believe me?"

"Under the circumstances, no."

The music was coming to an end and, despite Anne's startling declaration, he was determined to claim Brandy for the next dance. "Will you excuse me?"

"Of course," Anne whispered, shocked by her outspokenness. She watched him stride toward the dancers, this tall, dark, handsome man. Her cousin was insane. If she weren't so afraid of him, she might just go after the duke herself.

Chapter 26

Brandy really did try to enjoy the evening. She deliberately set Chandler from her mind and concentrated on having a good time. She danced nearly every dance, a different partner each time, and drank several glasses of champagne. Chandler claimed one other dance, but neither one of them enjoyed it. When the piece ended, Chandler escorted her to the edge of the dance floor and deposited her with Anne.

Chandler spent a good part of the evening in the company of the many beautiful women vying for his attention. They batted their lashes, exposed their bosoms, and twitched their backsides, all hoping to gain his singular attention. Watching them hang on his every word, as if he knew the secrets of the universe, Brandy became disgusted with the lot of them. She tried to ignore him, but not a second later she was once again seeking out his tall frame in the crowd of women that seemed to multiply over time.

Brandy would have been pleased to know Chandler was just as covertly watching her, with just as much intensity, and becoming increasingly annoyed by her many dance partners.

Chandler wasn't the only one who watched Brandy. Roger Blackwell's eyes followed her every move. Only after she had disappeared upstairs did he abandon his vigil and approach his sister, who stood with several other women in one corner of the room. "May I have a word with you, Lacey?" But for the age difference, she could have been his twin, tall, blonde and brown-eyed.

Lacey nodded and, excusing herself from her group of friends, allowed Roger to escort her to a quiet alcove where they could speak without being overheard. "Where is Thomas?" Roger asked. "I don't believe I've seen him this evening."

"He was detained in London. I decided to come anyway, with Lady Aranson." She hesitated a moment, her brown eyes narrowing. "What do you want, Roger?"

"I believe I have stumbled across something that could, if it became known, cause quite a scandal." Lacey arched a brow in bored curiosity as Roger continued, "'Tis the matter of a certain young lady." He watched her like a snake about to strike its victim.

"Really, Roger, do get to the point, will you?" She raised her fan and batted the air, glancing around the room with shadowed eyes.

"She bears a striking resemblance…don't you think?"

"To whom?"

"To *her*."

Lacey became still.

"So, you know of whom I speak?" Roger watched his sister closely, waiting. When her shoulders slumped, he struck. "Don't worry, my dear sister, your secret is safe with me. Of course, I do require something to ensure my silence."

"You were supposed to take care of it," she retorted. "And, if it is true, you are just as guilty!"

"Maybe, but I have nothing to lose. And you, well, you do." His smile was evil personified. "Whatever happened to her? Still languishing away in a convent?" He laughed, an ugly sound.

"I'm sure I don't know what you mean," she hedged, her fan flicking back and forth.

"Give it up, Lacey." His gaze swept the room. "I have a bigger problem." He found whom he sought. Brandy was once again ensconced on the settee with her cousin. Lacey, following his gaze, laughed. "Still won't marry you?"

"The chit refuses to honor Drummond's promise. I have to figure out some way to force her hand. I need that bit of land. I may have to resort to other tactics...and that is where you come in."

"You want me to convince her to marry you?"

Roger frowned, not amused by her sarcasm.

"I won't kill her."

"I don't want her dead."

"Then how can I possibly be of help?"

"By obtaining what I need."

"What do you need?"

"Information. Quite simply, I want to know what Blanchard and your husband are up to."

"How in the world am I supposed to know that? Thomas doesn't discuss his business affairs with me. Besides, what have Thomas's shipping interests to do with you?"

"I'm not interested in his shipping business. I want to know about his meetings with Blanchard and Townsend."

"I don't know anything about these meetings. Moreover, he never confides his secrets to me."

"Then I suggest you wheedle them out of him. I don't care how you do it, just do it."

"How do you know Thomas is involved with Blanchard?"

"I have my sources. Just get what I need. And do smile, my dear. People are looking this way." He flashed her a grin, patted her cheek, and walked away.

Chandler was keeping a sharp eye on Blackwell, when he wasn't watching Brandy, while enduring the veiled invitations from the group of women surrounding him. Their laughter grated on his nerves and their combined fragrances were making him lightheaded. Nevertheless, they were the perfect decoy for keeping watch on Blackwell. He chuckled. It was also making Brandy mad as hell.

He had noted with interest Blackwell's conversation with his sister and wondered at the lingering expression of fear on her face after he left her standing in the alcove. He saw Blackwell move to stand by the library near a set of double doors that led outside. When he saw him make eye contact with a gentleman across the room and slip out the door, Chandler immediately looked for Jeffrey. He, too, had been watching Blackwell. Their gazes locked and Chandler, with a nod, disengaged himself from his crowd of female admirers and slipped out the door behind Blackwell.

Brandy, who had been watching Chandler unceasingly, saw him leave. She told her cousin she needed a moment, and hurried through the door Chandler had disappeared through, just in time to see him slip around the side of the house.

The temperature had dropped considerably. She shivered, longing for the warmth of her cloak. The mist that had thickened to a dense fog was dissipating, and the full moon was spreading a thin layer of light over the land. She darted through the forest. For the first time she was grateful for her stint as a thief—she knew how to travel without making a sound. Her skirt did hinder her progress, and she ardently wished for the ease the lad's clothing afforded, but she kept Chandler in sight as best she could while staying far enough behind so he wouldn't sense her presence. She tripped over a dead tree branch, heard the tearing of her silk skirt, and fell headlong onto the forest floor. She held her breath, waiting for the clamor of alarm. But the carpet of leaves had softened her fall and she hadn't made a sound. She waited until her breathing evened out, the smell of damp earth pungent beneath her cheek, then hauled herself to her feet and started out again. The smell of salt on the air became strong, so she knew she was heading toward the cliffs. She paused and looked around. She had lost sight of Chandler. Remembering the night she had stumbled upon the circle of men on the beach, she instinctively continued toward the cliffs.

Lifting her skirt high, she moved stealthily through the trees. She paused to listen, her head tilted to one side. Muffled voices drifted to her on the cool night wind. She picked her way carefully around fallen tree branches and thick roots until she reached the edge of land, where she lay flat on her stomach and peered over the side of the cliff. It was not a long drop to the beach, and she could see the scene below quite clearly. She counted three men in a circle, talking fast and gesturing wildly. One man held aloft a lantern. In its band of light, she could make out one face clearly—Roger Blackwell. Somehow, she was not surprised. Her gaze was drawn to a man lying prone at their feet. She swallowed a horrified scream. Sprawled on the sand, motionless, was Chandler.

Brandy's first instinct was to scale the cliff and race to his side. Looking around, frantic, she spotted a boat heading toward the shore, bobbing drunkenly on the waves. As the boat scraped bottom, one of the men jumped out and dragged it onto the sand. Two other men leapt from the boat. A quiet conversation ensued. Roger handed a package to one of the men, then looked up, his gaze seeming to pierce the spot where Brandy lay hidden in the shadows. She froze, her heart in her throat, until he turned back to the others.

Two of the men climbed back into the boat as a third pushed it out into the Channel. The craft set out across the water, the lantern hanging from the mast dancing ghostlike against the black sky. The other men disappeared into the night. Roger gestured to the large man who had remained behind and pointed to Chandler. The man bent down and hefted Chandler across his shoulders as if he were a sack of grain and not a man fully grown. They started down the beach away from her, the fog now rolling in from the Channel swallowing them up.

Brandy waited for the witnessed scene to crystallize in her mind. Then, retracing her steps, she hurried back to Alden Ridge. She slipped unseen into the ladies' retiring room. She smoothed her hair and brushed away the debris clinging to her gown. She gasped in dismay when she noticed a small tear in the bodice and the mud caked on the hem of the skirt. She grabbed a shawl someone had thrown across a small settee and, in an effort to hide the torn material, draped it down the front of her gown. She prayed no one would notice her shabby state of attire.

Stopping at the entrance to the drawing room, she

searched for Jeffrey. She saw him standing with a group of guests and hurried to his side.

"I need to talk to you," she stated through a smile. She had not seen Roger, but he could well be there watching her.

Jeffrey took one look at her drawn expression, her eyes filled with worry, and took her by the arm. He started to escort her onto the dance floor, but she shook her head, dropping her gaze to the hem of her skirt. He immediately understood. "I will meet you in the front salon."

She made her way through the crowd, nodding here and there to those of her acquaintance, and after reaching the salon took a seat in one of the overstuffed chairs in front of the hearth. She clasped her hands in her lap.

Jeffrey entered the room and shut the door behind him. "What is it?"

"It's Chandler. They've taken him."

"Who?"

"I don't know. I followed him—"

"Why did you follow him?" Jeffrey busied himself pouring a draught of cognac.

"I saw Roger Blackwell go out the door by the library and then Chandler."

"Why did you feel the need to follow him?"

"Well, I'm not sure. I just felt I should. But when I fell, I lost sight of him. When I reached the cliffs and looked down at the beach, I saw a circle of men and at their feet was Chandler. He wasn't moving."

"Are you quite sure it was Chandler? I mean, why would he go out into the night? And who would want to waylay him?"

"Stop it! Please don't patronize me. I know what I

saw."

Jeffrey was at a loss. He knew Chandler had his doubts about her loyalty, but of late they were hard for Jeffrey to accept. His instincts told him she could be trusted. Still not understanding why she followed Chandler, she did seem genuinely distraught. And the state of her attire attested to the fact she had been outside and into something. It seemed to fit her story. He handed her a delicate-stemmed glass of sherry and decided to tread carefully.

"Suppose you tell me exactly what happened." He sat down in the other chair and listened intently as she quickly related what she had seen. When she finished, Jeffrey was scowling. He stared at her, eyes narrowed in thought, and seemed to come to a decision. He opened the door and signaled for his butler. "Ham, ask Miss Anne MacCartin to join Lady Brandy and me. Then retrieve their wraps and have the coach pulled around front to see them to Stonebrooke Manor." To Brandy, he ordered, "You are to go home. And don't worry," he added, a little more kindly. "I'll take care of it."

Anne rushed into the room, followed by Ham, the ladies' cloaks draped over his arm. "Brandy, is everything all right? I was dancing with one of the nicest gentlemen when—"

"We're going home."

"Of course," Anne said, concerned by her cousin's tone of voice.

Jeffrey bid them farewell with a promise to see them on the morrow. He strode out of the room in search of Blanchard, while Ham escorted the ladies to the door and into the Alden coach.

Brandy settled back against the supple leather squab

across from Anne. She huddled beneath the heavy blanket and stared out the window into the darkness. It had begun to snow, the white flakes drifting outside the window as the coach raced toward home. She pulled the curtain closed and with a trembling sigh, leaned back against the head rest. Where had they taken Chandler? And why? *Oh Lord, please let him be safe.*

Anne didn't say a word for the expression on her cousin's face forbade conversation. She knew instinctively something was frightfully amiss.

When they arrived home, Anne could no longer keep silent. "Brandy, what happened? Why, just look at your gown!"

Brandy had removed her cloak and now glanced down at her torn, soiled gown. "They've taken Chandler."

"Who has?"

"Well, Roger Blackwell, for one."

Anne grabbed her wrist. "Did he try to take you too?"

"No, he didn't see me. I was hiding." She hugged her cousin. "Lord Montaldene is going to find out what's happening. He'll be here on the morrow. There's not much to do until then. Let's retire, and we'll continue this discussion in the morning."

They climbed the stairs together and hugged good night. Anne waited until Brandy had disappeared into her chamber before turning toward her own, fraught with worry.

Brandy tossed and turned, unable to dismiss the image of Chandler prone—and vulnerable—on the sand. She rose from the bed, shrugged into her robe and padded down the stairs, pausing on the bottom step in alarm. A light shone from beneath the door to Philip's study. She crept to the door and pressed her ear against the solid wood. Hearing nothing, she reached for the knob and turned it slowly, biting her lower lip and praying the door wouldn't squeak on its hinges. She pushed it open a crack and peered around the edge. The room was empty. She swung the door wide and stepped inside.

A candle sat on the corner of the desk, nearly gutted by the cold breeze blowing in from the open window. The curtains billowed like eerie apparitions, and a light coating of snow covered the windowsill. Brandy closed and locked the window.

She turned back to the desk. Papers were scattered across the top and an inkwell had been overturned. She frowned in confusion, clearly remembering leaving the desk in an orderly fashion, the papers neatly stacked. Who had been in here? And what were they looking for?

She picked up the candle and turned to leave when she spied Arthur lying on the floor behind the door. She rushed to his side and knelt beside him. She rubbed his forehead until his eyes fluttered open.

"Arthur? What happened?" She held his hand as he struggled to sit up.

"I was locking up for the night when I heard a noise. When I came in, I was hit over the head. I didn't see who it was, Miss Brandy." He sounded disappointed.

"'Tis all right, Arthur. Does your head hurt very much?"

"No, but I think there will be a good-sized lump, come morning."

"Well, off to bed with you. Whoever was here is gone now."

Brandy returned to her chamber more frightened than ever. Chandler had been captured, her home had been invaded, Philip's papers had been rifled through, and her butler set upon.

What would happen next?

Chapter 27

The next morning, Brandy pulled open the front door. A scruffy-looking man stood on the landing, shifting from one foot to the other as if standing on burning embers. He was short, a mop of dirty brown hair atop his round head, his clothes looking as if he had slept in them for months. She kept one hand on the door ready to slam it in his face at the first sign of danger.

"May I help you?"

"I be lookin' for Lady Brandy Drummond." His teeth were stained brown.

"I am Lady Brandy Drummond."

The man pulled a crumpled envelope from his overcoat pocket and held it out. She saw her name scrawled across the front in bold black letters. She took it from him and turned it over in her hand. She looked back at him. "Who sent it?"

"Ain't no business o' mine." He turned and bolted down the steps to his horse. He swung up into the saddle, kicked his heels into the horse's flanks, and tore down the drive.

Brandy watched him disappear, sensing trouble in the air. She shut the door and went back into the salon, where Jeffrey waited. "A man just delivered this." She held up the envelope, then ripped it open. The blood drained from her face. "It's from Roger Blackwell." She handed the letter to Jeffrey, who quickly scanned the contents.

If you want to see Townsend alive, bring me your father's journal. It was signed *Blackwell.*

Jeffrey glanced up at Brandy. "What journal?"

"After my father died, I found a journal he had been keeping for years."

"Have you read it?"

"I have, but I didn't find any incriminating evidence against Blackwell, not that I could decipher anyway." She added with a grimace, "other than him blackmailing Philip for my hand in marriage." She thought a moment. "I wonder why it's so important to him."

"Where are you going?" Jeffrey questioned as she turned to leave the room.

"Blackwell Hall."

"Oh, no, you are not!" Jeffrey grabbed Brandy's shoulders. "It could be a trap."

"If Chandler is there, and in trouble, then I must go."

"Brandy...wait!" His hand made a path through his already rumpled hair. Chandler would kill him if harm came to Brandy, regardless that she had yet to be fully exonerated. If she was in league with Blackwell, she wouldn't be harmed. But if she wasn't... He thought quickly but couldn't come up with another plan. "May I see this journal?"

Brandy hesitated but a moment, then came to a quick decision. "Of course. I will get it for you. But I have no intention of giving it to Blackwell." She hurried to her room to retrieve the journal and was back in a moment. "I couldn't make sense of most of it. Perhaps you can. I just know that if Blackwell wants it, it can't be good for him."

Jeffrey flipped through the pages. "May I keep it?

I'd like to read it." At her inquisitive look, he explained, "Curious, 'tis all." Knowing there was more to it than he was saying, she nevertheless nodded as he slipped it into his waistcoat. "I don't think it's wise for you to go rushing off to Blackwell Hall. Why don't we talk to Blanchard first? We'll show him the letter and let him decide what to do."

"Lord Merrick? What has he to do with this?"

Jeffrey glanced out the window avoiding her question.

"Lord Montaldene, why did Roger take Chandler?" Brandy asked slowly, suspecting there was a great deal more here than she was being told. Especially if Jeffrey wanted to involve Blanchard.

"It's a longstanding feud, 'tis all. I'm sorry, but I can't go into further detail."

Brandy didn't believe him for a moment, but Chandler's welfare took precedence. She would get to the bottom of it later. "I will tell him that I know nothing about a journal and convince him to release Chandler." Brandy watched Jeffrey pace the length of her salon. When he passed by her, she clutched his arm. "He will kill Chandler—I just know it! The man is ruthless. 'Tis the only way to free Chandler."

"It's too dangerous." Jeffrey's hand plowed through his hair again. He stared at her, and something in her eyes made him pause. "You really care for him, don't you?"

"I…I suppose I do," she hedged, not ready to declare aloud her love for Chandler. "Anyway, I don't want him hurt—or dead." She turned away from the probing questions in his eyes.

"All right. Find out what you can, but then I want you out of there. I will be waiting in the north woods. If you haven't appeared in thirty minutes—"

"You'll what? Come in after me? Really, milord, I'll be perfectly safe. Roger Blackwell wants to marry me. He would not dare harm me." At Jeffrey's reluctant nod, Brandy raced up the stairs to change into her riding habit before he could change his mind.

Anne walked in just as Brandy was placing a small muff pistol inside her reticule. "Brandy, where are you going—and with a gun! Where did you even get a gun?"

"Michael left it with me the last time he was home. There's another one in the salon. Oh, never mind that now, Anne." She read the fear in her eyes and, relenting, told her quickly of her conversation with Jeffrey as well as the note received from Roger. "I will be fine. Please don't worry about me."

"Brandy, this is not a game. You don't know what Roger is capable of. He is evil." Reading the determination on her cousin's face, she knew she would never turn her from her determined course. "You will be careful, won't you?" she asked needlessly, her hands twisting in her skirt.

"Of course. I will be home in no time, you'll see."

Still not convinced, and terrified for her safety, Anne watched forlornly as Brandy made her way downstairs to the salon. There, Jeffrey detained Brandy, wrapping his hand around her upper arm. He gazed down into her eyes and said softly but firmly, "Remember, thirty minutes…"

Brandy urged Misty into a canter. She took deep breaths until the hysteria threatening to turn her around dissipated. She topped a small rise near a wooded copse and Blackwell Hall loomed before her. She nudged her horse on, fear gripping her with icy hands as she dismounted in front of the house. She clutched her reticule tightly, felt the outline of the pistol hidden inside, and felt a little calmer. As she reached for the bell pull, the door was snatched open. Startled, she jumped back, her hand at her throat.

"My dear Brandy, how good of you to come. I wasn't sure you would. Have you the journal?" Roger's hand shot out and closed around her arm, pulling her inside the foyer. The door slammed shut behind her.

"I came when I received your note because I was concerned about the duke. I'm sorry, but I don't know anything about a journal. If my father kept one, he must have destroyed it before he died."

Roger gritted his teeth and turned, taking a moment to compose himself. He turned back with a smile. "Well, do come in, anyway."

Brandy followed him into the drawing room. At first glance, it was apparent the house had fallen into disrepair. Striped, brown-and-white silk paper peeled away from the walls, and the room was barren, as if most of the furniture had been sold, save for a well-worn settee and scarred table. The carpet was worn in spots, the once-bright color faded, and the windows were devoid of drapery. A fire burned in the hearth, warming the chilly room. Brandy stepped closer to it, raising her hands toward the heat. Roger murmured something to his butler, who left to do as bidden.

"Your beauty graces this humble room. I am truly honored by your presence."

She smiled brightly. "Milord, you do wax poetic. I didn't know you were such a romantic."

"There are many things you do not know about me. Perhaps, in time…" He shrugged his shoulders and motioned to his butler, who had returned with a tea service. "Set it there. Would you care for some tea, my dear?"

Brandy accepted the offer and perched on the edge of the settee. She watched Roger over the rim of her cup, waiting for his next move. After a long moment of silence, she set the cup on the saucer with a noisy clatter, her nerves stretched taut. He sat down beside her.

"Brandy, won't you reconsider and marry me? You would make me the happiest man in England."

"I have been thinking about your proposal, milord. Papa obviously thought he was doing right by me with the betrothal agreement. Since Michael has not returned, quite frankly, I need a man around the house." She lowered her eyes, choking on the lies.

He grasped her chin in his large hand and lifted it until he could look into her eyes. "Come now, Brandy, you can do better than that."

Choking down her panic, she tilted her head to one side. "Whatever do you mean, milord?"

"I mean, my dear, you can drop the charade. Do you take me for a fool? I have badgered you for months to marry me, and you were quite adamant in your refusals. Why, now, are you willing? Does it have anything to do with my houseguest?"

Brandy jerked her chin from his grasp. "I did not say I would marry you, but that I would consider it. Perhaps it isn't as horrendous an idea as I had previously thought. However, with your present manners, I see I was correct in my initial stance." Anger simmered just below the surface, yet she kept her expression calm.

"Tell me, my dear, aren't you the least bit curious about Townsend? After all, you did arrive rather quickly after receiving my note."

"What is the duke doing here?"

"I think you already know the answer, my dear."

"No, I don't. What has he done to warrant killing? Especially over a hypothetical journal?"

Roger studied her for a moment, then shook his head. "That's not important. Suffice it to say he's had this coming for a long time."

"A longstanding feud?"

"Something like that." He cocked his head to one side, grinning. "Would you like to see him?" Without waiting for an answer, he pulled her to her feet and out into the foyer. Under the main staircase, a door hidden in the wood paneling opened with a push to one side. He took her hand and led her down a darkened stairway into the bowels of the house. The air smelled musty, and cobwebs hung from the rafters, the gossamer strands glistening in the light from a torch set into a crack in the wall. Seated on a chair was a man she recognized as Mr. Osbert, the man who had visited Philip just before he took his life. He bobbed his head.

"You have a visitor, Townsend."

Roger pushed Brandy from behind, causing her to stumble. She steadied herself and peered into the dim light. Looking between metal bars, she saw Chandler seated on a straw mattress, his black evening attire now dirty and torn, the once intricately tied cravat missing from around his neck. His shoulders slumped against the concrete wall, his wrists and ankles bound with leather straps. One strip of leather stretched from his bound feet to a ring of metal attached to the opposite wall, effectively keeping him in place. A thin motheaten blanket was his only protection against the damp chill room. Brandy shivered, running her hands over the goosebumps dimpling her arms; her heart breaking at the sight of the strong beautiful man bound against his will.

"Chandler," she said in a choked whisper, instinctively reaching out to him.

His face was in shadows, but she saw his eyes lift to her face. They widened in shock before narrowing. "What in the hell are you doing here?"

She flinched as if struck, her hand on her throat, never having heard such raw fury in his voice.

"I told you he was fine," Roger said to Brandy. He turned to Chandler with a shrug of his shoulders. "She didn't believe me, you see. Insisted on seeing for herself," he added, as if attesting to the faithless persuasion of women. "From the beginning, I assured her you wouldn't be harmed." He waved his hand toward Chandler. "There he is, my dear, safe and sound, just as I promised."

She looked at Roger, her brows drawn down in confusion. He made it sound as if she had been involved in Chandler's capture! She stole a quick glance at Chandler, noted his impassive expression, and experienced a sinking feeling in her stomach. And Chandler believed him!

She opened her mouth to refute the lie, but Roger leaned down and whispered in her ear, "If you deny my words, Townsend dies."

She bit her lip. Chandler would undoubtedly believe Roger's lies. He already thought her a thief and a liar—why not kidnapper as well? Since he didn't entirely trust her, this would merely confirm his convictions, false as they may be. She thought to reach for the pistol in her reticule, but Roger held her arm in a steel grip. In addition to that, a huge brute of a man, whom she hadn't seen until now, stood off to one side, a human deterrent to aiding their imprisoned guest.

"Come along, my dear. You have seen for yourself he has not been abused." Roger pushed her up the stairs. She turned back to catch a last glimpse of Chandler. She couldn't bear to leave him believing she had betrayed him. She looked hard at him, all the love she possessed for him glowing in her eyes, willing him to believe in her. He merely gave her a long look of contempt and turned away.

Roger leaned down and whispered, "Remember, one word and he dies." She had no recourse but to turn and precede him up the stairs.

Roger pulled her into the drawing room and slammed the door shut. She jerked from his grasp and swung to face him, arms akimbo. "I had nothing to do with his capture. Why did you make it sound as if I did?"

"It was amusing to let him think so. Does that bother you?"

She caught herself before she lashed out at him and shrugged her shoulders. "No, it doesn't matter one whit. I can barely tolerate the man. It's just that I don't like people thinking ill of me. It wasn't nice of you to let him think I was involved." She kept her voice even while she desperately tried to convince him that she didn't care for Chandler. Oh, but she did! Her heart had broken in two when she saw the dynamic man, her beloved, bound as tight as a corset. "Roger, when word of this becomes known, you will find yourself in a great deal of trouble. He is the Duke of Marbury. You can't just kill him without suffering the consequences."

"Word will not become known."

She stared at him a moment, then started to pull on her gloves in a show of nonchalance. "Well, 'tis your life. Now, I really must be going. Thank you for the tea."

"I'm sorry, Brandy, but I can't let you go. Not now, not when you know about Townsend."

"But I told you, I couldn't care less about him. I don't know why you took him, nor why you have him bound in your cellar, nor do I want to know. He means nothing to me."

"Nice try, sweetheart. No, you will stay here. Besides, there is something you have that I want. I believe I mentioned it earlier?"

"The journal? I know nothing about a journal. I've told you that repeatedly."

His sigh was loud and drawn out. "Brandy, please don't be difficult. I don't want to get rough with you, but I will. That journal is very important to me."

"Why is *my* father's journal so important to you?"

"That is not your business."

"Roger, if my father kept a journal, I have not found it." She headed for the door. "Now I really must be going."

Roger let out a sharp whistle and the door swung open. The large man from the cellar blocked the doorway. She glanced over her shoulder at Roger, a slim brow raised in query, her mouth dry. Roger nodded and the man swung his meaty fist into Brandy's chin.

She crumpled to the floor in a world gone black.

****

Brandy came slowly awake. She shook her head to clear it of the fog, wincing at the pain in her chin. She worked her jaw back and forth. At least the brute hadn't broken it.

She was on a hard cot, a rough blanket covering her, a coarse pillow beneath her cheek. The room was pitch black and smelled stale, airless. It was when she tried to sit up that she realized her wrists were bound. She moved one leg and found her ankles bound as well. She forced herself to lie still and take stock of the situation, willing herself not to panic.

A key turned in the lock, and she glanced toward the sound. The door creaked open, the wedge of light expanding as it swung wide. A man stood outlined in the doorway. He stepped into the room, lit a candle on the bureau, and turned toward her. It was Roger.

"Good, you are awake. I was afraid Bart may have been too rough on you." He sat on the edge of the bed and reached out to push an auburn curl from her forehead. She flinched and pressed back into the pillow.

"So, you cringe at my touch. We shall see about changing that, eh?"

"For heaven's sake, milord, this was not necessary. What did that ogre use on me, a cudgel?"

"I have already chastised Bart for his heavy hand. I explained that, because you are a woman, you are not accustomed to the rough handling that he is infamous for. But he does come in handy, so I keep him around." He chuckled.

"Why am I here?" she demanded, anger overriding her fear. "I demand that you release me at once!"

"You have seen too much." He stroked her chin with his fingers.

She jerked from his touch, grimacing in pain from the sharp movement. "What are you talking about? What have I seen? I told you I thought you careless with taking the duke, but other than that—"

"I saw you that night, you know. You were disguised as a lad, yes, but you were followed back to Stonebrooke Manor. Then last night, one of my men circled back, on a hunch, and you were followed back to Alden Ridge. You do not make a very good spy, Brandy."

"I don't know what you're talking about. I do not wander around the countryside at night. Dressed as a lad, indeed." She turned away from his amused expression.

"I want your father's journal."

"How many times do I have to tell you? I don't know anything about a journal." She looked him directly in the eye. "What's so important in the journal anyway? What could my father possibly have known to write down and keep hidden?"

"If you had read it, then you would know."

"Doesn't that prove I know nothing about it? I can assure you that if I had found it, I most certainly would have read it."

"Where is it?" he demanded, raising his fist as if to strike her.

Brandy shrank back, her thoughts banging into each other as she frantically thought of a way out of this dilemma. She watched him closely, then her eyes widened. She struggled to sit up. "It was you! *You* were in my father's study last night! You rifled through his desk and hit Arthur on the head when he walked in on you!" she shouted in accusation.

"Guilty. And now, my dear, if you do not give me the journal, it will go very hard for you. Not to mention Townsend." He paused as if considering his next words. "Think of your brother, Brandy. You want him safe, don't you?"

"Michael?" Her heart sank.

Roger smiled, a grin without mirth. "If you don't deliver what I want, I have it in my power to take Michael away from you, too."

Brandy turned from his evil countenance and faced the wall. He reached out and ran his hand down the length of her body. "You will do as I say, do I make myself clear? I will leave you alone to think on it."

She felt the bed move as he stood up. The room was again plunged into darkness when he doused the candle and left, locking the door behind him. She was left alone in the dark with her troubled thoughts. What did Roger know of Michael? Was he responsible for him being away so long? Did Chandler know this? Is that why he followed Roger from Alden Ridge last night?

She curled into a ball, hugging her knees to her chest. Tears of frustration and fear pooled on the rough pillow beneath her cheek. She sniffed and brought her bound hands up to wipe away the salty drops. She should have been more careful. Anne was right—Roger Blackwell was a dangerous man.

They had all warned her about Roger. She had scoffed and dismissed their worries as nonsense. She had been so self-assured, so certain she could handle the Earl of Norwood. What a fool she had been! Just look where it had landed her—a prisoner of the man she hated above all others. The man responsible for Philip's death and possibly Michael's welfare and threatening the life of the man she loved.

Downstairs, Roger reclined on the settee, his hands stacked behind his head, staring at a crack in the ceiling. Brandy was being stubborn. He desperately needed the journal, and she was the only way to gain that end. If it fell into the wrong hands, the results would be devastating. There was no doubt she had discovered it. That it was most likely encrypted mattered not. Brandy was a smart girl and would figure it all out. Of course, if she continued to play dumb, he would use force to retrieve it. He chuckled, pleased with the plan he had devised just in case she proved difficult. With Michael soon to be dead, if he wasn't already, he would marry her and obtain her lands. If she caused problems, she could always suffer an unfortunate accident. His sinister thoughts twisted his face. He would enjoy breaking her.

****

Jeffrey was worried. The afternoon was waning, and Brandy still had not returned. Bloody hell! He should never have allowed her to go to Blackwell's alone. He couldn't go in after her. He didn't know what he'd be walking into. A horrible thought arose, terrifying in its possible reality. Could she be in league with the bounder? Was this all a setup? Had he been duped? He thought on that but knew deep down she was innocent of any collusion, and in very real danger. He had seen the look in her eyes, eyes that had shone with concern for Chandler's safety. That wasn't something that could be faked, not to her depth of distress. She was in love with Chandler, as the duke was with her. When he was in their company, Jeffrey could feel the attraction, feel the emotional currents surging between them. Of course, they were both too stubborn to admit it, and after this fiasco was over, he would make sure they confronted their feelings. But first things first. He threw his leg over his horse and quickly rode back to Stonebrooke Manor.

Shadows were beginning to lengthen across the carpet as the sun, in its daily descent, dipped behind the treetops. Anne stood in the doorway contemplating Lord Montaldene's rigid back as he stared into the fire. He held a missive in his hand. She moved to the sideboard and splashed a liberal amount of cognac into a glass and crossed the room to his side. She pressed the glass into his hand. "There has been news?"

"Blanchard has sent word to his men in London. They should be here late this evening. I am going back to Alden Ridge to wait for them. Would you like to accompany me? Stay the night at Alden Ridge?"

"No, I want to be here when Brandy returns home."

"Will you be all right by yourself?"

"Yes, I will be fine." She walked over to a spindle-legged oak table and pulled a small pistol out of the drawer. "I won't hesitate to use it."

Jeffrey smiled at her bravado.

"Do you know how?"

"No." She shrugged her shoulders. "I'm hoping it'll scare them away."

"Well, if you should hear or see anything unusual, please contact me immediately."

"Of course. Milord…you don't think Blackwell would hurt Brandy, do you?"

He looked into her frightened face and lied. "No. He is dangerous, true, but I don't think he will do her harm."

Anne accepted his answer, knowing full well it was said to calm her. She accompanied him to the door, then slowly climbed the stairs, pistol clutched tightly in her hand. She retired to her chamber to wait out the remainder of the day, thankful her mother was in London. It was also a blessing she wouldn't have to explain Brandy's whereabouts to Maddie and Arthur, for they were away visiting Arthur's ill brother until late that evening. Brandy would certainly be home by then—Anne prayed it would be so.

Chapter 28

Brandy watched Roger's henchman enter the room with what appeared to be a tray of food. He placed it on the table beside the bed, lit the candle on the bureau, and turned to leave.

"Bart, isn't it?" He nodded. "How do you expect me to eat with my hands tied?" She held up her bound wrists.

He looked down at her hands, back up at her face, and shrugged his massive shoulders. "Ye'll manage."

"Please, won't you untie them just long enough for me to eat?" She hated to beg, but her arms were numb, and her shoulders ached.

He hesitated and shrugged again, his large shoulders nearly touching his ears. "I guess it'll be all right. But don't do nothin' funny." He untied the knots, pocketed the ropes, and left her alone, locking the door behind him.

Brandy sat up, rubbing her arms up and down, groaning. The blood, now free to flow, coursed painfully through her veins. It felt like a thousand needles puncturing her skin. She glanced over at the tray. She didn't want to accept Roger's hospitality, such as it was, but she was nearly faint from hunger. Besides, she would need her strength for the ordeal to come. *Whatever that happened to be.* She swung her bound legs over the side of the bed and reached for the tray, placing it on her lap. She took a bite of the stew, found it tasty, and soon devoured it, along with the small loaf of crusty bread. She placed the tray with the empty dishes back on the table but kept the small glass of red wine.

She sipped the wine as she looked about the room. It was small, windowless, and the ceiling was vaulted as if it were at the top of the house. Other than the bed she sat upon and the small table next to it, there was a small bureau pushed against the wall opposite the bed. She spied her reticule on top of it. She stood up and nearly keeled over, having forgotten her ankles were tied. She hopped toward the bureau, tripped on the edge of a small rug, and promptly fell flat on her face. She drew herself up, pain shooting up her arms, and leaned her stomach against the bureau's edge. She opened her reticule and thanked the Lord for small miracles. The pistol was still tucked inside. She pulled it out and set the reticule back on the bureau. She heard footsteps outside the door and quickly hopped back to the bed. She shoved the pistol under her pillow just as the door swung open.

Roger strode into the room. "Did you enjoy your supper?" he queried, smugly. He stood with his hands clasped behind his back, the epitome of self-assuredness.

"What are you planning? Keep me in here forever? I will be missed at home, you know."

"I sent a note to your cousin informing her that you would be staying for supper and would be home quite late. That should take care of matters for now." He lifted a brow. "I have also sent a note to Father Donnreed."

"To pray for your soul?"

"No—to marry us."

"I will not marry you," she stated calmly. Then, as a thought occurred, she continued, "We cannot be married this quickly. What about the—"

"The good Father has connections for obtaining certificates of marriage without delay, no posting of the banns. It will all be quite legal, I assure you, especially as I informed him of your delicate condition."

"My delicate condition?" She tilted her head to one side.

"Yes, the new addition to our family we'll be welcoming soon."

"You told him *what*!" She took a deep breath, mortified. "You will not get away with this," she shouted, hysteria beginning to take over, banishing her resolve to remain calm.

"I can and I will. Now, promise me you won't cause a scene in front of the good Father." He sat down on the bed, taking one of her hands in his.

She snatched her hand away and lifted it to slap his face. "You bastard!" she hissed.

He grabbed her hand and twisted it. The pain brought tears to her eyes. "I want you to be meek, if you can manage it. One wrong word out of you, or any display of disobedience, and Townsend will die."

Brandy nodded her head, keeping her eyes downcast. He didn't even try to conceal his maliciousness. He had been backed into a corner and meant to use any means possible to obtain what he wanted. She had to remain calm, to appear willing, and when the opportunity arose, she would shoot a hole through his black heart!

He pulled a length of rope from his jacket pocket and quickly retied her wrists. He pushed her back against the pillow, followed her descent, and covered her mouth with his. Gagging at his sour breath, she tried in vain to push him away.

He pulled back and brushed a lock of hair from her face. "You won't be rejecting my kisses once we're married, my dear. I mean to have you. Then, with you as my wife, we will return to Stonebrooke Manor and look for that journal. No one can gainsay me then." His hand slid down her throat and lifted the gold chain from around her neck. An odd expression came over his face as he gazed at the locket. Then he smiled.

"What is so important in the journal?"

"There is some incriminating evidence your father was stupid enough to write."

"How do you know?"

"He told Mr. Osbert."

"Who *is* Mr. Osbert?" Brandy asked, remembering the evil man who was the last person to see Philip alive.

"One of my men. He would inform your father of his next assignment."

"Were you responsible for involving Philip in your schemes?" When he didn't answer, she continued, "What are you all caught up in? Spying?" she asked, her eyes narrowed.

"So, you have heard the rumors."

"Are they true? Was my father a spy?"

Roger stared at her a moment, then shrugged. "I suppose since you will soon be my wife and cannot testify against me, it wouldn't hurt to tell you. No, your father was not a spy. But he was instrumental in bringing them into England."

"How?"

"Your father owed a lot of people a great deal of money. I, of course, had recommended a certain acquaintance of mine who was happy to generate a loan. When it became apparent that he was unable to repay the money at the allotted time, he was allowed to work for us as repayment."

"You forced him into it."

"Not exactly. It was simply a way for him to repay his debts. He allowed us to use Stonebrooke Manor as a warehouse for goods brought into England as well as those waiting to be shipped to France. He was responsible for scouring the countryside for other likely places to store goods as well as for people to assist us in our little operation."

Brandy digested this bit of news. She had no knowledge of goods being stored at Stonebrooke Manor, but she had heard about the smugglers. They often carried on quite openly because they knew they could instill terror in anyone who thought to bring them to justice. They were that powerful.

"So, you are nothing but a common smuggler."

"We like to think of ourselves as *free traders*."

"And a traitor to your country," she continued. "And you forced my father to do your dirty work."

Anger suffused his face, turning it bright red. "Your father was an incompetent rube. He messed up every assignment we gave him, then took the cowardly way out."

"My father was not a coward! He was nothing but your scapegoat. You used him! How dare you slander his name when you tricked him into joining your traitorous activities against his will!"

Roger stood up, shaking a fist at her. "These bloody English snobs will get what is coming to them. The French will win the war in Portugal, and I will be on the winning side. I have been spurned by the English for far too long. We'll see who comes out the victor in the end!"

He waved his arms about the room, a maniacal light in his eyes.

Brandy huddled in the corner of the bed, suddenly very afraid. He was most definitely crazed. Good heavens, but she had to get out of here!

Roger took a moment to calm himself, then strode to the door. He turned back to her. "I will come for you when Father Donnreed arrives. 'Til then, sweetheart, try to get some rest. You look awful."

She stuck her nose in the air. "I don't care a bloody fig what I look like, you...you cur!"

Roger merely laughed and locked the door behind him.

Brandy tried to rest. She needed her strength for whatever might come. She tossed and turned on the bed, her dreams active. Suddenly she began to shake. Her eyes flew open, her gaze taking in the hand shaking her shoulder. She screamed, her shriek shaking the rafters. Those hands! The ones from her nightmare!

Roger took a step back, staring at her in shock. "What the devil is wrong with you?"

Brandy came fully awake and sanity dawned, remembering where she was and why. Managing to sit up, she shook her head clear of the nightmare, and murmured inaudibly under her breath. Her hair, long ago unpinned, spilled over her shoulders in an auburn waterfall.

Roger looked down at her, noted her calmer demeanor, and his expression twisted into a lascivious grin. "'Tis time, Brandy." He untied her wrists and moved to unbind her ankles, his hands sliding down her legs. As he worked the knots in the rope around her ankles, Brandy slipped her hand under her pillow and pulled out the pistol.

She raised her arm, the small gun clutched tightly in her hand, her finger wrapped around the trigger, and leveled it at Roger's face. "Step away, Roger. Over there." She motioned him across the room. "Now!"

Roger looked momentarily shaken, then sneered as he rose slowly to his feet. "Now why would you want to do something so foolish?" He inched toward her, watching her intently.

"I mean it, Roger. I will shoot you if you come one step closer."

Roger lunged forward and Brandy instinctively pulled the trigger. The shot reverberated throughout the room as the pistol slipped from her numb fingers and clattered to the floor.

Roger stared at her incredulously, one hand pressed against his face. Blood seeped through his fingers and ran in narrow crimson rivulets down his cheek.

"What the hell—!" Bart came rushing into the room. He took in Roger's bleeding cheek, the gun on the floor, and the woman sitting in stunned silence on the bed. He laughed as he bent to retrieve the pistol and place it in Roger's outstretched hand.

"It ain't nice to shoot yer future husband on his weddin' day," Bart said, his voice full of laughter. He caught a glimpse of Roger's murderous expression and sobered. "The priest be waitin' downstairs."

"I am not going to marry you!" Brandy shouted, fear covering her like a blanket.

Roger swung his hand and slapped her across the face. Brandy fell back with a gasp, pain exploding in her cheek. It wasn't nearly as hard as the blow Bart had dealt, but nevertheless it rendered her momentarily stunned.

Roger reached into his pocket, pulled out a handkerchief, and pressed it against his injured cheek. He grabbed her arm in a vicious grip and looked down at her. "One more word out of you and Townsend is a dead man. After this little stunt, I just might kill him anyway." He shook her hard. "That was not very wise of you, my dear."

Brandy said not another word. She scooted off the bed and followed him from the room, down the stairs and into the salon. Her cheek throbbed in pain and she was lightheaded from the blow. A heavyset man dressed in black stood before the window, his back to the room. He turned when they entered, his gaze riveting first on Roger's bloody cheek before taking in Brandy's face, swollen and discolored. Brandy spied the white collar around his neck and the Bible clutched in his hand. Her mouth went dry.

"Good evening, Father—you're not Donnreed!" Roger exclaimed in surprise.

"That is correct, my son. Father Donnreed was called away on an urgent matter with one of our parishioners. I am Father Dinnmiddle, a close associate. He has informed me of your circumstances."

Roger shrugged. "One priest is as good as another, I suppose. Shall we begin?"

"My son, you are injured. We should tend to your wound first. And the lady, her cheek is quite swollen."

"'Tis nothing, Father," Roger answered with a wave of his hand and an air of dismissal. "Lady Brandy took a bit of a tumble, 'tis all." He glanced at Brandy. "I believe we're ready now, aren't we, my dear?" At Brandy's silence, Roger squeezed her arm. She grimaced in pain and nodded her head.

Without further ado, the priest opened the Bible and

began the marriage ceremony. His voice droned on, and Brandy, lost in thoughts of escape, was not paying attention. When Roger nudged her sharply in the ribs, she looked up to find the priest waiting patiently for her answer.

"What did you say?"

"Will you take this man to be your lawful wedded husband?" the priest repeated, solemnly.

She opened her mouth to answer *no*, but after another sharp jab to her side, she nodded.

"We can't hear you, my dear. Please tell the good Father you will." Roger's voice was laced with underlying threats.

"Oh, all right—yes!" Brandy jerked her arm away from Roger's grasp and glared at the priest.

"I now pronounce you man and wife." The priest shut the Bible with a thud and nodded to Roger. Roger kissed Brandy on the mouth. She kept her lips firmly closed until he had moved away. He pulled a bulky envelope from his waistcoat and handed it to the priest. "Thank you, Father."

With a last lingering look at Brandy, the priest followed Bart from the room leaving her alone with her unwanted husband. She waited for his next move; her stomach sinking with his first words. "Well, my dear, it seems we are now legally wed. And I, for one, am quite eager to claim my rights. Shall we retire? Tomorrow, we'll go to Stonebrooke Manor and get your father's journal."

Brandy backed away, but he reached out and grasped her arm. He leaned down until he was mere inches from her face. "You listen to me, girl. We are married and you will act the dutiful wife. If you don't, you know what will happen."

Yes, Brandy knew what would happen. He would kill Chandler and who knows what he'd do to Michael. Good Lord, what was she to do? The thought of Roger's hands on her body sickened her. She shuddered in disgust, trying to keep the bile from rising and choking her.

Without a word, Roger dragged her upstairs and deposited her into what she guessed was the master bedroom. It was in disrepair like the rest of the house—cracked ceiling, paper peeling from the walls—but there were more furnishings and in slightly better condition. Taking up most of the room was a massive bed covered in a red-and-gold coverlet, a small bedside table, a mahogany armoire and matching bureau, and a simple wooden table with two chairs. On the table was a tray, a carafe of red wine and two glasses upon it. On the bed was a lacy pink nightdress and matching robe. She blanched and reached for the wine, pouring herself a small draught of the liquid courage.

She was kept locked in the room for what seemed like an eternity. She waited out her destiny on the edge of the chair, sipping the wine. At least she wasn't bound and had the full use of her limbs. She wavered between anxiety and relief that the wedding night had yet to commence and knew Roger was keeping her waiting on purpose, heightening her anxiety of what was to come. Well, his plan was working. Her nerves were stretched to the breaking point, and she jumped at every little sound. *How can I stop him from bedding me?*

She thought of Chandler, bound like an animal in the bowels of the house, and hot tears blurred her vision. She could still feel the hatred in his gaze, it had been palpable. When she heard the key turn in the lock, she set the glass back on the tray and clasped her hands in her lap.

Roger pushed open the door. He had changed into a blue-and-gold robe, belted at the waist. His cheek had been bandaged. Tucked under one arm was a bottle of champagne, two crystal fluted glasses in his hand. He set the bottle and glasses on the table, locked the door, and dropped the key into the pocket of his robe.

"And how is my lovely wife? I'm sorry to have kept you waiting so long." He glanced at the bed. "You haven't changed into your wedding night outfit. Tsk, tsk, Brandy." While he baited her, he made a show of opening the bottle of champagne and pouring the sparkling wine into the glasses. He offered one to Brandy.

"I insist that we toast our marriage." He frowned when she shook her head. "Do I have to warn you again what will happen?" His voice sounded tired, as if bored with the banality.

Brandy's tenuous hold on her composure broke. "What kind of man are you? Is that the only way you can get a woman to cooperate, by threatening someone else's life?" She paused, thinking rapidly. "If you harm one hair on Chandler's head, you will never get the journal!"

"Aha, so you admit its existence!"

"No, I do not. But you seem so bloody set on the idea there is such a journal, perhaps there is." She waited, quivering with fear. "Well?"

He cocked his head to one side, as if considering her offer. "So, you do care for His Grace. I thought as much."

"No, I do not. It's just that, unlike you, I care for all living things, be they human or animal."

"Good Lord! You're not thinking of that bloody bird, are you?"

"Yes! You were a monster then and you are a monster now!"

His eyes narrowed and his lips became thin white lines. He placed the glasses on the table, and without breaking eye contact, shoved her onto the bed. She fell back and sidled across it until she could go no further, her back against the wall. He laughed, the ugly sound making her quake in fear.

He withdrew a pistol from the pocket of his robe and placed it on the bureau. He knelt on the bed and fell on top of her, trapping her body beneath his. Planting his mouth on hers, he kissed her hard, bruising her lips. She twisted her head back and forth, trying to escape his sickening touch. To keep her still, he placed his hands on either side of her face and continued his assault, shoving his tongue roughly into her mouth. He pulled back to whisper against her lips, "You are so beautiful. And you are mine," he cried jubilantly.

He twisted his hand in the folds of her riding jacket and, with a powerful jerk, tore it in two. He tugged the tattered garment off and threw it on the floor. He ripped the cotton bodice apart, exposing her breasts to his leering gaze. She tried to push him away, yet she was no match for his strength. He ran a hand over her breasts and taunted, "Your tits are lovely, my dear. Just as I knew they would be." He fastened his mouth on one and sucked noisily. Without warning, he bit down on the pink crest. She whimpered, squeezing her eyes tight against tears of pain.

She prayed Chandler would come for her before the nasty deed was done. As if in answer to her prayers, a loud knock on the door interrupted Roger's prelude to debauchery.

He cursed and sat up. "What is it?"

"You have a visitor, milord. I tried to explain that you were otherwise engaged, but she would not take *no* for an answer."

Roger jumped to his feet with a muttered curse. "I'll be back, my dear." As he strode to the door, he grabbed the pistol from the bureau and pocketed it in his robe. Brandy pulled the coverlet over her exposed breasts and murmured her gratitude for this brief reprieve from hell.

Roger entered the salon to find his sister standing before the window gazing out into the inky blackness, her hands behind her back. She turned when he entered the room and folded her hands in front of her.

"What do you want, Lacey?" Roger snapped as he crossed to the sideboard and poured himself a whiskey. He didn't bother to offer her one.

"It's been a long time since I've been here. Not since Mother died."

"Father was a terrible brute, wasn't he? The bastard made sure he spent the family fortune before dying."

"I—I have information for you," Lacey began tentatively. When her brother merely cocked a brow, she continued, "They suspect you, Roger."

His hand stilled, the glass halfway to his mouth. "Suspect me of what?"

"Spying, smuggling—among other things."

"Do they have evidence?"

"I'm not sure."

"What do they plan to do about it?"

"I don't know."

"Well, find out, damn it!" He grabbed her elbow and

escorted her toward the door. 'I will meet with you the day after tomorrow." He hesitated, before letting go of her arm. "I will let you in on a little secret, my dear. Lady Brandy Drummond and I were married this afternoon."

Lacey stared at him in shock. "You what?" she shrieked.

"She will come in handy, I think. Especially now. Not to mention I intend to thoroughly enjoy her delicious body."

"Don't be crude."

"Even as we speak, she is impatiently awaiting my return upstairs. You, ah, interrupted us at a most inopportune time." He smiled in amusement at his sister's horrified expression.

"Roger, she could ruin everything! If the truth were known—"

"The truth will not become known unless, of course, you don't deliver. Besides, we don't know for sure, do we?" He pushed her out the door. "You know what I need from you, sister dear. Do not disappoint me."

"You will get it," she snapped and without a backward glance, swept from the room and out the front door. Roger watched as she climbed into her carriage and disappeared into the night. He stroked his chin thoughtfully. He would have to do something about Lacey. She could become troublesome. His thoughts turned to Brandy, envisioning her lying naked on the bed, waiting for him. He became hard just thinking about what lay ahead. He rubbed his groin in anticipation, and with a harsh laugh, downed the whiskey. He set the empty glass on the table and quit the room.

Chapter 29

Chandler fought against his shackles, wrists raw from the leather bindings cutting into his skin. He laid his head back against the cold wall, gritting his teeth in rage.

He had been duped, betrayed by that bitch! He couldn't believe it, didn't want to believe it, but the evidence was there. He would never again trust a woman, especially her! Of course, it no longer mattered—the deed was done, and he was tied up tight. He'd let down his guard and she had taken full advantage. If he had kept up his vigilance, he would not have been set upon by Blackwell's men, who had obviously been tipped off by *her*. Now, he was trapped like an animal, awaiting the whim of a mad man. And he had thought he loved her! Oh, more fool you, he chided himself bitterly.

Chandler had spent last night thinking of her, of her perfumed body pressed tightly to his, her soft mouth pliant under his demanding kisses. His heart had swelled with love. Then she had appeared in this hellhole with Blackwell, showing her true colors. His lips curled into a snarl. When he got out of this Godforsaken prison, he would strangle her for her deception—right after he killed Blackwell!

Chandler heard someone descending the stairs, and his body tensed in anticipation. Thoroughly expecting to see his jailor with an expression of unabashed joy, he sat up fully alert when he heard the shadow hiss, "Chandler?" He recognized that voice.

"Good Lord, Jeff, 'tis you! Get me out of this bloody cell!"

Jeffrey couldn't contain his smile. Even incarcerated, Chandler had the tone of one totally in command. "As you wish, Your Grace."

Chandler waited impatiently for Jeffrey to unlock the door. "How did you get the key?"

"Compliments of that huge beast who was guarding you."

"Ah, that would be Bart. You didn't kill him, did you? I want that pleasure for myself. He went to great lengths to inflict pain. I'd like to return the favor." In the dim light from the torch on the wall, Jeffrey could see his friend's bruised and battered face.

Jeffrey stepped into the cell and, with a sharp knife, made quick work of sawing through the shackles. When the last leather strap had been cut, Chandler jumped to his feet, rubbing his sore wrists. His legs nearly buckled under him, but he stood steady.

"Where's Brandy?" Jeffrey asked, looking around the room.

Chandler shrugged his shoulders. "I don't know, nor do I care." He preceded Jeffrey up the stairs yet stopped at the slight pressure on his arm and looked back.

"Chandler, what happened? You look as though you would like to murder the lady."

"I would."

"What happened?" Jeffery repeated, still holding onto his arm.

"She was in on this," he added, his voice void of

emotion.

Jeffrey's heart sank. It couldn't be true! "I don't believe it. If you had seen her face when she came running back to tell me you had been captured, you wouldn't believe it either. She was quite distraught, Chandler."

"How did she know I had been captured?"

"She followed you when you left the rout. She spotted you unconscious on the beach with Blackwell and his cohorts and came back to tell me. It was her idea to come here." He ignored Chandler's snort of disbelief. "However, the plan must have backfired, because she didn't return home." He gazed intently at his friend. "She loves you, Chandler."

"Loves me? Then I am eternally grateful she doesn't despise me. Bart was quite talkative. It seems that Brandy and Blackwell were married this afternoon."

Jeffrey laughed, then sobered under Chandler's dark scowl. "Relax, old chap, the priest was a fake. He was one of our own. We waylaid the real priest. Posing as a man of the cloth, Flynn performed the ceremony."

Chandler turned to climb the stairs but stopped, his expression shuttered. "Do you mean to tell me that Brandy risked her neck to get me out of here? You put her in that kind of danger?"

"I didn't have much say in the matter. She received a note from Blackwell informing her that he held you captive. He wanted her father's journal in return for your life. There was no arguing with her. She was hell-bent on rescuing you."

"What journal?"

"Her father kept a journal. She gave it to me, but she was not going to give it to Blackwell. She's been

309

insisting for weeks that no such journal existed, but he refused to believe her. She thought if he wanted it that badly, it contained some damaging information. I gave it to Blanchard."

Chandler was not yet ready to even hope she was innocent. His emotions had taken a beating these past hours and he wasn't prepared to give up his thoughts of betrayal. He glanced at Jeffrey, who was still talking.

"I tried to talk her out of it, but, as you well know, she has a mind of her own. Now, don't look at me like that. I wasn't happy with the plan either, but we had no choice. Brandy was going to come here, no matter what. Besides, she was the only way to get to Blackwell...and you."

"Where are they now?"

"I don't know."

"I do. I can bloody well bet that at this moment Blackwell is trying to consummate the purported marriage. And if he has dared to touch one hair on her head—he's a dead man!"

Jeffrey hurried to catch up with Chandler, who was bounding up the stairs as if demons were snapping at his heels.

****

"Go away, Roger." Brandy tried to talk reasonably with the man looming over her, while masking her fear. "I will never submit to you willingly."

Roger took the pistol from the pocket of his robe and laid it on the bedside table. He sat on the bed and reached out to her. "We are married, Brandy. You are my wife, hence you will obey me. I wish to make love to you."

Her mind worked frantically for a plan as his mouth descended on hers. She moved her body from side to side, kicking her legs, struggling to dislodge him, but he was determined and therefore unyielding. He slanted his mouth over hers, the odor of whiskey making her gag.

She bit his lip, drawing blood, and he howled in pain just as the door crashed in. Both occupants of the bed turned toward the gaping doorway. Chandler took in the scene in one quick glance, his visage black with fury.

"Chandler," breathed Brandy, relief making her weak. Her gaze swept over him, and she sucked in her breath. Good Lord! What had they done to him? One of his eyes was nearly swollen shut, and dried blood was clustered at the corner of his mouth. His face was bruised.

Roger rolled over in a flash and grabbed the gun off the table. He raised the barrel and aimed it at Chandler's chest. With his other hand, he caressed Brandy's bare breasts. "You're just in time, Townsend. We were about to consummate our marriage." He smiled cruelly as he twisted Brandy's nipple. She grimaced in pain and tried to push his hand away.

Chandler growled and took a step into the room. "Get your hands off her, Blackwell." He had noticed her discolored jaw and cheek, the sight of the large bluish-purple bruises further igniting his rage.

Roger grinned without mirth. He had not missed the emotion crossing the duke's face. Changing tactics, he warned, "One more step, Townsend, and she's dead." He swung the pistol around to Brandy's head. To Jeffrey, who had just come down the hallway and was now standing behind Chandler in the doorway, he ordered, "Throw your gun under the bed, Alden." Jeffrey did so, reluctantly.

"Let her go, Blackwell," Chandler said, his tone

murderous. "You are already a dead man. What you do now will decide whether you die quick or slow."

"I mean to have her. If you care to watch, by all means, make yourself comfortable."

"Over my dead body."

"That can be arranged." He laughed and, with the barrel of the gun, brushed an auburn tress from Brandy's face, all the while taunting Chandler. "She is beautiful, isn't she? Hair the color of fine French cognac—eyes like emeralds. And her breasts, my mouth aches to kiss them. In fact, I already have." He ran the pistol over one, the contact with the cold metal making the peak harden. He lifted the delicate chain around her neck and watched the locket swing back and forth before he snatched it off her neck and pocketed it. But he had made the fatal mistake of looking away. It was all Chandler needed to strike.

He leapt onto Roger, knocking the pistol from his hand and sending it sailing across the room. He wrapped his hands around Roger's throat and squeezed. Roger clawed at the hands around his neck, his eyes bulging, his complexion ashen. With renewed strength, he shook off the duke, and the two tumbled to the floor in a flurry of fists.

Brandy jumped from the bed and ran to Jeffrey, clutching her torn bodice together. She watched in horror as Chandler pulverized Roger with his fists. She turned her head away, unable to watch the horrible scene unfold.

Chandler picked Roger up off the floor and threw him across the room, slamming him into the far wall, where he slithered down, his legs stretched out in front of him. When Chandler came near, Roger raised his legs and shoved them into Chandler's stomach, sending him flying back against the bed. Roger rolled over and reached for the pistol. He grinned at Chandler, blood streaming from a cut above his left eye, another at the corner of his mouth. He raised the pistol, leveling it at Chandler's heart.

"Drop it, Blackwell." Ross Blanchard stood in the doorway, a pistol aimed at Roger's head.

Roger glanced at the door in surprise, and Chandler leapt forward, knocking Roger's arm upward just as he pulled the trigger. The bullet discharged and whizzed past Brandy to lodge in the door jamb.

Roger's shout of laughter drew the men's attention. "An eye for an eye, eh, Brandy?"

As a group they looked at him in confusion, then over at Brandy. Chandler's eyes widened in alarm when he saw the blood trickling down her arm. Dazed, Brandy followed his gaze to where a searing pain had sprouted. Seeing the blood seeping from the wound, she did something she had never done in her life—she fainted.

Jeffrey caught her before she hit the floor. "The bullet must have grazed her arm," he observed, withdrawing a handkerchief from his jacket pocket. He quickly wrapped it around the wound, stopping the blood.

"You're lucky I don't kill you now," Chandler snarled. He pulled Roger up from the floor and threw him at Blanchard.

"Where he's going is worse than death," Blanchard replied tightly.

"The bitch shot me!" Roger shouted, pointing to his bandaged cheek.

Blanchard looked down at a still unconscious

Brandy with something akin to admiration. "You most likely deserved it." He left the room dragging a defeated Blackwell with him.

Chandler gathered Brandy in his arms, mindful of her injured arm, and, holding her close, followed Jeffrey downstairs to the drawing room. A group of men was gathered there, but with a nod from Blanchard, they disappeared outside.

Chandler laid Brandy on the settee. She was out cold. He reached for one of her hands and enclosed it in his own warm one, rubbing it gently. "She's in shock," he said to no one in particular. Jeffrey handed him his cloak with which Chandler used to cover her.

"All right, Blackwell. Let's hear it." Blanchard trained his pistol on Roger.

"I have nothing to say."

"Have it your way. I believe you'll talk to the authorities. You, man!" He gestured to the butler who hovered in the doorway. "Fetch appropriate clothing for your master." He eyed Roger evenly. "An extended stay at Newgate will loosen your tongue, I think. I'm sure Lady Brandy will have quite a tale to tell."

"She can't testify against me! She's my wife!" Roger crowed triumphantly.

"Think again, Blackwell. It was a ruse. The priest was one of our men," Jeffrey informed him with a grin.

Roger paled, then nodding his head in Brandy's direction, asked with a sneer, "Have you taken a good look at her?"

"What are you babbling about, Blackwell?" Blanchard demanded, glancing over at Brandy in bemusement.

"Almost like a ghost from the—"

Blanchard flicked his wrist in annoyance, grabbed Blackwell's arm, and led him from the room.

Chapter 30

Every window in Stonebrooke Manor was illuminated. Chandler slid off the horse's back, Brandy cradled in his arms. He bounded up the front steps and pushed open the door with his boot. He strode into the foyer, past a startled Arthur, and up the stairs. He opened the first door he came to and laid Brandy on the bed. He sat down beside her and, with a tender touch, brushed the hair off her forehead.

Maddie came rushing into the room and stopped with a horrified gasp, her hand clasped over her mouth. "Miss Brandy! What happened? Is she hurt?" She hurried over to the bed and stared down at her young mistress. She turned to glare at the bruised and battered man. "What have you done to her?" she accused him, her eyes narrowing. "I'm calling the authorities."

"She is not harmed by my hand."

"But the bruises… And why is she sleeping?"

"She's fainted, 'tis all." His voice was tired, edged with worry.

"Miss Brandy does not faint."

Chandler ignored her indignant tone. "She's been shot and most likely is still in shock. The bullet grazed her arm. 'Tis a small injury and shouldn't do any residual harm. You'll need to dress the wound." He paused and looked around. "Where in the hell is everyone?"

"Lady Whyte is in London. Miss Anne is—"

Maddie didn't finish her sentence as she ran from the room to gather the supplies needed to tend to her mistress.

"I'm here, Maddie. Good Lord—Brandy! What has happened? Why her clothes are torn—and blood!" Anne rushed over to the bed and gazed down at her cousin just as Brandy's eyes began to flutter open.

"Chandler?" Her voice was no more than a whisper.

"I'm here, sweet." He turned to Anne. "She's had quite an ordeal. Do you have any whiskey or cognac in the house?"

Anne nodded and hurried from the room, returning soon with a short glass of cognac. Chandler slipped his arm around Brandy and, supporting her back, placed the glass to her lips and commanded her to drink. She obeyed, stiffening as the liquor burned its way down her throat. She slumped back against the bed.

"Is it over, Chandler?"

"Yes, you are safe now. But I must leave. I shall return in the morning." He stood, taking a last look, his expression inscrutable.

Brandy sagged against the pillows, watching him retreat. *He blames me. He hates me.* She closed her eyes; she was miserable. Her arm throbbed and her face ached.

Anne moved to the other side of the bed as Maddie entered the room with a tray and set it on the bedside table. She pulled the handkerchief from around Brandy's arm and, grabbing a clean cloth, dipped it in the bowl of warm water and gently cleaned the wound. She applied a thick salve and wrapped her arm in a clean linen cloth. "This be from Arthur's sister's larder. She's quite knowledgeable about balms and such." She stood up and smoothed her skirts. "There, that should do the trick," she announced with a nod of her head. Declaring that some hot broth was just the thing, she went scurrying from the room.

After she left and they were alone, Anne sat on the bed and reached for her cousin's hand. "What happened, Brandy? And don't whitewash it. I want the truth," she demanded.

Brandy quickly related the sordid story, including how she had shot Roger and in return he had shot her, although by pure happenstance. She ended with, "So, you see, I am married to the blackguard."

"Well, then you will just unmarry him."

"Chandler blames me for his incarceration. Roger made a point of letting him know that I was in on it."

"But you weren't!"

"I know, but Roger made Chandler think I was. I couldn't say a word for fear Roger would kill him. Oh, Anne, he hates me."

"Oh, I don't think he hates you. Quite the opposite, if you ask me. Lord Montaldene will explain everything to him. You'll see. It will all turn out for the best."

Brandy seriously doubted that, but to appease Anne, she nodded in agreement, stifling the overwhelming urge to burst hysterically into tears.

****

During the night, Chandler had gone over in detail the entire macabre scene in Blackwell's cellar. Jeffrey had filled in the gaps, beginning with what Brandy had witnessed on the beach to when she had disappeared inside Blackwell Hall.

Looking back, Chandler had thought that she'd seemed genuinely distraught at his imprisonment and a spark of uncertainty at her collusion with Blackwell had flared. Further, on reflection, the last look she had cast him while ascending the stairs had been full of anguish and—something else.

Chandler wanted to trust her, he loved her, for bloody sakes, but, if he trusted her, then everything he'd believed in since childhood would have been for naught. It wasn't easy to dismiss a lifetime of beliefs. He had yet to read her father's journal and had only her word she was not in league with Blackwell.

Time would tell.

The next morning, Chandler strode into Brandy's bedchamber, stopping beside the bed. He stood, staring down at her, his blue eyes inscrutable. "How are you feeling?"

"Much better. Anne insisted I stay in bed today. I'm not a'tall ill, and the wound is healing…" Her words trailed off, his rigid stance and unflinching stare making her nervous.

"I'm sure you are sorry that your little ruse didn't work."

"There was no ruse."

He raised a brow, watching her carefully with his next words. "I will concede that you were not in on my capture and imprisonment. However, there is still the matter of whether you were in league with Blackwell on the rest."

Brandy, deflated, turned her head away. "If you are determined to think the worst of me, so be it. My denials fall on deaf ears."

Chandler leaned his hip against the bedpost and crossed his arms over his chest. "You are not married to Blackwell. The priest was one of our men."

She swung back to him. "Truly? Oh, thank the

319

Lord!"

"However, Roger believed you were. Not that it would make a difference to him, mind you. Did you consummate the marriage?"

Brandy gasped at the insult and raised her chin in indignation. She regarded him with a fierce look, a scathing retort on her lips, but beneath his icy stare, the reply just as quickly died. And then her heart began to shatter.

"Chandler, please, listen. I detested Roger Blackwell. How could you possibly believe I would marry that bounder of my own free will, much less consummate it with him? And I have told you repeatedly that I am not in collusion with him—on any matter." She stared up into Chandler's forbidding countenance. "Didn't Lord Montaldene explain what happened?"

"Oh, yes, my dear, he did indeed. But I know how good an actress you can be."

"But I *shot* him!"

"That merely proves you didn't want to bed him."

Brandy stiffened with pride. "Go ahead, believe what you will. You are impossible." She turned to stare out the window. From the corner of her eye, she saw him turn away. He hesitated at the door, looked back at her briefly, then strode from the room, his booted footsteps rapping along the wooden floor.

She sagged against the pillows and, burying her face in her hands, cried until there were no more tears to shed. Her dry racking sobs filled the room.

Anne rushed in, took one look at her cousin, and wrapped her arms around her. "Oh, Brandy, he'll come around. You'll see."

Brandy mumbled into Anne's shoulder. Anne pulled

back and raised Brandy's tear-streaked face. "What?"

"I said, I don't give a bloody fig if he comes around. He is an arrogant cad, and I hope I never lay eyes on him again. To think I actually cared about him—risked my life to save his miserable hide." She disengaged herself from Anne's embrace and rose from the bed. She walked to the fireplace and, grabbing the poker, stoked the dying embers into leaping flames. "He can go to the devil!"

****

Lydia Alden paid a visit later that day. Brandy received her in the drawing room, surprised by her gesture of friendliness. She asked Maddie to bring tea and took a seat on the settee next to her guest.

"How are you, Lady Brandy? I must say, we were all very worried about you." Elegantly dressed in a bright yellow day dress, the Marchioness of Montaldene looked like a breath of spring in the otherwise dull winter day.

"It was quite an experience. My arm pains me a bit, but other than that…" She shrugged her shoulders.

"I can certainly understand. Jeffrey told me where he and Chandler found you."

Brandy blushed and lowered her gaze. Lydia reached out and clasped her hands. "There is no need to be embarrassed. I'm only glad they found you in time."

"Yes, it could have been much worse."

"Jeffrey told me you shot Blackwell."

"Yes," she answered with a lopsided grin.

"Well, good for you. I can only hope I'd be that brave if I were in the same situation."

Maddie brought in the tea service and placed it on the low table in front of them. She poured and offered the marchioness and Brandy each a cup. She settled Brandy back against the settee, tucking one of the embroidered pillows under her injured arm. "You must keep your arm elevated, Miss Brandy."

Brandy accepted Maddie's ministrations with a smile and waited for her to leave before turning back to Lydia.

"What's happened to Roger?"

"He is in Newgate Prison. I hope he rots there. I'm sure I sound quite cold, but that man is not only a traitor to his country but also responsible for many deaths."

"My father's included. Is—is Chandler still at Alden Ridge?" Brandy tried to sound nonchalant—after all, she didn't care where he was—but even to her own ears she sounded far too interested.

"Yes, he is. He and Jeffrey have been closeted with Blanchard all morning."

Arthur appeared in the doorway. "Excuse me, Miss Brandy. That man is here." He sounded irritated. "Along with two other gentlemen."

"What man, Arthur?"

"*That* man."

"Oh, I see. Send them in." She turned to Lydia. "It must be Chandler. Arthur isn't too fond of the duke."

"Then the other two must be Jeffrey and Ross." Lydia looked up as the three men strode into the room. She rose to her feet and went to Jeffrey's side, linking her arm through his.

Brandy watched Chandler enter the room, and her heart melted at the sight. He was breathtakingly handsome, his presence filling the room. He nodded to her, smiled at Lydia, and moved to the fireplace, where he rested his arm on the mantel.

"You're looking much better this afternoon, Lady Brandy," Jeffrey remarked, drawing his wife down beside him on the opposite settee. "Your bruises are starting to fade. How's the wound?"

"It pains me a little, but otherwise I hardly know it's there. Lord Merrick, I owe you a debt of gratitude."

Blanchard did not rejoin nor return her smile—it was doubtful he even heard her. His gaze was riveted at a spot above Chandler's head, on the portrait of Brandy that Anne had recently painted and now hung above the fireplace.

Brandy glanced over in consternation at Lydia who gave her an encouraging smile. Still, her chest tightened with anxiety. Why were they all looking so serious? Was there more bad news? Were they all still convinced she was guilty, and they were here to haul her off to prison? She trained her gaze on Blanchard, who had abandoned the portrait and was now regarding her evenly.

He cleared his throat and, after a quick glance at Chandler, turned back to Brandy. "Lady Brandy, first let me say how happy I am that you were not harmed any more than you were. Obviously, it could have gone much worse." He held out his hand and in his palm was her locket. "I believe this is yours."

Brandy reached out and took the locket. "Thank you, milord. I thought it was lost forever."

"I found it in Blackwell's pocket. He claimed it was a token of your affection." He cleared his throat and continued, "I have a few questions to ask you."

"Certainly." Her heart pounded, and she wished Chandler would give her a sign, any sign of reassurance. However, he just stood there avoiding eye contact and staring at a spot on the rug.

"I have read your father's journal. He was involved in some rather illicit activities. Blackwell was behind those dealings. I understand you were friendly with Blackwell on several occasions."

Brandy eyes widened in dismay. Her efforts to make Chandler jealous had come back to haunt her. "Milord, I can assure you that I was not on friendly terms with Roger Blackwell. I will admit that on occasion I might have used him in some small way, and it may have seemed that I cared for him." She tried not to blush when she felt Chandler's gaze on her and continued to focus on Blanchard. "Quite frankly, I despise the man. My father had betrothed me to him without my consent. From what I have gathered, Roger threatened him with blackmail. And I was the prize. I can assure you I truly detest the man." She cocked a brow. "I even shot him when he tried to drag me downstairs to the priest."

"Yes, he exclaimed quite loudly that you had shot him. Well done." Blanchard cracked a small smile. "As I said, I have read your father's journal. Would you permit us to search his study as well? There may be more we can ascertain from his papers."

"Of course." Her glance took in the group around her. Chandler was still avoiding her gaze, but his countenance was now thoughtful. Jeffrey and Lydia looked sympathetic.

"Milord, I am not nor was I ever involved in Roger's activities against the Crown," she reiterated. "The only thing I am guilty of is ignorance. I was not aware of my father's activities until after his death."

Blanchard's countenance softened, and he smiled. "Yes, we know that now. It's just that there is some very pertinent information in your father's journal about your brother, and I'd like to see if there is perhaps more hidden in his papers."

"Michael? He would never betray England! In fact, Roger made mention of him. I do believe he is responsible for his disappearance. I can only call it that, as I have had no word from him in months. He also said that it was in his power to see him dead." She stopped talking when she witnessed Chandler and Blanchard exchange a startled glance.

"We will be sure to question him on that as well," Blanchard assured her. "However—"

Chandler straightened. "Ross, we should not say another word until we are sure of his whereabouts."

Brandy looked back and forth between Ross and Chandler before settling her heated gaze on Chandler. She stood up and faced him. "Just what do you know about my brother? You were fully aware I have been worried sick about him." She waved her hand around the room. "You, more than anyone, know what I've been through, what I've been forced—" She stopped, not wanting to say too much. "You've given me one vague excuse after another. And all this time—" She turned on Blanchard. "I've had just about enough of this intrigue! If you have word of Michael, I would appreciate it if you would tell me."

Chandler stepped forward and for the first time looked Brandy in the eye. "I'm sure your brother is fine."

"You know where he is? All this time, you've led me to believe you knew nothing."

"It was in his best interest, as well as yours." He wrapped his hand around her uninjured arm in a gentle hold. She jerked out of his grasp.

"You, Your Grace, can go to the devil. If you will excuse me, I feel a headache coming on that will probably last the rest of my life." She swept from the room but stopped when Blanchard spoke out.

"Lady Brandy, do not blame the duke. He was sworn to secrecy. Believe me, when we have definite word of Michael's whereabouts, I myself will personally inform you. In the meantime, please know we are doing everything we can to keep him and Andrew safe."

At the mention of Andrew's name, Brandy turned to Chandler and for the first time noticed the worry hidden deep in his sapphire-blue eyes. He was concerned about his brother, and here she was screaming like a banshee. "I apologize for my lack of compassion, Your Grace. I hope that Lord Andrew, too, is safe." Without another word, she turned and left the room. Lydia stood up intending to go after her newfound friend but was stayed by Jeffrey's hand upon her wrist. He nodded his head toward Chandler, who was already striding after Brandy. Lydia smiled and sat back down beside her husband.

Blanchard pulled Philip's journal from his coat pocket and flipped through the pages until he came to the entry he had read last night. He reread the words and again his gaze sought the portrait above the hearth. He frowned, shook his head, and pocketed the journal. "I will be heading back to London after I look through Drummond's papers." He turned to Lydia. "I thank you for your hospitality." He nodded to Jeffrey. "I will be in touch soon." He headed toward the old earl's study to see what he could find hidden there. Jeffrey and Lydia took their leave as well, leaving the duke and Brandy alone upstairs.

Chandler caught up with Brandy as she was closing her chamber door. He stayed it with one booted foot and pushed it open. Brandy stepped back into the room, clutching the bodice of her gown. "What do you want?"

"I think we had better talk." Chandler shut the door and moved toward her with catlike grace.

"We have nothing to talk about. You have made that perfectly clear. Stupid little actress that I am, I did understand that much." She walked to the window and pulled back the curtains to stare blindly out at the drive, acutely aware of the charismatic man behind her. "Besides, it's not proper for you to be in my chamber, Your Grace."

"It might not be proper, but we are not strangers, Brandy."

She spun on her heel, her face tinted pink. "Do you have to remind me of that? You are no gentleman, Chandler."

"True, but I never claimed to be." He watched her with a look of regret in his eyes. "I want to apologize for doubting you. I should have known Roger would use you to trick me."

Brandy tossed her head, her heavy auburn plait snaking over her shoulder. "I think it's a little too late for an apology." She stamped her foot in exasperation. "I can't believe you would actually think I'd collaborate with that—that bounder!"

"Your beauty blinded me and I lost my head?" he offered with a crooked smile.

"I find nothing amusing in any of this."

"But life is so much more fun when touched with humor. 'Tis good for the soul."

"Hah! Since when have you embraced that belief? You are the consummate picture of inflexibility and ill humor." She heaved a heavy sigh and waved her hand through the air. "There is no hope for you, I'm afraid. You have led a sadly depraved life, Your Grace. Besides, you're dangerous," she added as an afterthought.

As he came closer, she backed away until, bumping into the wall, she could go no farther.

"Dangerous, am I? You throw yourself headlong into anything that comes your way without a thought to the risks. Yes, Jeff told me how you pleaded with him to let you go to Blackwell Hall. What could you have been thinking? Rescue me, indeed! Damn it, Brandy, you endangered your life!"

Chandler was working himself into a fine rage, and Brandy, watching his fury build, smiled to herself, filled with abundant happiness. He cared, her heart sang, he did indeed care!

"I would have helped anyone in need. A dog, a bird. Besides, I never liked Roger and I didn't want him to get away with it. I enjoyed thwarting him at every turn."

"You allowed me to believe you cared for him, even a little. Why?"

Brandy blushed. She had hoped he would have forgotten that part. "Hmmm, I, ah—"

She stepped sideways along the wall, willing her head to stop spinning. His nearness was affecting her physically, and she felt faint.

Chandler was watching her with interest, fascinated by the play of emotions crossing her face. When she looked up at him, her eyes were a stormy green, and he smiled inwardly. So, she was as affected as he. His expression set, a wicked gleam in his eyes, he hauled her into his arms and kissed her, a long, slow kiss that succeeded in propelling her over the edge.

She breathed a sigh of surrender and wrapped her arms around his neck, her fingers tangling in the soft curls at his nape. He bent her over his arm, molding her soft body to his hard frame, and deepened the kiss. She murmured low, kissing him back with all her pent-up passion.

A sound outside the door brought her to her senses. She unfurled her arms from around his neck, straightened, and stepped aside. "Chandler, this isn't a'tall proper." Her voice was shaky, her reprimand not at all firm.

Chandler laughed and conceded, albeit reluctantly. "As you wish, milady." Then, suddenly, he gathered her back into his arms, and holding her tight, he whispered against her hair, "I'm sorry. I'm so very sorry for doubting you."

Knowing how proud he was, this admission was most assuredly hard to admit. She stroked his back as he continued. "You don't know, Brandy. I have spent my entire life mistrusting women. I should have known better with you."

She leaned out of his embrace and reached up to stroke his cheek. "I can understand why you might have thought me guilty of following in Philip's footsteps. How were you to know? But how could you have believed I'd work with Roger? You were so cruel after I had been shot. You wounded me further with your words."

"I had to be sure."

"My words should have sufficed as the truth."

He gazed down into her face, his eyes soft with remorse. "I'm a fool, Brandy. A bigger fool than you know."

"I'm not like the others, you know. I'm not like your mother."

He drew back. "How did you—?"

"Abigail."

He pulled her into his embrace, holding her as if she might disappear if he but loosened his grip.

"When did you start to trust in me?"

"The moment I learned you'd shot Blackwell confirmed what I had already begun to believe. And then, of course, when you implied you may have used him to make me jealous."

Brandy started to argue the point, but instead shrugged her shoulders as if admitting defeat, and smiled.

"Can you forgive me?"

She laughed, lightening the mood. "Only if you promise to come back and kiss me again."

He smiled and placed a warm kiss on the side of her mouth—lest it turn into something more. Turning to leave, he paused to look back at her from the doorway. "Rest assured, sweet, I will be back." With that he quit the room, his hearty laugh echoing behind him.

Brandy stared at the empty portal, still feeling a small bit of uncertainty. He might believe in her now, and feel sorry for his misplaced censure, but he had yet to tell her he liked her, much less profess his love. Desire her? Most assuredly. But love her? That remained to be seen.

Chapter 31

Chandler returned sooner than expected. Later that evening, he was in Brandy's bedchamber not caring a whit about the impropriety. "I have to return to London."

"When do you leave?"

"In the morning."

"So soon?" Brandy was crestfallen. She had hoped to spend some time with him. With her blossoming love coupled with her concern for Michael, she needed to be near him, to draw from his strength.

Chandler laughed at her forlorn expression. "I'll be back soon, sweet. I need to stop at Marbury Hall on the way to town. I'm afraid I've neglected my duties for far too long. I will leave for London from there." He studied her closely. "What is it, sweet? Will you miss my kisses that much?"

His teasing remark slid right past her. A sick feeling knotted in her stomach at the mention of London. London meant Vivian Beaumont. "Chandler," she started out casually, "I had an interesting conversation with Lady Vivian at the Blanchards' soiree." She took a deep breath before blurting out, "Are you betrothed to her?"

Chandler, incredulous, leaned his shoulder against one of the bed posts. "Why, did she say as much?"

"Well, she hinted at it, yes." When he didn't respond, "Well, are you?"

"Jealous, sweet?"

"Bloody hell, Chandler, just answer me!"

"Tsk, tsk—such language from a sweet little country girl." He stopped teasing when he saw her gritting her teeth in frustration. "I am as much betrothed to Vivian as you were to Blackwell. Satisfied?"

"Hmmm, very." She was staring at his mouth. She closed the distance between them, stood on her toes, and circled his neck with her slim arms. She was surprised by her boldness, but she wanted him to kiss her.

Chandler didn't need any more of an invitation. He caught her up against him, his hands tangling in her flowing hair as he brought her face up for his kiss. He growled low in his throat as she naively kindled the flames lurking just below the surface. His hands slipped down her back to cup her soft backside, nestling her against his arousal. Brandy molded her body to his, and kissed him back, putting every ounce of love and desire behind it. The kiss was one of long-starved passion.

Chandler came to his senses first and gently, but firmly, set her away from him. "There are people about, my love. They could walk in at any moment." He laughed at her disgruntled expression. "I'll be back soon. We'll pick up where we left off." He took her hand. "Walk me downstairs." Brandy muttered something about the lack of privacy and allowed him to lead her from her chamber.

On the front stoop, he brushed his lips across hers. "Try not to get into any trouble while I'm gone, sweet."

She grinned. "Certainly, Your Grace."

He smacked her lightly on her bottom, then mounted his horse and cantered down the drive. As she watched him fade from view, her thoughts turned inward. She wished she knew where she stood with him. He believed her innocent of his capture and of being in collaboration with Roger, but would something come along to test that trust? To cause the doubt to flare up again?

Her thoughts veered to her latest concern, a worry she'd tried hard to ignore. Her time of the month was late. She slid her hand down to rest on her belly. What if she carried his child? How would he take the news? Marriage, of course, would be out of the question. She knew all too well what he thought of that sacred rite.

Anne came up beside her. "He is gone?"

"Yes. He is off to Marbury Hall, then on to London. He bade me wait here for him. He will be back in a fortnight."

"What are you going to do?"

She gaped at her cousin in surprise, thinking she had read her thoughts. "About what?"

Anne was gazing after Chandler. "Him."

"Oh, I don't know. 'Tis odd. I didn't like him for the longest time. He would insult me at every turn and kiss me whenever it pleased him. Then he thinks I betray him, and he bends his anger on me. But the more I'm with him, the more I want to be with him." She turned to Anne with a sigh. "I think nothing will come of it, Anne. When Michael returns, we will live here quietly, with you and Aunt, of course. What is so funny?" she demanded.

"Do you actually believe all that drivel?"

"I most certainly do!"

"Oh, cousin, you love him."

She hesitated only a moment. "Yes, I do. But he doesn't love me," she whispered brokenly.

****

Lacey Alexander closed the door to her husband's

study and made her way to his large desk set in one corner of the room. She paused, listening for sounds, but the house was quiet. She went through the papers on the desk, careful to place them neatly back in order. When she could find nothing of any consequence, she began to panic. For all her bravado, she was terrified of her brother. Roger Blackwell knew the one secret that could ruin not only her marriage but her life as well.

"What are you doing?" Thomas stood in the doorway, watching his wife rifle through his papers. Lacey, unaware he had come into the room, thought quickly. "I—I thought I would straighten your desk." She watched him approach, clasping her hands together to still their trembling.

"What is it, Lacey? You seem quite out of sorts."

"'Tis nothing, Thomas."

He went behind the desk and sat in the tall leather chair. Leaning back, he watched closely for his wife's reaction to his forthcoming news. "Your brother is in Newgate."

"Newgate? Whatever for?" She turned her back on him, studying the oak paneled walls, avoiding her husband's searching look. Roger in prison! She wavered between relief and despair. Would he take her down with him?

"Spying, smuggling, among other things," he said. "Did you know?"

She swung back around. "Of course not! Although, nothing he does surprises me. We—we weren't very close, you know." Her pale brown eyes were void of emotion.

"So, were you looking for anything special?"

"What? Oh, no, I was just straightening the papers."

"I appreciate it, of course, but in the future, I will see after my own affairs."

"Of course, dear. Well, I must be off. I have a fitting for a new gown." Lacey waved her hand and hurried from the room.

Thomas watched her leave, a frown furrowing his brow. He picked up his pipe, filled it with tobacco, and lit the bowl. The fragrant smoke circled his dark head as he contemplated his wife's strange behavior.

Chapter 32

"We're going to London," Brandy announced without preamble.

Anne looked up from her painting, the brush poised above the canvas. "When do we leave?"

"Tomorrow." She narrowed her eyes at her cousin. "Why aren't you surprised?"

Anne laughed. "I've been waiting for you to come to this decision. I can see how restless you've become."

Brandy joined in her laughter. "Well, then, let's get packed and be on our way."

"What about the duke? Isn't he expecting you to be here when he returns?"

"It's been over a fortnight and he has not shown up at my door. I'm tired of waiting."

"Well, whatever the reason, I'm anxious to see Mama again."

The winter day dawned crisp and clear, and they arrived in London by early evening. The setting sun illuminated the city and once again Brandy marveled at the skyline. Today, however, her spirits were higher than they had been that day several months ago when she had arrived in London filled with trepidation and uncertainty. She was anxious now, but for a different reason, for the task she had set weighed heavily on her mind. Could she pull it off?

Abigail and Jessie were delighted to see the two girls

again. By mutual consent, Brandy and Anne had decided not to tell them of the near disaster at Blackwell Hall. Brandy's bruises were all but faded and her arm had healed to where she winced in pain only if she moved it too fast.

"Chandler is out right now, Brandy. But he should be home soon," Abigail offered, shortly after they had arrived at the townhouse.

"Oh, no matter," Brandy said with a slight shrug of her shoulders, trying her best to sound nonchalant. She hid her apprehension that Chandler might be spending his time with the lovely Lady Vivian despite his reassurances to the contrary. She had spent many a fitful night troubled by her fanciful imaginations of them together.

They were just sitting down to dinner when Chandler strode into the dining room. He paused in the doorway, his eyes widening in pleasure when he spotted Brandy seated at his table. He greeted the other ladies, then, gently taking hold of Brandy's arm, he drew her out of her chair and out of the room. "Excuse us," he said over his shoulder as he led Brandy into his study. He shut the door, leaned back against the hard wood, and pulled her into his embrace.

"What are you doing here?" he asked with a lazy smile, lifting her hand to his mouth and kissing each fingertip—one by one.

"I, ah, was bored at Stonebrooke Manor," she offered, becoming lightheaded from his nibbling. "And you did say you'd return in a fortnight. I became worried." She rested her free hand on his shoulder.

"I'm sorry. My duties at Marbury Hall took longer than expected. I was going to send you a note on the morrow." His gentle caresses were warming her toes.

"You don't mind that I've come to London, do you?" Her fingers tangled in his hair.

"Not at all. I'm quite pleased to see you." He captured her lips in a searing kiss. "I've missed you, sweet," he whispered against her mouth before his lips traveled down her neck, placing soft, wet kisses. Her head fell back exposing her slender neck to his exquisite torture. She clung to him for support.

"We should return. They will wonder where we are and what we're doing," Brandy murmured after several long minutes of bliss.

"Mmmm," was his response as he recaptured her mouth. As the kiss deepened, she gave in to the sensations he was creating, wanting more, until, ready to spiral out of control, she broke contact first. "This is most inappropriate," she admonished, with no conviction, her arms still wrapped around his neck.

Chandler reluctantly agreed and, loosening his hold, allowed her to step back. She patted loose tendrils of hair back into place and tried to calm her erratic heartbeat.

"Ready, sweet?" he asked, holding out his arm. Brandy, still breathless from his kisses, and Chandler, trying desperately to calm his raging desire and obvious arousal, returned to the dining room. He assisted her back to her chair and took the empty seat at the head of the table.

Abigail hid her delight behind a composed façade, Jessie blushed to the roots of her hair, and Anne counted the peas on her plate—all pretending not to notice Brandy's flustered countenance and Chandler's contented grin. As they resumed their meal, the two elder women looked at each other and shared a smile.

After the initial silence dissipated, the remainder of dinner was filled with gay laughter and chatter as they enjoyed the fine fare. Afterward, the group retired to the salon where Chandler poured each of the ladies a sherry, a cognac for himself. The lively conversation continued until a short while later, Chandler excused himself, informing them he had an appointment. He bid the ladies goodnight, tossed a discreet wink Brandy's way, and left. Soon after, the women made their way to their bedchambers for the night.

The next morning, Brandy found the butler in the kitchen conversing with Mrs. Farnham. "Deaton, may I have a word with you?"

"Certainly, milady." He followed her into the foyer.

"I was wondering…if someone wanted to go to, say, France, how would one go about it?"

His eyes widened. "I'm sure I don't know, milady."

"Deaton, you strike me as a man who knows quite a bit about many things. Are you sure you don't know someone who could help in this matter?"

Deaton glanced around the empty foyer. "Who is wanting to go?"

She averted her gaze. "'Tis a friend of mine. I'm not at liberty to divulge his identity."

Deaton nodded. "I will see what I can do, milady."

"Thank you, Deaton. I knew I could count on you. Oh, and please don't mention this to anyone. Especially, well, just not to anyone."

"Yes, milady." He waited until Brandy had disappeared up the blue-carpeted stairs, then promptly went to inform His Grace of the conversation he'd just had with Lady Brandy.

****

Under the blanket of night, and dressed as a lad, Brandy slipped out of the townhouse and made her way to the stables. She quickly saddled a chestnut mare and led her quietly out of the stall and down to the street. She mounted, pulled on the reins, and headed out of town. She rode swiftly through the city, keeping to side streets and shadows.

As she trotted across the bridge, she breathed a sigh of relief. *So far, so good.* She had thought her plan would fail when Deaton realized it was she who wanted to go to France. He had argued vehemently, threatened to tell His Grace, but Brandy had held her ground and won in the end, extracting a promise of secrecy from the disgruntled butler. She was thankful Chandler had been out for the evening or she would never have made it out the front door.

While she was at Stonebrooke Manor, she had come up with this scheme to go to France to find Michael. Since the debacle at Blackwell Hall, and the ensuing get-together with Lord Merrick, Chandler had stayed close-mouthed on the subject. Now that the plan was upon her, she prayed she could accomplish this daring escapade, unscathed.

She went over the arrangements that had been made. Deaton had assured her that two men would be waiting for her in the small harbor town of Deal. They would take her by boat across the Channel and into France. Once there, she was to contact a Monsieur Dubois. He was familiar with the activities of the English underground, and Deaton was certain he would help her—if he could.

After several hours of hard riding, Brandy entered Deal and followed Deaton's directions to the docks. She slowed the mare to a walk and, rounding a corner, the dim glow from a streetlamp illuminated two men leaning against a dark building, watching her approach. She swallowed the panic lurking just below the surface.

"Bradford?" one of the men called out, taking a step toward her.

She breathed a sigh of relief. "Aye," Brandy answered, responding to the alias she had decided upon. She pulled the brim of the woolen cap lower over her forehead. When they stepped away from the building, she got a good look at them. They were a seedy pair, scruffy, with whiskers covering their faces, and clothes that looked as if they'd been slept in for days. She once again doubted the wisdom of her venture.

One of the men grabbed the reins and led the horse behind the building. Brandy recognized it as the local livery, and after she dismounted, the man led the mare into an empty stall.

"Come along, we ain't got all night." They flanked her as they proceeded down the road to the pier. They headed toward a small boat rocking gently on the water, anchored amidst other vessels moored for the night. As they neared the craft, she wrinkled her nose at the pungent odor of fish. She glanced inquisitively at her escorts.

"It's a trawler—used for catchin' herrin'," he explained. "We won't be out of place if we're spotted crossin' the Channel."

Before they climbed into the boat, one of the men stopped her. "Do ye have the money?"

She fumbled inside her coat, withdrawing a small pouch of coins. She handed it to the man. "'Tis all there," she assured him.

He shook the leather pouch, the jangle of coins

clanging in the quiet night. She watched forlornly as he pocketed it. There went the beautiful diamond earbobs Michael had given her for her birthday. She silently thanked Deaton for giving her the needed coin by taking the earbobs as recompense.

The man took her by the arm to assist her into the trawler. "Come along, laddie, if ye be comin'."

She hopped into the boat and took a seat on the bench facing the docks. One of the men scrambled in and grabbed the oars as the other man untied the ropes, pushed the boat from the pier, and jumped in. The boat swayed, causing Brandy to grab onto the side until it righted itself. The men plied the oars, and the boat moved out into the dark waters of the Channel.

Her escorts were silent as they rowed swiftly across the water. Brandy stared up at the midnight sky. The moon, a crescent of light, hung suspended over the water, the stars mere dots glowing faintly against the coal-black sky. She marveled at the tall cliffs looming over the Channel, bleached white in the pale moonlight.

The trawler skimmed over the water. The Channel was calm, the wind not much more than a gentle breeze. They were fortunate—the Channel crossing could be treacherous if the wind blew in from the North Sea. Those gales had been responsible for many shipwrecks and lost lives.

She took a deep breath, trying to calm her nerves. With each stroke of the oars, she chanted her brother's name, stiffening her resolve to continue this journey before she shouted at them to take her back to England. She had to find Michael! She could no longer sit idle and wait for him to return—if he returned.

The men were silent, busy watching for sandbars

and rocks, fully aware one wrong move would find them wrecked upon a reef. Brandy gripped her seat and prayed her luck held.

As they neared the coast of France, the wind picked up in intensity, tossing the small craft upon the white-capped crests. The night had cooled, and the smell of rain was thick in the air. She held fast to the boat as it bumped against the pilings of the wooden pier. One of the men jumped out and tied the boat's rope to a post, then reached down and assisted Brandy from the trawler. He pointed to a spot of light.

"You will find Monsieur Dubois in there. He owns the inn." Brandy was about to ask him how he knew who she was looking for when suddenly he crouched down, pulling her with him. He held a finger to his lips for silence.

A group of soldiers was coming down the street, reeling from side to side. They were singing, their raunchy ditty punctuated with shouts of raucous laughter, and holding onto each other for support.

After the drunken group passed, and it was safe to do so, Brandy rose to her feet, thanked the man, and moved from her hiding place. The docks were now deserted, the outline of the ships moored in the harbor casting undulating shadows like cavorting ghosts against the dark night. She glanced back to find her escorts watching her, as if waiting for her to reach her destination.

She hurried to the inn and, taking a deep breath, pushed open the door. The room was cast in shadows, the fire in the hearth reduced to a bed of smoldering embers. She glanced quickly around the deserted room, shutting the door behind her.

A short, rotund man appeared from the back of the room. He had a large nose, a bushy black mustache nearly hidden beneath it. He limped toward her, leaning heavily on a cane.

"*Bonsoir*, may I be of assistance?"

"I'm sorry, I don't speak French." She bit her lip.

"You are English then?"

Brandy hesitated before answering, unsure of what to say. She decided to ignore his question and said, "I am looking for Monsieur Dubois."

"Ah, *oui*, that is me. You are Bradford? *Très bien*! I have been expecting you!"

She gaped at him in surprise. He had been *expecting* her? She became increasingly uneasy when he beckoned her to join him at one of the rough-hewn tables against the back wall. She patted her pocket, felt the outline of her pistol hidden there and, deciding she would be quite safe, sat down in one of the ladder-backed chairs. He sank into a chair across from her, leaning his cane against the edge of the table.

"I am looking for my brother, Michael Drummond."

"I do not know this man." His black eyes watched her carefully, his expression blank.

"But I do," a familiar voice answered from behind her.

Brandy jumped to her feet and whirled in amazement. Chandler was there, hidden in the shadows. She sagged with relief. "How did you—what are you doing here?"

Chandler nodded to Monsieur Dubois. That one heaved himself to his feet, grabbed his cane, and disappeared behind the long wooden bar.

"I believe that question is mine to ask." He pointed

to her chair. She sat back down, her relief short-lived. He was furious. She didn't like the look on his face nor the anger blazing blue fire in his eyes. She plowed ahead anyway, her words coming out in a rush.

"I came to find Michael. No one else was doing anything, and I, well, I thought perhaps if I tried…oh, Chandler, I just had to come!" Tears threatened to spill. "How did you know?"

"Deaton is loyal to me."

"Oh," she murmured. The butler!

"Casey and Jon, the men who brought you over the Channel, work for me as well. When Deaton first informed me of your conversation with him, I became suspicious. Familiar with your habit of running headlong into danger without thinking of the consequences, I made it my business to find out what you were up to. Deaton supplied the rest. I also made sure it was Casey and Jon who brought you over. Did you honestly think it would be that easy to enter a country we're at war with?" He looked at her incredulously, his anger boiling even hotter. "Honestly, Brandy, why would you do such a foolish thing?" He took the seat Monsieur Dubois had vacated at the table.

"Because I must find Michael. Don't you understand? He's all I have left!" Brandy burst into tears—tears of frustration mingled with relief. She'd had no idea until that moment how frightened she'd been these past hours.

"You have me," he said quietly, but beneath the sound of her sobs he doubted she heard his softly spoken declaration.

Monsieur Dubois approached with a bottle of red wine and two glasses. He set the tray on the table and disappeared again. Chandler poured them each a glass of wine and waited patiently for her tears to dry. He fished a handkerchief from his vest pocket and handed it to her.

When her sobs turned to hiccups, she took a long swallow of wine. "Well, I did wonder that it hadn't been more difficult to enter France." She bent her head in embarrassment, not wanting to see his expression. She could stand just about anything right now but his mocking grin. "You must think me quite the fool."

He leaned forward and lifted her chin with his finger. "What I think is that you are very brave. Misguided, yes, but brave. And that you love your brother very much. I admire a woman who takes matters into her own hands, despite the risks involved. However, I am not happy with this situation. This was far too dangerous."

"Yes, I see that now. It could have gone much worse. But you've been evasive and secretive, so I thought I should do something."

"Running headlong into France is not the answer."

"It's this bloody waiting."

"I know, I have felt that way many times. And I did exactly what you did—took care of it myself." He studied her tearstained face, his heart swelling with pride at her determination. "We will get a room for the remainder of the night and return to England at dawn."

"No."

"No?" One black brow shot skyward.

"I came to find Michael, and I will not leave until I do." She set her glass down, preparing for an argument.

"I see." Chandler leaned back in his chair, regarding her silently. He signaled to Monsieur Dubois. "Have you a room ready?"

"*Oui, Monsieur.* If you will follow me?" With one hand, he gathered up the tray, the bottle of wine and glasses upon it, and turned toward a dimly lit stairwell hidden in the back of the inn.

Chandler led a none-too-happy Brandy upstairs. She had no idea what Chandler was thinking or what he would do. It would be just like him to ignore her wishes and drag her home instead. They entered a small, rather stark, room furnished only with a bed, a small wooden table with two chairs, and a surprisingly comfortable-looking chair. One narrow window on the corner wall was framed by heavy, brown curtains, shut against the night. A small oil lamp threw out a thin circle of light. Monsieur Dubois deposited the tray on the table and closed the door behind him. Brandy sat on the edge of the bed, pulling the woolen cap from her head, and waited.

"I don't suppose you considered the consequences of your actions if you had been caught." It was more a statement than a quest for information. "At least you were smart enough to dress as a lad," Chandler observed, refilling their glasses with wine.

"I do have some wits, even for a female," she muttered, accepting the glass he offered.

Chandler chuckled and sat down in the chair across from the bed. "Why don't we start from the beginning."

"The beginning of what?"

"Your life."

"You want to know my life story? Now?"

"Maybe then I can figure out why you do what you do."

"Oh, of all the— Stop laughing! This is serious!"

"I know," he said, suddenly somber. "Brandy, I

can't tell you anything just now. Suffice it to say I believe our brothers to be safe."

"How do you know?"

"Listen, love, your life could be in danger if you knew too much."

"You're keeping me in the dark again."

"Won't you believe me when I say it is so?" He leaned forward, his arms resting on his knees.

Brandy stared into his blue eyes. She could tell he was being sincere. "All right, I will believe you—for now."

"Why don't you tell me about your father?"

"You mean Philip?"

He gave her an odd look. "Yes."

"Chandler, there is something you should know. Ah…" She hesitated, then blurted out, "I'm adopted." She awaited his reaction and was rewarded by the raising of his brows. "'Tis true. The Drummonds were not my natural parents. I only found out after Philip died, when his solicitor called to go over his affairs. He gave me this locket, too." She fingered the chain around her neck. "I understand I was wearing it when Doreen found me in her gardens." Brandy reached inside her shirt and withdrew the thin gold chain.

"May I see it?"

Brandy presented her back to Chandler, who unclasped the chain from around her neck. He walked over to the oil lamp on the table and, holding the locket beneath the light, studied it closely. He flipped open the latch and stilled. "Who is this man?"

"My father, I suppose."

He composed his features and turned back to Brandy. "Very nice," was all he said and replaced it around her slender neck. He paused to run his fingers lightly over her skin.

Brandy, shivering at his touch, looked over her shoulder at him with eyes narrowed. Catching her expression, he chuckled and moved to sit back down in the chair. He leaned back with an expectant look on his face. "Go on," he ordered, sipping his wine.

"I had been concerned with why Philip took his own life," she continued thoughtfully. "As well as betrothing me to Blackwell. I was at a loss. Then I learned Roger had something to do with it, all of it."

"How do you know this?"

"At first, I learned it from Philip's journal. Then, that night at Blackwell Hall, Roger told me." She fell silent. "He forced him into it, you know. All of it—the smuggling, the activities against the Crown, the betrothal agreement. Philip must have felt the weight of the world on his shoulders. I guess it just became too much for him." She glanced up sharply. "I, however, had nothing to do with Blackwell," she reiterated.

"I know," he replied softly and moved to sit beside her on the bed. "You are far too expressive. You wouldn't be any good at espionage, sweet."

"I wouldn't?" she whispered distractedly, flustered by his proximity. He was sitting far too close; she could feel the heat emanating from his body.

"No," he answered softly, "you wouldn't." He cupped her face with his hands—softly kissed each corner of her mouth. His lips then moved over hers, capturing them in a soul-searching kiss.

Wrapping her arms around his neck, she pulled him close. No longer could she fight the feelings he aroused—no longer did she want to. She surrendered to his touch and rode the passion he awakened.

He pushed her onto her back, followed her descent, and with his large body covered hers. After several long hungry kisses, he pulled away, quickly divesting her of her clothes, his joining hers on the floor. Unbraiding her hair, he spread the silken tresses across the pillow, and began to make slow passionate love to her.

Chandler trailed warm kisses down her throat, down to her pink-tipped breasts. He captured a velvet bud in his mouth, bathing it with his tongue, before moving lower, to her stomach, and circling her navel with his tongue.

"Chandler," she whispered. Upon hearing the uncertainty in her voice, he ceased his journey and slid up her body to recapture her lips, with a kiss that shot a current of electricity between them.

With his knee, he nudged her legs apart. "You're ready for me, aren't you, love?"

Brandy, lost in a cloud of desire, whispered his name a moment before he thrust inside her, sheathing himself within her pulsating warmth. She clutched his shoulders, her nails digging into his skin, feeling his muscles bunch, the damp sheen of moisture covering his skin, as they traveled to the stars together, on a magical voyage of love. They returned to earth glowing in the aftermath, their breaths mingling with their sighs of spent passion.

Chandler kissed her full on the mouth, and rolled onto his side, drawing Brandy with him. He held her close, tucking her head beneath his chin. His breath stirred her auburn tresses and the subtle scent of lavender drifted up.

A flash of lightning and a batter of rain at the window heralded a storm. An answering clap of thunder reverberated through the room, rattling the glass. Brandy snuggled closer to Chandler. He chuckled. "You run headlong into France, ignoring the dangers of war, yet are frightened of a little storm?"

"I'm not afraid," she countered, yawning, not the least bit bothered by his teasing. As far as she was concerned, the earth could shift, the mountains could crumble, and she would not be frightened—as long as she was wrapped in his embrace.

Her even breathing told Chandler she was fast asleep. *Must be exhausting running into enemy territory.* When Deaton had come to him with his bizarre story, Chandler's first inclination was to go to Brandy and forbid her to go. But he knew that would only get her back up and she'd come up with another crazier scheme—one he may not be made aware of beforehand. So, he had played it through, enlisting the help of some of his men, to ensure her safety into France.

He kissed the top of her head. He had to admire her, though. She was one determined woman who definitely kept him on his toes. Life was certainly not dull since Brandy had stumbled into it.

Chandler smiled to himself, enormously pleased with this impetuous, willful woman he now held so close to his heart.

****

Jessie and Anne were blissfully unaware of Brandy's madcap dash into France. Abigail, however, was not. She took Brandy aside and gave her a good scolding.

"I'm sorry, Your Grace," Brandy said, contrite. "But I had to try to find Michael."

"I know, dear. But racing into France is not the

answer. You could have been killed or worse! Good heavens, child, we're at war!" Her tone softened. "Chandler will bring Michael home, you'll see. Please, don't do anything so foolish again. I'm afraid you gave my old heart a start."

Brandy hugged her tightly. "I am truly sorry for worrying you." She pulled back. "How did you know? Wait, let me guess—Deaton?"

"Of course, Deaton. He is as loyal to me as he is to Chandler." She patted Brandy's cheek. "'Tis a good thing he is, too. If Chandler had not been made aware— I shudder to think what could have happened."

Upon leaving the room, Brandy promised not to do anything so rash and impulsive again. Abigail watched her go, a sad smile playing about her mouth. Poor girl. So much sadness in one so young. She then went in search of her grandson. It was high time she got some answers. She found Chandler in his study, seated at his desk, a mound of papers at his elbow.

"Chandler, a word, please?" She sat down in one of the leather chairs opposite the desk.

Chandler leaned back, her tone putting him instantly on guard. "Yes, Grandmother?"

"Where is Andrew? And Michael Drummond? Are they together?" She held up her hand. "Do not feed me any more poppycock. I want the truth."

"I'm not at liberty to tell you."

"Do you know where they are?"

"I believe so."

"Are they safe?"

"I hope so."

"What do you mean?" Her face creased with worry.

"We aren't *exactly* sure where they are, but we are

doing everything we can to locate them and bring them home. Last we heard, they had not been harmed. Don't worry, Grandmother. And please don't say anything to Brandy. She's anxious enough, and I wouldn't put it past her to sail off to France again, raising a ruckus along the way."

Abigail nodded. "All right, Chandler. I trust you, my boy. If anyone can find them, you can." She rose to her feet and left the room, her posture not quite as erect as when she entered.

Deaton found Brandy reading in the morning room. He stood waiting to gain her attention. Sensing a presence, she looked up. "Yes, Deaton?"

He dropped the velvet box into her lap.

She lifted the lid and smiled. Her diamond earbobs twinkled in the sunlight. "Thank you, Deaton. I will repay the coins you gave me."

"It is not necessary, milady. The money came from His Grace."

Brandy blushed. "You must think me a veritable fool."

"Not a'tall, milady. I think you are very brave. However, it is fortunate you have His Grace to protect you." With that, he bowed, and left the room.

Yes, Brandy agreed, she was indeed fortunate.

Chapter 33

Michael Drummond came slowly awake, his tired mind taking in the strange surroundings. He was on his back, staring at wooden rafters, a soft mattress beneath him, a downy pillow under his head. *So, it was not a dream. I did escape that bloody prison.* He moved, grimacing at the searing pain shooting through his head. He carefully tested the other parts of his body. One of his legs was wrapped tight, but other than that, he seemed to be in one piece. Hearing the creak of a door opening, he stiffened, waiting. A woman entered his line of vision. She was petite of stature, with chestnut-brown hair and haunted green eyes. She was wearing a faded gray muslin dress that had seen better days.

When she saw his eyes were open, she sighed in relief. "So, you are awake. That is good. We were afraid we would lose you." She spoke in French.

"Where am I?" he answered in kind.

"You are in my home, *Monsieur*. My son found you in the woods. You were delirious with fever."

"Why does my head hurt? And my leg?"

"You have a nasty gash on your forehead and have lost a great deal of blood. It is bandaged now. You also have a broken leg."

"The man who was with me—where is he?"

"He is asleep in the other room."

Michael's body relaxed. "Who are you? And where

is your home?"

"I am Madame Fouillet. We live in Mouilleries." She gazed at him curiously, a thousand questions on her tongue. She asked only one instead, "May I tend to your wounds?"

He closed his eyes. Her hands were gentle as she changed the bandage around his head and the dressing on his leg. Under her gentle ministrations, he was soon fast asleep.

Madame Fouillet gazed down at the young man, pleased that he would live. It had looked doubtful, but at last the fever was broken and his progress was good. She had been frightened when her son, Oliver, ran in from the woods raving about two men. She'd hustled him into the cottage and locked the door. But when he told her there was blood everywhere and the men were asleep, she began to fear for their lives. She had grabbed her husband's pistol and ventured into the woods with her son, clutching his little hand. She found the two men lying beneath a tree. One of them was out cold, his face covered with blood. When she glanced at the other one, she found him watching her, his gaze vigilant.

Now, caressing the wounded man's cheek, her fear returned. France and England were at war. True, the conflict was in Portugal, but nevertheless, to the French, she was hiding and abetting the enemy.

Madame Fouillet left Michael to sleep and entered the common room, where her son was waiting for her. She ruffled his red hair as she walked past him on her way to the hearth.

"He will live?"

"*Oui*. You have done a very brave thing, Oliver. Thanks to your quick thinking, they will both live."

"But they are English, no?" Oliver asked with the bluntness of a ten-year-old.

"*Oui*, but they are human beings first. God willing, they will arrive safely back in England." *Before I am caught harboring the enemy.*

"Did you tell them you are English, too?" Oliver gazed up at his mother with round brown eyes.

She shook her head. "It is best they do not know." That part of her life was over. The less these two strangers knew of her history, the better.

"But *Maman*—"

"I said no, Oliver. Now, that is quite enough. Will you please bring in more wood? The fire is dying."

"*Oui, Maman*." Oliver raced from the cottage to do his mother's bidding.

Andrew Townsend pushed open the door from an adjacent room and stepped into the common area. It was spacious, with little furnishings save for a large oak table with several chairs, a sideboard, and a matching cupboard. It was clean and had a comfortable feel to it. Madame Fouillet stood at the table cutting vegetables. Her chestnut-brown hair was bound tight at her nape, a few strands hanging limply about her face. She looked up as he entered and wiped her hands on a well-worn apron.

"*Bonsoir, Monsieur*. You are feeling better?"

"*Oui, Madame*. How is my friend?"

"He is conscious now, but still in a great deal of pain. He has fallen back asleep. It is what he needs most now. Are you hungry? Supper should be ready shortly." She tossed the vegetables into a pot simmering over the open fire.

"Yes, *merci beaucoup*." Andrew took a seat at the

scarred table and accepted a glass of wine. Madame Fouillet was a beautiful woman, or had been before her toils had left tired lines around her eyes and streaks of gray in her hair.

"We owe you and your son our lives. If your son had not found us, I fear we would be dead. I am glad he harbors no prejudice. Nor you," he added softly.

"As I explained to Oliver, when it comes to helping others, nationality is not an issue."

Oliver entered the cottage, a stack of wood in his arms. He placed the wood in the grate next to the hearth, threw a couple of logs on the fire, and took a seat next to Andrew. He looked up at him in curiosity.

"My *Maman* would help anyone, especially one of her—" Oliver stopped talking at the sharp shake of his mother's head.

Andrew gazed curiously at the redheaded child. "One of her what?"

"He meant nothing," Madame Fouillet answered and gave her son a stern frown before busying herself with setting the table.

Andrew watched her, puzzled by her curt response. He decided to be blunt. "Madame Fouillet, are you English?"

She took a moment before answering, then brushing a loose tendril of hair off her forehead, she replied, "*Oui*, but I have not been to England in a very long time."

"Where is Monsieur Fouillet?"

"He is dead."

"Oh, I am sorry."

She nodded. "Please, I think it best if we did not talk of this. You see—" She spotted Michael limping into the room. "*Mon Dieu!* What are you doing up? You should be in bed, *Monsieur*." She had switched to English now that the truth was known.

Michael made his way slowly across the room and sank into one of the chairs arranged around the large table. "Ugh! I don't think I have ever been in this much pain. Not even when I fell off my horse and broke my arm."

"Other than that, how are you feeling?" Andrew leaned forward and clasped his friend's hand.

"Thanks to Madame Fouillet, I am well. Tired, but I think I will recover enough to leave soon." Michael accepted a glass of wine from Madame Fouillet and took a large swallow, savoring the sweet taste. It had been too long since he had indulged in this little bit of heaven. "How's your back?" he asked Andrew.

"Madame Fouillet applied a magic salve that has practically healed the welts." He smiled her way as she poured herself a glass of wine and joined them at the table.

Michael glanced around the spotless room. His gaze landed on Oliver stoking the fire in the hearth. "Are you the young man I should thank for saving my life?"

Oliver beamed with pleasure. "*Oui, Monsieur*, I am Oliver Fouillet. I found you in the woods."

"I owe you my life, Oliver. If there is anything I can do, you have only to get word to me." He stared solemnly at the young man who was apparently the man of the house.

"Tell me, how is it you both speak English?"

Before she could answer, Andrew supplied, "She is English."

Michael eyes widened. He stared intently at the woman who was diligently avoiding his gaze. Her profile, now presented to him, struck a familiar chord, but his weary mind couldn't comprehend it. He leaned forward and peered into Madame Fouillet's face.

"Monsieur, are you quite well?"

"Yes, I mean, I don't know. Have we met before?" She shook her head as he continued, "Where in England do you hail from? How long have you lived in France?"

"Please, I would just as soon leave the past—in the past."

Andrew raised a brow at his friend's persistent questions and shook his head when Michael opened his mouth to further his interrogation. Michael shrugged his shoulders. "As you wish, Madame."

After supper, Andrew assisted Michael outside. An overturned crate made an adequate seat, and Michael gratefully sank onto the wooden box. Andrew sat on the ground across from him, his back against a tree. He withdrew a coveted box of cheroots he had stolen from one of their jailers. The two men enjoyed a silent smoke in the pleasant chill of the French country night.

"Why were you questioning Madame Fouillet so intently?"

Michael glanced at Andrew in the lengthening shadows. "She seems familiar. Like we've met before. Which of course is impossible." He took a drag from the cheroot. "Odd, but she reminds me of my sister."

"My friend, the fever has robbed you of your senses," his friend teased, smoke spiraling.

"You're probably right." Michael laughed, shaking off the unfounded feeling of familiarity.

Chapter 34

The note was delivered during the night. The next morning, Deaton entered the foyer and, spying the beige envelope on the floor, bent down to retrieve it. He turned it over in his hand and read the small black lettering. Wrinkling his nose in distaste, he headed to the morning room where the Dowager Duchess was enjoying her tea.

"Madam, I found this under the door." He handed the envelope to the Dowager Duchess.

"Thank you, Deaton." Abigail was studying it when Brandy walked into the room.

"Good morning, Abigail. Have Aunt Jessie and Anne come down?"

"Good morning, dear. They are already up and off to the milliner. This is for you." She handed the envelope to Brandy.

Brandy ripped it open and quickly read the note. "Good heavens!" she whispered. "Excuse me, Abigail." She rushed from the room, ignoring the Dowager Duchess's concerned outcry.

Brandy ran upstairs and quickly changed into her riding habit, slipping the note into the pocket of the forest-green skirt. She left the house minutes later, slipping past the morning room door so she wouldn't be waylaid by the Dowager Duchess.

Deaton watched her sneak out the front door and shook his head. *There she goes again.* Unfortunately, this time, the duke wasn't at home to stop her.

Chandler did return a few hours later and strode into the morning room where he found Abigail at her elegant writing desk, answering correspondence. "Grandmother, have you seen Brandy?"

"Not since this morning. She received a note and after reading it she ran upstairs. I assume she is still in her chamber."

"Do you know who it was from?"

"No, but she did seem quite upset after reading it."

Chandler frowned, wondering who would have sent her a message. He ascended the wide staircase and tapped lightly on her door, pushing it open when he didn't receive an answer.

"Brandy?" He glanced around the empty room, puzzled. His head came up as he detected a familiar scent. He ran his hand through his hair, turned around and with angry strides returned to the morning room.

"She's gone," he announced from the doorway.

Abigail looked up from her sewing. "Oh, dear, not again. Deaton!" The butler appeared in the doorway as if he had been hovering outside the room.

"Have you seen Lady Brandy?"

"No, Madam. Not since she left the house this morning."

"She left the house, unaccompanied? Where did she go?" Chandler asked, his tone sharp.

"I don't know, Your Grace."

"Who delivered the note?"

"I found it in the foyer this morning. It must have been slipped under the door during the night." He glanced at the Dowager Duchess. "Is something amiss, Madam?"

"We're not sure. Chandler, where are you going?"

"To the stables to see if the mare is gone." He disappeared before Abigail could draw a breath.

"Thank you, Deaton. That will be all." She crossed to the window and pulled aside the drapes in time to see her grandson race off on his black stallion.

When Chandler reached his destination, he dismounted in one fluid motion and raced up the front steps. He pounded on the door until it was pulled open by the butler, who took one look at Chandler's furious expression and took a step back.

"Where is your mistress?"

"Lady Vivian is not at home, Your Grace."

"When will she return?"

"I'm not sure, Your Grace."

"Did a young woman call on her this morning?"

"Yes. She and milady left together. When she returns, I will tell her you called, Your Grace."

"I'll wait." Chandler strode into the drawing room and helped himself to a whiskey. He had the sinking suspicion that Brandy had been pulled into something dangerous. What possible reason would Vivian have to seek her out? He paced the floor, listening to the faint chimes of the hall clock. "Three o'clock. Damn it, where could they have gone?" Upon hearing the front door open, he stepped to the drawing room door.

Vivian Beaumont handed her cloak to the butler, turned and gasped when she spied Chandler standing in the doorway. Quickly composing her features, she glided toward him, her hands outstretched in welcome.

"Chandler, darling, what a pleasant surprise." She smiled brightly and linked her arm through his, leading him back inside the room. She shut the door behind them.

"Where is she?" Chandler asked bluntly, disengaging her arm.

"Who, darling?"

"Brandy."

"Your little houseguest? I'm sure I don't know. Now, do come and sit down. May I offer you a drink? No, I see you already have one." She went for his arm again but stopped at his thunderous expression.

"Vivian, if you value your life, you will answer my question—now!"

****

Brandy, bound and gagged, sat shivering on a cold floor, her back against a damp wall. She concentrated on staying calm, though she could see no way out of her present situation.

How could she have been so reckless? To believe that Vivian Beaumont would have news of Michael! It was ludicrous! She did not trust the messenger and should never have believed the message. Now look where her foolishness had landed her! She glanced around the bare, dank room. Just where had she landed?

She went over in detail the events of the past several hours. She had arrived at Lady Vivian's townhouse, and after being graciously ushered inside her opulent drawing room, had insisted on hearing what news she claimed she had about Michael. Vivian had informed her that they would need to travel outside of London to meet a man who had this information. He couldn't come here, of course, for it would be far too dangerous. Against her better judgment, yet anxious for any news of Michael, Brandy had accompanied Vivian in her carriage to the designated meeting spot. At the time, it hadn't occurred to her to wonder how Vivian knew her brother, much less that he was missing.

They had travelled the Kent Road until they were some distance from the city. Brandy's suspicions blossomed when, where they stopped, was deserted. She had just turned to confront Lady Vivian when the door to the carriage was snatched open and she was pulled outside, blindfolded, and thrown into another carriage. She was in trouble, serious trouble, and had no idea why she had been taken nor where she was being held captive.

A scratch at the door brought Brandy back to the present. She held her breath as the door swung open. A man entered, a black hooded cape covering him from head to foot. Another man, a pistol tucked into his belt, stood behind him. The caped man sauntered forward and removed the scarf from around Brandy's mouth.

"Who are you? Where am I?" Brandy croaked, her mouth dry, her tongue swollen from lack of moisture. She struggled to stand, but her bound feet kept her seated on the floor.

"Comfortable?" The voice was husky and tinged with laughter.

"Why have you taken me?" Brandy asked, peering into the shadowed face hidden by the hood, unable to make out any identifying features.

"You were supposed to die a long time ago. How you managed to survive, I'll never know. But I won't fail this time," the voice averred, his tone threatening.

"I don't understand. What have I ever done to you?"

"Enough of these questions. Suffice it to say you are in my way. You must die." He turned to the man standing in the doorway. "Do what you will, but I want her dead." He swept from the room, the cape billowing out around him.

Brandy's attention was immediately drawn to the man who stayed behind. He stepped further into the room and closed the door, leering.

Brandy closed her eyes against his ugly expression. When she opened them again, they widened in fear. He was fumbling with his breeches. Dear Lord, no! His intent perfectly clear, Brandy suddenly became afraid— very afraid. She struggled against her bindings as the man knelt beside her.

"Don't fight me, missy. Ye be enjoying what I have to offer. I'll make it pleasurable for ye, I will. Before ye die, that is."

"Please, I will pay you not to hurt me. Whatever he is paying you, I will double—no, triple—the amount." Brandy wondered hysterically where she would get that kind of money but hoped desperately her bluff worked.

The man hesitated a moment as if considering her offer. "Maybe—but either way I'll be havin' ye. Come now, little lady, don't fight me." With his grubby hand, he grabbed the top of her riding habit jacket and tugged, tearing the material and exposing the bodice underneath. As he moved down to untie the bindings from her ankles, Brandy lashed out with her bound hands, connecting solidly with his nose. He shrieked in pain and fell back on his heels, holding his bleeding nose. Just then the door flung open, crashing loudly against the wall. Brandy looked up and breathed a sigh of relief. *Chandler!*

The vile man turned toward the sound, his eyes widening in fear at the sight of the large, furious man filling the doorway. He inched his hand toward his gun hidden behind Brandy.

Chandler took one look at the scene in front of him, his expression murderous, before fastening his gaze on the man. "Step away from her."

The evil one brought up his arm, the gun clutched in his hand. "Ye can watch if ye want, but I got me orders. And I plan to pleasure meself first."

"Over my dead body."

"What's one more?" the man cackled, aiming the gun at Chandler. Brandy bit her lip, then took the chance and shoved her hands into his back. Startled, he took his eyes off Chandler for one brief moment. It was all the time Chandler needed. In a flash, he pulled his pistol from his belt and fired one shot that went cleanly through the miscreant's heart. As the body slumped over on top of Brandy, she pushed it away with a cry.

Chandler rushed to her side, gathered her in his arms, and carried her from the room. They were inside a house, and from what Brandy could see, it was deserted. The furniture was covered with white linens, cobwebs hung from the rafters, and a thick layer of dust covered every surface. Chandler placed her on her feet and quickly untied her bindings, ankles and wrists.

"Did he hurt you?"

She shook her head. "Thank God you got here when you did. He was going to—"

"Hush, sweet. He's dead. He can't hurt you now."

"I know." She stared at him happily. "You shot him…I'm glad you shot him. He was an evil man. He was supposed to kill me after he—you know. There was someone else here, too. I don't know who she was, though, for she was wearing a hooded black cape concealing her features."

"If her face was hidden, how do you know it was a female?"

"When she left the room, her cape billowed out and

I spied blue taffeta. Not many men wear blue taffeta, do they?"

"You're amazing. Most women would be weeping in hysteria right about now."

"I knew you would come," she stated matter-of-factly.

He laughed and scooped her up in his arms. "Let's get out of here before the blue taffeta one returns."

"But, Chandler, who would want me dead? She said I was supposed to die a long time ago," Brandy added, nonplussed.

"I'm not sure."

"You know who it is, don't you?"

"I have an idea."

"It was that hateful Lady Vivian who tricked me. She told me she had news of Michael."

"And you believed her?" He looked down at her, one brow cocked incredulously.

Brandy blushed. "I know it was foolish of me. I guess I've truly become desperate." She paused. "How did you know I was here?"

"Vivian told me."

"But—"

"I smelled her perfume in your room. It is rather distinctive, you know. I deduced that the note came from her. When I confronted her, she couldn't tell me fast enough."

Brandy snuggled up against his broad chest, wrapped her arms around his neck, wanting nothing more than to forget the entire episode.

Chandler, his heartbeat having returned to normal, now that she was safe in his arms, pulled her close. "I asked you before, and I will ask you again—please come to me before you run headlong into danger, understand?"

"Yes, Your Grace," she answered with a grin, her fear having abated with his presence.

They left the abandoned house and, riding together on his stallion, made quick time back to the townhouse. Deaton was the only one about and, with a slow shake of his head, watched them climb the stairs. He didn't envy the duke—she was most definitely a handful.

When they reached Brandy's chamber, Chandler followed her inside and shut and bolted the door behind him. Brandy glanced around in surprise. He was walking toward her, his steps measured, his eyes glowing with lust and something else she couldn't determine.

She stood still, waiting for him, feeling a rush of longing. When he reached her, she stood on her toes, and wrapped her arms around his neck. He smothered her mouth with his, kneading her soft lips, demanding her response.

She clung to him, molding her body against his, and kissed him back. After the past hours of fear and uncertainty, she wanted to get as close to him as possible.

Chandler's hands cupped her bottom, caressing the soft mounds. He sidled toward the wall until his back was pressed against it and undid his trousers. Then, pulling up her skirt, he lifted her off the floor and gently brought her down on his arousal, sliding into her warmth.

"Ride me," he commanded, his voice husky with unbridled passion, his hands encircling her waist.

And she did. She wrapped her legs around him, moving against his groin, sliding up and down his hard length. Their gazes locked as they continued the rhythm, their bodies fused together by unspoken love, reveling in the age-old act between man and woman. After their breathtaking release, Chandler held her until their trembling subsided.

He quirked a brow. "You are quite the horsewoman, sweet," echoing their first encounter in the lea.

Brandy laughed and kissed him full on the mouth. "You are quite the mount, Your Grace," she retorted saucily, blushing at her boldness. She slid down his body and smoothed her skirt as he arranged his clothing. His brow darkened as he fingered the torn bodice of her riding habit. She covered his hand with hers and whispered, "I'm safe, Chandler. All is well."

Their gazes locked before their mouths came together in a tender, loving kiss.

"I will let Grandmother know you are home. Both she and Deaton were quite worried about you." As he strode from the room, he said over his shoulder, "I will see you at dinner, sweet."

Brandy, weak from spent desire and delayed reaction from her harrowing experience, sank to the bed, her legs no longer able to hold her upright.

Chapter 35

Brandy, along with Jessie and Anne, returned to Stonebrooke Manor for Christmas. Abigail had been invited to the country estate of one of her closest friends, and they had declined her gracious invitation to join them for the Yuletide. Brandy longed for home, especially since Chandler was away on business with a promise to come to the manor after the new year.

The night before Christmas, the three women gathered in the salon, gaily decorated in honor of the season. Earlier in the evening, Arthur had wrestled in the huge Yule log now crackling cheerfully in the hearth. They each enjoyed a sherry as they shared stories of Christmases past.

After the others had retired for the night, Brandy lit a candle from the flames of the Yule log, whispering a prayer for Michael's safe and speedy return. Her thoughts turned to Chandler, and she smiled, eager for the new year to arrive, for the new year would bring him to Hathshire. Not only did she long to be enfolded in his strong arms again, he just might have news of Michael.

The next morning, a fresh layer of snow blanketed the countryside. After luncheon, Brandy took Misty out for a ride. Her breath misted in the crisp winter air, the chill invigorating. She rode to the small, secluded glade. The winter sun streamed through the bare branches of the trees, reflecting with blinding brilliance off the snow-covered ground. She slid off her mare's back and walked to the now frozen pond. She placed her saddle blanket on the ground and sat down, stretching her legs out in front of her.

She rested her hand upon her stomach. Soon it would be impossible to conceal the truth. She had suspected it for quite some time and could no longer ignore the fact that she carried the duke's child. She knew she should be ashamed to be expecting out of wedlock, but she wasn't and wouldn't pretend otherwise. The little one growing inside her was the result of a union of love. Maybe Chandler didn't love her, but she loved him—with all her heart. And she would love their child just as much. Time would tell what the duke's reaction would be to fatherhood.

The sun had lowered considerably by the time she returned to the manor house. It was late afternoon, and she was in better spirits, having drawn comfort from her secret glade.

"Brandy, look what just arrived!" Anne held out a gaily wrapped package.

"Is it from Michael?"

"No! It's from your duke!"

Brandy ripped open the package and gasped in delight. Nestled in soft green velvet were a pair of combs. Made of gold and studded with emeralds, they sparkled with green fire.

"Oh, my, they are beautiful!" Brandy exclaimed, as she rushed to the small oval mirror hanging above the table in the foyer. She pulled the pins from her hair and shook her head, the auburn curls tumbling down her back. She lifted her hair back on one side of her face and pushed one emerald comb into place. After she had done the same with the other, she tilted her head from side to side, admiring the gift.

"Maybe your duke cares more for you than you think, Cousin," Anne teased.

"Hmm," Brandy murmured. She turned to her cousin and hugged her tightly. "Oh, if it were only true!" she cried, her words catching on a sob.

"Brandy, what is it?"

"Come," she said, pulling Anne into the salon and shutting the door behind them. She took a seat on the settee, patting the place beside her.

Anne sat down, a worried look on her face.

"I carry his child."

Anne's mouth fell open. "His child?" she repeated as if trying to comprehend her cousin's announcement. After a moment, she placed her hand on Brandy's arm. "Does he know?"

"No."

"You are going to tell him, aren't you? What I know of the duke, he is stubborn and proud, much like someone else I know, but he's also honorable. He'll want to marry you."

"No, he won't. He doesn't believe in it. Besides, I don't want him to marry me because of the babe. I want him to marry me because he loves me."

"Are you going to tell him?"

"Of course," she said, biting her lip.

"When he arrives after the new year?"

"I don't know." Brandy looked out the window, watching the snowflakes drift lazily to the ground.

"Before long you won't have to tell him. He'll know when you grow as large as a pumpkin." Anne continued with a sigh, "Well, thank heavens you no longer have to wander around at night stealing food."

"Yes, it was generous of Aunt Jessie to share her inheritance. We will repay her, of course. And what with the money Abigail gave me, we should be fine until Michael returns."

"The Dowager Duchess gave you money? Again?"

"Yes, before we came home for Christmas. I believe it was Chandler's idea." She hesitated. "He knows about the midnight raids, Anne."

"He does?"

"I never told you he caught me one night. I didn't want to worry you, so I kept it to myself. Remember the night I came home late, and you were waiting up for me? The night I stole the chicken from Alden Ridge? Well, he caught me fleeing the grounds. Of course, at the time he didn't know it was me." She laughed in memory and declared proudly, "I escaped before he could unmask me!"

Anne erupted with laughter. "'Tis a good thing he didn't. Lord knows what might have happened." Then, sobering, she eyed her cousin. "Back to the issue at hand—what are you going to do about the child?"

"Keep it, of course! This one will not be left in someone's garden. Before Chandler arrives, I will figure out something," she announced decisively, in a valiant effort to convince herself.

****

It was more than a fortnight after they had been found by Madame Fouillet that Andrew deemed Michael well enough to travel. They bid the compassionate woman and her son goodbye, with a promise to repay their kindness. The sun was emerging over the horizon as Madame Fouillet watched them walk away, her green eyes solemn. She mouthed a silent prayer for their safe return.

It was late afternoon when Michael and Andrew arrived in a small coastal town, hoping to find one of their men. It had been designated a meeting place if any of their own became lost. They had begged a ride from a farmer on his way to market, so had made good time thus far. Their progress was now considerably slower as they walked through the town, for Michael used a cane, his leg not quite healed. The street was crowded with carts, people and animals, all vying for space in the allotted area. As they maneuvered their way through the throng, they kept their hats lowered, trying to remain inconspicuous. Madame Fouillet had lent them some of her late husband's clothing so they blended in more than they would have wearing their own torn and bloodstained clothes.

A man stood on the corner, watching them proceed slowly down the street. When he saw them slip into a tavern, he turned and disappeared around the corner.

Michael and Andrew glanced around the nearly deserted room and took a seat at a table near the back. They ordered wine from a buxom barmaid who sauntered over, eyeing the two brawny men. She returned shortly with a bottle of red wine and two glasses, bending low to place them on the table, and exposing her large bosom. Michael and Andrew exchanged amused glances but ignored the barmaid's blatant invitation.

Michael, anxious to return home, tapped the table with his fingers. With his father dead, Brandy was alone and, he was sure, frantic with worry. He hoped the duke had kept his promise and was watching over her until he returned from this mission.

They looked up as a man approached their table, his eyes alight with pleasure. He spoke in French. "*Mon Dieu!* It is you! Claude thought he recognized you."

Andrew smiled. "*Bonsoir*, Pierre. It is good to see you. Tell me, when can we get out of here? I long to smell the sweet soil of England." His voice had dropped to a whisper as Pierre took a seat beside him.

"Patience, *bon ami*. First you must tell me what happened. I, of course, will send word to Townsend that you are both well. The last news he received was not so good."

Andrew agreed. He knew his brother kept his emotions on a tight rein, but the news of his disappearance would cause him considerable distress. Not to mention the added burden of having to keep it from their very astute grandmother.

The three put their heads together, and Michael and Andrew took turns telling Pierre their story.

****

Michael topped the rise and looked down at Stonebrooke Manor. It was quiet in the early morning light and, at first glance, looked deserted. He sat for a moment savoring the sight of his home. The late winter sun didn't carry much heat with it, but just being here brought a warmth no sun could ever provide. He urged his horse down the grassy slope to the stables.

Cobey greeted him at the door. "Master Michael! Welcome home, milord. We've all been anxiously awaiting your return. Miss Brandy will be so happy to see you."

"Cobey, where is everybody? The place seems deserted."

"I'm the only one here, milord, along with Maddie and Arthur. Miss Brandy had to let the others go. Couldn't afford to pay 'em. But I stayed," he added proudly.

"Couldn't afford—?" Michael shook his head as he left the stables and headed toward the house. He had been told that circumstances had changed after his father's death, but not to this degree. He limped through the empty foyer, suddenly feeling uneasy. "Brandy?" he called out.

"Master Michael!" Maddie rushed down the hallway and clasped Michael to her bosom. "Thank the good Lord, you have returned!" She brushed tears from her eyes.

"Maddie, where is everyone? It's so quiet."

"Come, sit." She led him into the salon and poured him a whiskey, pressing it into his hand as he settled himself on the settee.

"Where is Brandy?"

"She's in the garden."

Michael grabbed his cane and stood, placing the whiskey on the table.

"Wait, child. There is a great deal you don't know."

Michael frowned, thoroughly puzzled by her solemn tone of voice.

"So much has happened since you've been away. You know of your father?" At his nod, she opened her mouth to continue but was interrupted by a squeal of delight.

"Michael!" Brandy rushed into the room and threw herself into his outstretched arms. He pushed her back to gaze lovingly down at her tearstained face. As his gaze traveled down her body, he gaped in astonishment.

Brandy blushed, averting her gaze from his incredulous expression.

"What is the meaning of this?" He pointed to her gently rounded stomach, frowning darkly. "You are married, I hope?"

She shook her head.

"Bloody hell! Who is he? I'll kill him!"

"Michael, please sit down. I will explain everything to you."

Jessie and Anne entered the room in time to catch the last of Brandy's words. They rushed forward to embrace Michael, and after they were all seated, Brandy drew in a deep breath, knowing this would not be easy.

"Michael, where have you been?" she asked softly. "I've been so worried, so very worried about you, and no one would enlighten me. They would just tell me that you were safe...as far as they knew."

"I can't discuss that right now."

"You know about Father?"

"Yes, I know about our father. What I would like to know is how you got yourself in this state." He looked pointedly at her stomach.

She blushed, laying her hands across her belly.

"Who is responsible?"

She squirmed under his scrutiny. "Ah, the Duke of Marbury."

Michael's face twisted in fury. Then he laughed, an ugly harsh sound.

"He takes his promises seriously, I see. Too seriously."

"What do you mean?"

His hand sliced the air. "'Tis nothing. Has he asked you to marry him?"

"Well, not exactly."

"What in the hell is that supposed to mean?"

"He doesn't know I carry his child. I haven't seen him in a while. He was due here after the first of the year, but— When he arrives, I will tell him." She stopped talking. Truth was she was worried. She had received a brief note from him telling her he had been detained in London. Her imagination had been running wild of late, wondering what or who had kept him in the city.

She glanced sheepishly at her aunt and cousin, who sat very quietly on the settee, looking like they wished they were anywhere but there, then back at Michael, who was striding from the room, his cane under his arm.

"Where are you going?"

Michael turned at the door. "To London."

Chapter 36

Chandler strode into the salon, pausing at the sight of his brother lounging in a chair, enjoying a whiskey.

"Welcome home, brother. I see the French couldn't hold you down for long." Chandler clasped his brother's hand. "Oh, hell," he muttered and drew his brother into an embrace.

"I'm glad to be home. I can assure you it was not pleasant."

"No doubt. I was worried as hell over you." He pushed Andrew away and looked him over. "You are all right, aren't you?"

"Yes. Thank God I'm out of that hellhole. You wouldn't believe—"

"Yes, I would. Where is Michael?"

"He stopped at Stonebrooke Manor. He was worried about his sister. Did you look in on her while he was gone?"

"Yes, I did." He strode to the sideboard and poured himself a whiskey as Abigail rushed into the room, crying out in happiness.

"Andrew, my boy, you're home at last!" She hugged him tightly, running her hands over his upper body.

"I'm in one piece, Grandmother, I assure you. Scotland is not a dangerous place."

"She knows, Andrew," Chandler said, pouring his grandmother a sherry.

Andrew glanced at his brother in surprise. Chandler shrugged his shoulders and sipped his whiskey.

"And I don't mind telling you how worried I've been. You will never do anything that dangerous again. Do you hear me?"

"Yes, Grandmother," Andrew laughed, settling himself in the chair.

Chandler sank into one of the other chairs. With his brother home, he could now return to Hathshire and court Brandy properly. He wanted to make her his wife. God's truth, that revelation never ceased to amaze him. He smiled softly, thinking of his love, and glanced up to find Andrew gazing at him with interest.

"What in the hell are you looking at?" Chandler scowled.

"You. You look like you're, well, daydreaming. What is wrong with him?" Andrew turned to their grandmother.

Abigail grinned. "I would bet it's a certain young lady that has him so preoccupied." She glanced innocently at Chandler whose muttered curse had not gone unheard.

"What is this? My big brother—the one who suspects every woman has an ulterior motive, the one who doesn't trust anyone in a skirt, the, and I quote, 'most sought-after bachelor in Society,' end quote—mooning over a lady? I don't believe it!"

"Believe it," Abigail averred happily.

Chandler stood up. "If you two are through discussing me as if I weren't in the room, we need to brief Blanchard. Grandmother, we shall return in time for dinner."

It was early evening when Chandler and Andrew

returned to the townhouse. They entered the salon and found Michael Drummond pacing the room, leaning heavily on his cane.

"Michael, what are you doing here?" Andrew asked in surprise. "I thought you'd be in Hathshire with your sister."

Michael ignored him and stepped toward Chandler, his face suffused with rage. "This is for Brandy!" he shouted, and Chandler only had time to take in Michael's angry countenance before his world spun dizzily before him, pain exploding in his chin where Michael's fist had connected.

"What in the hell was that for?" He stepped forward and grabbed a handful of Michael's shirt, lifting him clear off the floor.

"You bastard!" Michael disengaged himself from Chandler's iron grip and pulled back his fist to swing again. Chandler was ready this time and grabbed his arm, twisting it behind his back and throwing him against the settee. Michael landed with a solid thud, then jumped up and went for Chandler's throat. Chandler swung his fist into Michael's stomach, and that one doubled over as he gasped for air. He fell back onto the settee, clutching his stomach.

Andrew stood back, watching the scene dispassionately. "Have you both had quite enough?"

"Would you mind telling me what in bloody hell is going on?" Chandler rubbed his jaw, glaring at Michael.

"My sister! I asked you to keep an eye on her—an eye, damn it, not your hands!" He lunged again for Chandler, who merely stepped aside, stuck out a booted foot and sent Michael flying across the room to collide with a table and send a pretty porcelain bowl crashing to the floor. Michael grabbed his leg, wincing at the pain slicing through it.

"What are you talking about?" Chandler demanded.

"You are going to marry her, you hear? Or you're a dead man!"

Andrew glanced at the doorway to find his grandmother and a lovely young woman standing there, mouths agape. It was quite obvious they had witnessed the entire scene. He wondered idly if the pretty young thing was Michael's sister. He cleared his throat, gaining his brother's attention. Chandler looked over his shoulder at the door and groaned.

Brandy was in shock—to say the least. What had Michael meant? Had he asked Chandler to watch over her? To take care of her? Is that why—?

"Brandy." Chandler took a step toward her.

"Stay away from me, you—cad! To think that you…that I…oh—!"

Chandler, puzzled by her reaction and thinking she was outraged by him fighting with her brother, sought to set her straight. "Michael came charging at me. I was merely defending myself."

"Look at her, you bastard. Look at what you've done!" Michael shouted from across the room.

Brandy flushed bright red as three gazes swept her from head to toe. Chandler's eyes widened as he took in her rounded stomach. He took another step toward her. "Why didn't you tell me?"

"Stay away, not one step closer. How could you? I thought you cared—" She spun on her heel and disappeared up the stairs.

Abigail looked disapprovingly around the room. "I am ashamed of all of you. Yes, including you, Andrew.

You have all hurt that poor sweet girl. Broken her heart, you have."

"What have I done?" Andrew asked, incredulous. "I just returned from a very harrowing experience."

Chandler rolled his eyes and went after Brandy who, despite her growing size, was surprisingly quick on her feet. She rushed into the chamber she had previously occupied, slammed the door shut, and fell on the bed.

"Brandy, open this door!" Chandler demanded, his voice edged with concern.

"Go away!" she shouted through her tears.

The door came crashing in, slamming against the wall.

Brandy sat up, her hand going to her throat. Chandler spotted the hurt and anger in her tear-filled eyes.

"I have nothing to say to you."

"It is not what you think."

She lifted her chin. "Go away," she said, her tone devoid of emotion.

"'Tis true that Michael asked me to look in on you. I did, but you were already on your way to London. It was the same day I saw you at the inn. However, what passed between us had nothing at all to do with my promise to him."

She stared blindly out the window. "I never want to see you again."

"And what of the babe?"

"It is not yours." She faced him, challengingly, watching anger darken his eyes.

"Do you mean to say that you and Blackwell—I don't believe it."

"Believe it." She averted her gaze until she heard

him slam from the room. She covered her face with her hands and cried some more.

Michael entered a moment later, his face red with anger. "Well?"

"Well, what?"

"Are you going to marry him?"

"No. I don't want him. And he doesn't want me." She faced her brother. "How could you ask him to look after me? I am perfectly capable of taking care of myself."

"I was in France when he told me the news of father's death. I was afraid for you, especially knowing Roger Blackwell would come sniffing around. I wanted to be sure you were kept safe." Realizing she might resent him for thinking she couldn't look out for herself and thinking to defend his actions, he blurted out, "They also thought you might be involved with Blackwell."

Brandy's shoulders slumped. Chandler had only been following orders—first Michael's, then Blanchard's. She threw herself across the bed, her sobs quiet but bountiful, Michael's words echoing in her mind. *I asked you to keep an eye on her...*

She placed her hands on her rounded stomach and felt her heart begin to break.

****

Chandler retreated to Marbury Hall. The sight of the large rambling house soothed his troubled mind, and the prospect of work would help erase the vision of brandied-colored hair and emerald-green eyes. He rubbed his jaw, still sore from Michael's fist of fury. After tempers had cooled, they'd had quite an enlightening conversation, each apprising the other of what they hadn't known.

His steward followed him into the book-lined study as Chandler settled himself in the leather chair behind the large mahogany desk. He went quickly through the pile of papers awaiting his attention, answering invitations, dictating notes, and resolving issues with his tenants, all done rapid-fire, his steward scrambling to keep it straight.

After two hours, Chandler dismissed his steward and leaned back in his chair. He stared across the room, lost in thought. He had finally found a woman who met all his needs, indeed, far exceeded any expectations he'd ever had. Not only had she brought laughter and love into his life, but most importantly and unbelievably—he trusted her. He, the self-proclaimed cynic, trusted a woman. He loved her incredible enthusiasm, her lust for life, and how she tried to hide her sorrow behind a smile. She was nothing like his mother—Brandy would be true to him. He knew marriage to her would be heaven on earth.

He couldn't dream of living without her. He wanted to spend the rest of his life with her—making her happy, making her laugh, making love. He smiled, a lightness of spirit replacing the darkness he'd held onto his entire life.

He gazed at the portrait of his parents hanging above the fireplace, studying it as if seeing it for the first time. His father's eyes were haunted, a sad smile playing about his mouth. Why hadn't he noticed that before? His mother was smiling, a sparkle in her eyes, as if the world were hers and everyone played by her rules. Chandler had always thought his father a strong man who had allowed a woman to ruin his life. Over the years, his respect had turned to pity. How wrong he had been!

A wry grin graced his mouth. *I understand, Father.*

I finally understand. Love did make one vulnerable. It could gnaw at your insides until it struck you down, or it could be the most wonderful, enriching feeling in the world. Chandler knew that for himself, unlike his father, the latter would be true. Brandy was the only woman he wanted, had ever wanted. And her love would be true—always.

He thought back to the first time he had seen her, at the glade, the day he had thought to save her from her horse. How magnificent she had looked flying across the lea, her auburn mane flowing out behind her. She had stirred something in him, but he hadn't known then that he had found her—he had found the one. When he learned she was a chicken thief, his heart had gone out to her, yet she had not asked for pity. When she had gone to France to find her brother, he had been so proud of her bravery. She hadn't bent under life's pebbles thrown at her but had instead found a way to cope, all without a word of complaint.

Yes, he had found her. She was his woman, his soul mate, the mother of his child. He would take care of her—if she'd let him.

He jumped to his feet. He would go to her and demand she marry him. She would be his wife if he had to bind her, gag her, and drag her to the altar. Despite her words, he knew the child she carried was his, but that was not the reason he wanted to marry her. He had decided long before that scene in his salon. He would just have to convince her of that.

With that determined resolve, he called for his horse and rode swiftly toward Hathshire and the woman he loved.

Chapter 37

Brandy returned to Stonebrooke Manor with Michael. She had stayed in her chamber at the Townsend townhouse the entire night. Abigail was kind enough to have a tray sent up for supper. Where Michael stayed, she didn't know nor did she care. She did not see Chandler again.

She spoke not a word to Michael, but sat silently, staring out the carriage window at the landscape as they headed toward home. Spring was dawning, pushing aside the dreary blanket of winter. Michael, after repeated attempts to draw her into conversation, finally gave up and he, too, stared out the window, lost in thought.

After he had calmed down, and Michael had had a long talk with Chandler, he now knew how wrong he had been about the Duke of Marbury. Chandler had filled Andrew and him in on all that had transpired while they were incarcerated in France. After hearing the entire story, Michael was extremely contrite for the way he had behaved. The duke had saved his sister's life, as well as his own.

Chandler had told them about Blackwell and his treachery, about Brandy becoming destitute and reduced to stealing food, and about her traveling to France to find him. When Chandler had revealed to him that she had been adopted, Michael had been devastated. What she had gone through! Now, if only she would listen to him so he could apologize and tell her how proud he was of her.

Michael glanced sideways at Brandy's stony profile. If it was the last thing he did, he would make it up to her. He knew Chandler loved her, but she was too hurt to see it for herself. She had immediately thought the worst, as had he, and now Michael was unable to change her mind.

When they arrived home, Brandy retired to her chamber and did not leave it for two days. On the third day, she emerged in breeches and boots, and astride Misty raced across the land. She pulled up on the reins and trotted to the secluded glade. She dismounted and sat beside the little pool of water that had now begun to thaw. The canopy of branches had, almost overnight, sprouted pale green leaves. The early spring sun filtered through the branches, casting its soft light into the glade.

She heard a sound behind her and glanced uninterestedly over her shoulder. Seeing no one, she turned back and skipped a few pebbles across the pond's smooth surface, watching the ripples expand into an ever-widening circle. When a shadow fell across the water, she glanced up and spied a man across the pond. He was looking at her, scrutinizing her face as if comparing it to a mental description.

Brandy stood up and slowly backed away from the pond. When the man edged around the small pool of water and made to come after her, she turned and bolted. She ran past Misty, knowing she didn't have time to mount the mare, and continued on foot through the forest. She was soon breathless from running, a sharp pain gripping her side. She tripped over a tree root and fell headlong onto the forest floor, instinctively twisting her body to land on her side and thereby protecting her abdomen. Fortunately, her fall was softened by the carpet of pliable spring grass and fallen autumn leaves. She lay still a moment, trying to catch her breath. Sitting up, she tilted her head to one side, listening for the sound of pursuit. The crashing noise behind her was close, pushing her to action. She stood up and her ankle buckled. Gasping from the pain shooting through her leg, she knelt and rubbed the bruised joint before clenching her teeth together, stiffening her spine and running blindly though the woods. She tripped over a fallen log and flew through the air, landing smack into a tree—a tree covered in broadcloth! Her scream stuck in her throat when a pair of strong arms encircled her body.

"Hush, 'tis me." At the sound of the familiar voice, Brandy sighed and leaned into him. Chandler set her aside with a whispered word of caution. He noticed her grimace of pain and cocked a brow at her in an expression of concern. She shook her head and in a hushed whisper, explained she had twisted her ankle.

He nodded and crouched on his heels, waiting. When the man ran into the clearing, he pounced. Striking with lightning celerity, he flipped the ruffian into the air with one quick flip of his arm. The man found himself flat on his back, cold metal pushing against his neck.

"Who is paying you?" Chandler asked, his voice harsh with suppressed anger. When the man didn't immediately answer, Chandler pressed the pistol deeper into his throat.

"I don't know," he gasped. "I swear, gov'nor. A woman—she wore a dark cape, covered her head, it did. Don't know her name…" He sputtered to a stop as the pistol pushed deeper into his throat, nearly cutting off his air supply.

"Talk," Chandler ordered, and eased up on the pressure of the gun.

"She wanted me to kill the lady. Said she'd pay real well, she did. She was talkin' wild. Somethin' about the lady ruinin' her life and had to die." The man shook with fear, closing his eyes against the horrible light in the blue eyes boring down on him.

Chandler glanced over his shoulder at Brandy. She sat huddled at the base of a tree, her hands covering her stomach. He couldn't kill the man in cold blood. He turned back to the miscreant.

"If I ever see your miserable face again, you're a dead man. Understand? Now, get the hell out of here!"

The man stared at Chandler in disbelief. "Ye mean ye ain't gonna kill me?"

"Run, before I change my mind."

"Aye, gov'nor." The man scrambled to his feet and was gone in a flash, looking back only once to see if the fancy gent had changed his mind.

Chandler strode to Brandy and gently lifted her into his arms. "It's all right, love. He's gone." He walked back to the glade, and when they arrived, he set her on the ground, joined her there, and gathered her close.

"Why was he chasing me?"

He looked out over the pond so she wouldn't see his apprehension. "He probably found you as delectable as I do and only wanted to steal a kiss," he teased, trying to erase her anxiety.

"Chandler, this is not the first time my life has been in danger. What aren't you telling me?"

"Nothing, love." He hesitated before speaking again. "I honestly don't know why someone wants you dead. But if it's the last thing I do, I will find out."

Brandy was silent a moment, allowing his vow to soothe her nerves. "What of Lady Vivian? Do you have news of her?"

"I heard she left London rather suddenly with no immediate plans to return."

"Did you find out why she lured me out of London?"

"From what I could gather, Vivian did not know the identity of the person who approached her. Apparently, this person had something on her that would prove humiliating, if made public. So, Vivian did what was asked of her."

"And what of Roger?"

"He will enjoy an extended stay at Newgate. They will probably hang him for treason."

"Were you able to find out his connection to Philip?"

"It seems that Blackwell told you the truth. He had arranged for Philip to receive a loan, and when he couldn't repay it, he demanded he join his treasonous ring of men. Quite simply, Blackwell was blackmailing Philip. I've no doubt 'tis the reason Philip betrothed you to him as he stated in his journal."

"Roger wanted the land by the cliffs. He must have learned it's my dower property." She suddenly remembered, "Roger told me Stonebrooke Manor was used to store stolen goods. I've never seen any nor heard mention of it before."

"I'll be sure to relate that to Ross."

"What happened to all the money Roger was making from smuggling?"

"He gambled it away as fast as he made it. He was becoming desperate."

"What about the journal? Why was it so important to him?"

"I'm not sure. We didn't find anything that incriminated him. Your father—" He shook his head. "Philip must have lied to Blackwell's man. Either that or he destroyed any pertinent pages before he died."

"When I found Philip in his study, there were ashes smoldering in a tray on his desk. He could have burned the important pages."

"That would explain it."

"I wonder why," Brandy mused aloud.

"Perhaps to keep you safe."

Brandy thought on that a moment. In his last moments, was Philip truly thinking of her? Was he protecting her in death as he couldn't in life? Her heart softened. Perhaps he had loved her a little.

"Was Roger responsible for Michael and Andrew's disappearance?"

"Yes. We can add that to his list of nefarious activities. Apparently, he found out their identities and was responsible for having them imprisoned in France." He gazed over at her, his expression tender. "I am sorry I couldn't confide in you, sweet. I know how worried you were about your brother. But can you see now how dangerous it would have been?"

"I suppose," she conceded. "Roger was an evil man, wasn't he, Chandler?"

"The worst. He deserves whatever he is dealt. Now, enough about Blackwell and his sordid deeds." He cupped her chin gently in his hand and placed a soft kiss upon her lips. "You will marry me."

"No, I won't." She stiffened in his arms, drawing her righteous anger around her like a cloak. "You don't care a fig for me. You were only following orders," she stated, her nose in the air.

His sigh was loud. "Brandy, do you honestly think that anyone could make me do anything I didn't want to do?"

"You don't want to get married. You have told me that at least a dozen times, as well as your low opinion of women. They're not to be trusted," she mimicked, perfectly imitating his most arrogant tone.

"I trust you," he said softly.

"You are only willing to marry me because of the babe."

"I wanted to marry you long before I knew of the child."

"'Tis yours, you know."

"Yes, I know." He wrapped his arm around her shoulders and drew her close. "You will marry me."

"No."

Chandler, becoming frightened by her stubborn refusals, lost his temper. He pulled back to look down at her and shouted, "I love you, damn it!"

"You love me so much you stayed away for months! Where have you been all this time? If not Vivian, then who? You were supposed to have returned to Hathshire after the new year."

"I was trying to locate our brothers."

At that admission, the fire extinguished. Her shoulders sagged beneath the truth of his words. He was right, of course. She had once again let her imagination run wild, and in the wrong direction. Who didn't trust who now?

He pulled her to him and kissed her with all the love he possessed. "Brandy, my love, say yes. Say you'll marry me," he whispered against her mouth.

"Yes, I will marry you," she whispered back, her heart fairly bursting with joy. To deny this dynamic man anything was impossible. And why in the world would she want to refuse the one thing she most wanted?

"Tell me again."

"I love you, Brandy."

She sighed and kissed him full on the mouth. "I love you, Chandler." She pulled back. "What about your parents' faithless marriage? From what you've told me of their relationship, aren't you afraid—"

He placed his finger against her lips. "I've made my peace. I realize that, for me, loving you is the most special gift in the world. You are my soul mate, Brandy, I know that now."

She stared at him in stunned disbelief. "Why, Chandler, you sound—well, romantic!"

"I do, don't I?" he asked, not the least bit embarrassed at expressing his profound love. He turned and whistled sharply. His large stallion crashed through the trees and skidded to a stop in front of them. Chandler untethered Misty from the tree, and after handing Brandy the reins, he mounted his horse and leaned down, gently lifting her in his arms. They headed back to Stonebrooke Manor, together, atop his steed.

Chandler carried Brandy through the front door, past a disgruntled Arthur, who watched disapprovingly as his mistress was once again carried up the stairs to her bedchamber by that man. He laid her gently on the bed and stepped back to look down at her. His gaze travelled from her tousled auburn curls, over her extended abdomen, and down to her scuffed boots. He sat down, and she scooted over to make room for him. He took her cold hands in his large warm ones.

"What am I going to do with you?" he whispered, placing a soft kiss in the palm of her hand.

Her smile was saucy. "Why, you're going to marry me, Your Grace."

"Yes, I am." He sat with her until she fell asleep, which didn't take long, then leaned over and gently kissed her. He was quiet when he left the room, making his way downstairs. Upon entering the salon, he was confronted by three anxious faces.

"She's sleeping. Anne, you might want to go up later and check on her." He turned to Arthur, who had appeared in the doorway. "Send for a doctor. She had a fall in the woods and twisted her ankle. I also want to be certain the child was not injured. Jessie, I think some of Maddie's broth would be in order when she awakes." He grinned to the room at large. "She has agreed to marry me."

Everyone began talking at once. Jessie and Anne hugged, beside themselves with happiness. Chandler waved Michael over to his side. He quietly and quickly related what had happened at the glade. "I believe I know who has been after Brandy, but I'm not ready to reveal it until I have confirmation. I need to return to London. Keep a close watch on her. Do not let her leave this house alone."

"Don't worry, she'll be safe with me." He clasped Chandler's hand. "I owe you more than I can ever repay."

"I'll take good care of her."

"I know you will," Michael said, and watched the tall, proud man leave the room, confident he would indeed take care of his sister.

Later that evening, Michael knocked on Brandy's chamber door. At her request, he came in and perched on the edge of the bed. "I think we should talk."

She nodded in agreement, and they spent the next several hours relating their time apart. He answered her questions about his prolonged absence, and she in turn told him of the events that had transpired while he was away.

When they spoke of her adoption, he assured her he had not known, and it wouldn't have made a difference if he had. She would always be his sister, whether they were related by blood or not, and he would always love her.

After Michael left, with a promise to see her in the morning, Brandy sighed in contentment. Her brother— and she would always think of him as such—had returned safely. She would marry the man she loved. She caressed her rounded belly. And very soon she would bear his child. She snuggled beneath the counterpane, happy at last, and fell asleep, dreaming of her duke.

Chapter 38

Chandler stopped at Alden Ridge just long enough to collect Jeffrey. On their ride to London, Chandler filled him in on what had happened to Brandy and his subsequent suspicions. By the time they reached the Alexander townhouse, their horses were blowing hard, breaths misting in the chilly night air.

It was late and the house was dark. Ascending the front steps, Chandler knocked loudly on the door, Jeffrey just behind him. After several minutes, the door was pulled open by the butler, who was trying to maintain his dignity dressed only in his nightclothes, cap askew. He eyed the two men with disapproval at the lateness of the hour, lifting the candlestick high to see their faces.

"May I help you?"

"Inform Lord Ashton that the Duke of Marbury and the Marquis of Montaldene are here to see him."

"Lord Ashton is abed."

"Do it, man, and now!" Chandler reached to grab the butler by his nightshirt, but Jeffrey stepped forward and stayed him, saying over his shoulder, "I would suggest you do as you are bidden, or I cannot be responsible for my friend's actions." He cocked a brow at the butler who immediately turned and darted up the stairs, candle flame flickering.

Jeffrey shut the door behind them and followed Chandler into Thomas's study. They waited in tense silence until Thomas appeared. He entered the room, tying the belt of his charcoal-gray robe around his waist.

"Chandler—Jeffrey! What is it? You look like the devil."

"There is something we need to discuss with you that is rather delicate. Thomas, I have known you for many years, and what I have to say is disturbing. It's about your wife, Lacey."

Thomas sat in the nearest chair, his hazel eyes filled with concern. He motioned for them to take a seat and nodded his head to the butler who had appeared in the doorway now fully dressed in his black livery. "Some cognac, please." He waited for the butler to distribute the snifters before continuing the conversation. The butler made a wide circle around Chandler and beat a hasty retreat, closing the door behind him.

Chandler spoke, his words succinct. "It seems your wife is desirous of my fiancée's death."

"Your fiancée?"

"Lady Brandy Drummond."

Thomas swallowed a good portion of his cognac. Jeffrey jumped up and began to pace the length of the room while Chandler related the events of the past few weeks.

Thomas was silent until the duke had finished. "I have noticed Lacey has not been herself lately. I wondered about it, naturally, but could find no explanation. Why do you presume it is Lacey who is after Lady Brandy? I can't understand why—"

"Because she should have died a very long time ago." Lacey had quietly entered the study and overhead the last of their conversation. She strolled into the room, her hands hidden in the folds of her maroon velvet robe.

"You see, Thomas, she was supposed to have died after her birth. However, the man my brother hired to do the job botched it. I only found out a short while ago she lived." She sighed dramatically. "And when I hired a man to do away with her, he bungled it, too. And got himself killed to boot. Bloody idiots," she muttered. "This last time was no better than the previous two." She lifted her hands, palms facing upward. "It has been impossible to find anyone in London competent enough to do the job."

Thomas stood and faced his wife. "Lacey, what are you about? Why would you want Brandy Drummond dead?"

Lacey walked to the shelves behind her husband's desk and lifted a framed portrait of a young woman that was positioned among the books. She turned back to the room, the portrait held high over her head. "Why, you ask? Because of this—this whore!"

"Marian Blanchard? What has she to do with any of this? She disappeared years ago." Chandler leaned back in his chair, a look of understanding dawning on his face. Suddenly, everything was becoming quite clear to him.

"Yes, she did. She disappeared and her babe was supposed to have died."

"Her babe? Marian was pregnant?" asked Thomas in disbelief.

"Yes!" Lacey laid the portrait face down on the desk. "How do I know this, you may ask?" Her eyes sparkled with a feral gleam as she scanned the room.

Both Chandler and Jeffrey watched carefully for any sudden movements. Chandler noticed her hand hidden in the pocket of her robe. He placed his glass on the table, his muscles taut in anticipation as he caught Jeffrey's eye and slanted his gaze toward Lacey's robe pocket.

"Because I was responsible for her disappearance!" she shouted triumphantly. "The bitch! I told her that her baby died. She lost all will to live after that, you see." She stared wild-eyed at Thomas and laughed, an ugly sound. "You don't get it, do you? Did you honestly believe Marian would just disappear without a trace?"

"Is Marian alive?" Thomas asked quietly.

"I don't know. I haven't corresponded with her in years."

"You corresponded with her? Where is she?" Thomas was trying to steady the cyclone of emotions whirling inside him.

"I'm not sure. She could be dead, for all I know." Lacey shrugged her shoulders. "I led her to believe you no longer loved her, told her we were to be married. I also told her that her parents were killed in an unfortunate accident. So, you see? She had no reason to ever return to England." She paused for breath, and looked around the room, as if waiting to be congratulated on her well-planned scheme. Her gaze swung back to her husband. "You were too blind to see the resemblance, weren't you? But I noticed it right away. Her eyes are the same shade as that whore who created her." She took a deep, labored breath, spread her arms wide, and announced, "Brandy Drummond is your daughter!"

Thomas stared at her in shock. With his eyes, Chandler urged Jeffrey closer to Lacey, then turned to Thomas. Feeling acute sympathy at Thomas's expression of disbelief, he tried to soften the blow his wife had dealt.

"Brandy has confided to me that she was adopted by the Drummonds."

"The little bitch should have died! I've paid good coin to have her done away!" Lacey shrieked, one hand at her head, her fingers twisting her limp blonde hair.

Thomas sat down and hung his head in his hands. Chandler rose to his feet at the same time Jeffrey took a step toward Lacey. She brought her arm up, a pistol clutched in her hand. She swung it wildly from one man to the other, effectively keeping them in place. Her gaze riveted on her husband as her words echoed throughout the room. "Marian loved you so much. But I was smarter," she said proudly, tapping her head with one finger. "I was always smarter." She looked at her husband and frowned. "I loved you, Thomas. I couldn't let her have you. Don't you see? She had everything she ever wanted. But not you—never you." So intent was she on taunting her husband she didn't notice Chandler edging over to her side.

"You're wrong, Lacey. I never stopped loving Marian. You were just a poor substitute." Thomas, hazel eyes misty with unshed tears, looked at his wife.

Lacey's eyes widened in disbelief and, while her attention was focused on her husband, Chandler dove for the gun. Startled, Lacy swung around, pulling the trigger. Chandler was struck and, thrown backwards by the force of the bullet, landed on the settee. He grabbed his left arm and slumped back. Lacey swung the gun toward Jeffrey, who had stepped closer. He stopped in his tracks, the pistol trained at his chest.

Thomas rose wearily to his feet, calmly faced his wife, and held out his hand. "Give me the gun, Lacey."

Lacey cringed at the hatred in his voice. She raised the pistol and aimed it at his heart. "I loved you, Thomas. I only wanted you. She had everything. I only wanted you."

Thomas growled and lunged at his wife. In her madness, she had the strength of two men, but Thomas's anger overrode her power. As they struggled for the gun, a second shot rang out. Lacey slumped over Thomas's arm, then slithered to the floor. She gasped for breath and stared up at her husband, her eyes starting to glaze over. "I only wanted you…" Her last breath left her body, a labored rattling sound.

The three men stared at each other in stunned silence. The door burst open, and the butler rushed into the study, followed by three footmen who stumbled into the room behind him. "Send for Dr. Bloodsworth at once," Thomas bade his butler. That one rushed back out of the room, his coattails flapping, the three footmen on his heels.

Jeffrey knelt beside Chandler, who was shrugging out of his coat. He tore his shirt off his shoulder, then reached for a candle to examine the wound.

"You're losing a lot of blood, Chandler. Hold still, man!"

"I must get to Brandy."

"You will do no such thing."

"Jeff—"

"You won't be any good to her dead,"

"Dr. Bloodsworth will be here shortly, Townsend." Thomas looked dazed as he poured three more cognacs and passed them around. He picked up the portrait of Marian and crumpled into his desk chair. He stared at the likeness of the only woman he had ever loved. She was gone, but she had left behind their daughter. "You know, when I first met Brandy, I had the strangest feeling we were—connected. When I gazed into her green eyes, I felt as if I'd been transported back in time. Such a strong feeling." He shook his head and traced Marian's face with the tip of his finger. "I should have known," he whispered. "I should have known she was our daughter."

Dr. Bloodsworth bustled into the room, a large black bag in his hand. He knelt beside Chandler and tore away the rest of his shirt. After cleaning the wound, he applied a thin coating of salve before wrapping a bandage tightly around it.

"You were lucky, Your Grace. The bullet went clear through the fleshy part of your arm. Now, you must stay quiet. Any sudden movement will reopen the wound." He glanced around as the three footmen, who had reluctantly returned to the study, covered their mistress's body with a sheet, and fled the room.

"I've sent for the authorities," the butler uttered, his gaze averted from the body on the floor before he too departed the grisly scene.

Dr. Bloodsworth collected his black bag. "Please don't hesitate to send for me if I'm needed again. I will talk with the authorities on my way out." He bowed and left the room, just as Ross Blanchard rushed in, cloak billowing around him.

"Good Lord, what happened here?" As he was quickly filled in on the night's events, he could only nod, too stunned to say a word. He looked over at Thomas. "You have a daughter?" He shook his head in disbelief. "I have a granddaughter?"

"Soon to have a great-granddaughter—or grandson," Jeffrey piped in with a grin.

Ross looked over at Chandler with a frown. "You will marry that girl and make an honest woman of her."

Chandler's smile was weak but broad. "That's the

plan." He hesitated, then continued slowly, "I don't want to get your hopes up, of course, but Michael told me of an Englishwoman he met in France."

"Yes, a Madame Fouillet," Ross interjected with a nod. "Her son found Andrew and Michael in the woods near their home. She nursed them back to health."

"Michael found her startlingly familiar. At the time, he thought it odd, not having a basis for his feelings, unaware that Brandy was adopted. In light of what's happened here, I'm wondering if the woman might be Marian." He held up his hand. "It could come to naught, but I think we should follow up on it." He struggled to his feet, grimacing in pain. "I will go to France on the morrow and question her."

"I don't think you should be doing any traveling just now. Your wound would only slow you down. Don't forget, Chandler, it is still too dangerous for you to be in France," Jeffrey reminded him. "You were lucky not to get caught the last few times you ventured there."

"I am going," Chandler insisted.

"I will send a couple of men into France and have them escort Madame Fouillet to the coast. You can meet her there," Blanchard suggested, fully understanding Chandler's determination. "If she is Marian, bring her back to England. If she wants to return, that is."

"Once she hears the entire story, she will return."

All four men nodded, their individual expressions registering varying degrees of shock, hope, and pain.

Chapter 39

Chandler escorted Brandy into the drawing room, where a group of people was gathered. Ross and Madelyn Blanchard occupied one settee, Jessie and Anne had taken the other. Thomas Alexander stood by the fireplace, his hands resting on the shoulders of a woman seated in a mahogany chair before him, Abigail sat in the chair next to her. Michael and Andrew stood in front of the large picture window, drinking whiskey.

Brandy glanced up at Chandler, her eyes clouded with confusion. "What's happened? Why is everyone here?"

He gazed down into her upturned face and said softly, "'Tis all right, my love. Come, sit here." He pressed her into the soft cushions of an overstuffed chair, his right hand resting lightly on her shoulder, his left arm in a sling. Brandy studied the tense faces around her. Her gaze fell on Thomas Alexander, and she smiled. She looked down at the woman in front of him and tilted her head. She didn't recognize her but felt she knew her. A shiver went up her spine as she stared into green eyes so like her own. Her glance lifted to the portrait of herself above the fireplace, and her heart skipped a beat.

"Brandy, there is someone we would like you to meet."

Brandy nearly cried at the tenderness in Chandler's voice. She looked up at him and nodded slowly, drawing strength from his touch.

Marian gazed at the daughter she had never known. Tears filled her eyes as she reached up to clasp the hand gently squeezing her shoulder. She gazed up into Thomas's hazel eyes, reading encouragement in their depths. She stood up and moved to kneel in front of Brandy.

Brandy stared at the woman with a mixture of anticipation and fear. She knew who she was before she said a word. "You are my mother," she whispered.

Marian nodded, taking Brandy's face in her hands. She leaned forward and placed a kiss on first one cheek then the other. "I am Marian."

At her touch, Brandy felt a rush of warmth and love. She had always believed she would hate her mother for abandoning her, so she was unprepared for these emotions.

Abigail sniffed back tears. "Brandy, we have heard some of the story. Are you ready to listen, child?"

Brandy nodded, not taking her eyes off the woman in front of her—her mother.

Chandler began to speak, "First of all, you should know the Blanchards are Marian's parents. They are as much in shock as you, my love." Brandy looked over at Ross and Madelyn and was warmed by their kind, loving smiles. "Lacey, Roger's sister, was responsible for the whole sordid ordeal, including your abandonment as a child and the recent attempts on your life." He felt Brandy stiffen beneath his hand. "Remember, she is dead. She can no longer harm you." Chandler caressed her shoulder until he felt her relax.

"Michael and Andrew were wounded when they escaped from a prison in France. Marian took them into her home and nursed them back to health. They were both delirious from fever and hunger, but Michael saw in Marian a resemblance to you. At the time he did not know of your adoption, so he dismissed it."

"Lacey arranged for my disappearance and saw to it that I never returned to England," Marian added solemnly, her eyes sad.

Brandy glanced at Thomas and whispered, "You are my father." She fingered the gold locket around her neck, knowing now the likeness portrayed inside the ornamental case was of him as a young man.

Thomas stepped forward and knelt beside Marian. He drew Brandy's hands into his. "I know this is quite a shock. Believe me, Brandy, we are all as astounded as you. You see, I did not know that Marian carried my child. The war in France had started and I was busy overseeing my family's shipping interests. I bade Marian wait for me and then we would marry. I gave her that locket as a promise for our future together. Unfortunately, my work took me away from England for quite some time. Lacey took the opportunity to lead Marian to believe I no longer cared for her."

"I managed to keep my expectant state hidden for quite a few months," Marian said, continuing the story. "When my parents went out of the country on an extended stay in Scotland, I gave birth in secret. Lacey told me my baby died. I became despondent and, because my parents and Thomas were away, I had no one to turn to—except Lacey." Marian reached for Thomas's hand. "After the birth, Lacey presented me with a note from Thomas saying that he would be detained on the Continent and not to wait for him. In my depressed state, I not only believed it but didn't recognize it as a forgery.

Lacey convinced me that Thomas was losing interest in me, that he had most likely found another woman. She persuaded me to enter a convent, assured me the quiet solitude would help put the pieces of my life back together. Because England and France were at war, travel to France was a bit tricky, but not impossible. She told me her brother, Roger, had arranged for passage over the Channel to Calais and from there I would travel overland by coach."

"Why didn't you return to England?" Brandy asked in confusion.

"During my stay in the convent, I found peace within myself. Lacey had written many letters, but they were kept from me until the Sisters felt I was strong enough to read them. When they were finally given to me, I read each horrid word." She shook her head. "Lacey was shrewd. She planted the seeds of suspicion quite cleverly. She implied I had no life back in England, nothing and no one to return to."

Blanchard took a deep breath and interjected, "There was a terrible boat accident in the Channel during that time. It struck a reef in a storm and sank. There were no survivors. Lacey took advantage of that calamity to tell Marian that her mother and I had been aboard the vessel and died. She had also contrived to get Thomas to marry her and informed Marian of that as well. So, you see? It really did seem to Marian that her life in England was over."

Marian looked at Thomas, who took over the telling of the story. "When I returned from the Continent, I was met with the news of Marian's disappearance. I was devastated. I searched and searched for her." He paused, bringing his hand up to rub his eyes. "After a while, with absolutely no leads, we thought it hopeless. Lacey took advantage of my despair and pressed her suit, convincing me to marry her. Thinking Marian was lost to me forever, I took Lacey to wife." He looked so forlorn, Brandy wanted to reach out and comfort him.

Marian finished the story. "The convent where I was living burned down. I moved with some of the Sisters to a small town in the north of France. It was there I met Antoine Fouillet. We married and had a son, Oliver. Antoine died several years ago, and my son and I have been living quietly in Mouilleries." She clasped Thomas's hand and gazed at him, her green eyes shining with a love still strong after all these years.

Brandy closed her eyes, her head spinning. When she opened them, she focused on her mother's face. "You truly didn't know I was alive?"

Marian shook her head. "No, my child. I was told you had died at birth. It wasn't until my father's men escorted me to the coast and I met with His Grace that I had a glimmer of hope. I came back to England with him." She nodded toward Chandler.

Brandy looked up at her beloved. "You went to France to bring her here? You did that for me?"

He kissed her softly. "Yes, my love."

Brandy rose to her feet, her legs unsteady. "I—I need to be…" She turned and rushed from the room, running blindly into the garden. She stood there in a daze, having no idea what to do next. The spring flowers were in full bloom; the ornamental roses climbed the trellis by the gate—the spot where she had been left all those years ago. She sank to the bench and pulled out the locket. She gently traced the etching of the initials inside the entwined hearts—*T* and *M*. Thomas and Marian. Her father and mother.

A pair of shiny black Hessian boots came into view. She raised her gaze to her beloved's countenance. Chandler was watching her closely. "Are you all right, my love?"

Brandy flung herself at him, his one good arm enfolding her in warmth, safety, and love. He murmured against her hair, "Quite a lot to take in, isn't it?"

She nodded against his chest. "I just can't believe they're my parents. And they didn't abandon me. When Doreen died, I was heartbroken. She was so good to me, loved me unconditionally. She was the only mother I knew. Philip had always been distant, and then, due to unfortunate circumstances, abusive. I honestly didn't like him. I felt so guilty about it after he died and learned the truth."

"Perhaps he felt he had let you down in some way."

"If that is the case, then why wasn't he more kind?"

"Well, we know from his journal that some of his actions were due to Blackwell."

"True, but that was more recent. I grew up without Philip's love. And I tried so hard—"

"I'm sorry he hurt you, love." His arm tightened around her shoulders.

"And now my true parents have surfaced. When I first found out I was adopted, I didn't know what to think. Questions swirled in my head until I thought I would go quite mad. Why did they abandon me? Why didn't they want me?"

"It must have been difficult for you, sweet. But now that you've heard their story, isn't it clear that they suffered too? And you were very much wanted?"

"I was so angry—"

"I know," he whispered against her hair. "You had every right to be angry. Something as important as one's birth should never be kept from them."

Brandy nodded against Chandler's strong chest. He was right, of course. She couldn't blame Thomas or Marian for the web of deception Lacey had so cleverly woven. They were all victims of her maniacal mind. She pulled back to look up at Chandler. "When I first met Thomas, I felt a jolt of...oh, I don't know what—but it was a nice feeling. He has the kindest eyes." Her own eyes swam with tears. "She's beautiful," she whispered, "isn't she?"

"You look just like her, you know. When I first saw the portrait of Marian in Blanchard's study, it gave me pause. But my mind was so wrapped up with Andrew and Michael I didn't notice the resemblance. Later, when you showed me the locket, I recognized Thomas as the man in the portrait." He paused. "I'm surprised Ross didn't come to the same conclusion."

"I did."

Startled, they turned to face Lord Merrick, who had followed them out to the garden. "But I was afraid even to hope. Madelyn and I both had the strongest sense we were connected to Brandy. Also, something Blackwell said when we found you with him at Blackwell Hall strengthened that feeling. Something about a ghost—"

Brandy sniffed. "You didn't even like me. You thought I was a spy."

Ross laughed. "You have me there, my dear. However, in my defense, it was Chandler's suspicions that got me started down that particular venue."

Brandy swung on Chandler, arms akimbo. "You did what? All this time, it was you who stoked the fires?

Now do you believe I am innocent of all the wrongdoing you have ever accused me of?"

"Yes. Except, of course, for the chicken."

"Oh, for heaven's sake, when are you going to forget about that?"

Chandler threw back his head and roared with laughter. "Never, my love, never."

She snuggled back into his embrace. "That's a mighty long time, Your Grace."

Ross stared at the two of them, completely baffled by their conversation. He shrugged his shoulders and started toward the house, saying over his shoulder, "You two had best come back inside. There is a roomful of people anxiously awaiting your return."

Chandler leaned down and kissed her, his lips warm and tender. "Ready?" he asked against her mouth.

"Yes. With you by my side I can face anything."

"I would say that you could face anything with or without me."

"True, but it's so much nicer with you."

He smiled, drew her to his side, and they followed Ross back to the drawing room. The gathered group was indeed tense with anticipation.

Brandy stepped in front of Marian and hugged her tightly. "I'm so glad we have found each other." She unclasped the locket from around her neck and placed it in her hand. "I believe this belongs to you."

"Are you sure?" asked Marian, stroking the locket lovingly.

"I have my family—'tis all I need to know I belong." She smiled as her mother accepted the gift of love she had received from Thomas so many years ago.

Brandy turned to Thomas and hugged him. "I'm so

happy you are my father." She felt a tug on her dress and looked down to find a red-headed boy, hands tangled in her skirt.

"Are you my sister?" he asked, eyes wide with wonder.

"If you are Oliver, then yes, I am." She knelt down and enfolded the young boy in her arms. "You also have a brother." She reached out for Michael.

"You are my brother? Why didn't you say so when you were with *Maman* and me in France?"

"Because I wasn't aware of it until just recently. Are you fine with this?"

"*Oui!*" shouted Oliver gleefully, and the three of them hugged tightly.

Brandy, awash with a sense of love and belonging, smiled—she truly had a family now.

****

Chandler and Brandy were married the following day, the entire family, and close friends, in attendance. Dressed in a simple white crepe gown, Brandy's abdomen preceded her down the aisle as she walked arm in arm with Thomas, but the love shining from her emerald-green eyes kept everyone's attention focused on her face. Her brandy-colored tresses were swept up and pinned back, a few loose tendrils left to curl around her face. The emerald bejeweled combs Chandler had given her for Christmas twinkled in her hair.

Hidden behind the rose-covered trellis, Mick watched the proceedings. Over the years, he had checked on the little one he had left in the garden, watching her grow into a beautiful young woman. He had heard her laughter, had seen her tears, and each time he knew, without a doubt, he had done right by her.

He had heard on the streets about those fancy folks who had wanted her done away with, had heard of their fates, too. As far as he was concerned, they got what they deserved.

Mick's lot in life hadn't changed. He was still poor. He was still a thief. But he never again took money for anything nefarious—like murder. His mother would be proud.

As Mick watched the young woman make her way through the garden to the fancy gent waiting beneath a floral arch, his heart swelled with pride—just as if she was his own daughter. And in a way, she was—wasn't she?

Epilogue

Brandy watched her beloved husband holding their child. For the first time in her life, she had something no one could ever take away—her husband, her lover, her companion for life. And now their love's creation—their son.

Chandler laid their child in Brandy's arms and sat beside her on the bed. He took in the beautiful sight of mother and son and wanted to weep. For the hundredth time, he thanked the Lord he hadn't let his foolish ideas of love and marriage keep him from this most wonderful gift he'd been given.

"He is beautiful, isn't he?"

"He is indeed, sweet. What shall we name him?" He clucked the babe under his chin and was rewarded with a wide smile and a noisy gurgle.

"Alexander Jeffrey Townsend."

Chandler cocked his head to one side. "Jeffrey?"

"Yes. If it weren't for him, we wouldn't be together now," she explained, gazing tenderly at her black-haired, green-eyed son.

"How is that, love?"

"Well—it was his chicken," she replied with an impish grin.

Chandler threw back his head and laughed. Wrapping his arms around his wife and son, he held them close, utterly at peace. He'd found a woman he could trust, one who wanted nothing more in life than to love and be loved—by him.

He breathed in the subtle scent of lavender as he whispered against her auburn hair, "Brandy—my love."

A word about the author...

Christine has a passion for love stories. When not weaving romance and mystery to create her own, she enjoys floral film photography, watching classic movies, and chocolate. She resides in Virginia with her dog, Apache.

christine-davies.com

Brandy Drummond's life depends on finding her missing brother, and she will use any means available to overcome this adversity. Thrown together with the one man who can help her succeed, she must endure his arrogance and suspicion. Added to her frustration, she finds herself struggling with unfamiliar feelings while fighting her growing attraction to him.

Chandler Townsend, the cynical Duke of Marbury, agrees to help but needs to determine if she is England's friend or foe. Fighting demons from his past, he doesn't trust Brandy, but he wants her. Is she cut from the same cloth as his mother? Is she in league with her suitor?

To save each other, and find love, Brandy and Chandler must overcome obstacles both real and imagined.

ISBN 978-1-5092-5357-9

9 00

9 781509 253579